RED SPECTER

OTHER TITLES BY BRIAN ANDREWS AND JEFFREY WILSON

Tier One Series

Tier One
War Shadows
Crusader One
American Operator

WRITING AS ALEX RYAN

Nick Foley Thriller Series

Beijing Red
Hong Kong Black

OTHER TITLES BY BRIAN ANDREWS

The Calypso Directive
The Infiltration Game
Reset

OTHER TITLES BY JEFFREY WILSON

The Traiteur's Ring
The Donors
Fade to Black
War Torn

RED SPECTER

A TIER ONE THRILLER

ANDREWS & WILSON

THOMAS & MERCER

Published by Thomas & Mercer, Seattle

www.apub.com

Amazon, the Amazon logo, and Thomas & Mercer are trademarks of Amazon.com, Inc., or its affiliates.

ISBN-13: 9781542091527
ISBN-10: 1542091527

Cover design by Mike Heath | Magnus Creative

Printed in the United States of America

For Gina

PART I

Your own prison you shall not make.

—*The Code of Thieves, Vorovskoy Mir*

CHAPTER 1

Kreenholmi Joala Abandoned Textile Factory
Narva, Estonia
Five Hundred Feet from the Russian Border
June 10
0400 Local Time

"It's a trap," said the voice in his ear.

"Let's try not to jump to premature conclusions," John Dempsey replied as he piloted the silver Mercedes-Benz Sprinter around a tight fishhook turn. The panel van's tires grumbled in protest as he maneuvered off Kreenholmi Street onto the pothole-ridden dirt-and-gravel stretch that led to an abandoned Estonian textile factory complex. Despite the early hour, the sun was already breaching the horizon, painting the Baltic sky with brilliant pink and orange hues. The city of Narva was north of the fifty-ninth parallel, putting it a degree north of Juneau, Alaska, in latitude. Thankfully, it was summer, and it didn't feel like he was operating in Alaska.

"Another SUV just pulled up and parked behind the building. That makes three vehicles. I'm telling you, you're walking into a trap," Elizabeth Grimes repeated with annoyed, persistent conviction. Grimes—the team's designated sniper, overwatch, and devil's advocate in residence—was communicating via the microtransmitter stuffed deep in his left ear canal. When he didn't respond, she sighed and added, "This is one of your worst plans ever, you know that?"

Dempsey glanced at Dan Munn, who was riding in the back of the van. The former Navy SEAL and combat surgeon did a chatterbox impersonation with his right hand, his fingers and thumb forming a squawking bird beak. Munn and Dempsey had served together at the Tier One back in the day, in what felt like another lifetime. At the Teams, Dempsey had been a tool of the Joint Special Operations Command, fulfilling a role as one of America's most lethal special operators. Now, he was a tactical spook—an operator playing dress-up and taking on the identity the mission du jour demanded.

They named people like him Smith, Jones, or Johnson. In fact, John Dempsey wasn't even his real name, just the thing he called himself in this second incarnation of his life. As the head of Task Force Ember's Special Activities Division, the nation's best-kept counterterrorism secret, Dempsey was whoever America needed him to be to get the job done. Today, America needed him to be a scumbag bodyguard, and America needed Munn to pose as his boss, an even bigger scumbag international arms buyer. The pretext for the meeting was to inspect samples of the latest Russian weapons technology before placing a large order. The seller, Matvei Amarov, was one of Russia's most powerful Mafia bosses, known for his ruthless practices and propensity for extreme violence. But it was all good . . . this was just another day at the office catfishing the most dangerous, sadistic, and vile players in the world's criminal and terrorist underground.

Munn flashed Dempsey a crooked grin and said, "Dude, you know she's usually right."

"I know, but I'll never admit that," he whispered. Then, loud enough for Grimes to hear, he said, "I appreciate your concern, Alpha,

4

but these Vory guys are famously paranoid. I mean, how many guys could Amarov have possibly brought?"

"Since you asked, let me tell you," said Ian Baldwin, Ember's SIGINT chief back in Virginia. "There's the vehicle up front, which you see, but a second arrived at the same time and parked behind the north corner of the building. We hold one thermal signature in each vehicle—the drivers—and the two *gentlemen* standing out front to meet you. That makes four. There are four more signatures inside the building, who appear to be setting up equipment. For what it's worth, we observed them unload three crates from the second vehicle and carry them inside . . . They have one additional body on the roof, and a tenth patrolling the perimeter—although this last fellow is presently urinating on the wall at the north corner. The third SUV that Alpha just reported is hidden from your line of sight and has five signatures inside. This is probably their QRF on standby in the unlikely scenario that the two of you decide, despite being dreadfully outnumbered, to pick a gunfight."

"What the hell?" Munn said, shaking his head. "Amarov insisted that I come with a single bodyguard while he brings an army. Remind me why we agreed to follow the instructions of Russia's most ruthless Vory boss to the letter?"

"Well, we didn't follow them *to the letter*," Dempsey said. "We brought Long-Gun Lizzie with us, which, if you consider her KIA average per engagement, probably gives us a slight edge."

"While I appreciate your faith in me, Bravo, keep in mind that *Long-Gun Lizzie* is working with razor-thin margins," Grimes said from her sniper hide. "A millimeter could mean the difference between covering your ass and accidently putting you six feet under. Might wanna remember that when you're testing out new nicknames for me."

Grimes had been in position for an hour, after making her infil on foot when it was still dark. Dempsey glanced toward the upper level of a squat building. He pictured her lying on a table, or a stack of boxes, draped over the Heckler & Koch M110A1 sniper rifle she seemed to prefer lately. The HK was lighter than the bolt-action Remington, and semiautomatic, which saved her precious time between shots. Her angle was good, but the building unfortunately offered her no height advantage.

Dempsey pursed his lips as he slowed the van's approach to the south corner of their target building and contemplated the tactical picture Baldwin had just painted.

It's a lot of guys, he thought, before shrugging it off. *Doesn't matter. If today's the day I get my ticket punched, so be it. I don't care.*

This had been his mantra ever since the disastrous mission in Tehran. It wasn't that he had nothing left to live for. On the contrary, his life was about as good as it could get for a forty-year-old door-kicker divorcé who was officially dead to the world. He had a job that challenged him and made a difference in the world, teammates he both liked and respected, and a purpose. But if he was being honest with himself—something he was getting better at with age—it was time to recognize that he was past his expiration date. How many more missions could he play Russian roulette and spin that cylinder before fate finally got sick of saving his grumpy old ass and just let the hammer strike put him in the ground?

An uncomfortable quiet hung on the line, and Dempsey suddenly got the distinct feeling that everyone was waiting on *him* to say something.

"I wouldn't overthink it, guys. They're just being careful. If they wanted to kill us, they could have done it with one well-placed sniper sequence on our approach. As long as we don't pick a fight, everything will go fine. I have a good feeling about this meet." The last statement wasn't true, but Dempsey said it anyway.

"Alpha, how are your lines?" Munn asked Grimes, his own misgivings clearly not assuaged by Dempsey's *good feeling.*

"I have easy lines on their roving patrol and the guy on the roof, but I'm no help once you go inside," Grimes answered. "Unless all their shooters decide to hang out by the windows, there's not a whole lot I can do. Step through that door and you're taking your lives out of my hands and placing them entirely in Amarov's."

Dempsey nodded at the comment, despite the fact Grimes couldn't see him. He looked in the rearview mirror at the back seat. Munn, who normally was dressed and groomed like a lumberjack, was fresh-shaven, his hair slicked back and dyed for the role he was playing today.

"What's your gut sayin'?" Dempsey asked.

"My gut is saying I wish we had a Reaper in orbit with Hellfire missiles," Munn said.

"I was very clear in the pre-op that orbiting an armed Reaper five hundred feet from Russian airspace was liable to start an international incid—"

"We know," Dempsey said, cutting Baldwin off. "We're not blaming you." He looked back at Munn. "So, do we fish or cut bait?"

"Even with you on the SCAR, we're still just two guys—and only one of us with a rifle. If things turn ugly, our only hope is to talk our way out. Shooting our way to freedom is probably a nonstarter."

Dempsey tapped his fingers on the steering wheel and looked at the desert-tan SCAR-H model assault rifle leaning against the passenger seat beside him. Grimes and Munn were right; once they got inside, the factory floor would be nothing but wide-open space. They'd have no hides and no backup shooters to provide cover fire or watch their six. If the Vory surrounded them, they'd never survive. Whether they walked out alive or not came down to Amarov's motives and endgame. It wasn't surprising that Amarov had brought additional personnel, but more than a dozen?

Amarov was a big fish in the Vory sea. Geographically speaking, his operation was concentrated in the Baltics—Estonia, Latvia, and Lithuania—with nearby Saint Petersburg serving as his home and Klaipėda as his logistical hub. When Ember's Operations Officer, Simon Adamo, discovered that Amarov had a history of transactions with a

Chechen arms dealer and human trafficker named Malik, Dempsey had pushed aggressively for a meet and greet.

It was Malik who had orchestrated last month's murder of the American Ambassador to Turkey and kidnapped the Ambassador's Chief of Staff, Amanda Allen. It was Malik who had tortured Allen while holding her hostage in Syria. It was Malik who had arranged for an assassination attempt on the President of the United States and the Director of National Intelligence. And finally, it was Malik who had shot Munn in the neck, nearly killing Dempsey's best friend, and then slipped through Dempsey's fingers after a harrowing chase through the streets of Istanbul.

Malik had smarts and skills, and he was one of the most dangerous adversaries Dempsey had faced in his long and decorated career. Everyone in Ember and all the way up the chain of command to President Warner himself wanted this guy found. The problem was, since Istanbul, Malik had been a ghost. So Adamo had decided to change tack. If they couldn't find Malik, then they would try to develop a relationship with someone who would know where to look. Dempsey prayed Amarov would be that asset, but first they had to establish trust and confidence.

"Omega, any chatter we should know about?" he asked Baldwin.

"Nothing of concern, Bravo," Baldwin said. "Just personnel positioning instructions. Nothing to indicate your NOC is compromised."

"I still vote we abort, Bravo," Grimes said, her voice soft but insistent. "We should reschedule this meeting on neutral ground, or at least somewhere we can bring a bigger team."

Dempsey gritted his teeth. She made a good point, but what if this was the only shot Amarov was willing to give them? The Russian had been adamant about meeting at this derelict factory, only a stone's throw from the Russian border. If they burned this opportunity with Amarov, who would they try next? How long would it delay the search for Malik?

Dempsey eased the van to a stop five meters from where two of Amarov's armed thugs stood waiting outside the south building. His gaze fixed out the windshield, he said, "Amarov is the only vetted and viable lead we have. We don't have a fallback option. If we want to find Malik, I think our only choice is to see this through."

"Check," Grimes said, her tone resigned but full of disapproval.

Dempsey looked over his shoulder and locked eyes with Munn, who was stroking his chin. Munn nodded. "Let's get it on."

Dempsey swept his gaze across the scene one last time, then grabbed the SCAR and stepped out of the van. He closed the driver's side door and walked around to open the rear door for his "boss," an international arms dealer known in the underground simply as "the American." Munn was dressed in black jeans and black ostrich cowboy boots, and a silver chain hung around his neck. The black silk shirt he wore perfectly concealed the low-profile body armor beneath. A polished chrome Beretta 92G Elite—with a pearl handle, of course—was on display in a black leather shoulder rig, and he clutched a steel briefcase in his left hand.

He looked ridiculous.

Munn took a deep breath, stepped out, and combed his slicked-back hair with ring-covered fingers. With a scowl on his face, he cleared his throat and spat a loogie on the dusty gravel next to his boot. "The American" was a NOC carefully curated and used by the CIA over the years. Langley had been adamant that the officer currently living the legend participate in the op, but the DNI had pulled rank and now here they were.

The two waiting Russians approached, both holding state-of-the-art AK-12 assault rifles pointing up at a forty-five, but firmly in two-handed grips. Two new guys emerged from the building fifteen meters away, cradling compact machine pistols. Dempsey clutched his own assault rifle in a combat carry, ready to put it on target, while Munn walked with unbridled swagger, the pistol under his left armpit no more help than if it had been left in the van. One of the Russians let go of his forward grip and raised his hand, either in greeting or as a gesture for them to stop—his intention unclear.

Munn stopped and looked the two thugs up and down. The bigger of the two Russians muttered something to his comrade, and they both laughed.

Baldwin translated in their ears. "He said, 'Oh look, it's the American and his doggie.'"

Munn looked sideways at Dempsey, who raised his rifle, pointing it directly at the man's head. Munn then hollered back the only phrases in Russian he knew, *"Vy budete govorit' po-angliyski po do . . . i proyavit' nekotoroye uvazheniye."*

"He just told them to speak English and show respect," Baldwin translated, although Dempsey knew this one because he'd listened to Munn practice it at least a hundred and fifty times.

The Vory enforcer's grin disappeared and he raised both hands casually, though his eyes still flickered with a malicious fire. "Of course, of course," he said with a thick Russian accent. "We are meaning no offense. Mr. Amarov is excited to meeting the American. You are well known to us, and we are delighting to doing business. We are all same here."

"Somehow I doubt that," Dempsey said under his breath, stepping a half pace ahead of Munn but not lowering his rifle. He noted the sleeve of ornate Vory tattoos on the enforcer's forearms.

"All right, are we just going to stand outside pointing guns at each other, or are we going to do business?" Munn said in the relaxed, unflappable voice of a man who'd participated in a hundred armed standoffs like this and walked away from all of them.

"Yes, of course, but your bodyguard is very serious. Perhaps if he is to aiming his rifle away from my face?" the Russian said.

Munn nodded at Dempsey, and Dempsey lowered his rifle, pointing it at the ground between them.

"Where is Amarov?" Munn demanded. "It was agreed we meet in person. I do not negotiate with intermediaries. My time is too valuable to deal with *minions*."

The man laughed and commented in Russian to his colleague, who responded with a series of shoulder-shaking grunts.

"Aldy laughs out of not disrespect. He loves American movie about the minions." When Munn remained stern, the Russian said, "I assuring you we are being more than minions. You are to be working closely with Aldy and me if moving forward with our product. My name is Trak. We are—how do you say—managers for distribution in these region."

"Unacceptable. Where is Amarov?"

"Amarov is inside building," Trak said and reached inside the flap of his coat. Dempsey raised his rifle and pointed it center mass as the Russian's hand came out to reveal a mobile phone. "*Gde nakhoditsya doveriye?* Where is trust?" he said through a laugh and snapped a picture of them.

"Omega, Alpha. Amarov's guys just took Bravo's picture," Grimes reported back to the Ember TOC, her voice tense. "If they have an image database on the American, we're fucked."

"What are you doing?" Munn asked, his gaze locked on Trak.

"Before meeting Amarov, we make sure you are who you say," Trak said. "Is normal procedure."

Dempsey's throat tightened. Time shifted into slow motion, and his senses kicked in to that hyperaware perceptual state he experienced whenever Death was about to join the party.

"Someone inside the building is making a call," Baldwin reported.

"Bravo, this is Omega Actual," came a voice over the comms circuit. Shane Smith, Ember's Director. "I don't like it. I'm calling it. Mission abort. Bravo, it's time to start talking your way out of there. If this thing deteriorates on us, it's going to get real ugly real fast."

Dempsey glanced up at the roofline of the building and spied the barrel of the Russian sniper's rifle pointed down at them. Movement to his left caught his attention, and he saw the driver of the Vory SUV parked on their side of the building step out of the vehicle. The driver was holding an AK-12 and took up a firing position using the hood to support his elbow. Aldy and Trak still held their weapons in casual carries, and the two thugs guarding the door to the building behind them were still at combat ready but not sighting in. Grimes was good, but between the Vory sniper, the driver with a bead on them, and the four other shooters outside, the odds of escaping without being shot were low.

Dempsey looked at Munn, who despite the confidence he was projecting had worried eyes. "Hey, boss, we don't need this shit. I say we hit the road. These guys clearly aren't interested in your business."

Before Munn could respond to Dempsey's prompt, Trak said, "Good news. Mr. Amarov has agreed to see you." Then, flashing them a vulpine grin, the Russian added, "We have demonstration to be showing you inside. Then you be taking your sample weapons and leave us your deposit. Yes?"

"That is good news," Munn said, his voice hard. "But why don't you invite Mr. Amarov to join us outside. We can shake hands, breathe the fresh air, and look at the merchandise out here in the light."

"No, no, I am sorry, but we cannot do these things under watchful eyes from satellites overhead. American CIA and the Russian FSB might both be looking down on us—bad for everyone's business, you agree? Come inside and we are having vodka, a show, and all will being well. You must be trusting us."

"That's the problem. I can't trust you. We agreed to come as two, but you have brought many," Munn said, gesturing to all the Vory shooters. "Mr. Amarov clearly doesn't trust me, or he wouldn't be hiding inside the warehouse. So, you tell your boss that if he wants my million dollar deposit," he said, lifting the steel case and tapping it with his right hand, "he can come out here, apologize to my face, and tell all the men with guns pointed at my head to lower their weapons."

A strange expression washed over Trak's face, and in that moment, everything clicked in Dempsey's head. This wasn't a meet and greet, and it wasn't about the money. This was a snatch and grab—and he and Munn were the targets. That's why Amarov had picked a location so close to the Russian border, and why he'd brought so many men and vehicles. If Malik had made the same one-degree-of-separation deduction as Adamo—suspecting that this meeting was a covert operation to use Amarov to get to him—then it stood to reason that he would direct Amarov to take preemptive measures. Malik had seen both their faces in Istanbul, and Trak had just taken their pictures. After getting confirmation, all Amarov had to do was force them into a vehicle at gunpoint, and five minutes later they'd be in Russia, never to be seen or heard from again.

Grimes was right.

They had walked into a trap.

Dempsey leaned into his shooting stance, pressing the stock of the SCAR-H firmly to his cheek while putting the floating red dot of his holosight in the center of Trak's chest. Simultaneously, Munn drew the Beretta from its holster and aimed at the big Russian's head. In that moment, their minds were one. All the missions they'd run together, all the ops they'd planned, all the evil bastards they'd hunted in the suck together had synchronized their thoughts. Munn had experienced the same epiphany as Dempsey, and Dempsey knew the next line out of his teammate's mouth before Munn said it.

"Your shooters will get one of us, maybe both," Munn said with stone-cold certainty, "but not before one of us ends you."

Gravel crunched underfoot as they took a cautious and synchronized step backward toward their van.

CHAPTER 2

Grimes tensed on the long, low table where she lay watching the events below through her spotter scope. This op was now a shit show of epic proportions. If Dempsey survived, she would tell him that, and then, she would punch him in his big, stupid face for putting her through this hell.

Focus, she told herself. *He needs me in the game.*

She exhaled slowly while counting to four, calming herself.

She shifted her attention to the Vory on the roof. The sniper was watching the scene below through his oversize optics just like she had been, but nothing in his body language suggested he was about to engage. She was at the same elevation as the other sniper, and to keep a line on him and on the shooters on the ground required her to be closer to the window than she liked. She tilted her head to peer around her scope and keep tabs on the scene down below. Dempsey and Munn were slowly backpedaling, their weapons still pointed at Trak. The other Russian up front, Aldy, had brought his AK-12 up and was sighting on Dempsey. The two guards behind them were fanning out right and left so their bosses wouldn't be in their line of fire if this standoff turned into a shoot-out.

"Shit, this is not good," she cursed under her breath, belatedly aware that the whole team could hear her.

She leaned in to sight through her scope and positioned the dimly lit red arrow on the side of the Vory sniper's head. This guy was the biggest problem and she would have to take him first, but her mind quickly went to work, planning her follow-on sequence of shots. Dempsey and Munn were best positioned to kill Trak and Aldy, which were their closest and most immediate threats. Munn was stuck with a pistol so, knowing Dempsey, after shooting Trak he would slide left to take out both the two rear shooters. That left the driver leaning against the hood of the Russian SUV free to cut them down, which made that guy her second priority. The rear shooter on Munn's side was the third biggest threat, in case he took cover or Dempsey missed. Last were the reinforcements inside the building who would rush to engage and the roving patrol who she presently couldn't see. She scratched an annoying itch on the left side of her nose and decided on her kill sequence: one—rooftop sniper; two—SUV driver; three—door guards; four—clear the field of reinforcements as required.

She tilted her head off the scope for another look below. Trak lifted a closed fist high over his head and then glanced over his shoulder at the guards behind him, who both froze and lowered their weapons.

"Wait, wait," Trak said.

She could hear the Russian in her earpiece from Dempsey and Munn's ultrasensitive transmitters. "Let me telling Amarov. Let me using my phone. I am sure he had no idea this would upset you. No need to leave. Wait please."

Everyone down below froze except for Trak, who raised his phone to his ear and began talking.

She leaned into her scope to check the Vory roof sniper and found him tight in on his rifle now.

Damn it, she cursed, this time in her head. That sealed it. She was going to have to draw first blood. Otherwise, one of her boys was getting shot.

"Trak is saying Bravo is spooked and will not come inside," Baldwin translated in her ear. "I can't hear the reply . . . Oh wait, looks like we have an inbound call from a prefix in Vyborg, Russia, but we don't have decryption."

Several long, tense seconds passed before Trak signed off his call and lowered the phone from his ear. "Amarov is coming, my friend. We are being apologizing. We are meaning not discourtesy, I am assuring you." When neither Munn nor Dempsey reacted, he said, "Perhaps you could be lowering your weapons?"

When neither man complied, Trak took two paces to Dempsey's right, his hands still up and off his slung rifle.

What's he up to?

Still off her scope, Grimes shifted her gaze from the parking area to the rooftop sniper, assessing the firing angle, and she understood.

"Bravo, Trak is opening a lane between you guys and their sniper," she said, her voice tight as she eased her cheek against her weapon. She exhaled a long, slow breath and steadied her red arrow on the head of the Russian sniper and pulled gentle tension into her trigger finger.

"And I have more bad news," Baldwin said. "Thermals are moving inside the building. Three bodies leaving and two coming toward you. And uh-oh, they just mobilized their QRF vehicle. It's circling northwest to flank you and block your exit."

"Alpha, this is Omega," Smith's voice said in her ear. "You're clear to engage."

"Roger," she said. "Bravo, call the ball."

The urge to check the scene below was overpowering, but she didn't dare take her eye off her optics. No matter what, no exceptions, she had to take the first shot . . . but she had to give Dempsey and Munn the opportunity to work the angles and the tactical situation on the ground to their optimal advantage before the shooting started.

"Forgive me, my new friend," Munn said to Trak. "I have been betrayed before, and it cost me the lives of my men. I'm sure you understand. So, as a gesture of good will, let me open the case and show you the money . . ."

She imagined Munn setting the steel briefcase down on the ground and slowly opening the lid. The point of all this showmanship was not to stall but to reposition in a way that would change the Russian sniper's firing angle. This was invaluable information that she could not ascertain from her perpendicular perspective: Who was the Russian sniper's primary target—Munn or Dempsey?

You're a genius, Dan, she thought as she watched the Russian shooter hold perfectly still.

"Bravo Two is the target," Grimes said, letting the team know Dempsey was the primary.

"This way we can have trust," Munn continued. "You can count the money and tell Amarov that everything is legitimate."

"I am sure that is not being necessary," Trak said, moving slightly back to the left. "We trust you have been bringing what you have said. Mr. Amarov bringing sample missile and then we can concluding our business for the day. Perhaps we are having more trust in next time we are meeting."

The red arrow centered on the Russian sniper's temple and, as she slowed her breathing and pulse, it slowed its bounce, finally becoming still. She watched the Russian press in on his own rifle, and she took a long breath.

"The window is closing, Alpha. The QRF is rounding the building," Baldwin said with uncharacteristic urgency.

"Ready," Grimes said. She was in her zone now, her voice ice.

"Take him," Dempsey said softly.

"What?" Trak said, confused.

She exhaled and squeezed the trigger.

The sniper's head barfed up a red cloud, and his rifle slipped from his grip, clattering over the tile roof and catching on a vent pipe by its sling. His dead body slowly slid down the roof after it.

Trak turned and looked over his right shoulder and shouted at the Russian sniper he thought had fired. *"Prekrati* idiot! *My dolzhny ikh v zhivykh!"* Then he turned back, and his eyebrows arched in surprise to see Dempsey and Munn still standing.

"He is telling them they were supposed to take you alive," Baldwin reported in her ear, but she didn't care. Speed and accuracy were all that mattered. She was a killing machine now as she swept the barrel of her rifle onto her next target, the shooter crouched behind the Russian SUV.

Her targeting arrow found the shooter's forehead . . .

Exhale.

Trigger squeeze.

The Russian's head exploded like a piñata, and she swept her sight toward her third planned target, the rear shooter on Munn's side. As she whisked across the field of battle, her brain rapidly reconstructed the blur of imagery into a comprehensible picture. She'd seen a muzzle flare from Dempsey's SCAR as he shot Trak. She'd noted Munn using the steel briefcase as a shield as he unloaded on Aldy, and that was it. She made a quick correction while leading the flanking Russian shooter on Munn's side and dropped him with a headshot. She scanned up, worried that the other might have the jump on Dempsey, but saw the man's body crumple amid a volley from the SCAR. She scanned right, back to the building entrance, just in time to catch two shooters squirting out the door, shoulder to shoulder, with guns blazing.

Trigger squeeze.

Trigger squeeze.

She dropped both shooters in succession. Less than two seconds had elapsed.

Five rounds left in this magazine.

"Alpha, Russian QRF vehicle is engaging. Will be in your line of sight in three . . ."

She trained her sight to the expected elevation of the driver's side window . . .

"Two . . ."

Dialed in a small correction for the range . . .

"One."

The Russian 4x4 came tearing around the corner of the building. Her elevation estimate was off, but she quickly compensated, exhaled, and squeezed the trigger. The round punched a hole in the driver's side window and slammed into his head just above the ear. The vehicle slowed and abruptly veered right, turning away from her before she could pop the other occupants. Instead of wasting bullets, she waited for them to climb out.

"Bravo, we hold three thermals moving toward the rear exit," Baldwin reported. "I assume they are exfilling Amarov to vehicle number two, which is waiting on the other side of the building at idle with a driver ready."

Grimes followed Baldwin's report with, "Bravo, Alpha, I'm on the QRF vehicle. The driver is dead, and I have your backs if the shooters exit. You are clear to egress to the van and bug out."

But Dempsey wasn't running to the van. He was staring at the factory building.

"What are you doing?" she barked into her mike. "Get the hell out of there!"

CHAPTER 3

Dempsey looked down at the kneeling Trak, and the Russian glared up at him. Blood was pouring down Trak's right arm, but he tried to raise his rifle anyway. Dempsey squeezed once on the trigger, the SCAR burped, and the Vory man fell forward, dead at his feet. Dempsey snatched the man's rifle, put a foot on his chest, and wrenched it free of the sling. He tossed the rifle to Munn and scanned the building in front of him.

"What are you doing?" Grimes hollered. "Get the hell out of there!"

"I'm going after Amarov," he growled. And then he shouted, "Follow me," to Munn as he took off at a sprint. His plan was to loop around the building and intercept Amarov's vehicle from the other direction, flanking Amarov and putting the building between him and the QRF vehicle Grimes had pinned down.

Munn was beside him in a flash. "Dude, there's only two of us."

"I don't care," Dempsey fired back. "I want to take Amarov."

"Bravo, this is ill advised," Grimes protested in his ear. "I can't protect you on the other side of the building."

"Copy, Alpha. Good shooting, but it's time for you to get out of here and move south to the secondary exfil."

"What about you?" she said.

"Not sure. Depends on how this goes down," he said. "Stay fluid."

Dempsey heard her unload four rounds behind him, likely at the QRF vehicle.

"Shit," she murmured on the open channel. "They dumped the driver and they're circling northwest back around the building to meet up with Amarov or intercept you. I put four rounds into the cabin before I lost my line. Overwatch is out."

"Check."

Dempsey rounded the corner of the building, his assault rifle up, and scanned back and forth as he hunched in a combat shuffle with Munn right behind him. He stayed tight against the filthy brick wall.

"Status?" Munn asked, prompting Baldwin for a bird's-eye-view report.

"Amarov has just climbed into a black UAZ Patriot. As Alpha reported, the QRF vehicle is going to provide cover fire to safeguard his escape. You have seconds to disable Amarov's vehicle before he's on the move," Baldwin reported.

Without a word, Dempsey surged forward, his SCAR blazing. Munn was at his right shoulder, unloading a prolonged volley with his AK-12 at the tires and engine compartment of the Russian-made 4x4. The barrage didn't last long, however, because the QRF vehicle drove into the line of fire, shielding Amarov's vehicle.

Vory shooters emptied out of the QRF vehicle to engage Dempsey and Munn, while the vehicle with Amarov inside sped away leaving a trail of dust behind it.

"Damn it," Dempsey cursed as he dropped the shooter from the front passenger seat with a headshot. "We gotta get back to our van and pursue."

"Negative, Bravo," said Smith, sounding very much in charge. "Too risky for too little return. Get back to your vehicle and—"

An explosion on the other side of the building sent a fireball skyward, followed by a pillar of black smoke.

"What the fuck was that?" Munn asked as he and Dempsey backpedaled to the corner of the building for cover. Two Vory shooters were still engaging them from the QRF vehicle, one crouched behind the back bumper and one at the front.

"That was your van," Smith said. "Someone just blew it up with a rocket fired from inside the building."

"What someone?" Dempsey snapped. "I thought you said the three remaining shooters exited with Amarov."

"It appears I was mistaken," Baldwin said. "It is a very old building, brick construction, with a lot of interference. One may have remained behind, or there may have been an additional shooter we missed."

"Well, now we know the sample we were going to buy works," Munn said with a sarcastic smile.

"Do you think he has another one?" Dempsey said, taking a knee and sighting a half foot left of the Russian SUV's rear bumper.

"I fucking hope not," Munn said. "But just in case, we should probably get the hell out of here."

The QRF shooter popped out for a volley, and Dempsey split his head open with a perfectly placed round. "All right, let's go," he said.

"Bravo, you're about to be flanked," Smith said. "The shooter from inside just stepped out. He's sweeping around the corner behind you."

"Copy that," Dempsey grumbled in reply to Smith. "You take him, Dan. I'll get this last asshole over here."

"Check."

Dempsey's SCAR burped out a 7.62 round, and the higher-pitched bark of a 5.45 x 39 mm round from Munn's AK-12 followed a half second later, both targets downed instantly.

"We're done here," Dempsey barked. "Secondary exfil. Omega, remind the boat captain to stay on the Estonian side of the river mouth, please."

"Copy, Bravo," came Baldwin's reply.

"Do you hold any more signatures in the building? Do you think this guy Munn capped was the dude who fired the rocket?"

"Eighty-five percent probability. I hold no other thermals inside."

"That's what he said last time, too," Munn grumbled.

"Alpha, report?" Dempsey said as he picked up the weapon from the thug Munn had shot. The Russian was lying facedown in the dirt, but he was still alive.

"I'm three minutes away," Grimes replied breathlessly. Then, using the evac boat's call sign, added, "Charlie is in position and standing by."

"Check," Dempsey said, standing over the Russian, who was bleeding and squirming at his feet.

"Dude, what are you doing?" Munn said.

"I wanna take this guy with us," Dempsey said, ejecting the magazine from the AK-12 he'd picked up and passing it to Munn.

"What? No, this guy is nobody. We gotta go, bro."

"I want to find out what he knows. I want to know why Amarov was going to take us," Dempsey said.

"Oh dear," Baldwin said, sounding like jelly had just dripped off his English muffin and landed smack-dab in the middle of his favorite necktie. But Dempsey had been working with the Ember Signals Chief for over two years, and he knew better.

"Oh dear what?"

"I hold multiple heat signatures across the Narva River coming from the *east*."

"From the east? You mean from Russia?" Dempsey asked.

"Yes, Bravo, from Russia."

"Another QRF?" Munn asked.

"I think this *is* the QRF," Smith said. "The guys we were calling the QRF before were just the B-team."

"Help me get this fucker up," Dempsey said. Munn hoisted the wounded Vory to his feet, and Dempsey slung the dude's arm around his neck. The guy groaned in pain and protested feebly. "I don't speak Russian," Dempsey said, "but it's simple. I leave you here, you bleed to death and die. Come with us, you live."

The Vory man nodded and got his legs moving in a respectable hobbling run, with Dempsey providing the lion's share of the locomotion. With Munn leading, they pushed through the trees surrounding the factory lot to the rocky, mostly dried-up riverbed. Dempsey scanned a wide arc but didn't see the approaching assaulters.

"SITREP, Omega?"

"I have multiple—make that seven—signatures. They are north and east of you, and I don't think they see you yet . . . Oh, disregard. They see you now . . . They're coming."

"Awesome," Munn said as they picked up the pace, pushing south. "I'll cover our six; just go."

"We're not going to make Charlie pickup," Dempsey said, humping it over the rocky riverbed, his boots splashing in and out of puddles. "The boat is going to have to come to us."

"Copy, Bravo," Grimes said over the roar of a revving marine engine. "Charlie is en route."

"Fast-water exfil," he shouted over his shoulder at Munn. "Just like the good old days."

Munn mumbled something, but all Dempsey could make out was "drown" and "ass."

"Hurry, gentlemen," Baldwin said. "The shooters behind you are splitting into east and west teams. It appears they intend to box you in and cut off both avenues of escape. They probably don't suspect we have a boat, so we have that going for us at least."

"Oh and look, there's a rainbow on the horizon," Munn grumbled.

"C'mon, asshole," Dempsey barked at the Russian, who was beginning to drag now. "Move your feet!"

Dempsey contemplated carrying the Russian as the trio ditched the open riverbed for a little finger of trees that stretched south to where two branches of the shallow river flowed into Narva Reservoir, a third of which was in Estonia, the remainder in Russia. Gunfire erupted from his right as he ran, and bits of bark blinded him for a moment as a high-velocity round tore apart a chunk of tree just inches from his face.

"Shit," he hissed and lowered his body in an awkward crouch.

"Bravo, hold," Grimes's voice said in his ear, confident and in control. His lips curled up into a grin. His guardian angel of death was back. He took a knee, scanning right through the trees, and again felt Munn spin around beside him, checking to their left.

"Now what?" Munn said. "They're closing in on both sides."

"Now, I go to work," Grimes said, answering for Dempsey.

Dempsey heard a far-off whump—the sound of salvation—followed by a dangerously close whistle on the other side of the trees.

"One," Grimes said softly.

Another whump from her sniper rifle. Another scream.

"Two . . ."

"The west team is pulling back towards the building. The east team is in the riverbed and, well, I think the expression is 'shit out of luck,'" Baldwin said with bravado as sniper rounds continued to fly from the south.

Dempsey needed no further encouragement. He tapped Munn on the leg as he pressed up to his feet, now hauling the full weight of the Russian. Munn fired several rounds out of the woods toward the factory to keep the western team pressed back, while Grimes picked off eastern assaulters. They ran south. A few yards later the tree line thickened, giving them decent cover. Dempsey was full-tilt sprinting now as two more sniper shots, less than two seconds apart, echoed from the lake.

"Three . . . four," Grimes said, a deadly satisfaction in her voice. "Five . . . the east side is clear. There's a pair on the west, but I can't see them."

"Shit-hot shooting, girl," Munn huffed. "Where are you going to pick us up?"

"On the point, past that railroad bridge," she said. "Go now."

Dempsey grunted and they made the break from the woods toward the water. The boat was turning a fishhook in the dark-green lake only twenty-five yards beyond a field of calf-high grass—only twenty-five yards, but twenty-five wide-open unprotected yards. Their Russian captive was all deadweight now, and Dempsey was beginning to run out of gas. He glanced and saw the man's shirt was completely soaked in blood and his skin had gone an unnatural pale. "You dead?" he shouted and to his surprise got a grumbled response from the thug. Suddenly, the load got exponentially lighter as Munn fell in on the other side and hooked his arm under the Russian's armpit. Dempsey looked sideways at his brother, and Munn smiled at him.

A beat later, Munn's smile disappeared and he made a dull "nuh" sound and stumbled in the grass, just as the throaty crack of a high-power rifle shot echoed behind them. Losing Munn sent their human tripod off balance, and Dempsey barely managed to stay on his feet.

"Munn!" Dempsey shouted, turning to look at his friend.

"Dude, keep going," Munn choked, scrambling to his feet. "Got me in the SAPI plate. I'm in the fight—but, ow—shit, that hurts."

Another crack reverberated and Dempsey tensed, waiting for the high-velocity round to smack into the back of his skull and put out his lights once and for all. Instead, his new Russian friend lost his head, and his body collapsed face-first into the dirt at Dempsey's feet.

"Alpha, we're in trouble. Unless you can kill the motherfucker sniping us, we're not making the exfil," Dempsey said, dropping prone in the weeds next to Munn.

"Apparently, one of the two western assaulters has obtained a position of elevation inside the factory building," Baldwin said.

"No shit, Sherlock," Dempsey fired back.

Another crack sounded as a puff of green kicked up just ahead of him and off to the left.

"I can't see him, Omega," Grimes said. "A little help."

"Southeast corner of the building. Can't tell which floor."

"All right . . . still can't see him, but I can keep him pinned down," she said.

A split second later there was the steady *whump whump whump* of her long gun and muzzle flashes from the approaching speedboat. Dempsey grabbed Munn by the sleeve and broke in a straight line to the water's edge.

"Let go, bro," Munn shouted with irritation and shook his arm free as they both dove into the frigid green water.

The cold took Dempsey's breath away as he dove deep, dropping the SCAR and pulling the water with long symmetrical underwater strokes at an angle from the boat, knowing the Russian sniper would fire on that line. No bullets shot past him in the murky water, but he pulled hard, over and over, to separate himself from his point of entry. Then he angled back toward the center of his course, knowing Munn would do the same. Three seconds later they broke the surface, side by side, nearly simultaneously.

Dempsey inhaled deeply, again expecting a high-velocity round to hit the back of his head, but it didn't come. Instead, a thick green rope looped around them like an anaconda as the thirty-seven-foot Venegy executed a tight power turn fifteen feet away, kicking up a monster rooster tail of spray. Dempsey clutched the rope in his ungloved hand and grimaced in preparation for the brick wall of pain that would hit when the Venegy pulled all the slack from the rope.

"You on?" Dempsey called to Munn.

"Yeah—on . . . ," Munn bubbled from beside him.

Dempsey tightened his grip, twisting both hands outward to make the grip as firm as possible, and then felt a wrenching pain in his shoulders as the boat jerked them forward, pulling his face into a large wake of water. He exhaled from his mouth and nose as his body became a helpless human torpedo and then scissored his legs and pulled hard with his right arm, rotating his body until he was being dragged on his back.

He tucked his chin to his chest, forming a little cocoon of water around his head where he could breathe. As the boat accelerated, the strain on his arms from the drag became almost unbearable.

Despite the exhaustion, despite the pain, he refused to let go.

The Venegy dragged them through the frigid water for what seemed like a half hour but was doubtless less than two minutes. Finally, the boat slowed, then stopped. Dempsey held the rope loosely and kicked his legs in small circles to stay atop the water as the sleek white-and-mahogany cruiser drifted beside him. He looked up and two dudes he did not recognize, standing shoulder to shoulder, leaned over the side. Hands pulled at his armpits and he scissor-kicked hard, propelling himself up and over the edge of the boat and falling with a wet splat on the deck. Moments later Munn was half beside him and half on top of him.

"Hit it," one of the crew yelled, and the pilot punched the throttle.

Dempsey and Munn lay in a clump of tangled, exhausted flesh as the boat accelerated to safety. He blinked the lake water from his eyes and looked up to see Grimes peering down at him.

"That went well," she chided.

Dempsey gave her a tight-lipped grin and struggled to his knees as the rocking boat angled south to clear a long, thin island of trees. The man at the wheel gave him a grin and a two-finger salute, and Dempsey nodded his thanks back to the man, who he was sure, from both his appearance and the way he handled the boat, must be a SWCC operator—the expert boat handlers from Naval Special Warfare who support the SEALs. The bearded man beside him, arm draped over an assault rifle on his chest, leaned in and said something to the pilot. Dempsey couldn't hear over the wind and the roar of the engine, but both the young operators laughed. Dempsey turned to Munn, who was half sitting against the rear bench seat, his face contorted in pain, and snorted. Had they been that young once? It seemed like yesterday they were in their first platoon together at SEAL Team Four. And now . . .

"Talk to me, Dan," Dempsey said, reaching a hand behind the former combat surgeon, his ice-cold fingers checking for warm blood under Munn's vest.

"It didn't penetrate. It just—ow, shit dude. That's the spot. Might have cracked a rib . . . Dude, your hands are fucking freezing."

Dempsey felt a hard, swollen knot under the skin of Munn's back, just to the left, but no hole and no blood.

"Omega, everyone is five by five," Dempsey announced on the open channel.

"Excellent," Baldwin said in his ear, sounding like a proud parent whose kid had won first place at the science fair.

"Yeah, thanks for having our backs," Dempsey said, steadying himself on the gunwale and then pulling himself to his feet. He immediately felt Grimes's reproachful stare. "What?"

She held his gaze for a painfully long moment, lips pursed. Finally, she said, "We were very, very lucky today. Promise me we'll never do something like that again."

He shook his head. "That's one promise I can't make. Sorry, Elizabeth."

"If I hadn't been there—"

"I'd be dead, I know," he said, cutting her off. "But you were there, and you did your job perfectly, which is why I'm not. That's why we're a team. This is what we do."

After a long pause she said, "I don't think Amarov was being paranoid or overly cautious. And it wasn't intended to be a hit job. From what I saw, this whole meeting was a ploy to take you. The location, the way the vehicles were positioned, the way Amarov stayed inside and used a welcome party to coax you in . . ."

"They brought real merchandise," Munn chimed in. "The rocket that blew up our Sprinter was the sample unit."

"I know," Grimes said. "They set the table to play the game until the very end, but I'm convinced the ultimate plan was to take you."

"I came to the same conclusion," Dempsey said, nodding.

"The empirical evidence suggests you're right, but the NOC was solid," Baldwin weighed in, even though they weren't talking to him. "Why would Amarov want to kidnap the American?"

Dempsey looked over his shoulder at the derelict textile factory complex fading away in the growing sunlight. "Maybe the American wasn't Amarov's target . . . maybe it was *us*."

"Impossible," Baldwin said. "He doesn't know you exist."

"He took our picture," Dempsey countered.

"Yes, but that was after your arrival, which means the picture was taken for confirmation to go ahead with a plan already in place."

"What if Malik thought of the same thing we did—that we might try to go through one of his associates to get to him?" Dempsey said.

"I suppose it's possible, but that still begs the question how he knew you were coming. Someone would have had to photograph you in your NOCs and pass that on to Malik, and you've only met with one other contact while posing as the American and his bodyguard."

Dempsey's face flashed hot and he turned to look at Munn, who was sitting on the bench seat taking long, slow breaths. "That sneaky, double-dealing . . ."

"Backstabbing German," Munn said, completing Dempsey's sentence.

"Michael the Broker?" Grimes asked, pronouncing the name *mish-ay-el*.

"Michael the fucking Broker," Dempsey grumbled through gritted teeth. "I think it's time me and *Mish-ay-el* have a little talk—one lying asshole to another."

CHAPTER 4

Saint Petersburg, Russia
June 11
1530 Local Time

"Mr. Malik," the female attendant said, glancing at his face but then quickly averting her eyes. "She's ready for you."

"No matter what you hear, we are not to be interrupted. Is that understood?" Malik instructed, his glacier-blue eyes boring into her. Malik wasn't his real name, merely the legend he occupied. The number of people who knew him as Valerian Kobak he could probably count on two hands—a natural repercussion of his profession. As a member of Spetsgruppa Zeta, Russia's most elite and covert black ops activity, he'd been forced to disavow his old life and say goodbye to his friends and family forever. Thankfully, he didn't have either friends or family to worry about.

"I understand," she said before scurrying away, mumbling in Russian under her breath.

With a surge of anticipation, he pulled the key from his pocket, unlocked the door to the room at the end of the hall, and stepped inside. The room was completely devoid of furniture, the hardwood floor scraped and worn. The faded wallpaper, printed with a braided-rope and fleur-de-lis pattern, was peeling, and the smooth plaster ceiling was stained yellow with cigarette smoke. The only light in the room came from twin slivers of daylight streaming between the closed exterior shutters on two windows. Huddled in the corner sat a young woman clutching her knees, naked and shivering. A dingy metal pail sat in the corner opposite.

Valerian walked over and looked down into the pail. Finding it empty, he picked it up by the curved wire handle and carried it over to the girl.

She did not look up at him but made no effort to hide the scowl she wore.

He flipped the bucket upside down, placed it on the floor a meter from her, and sat on it.

"Hello, Amanda," he greeted her in English.

She didn't answer him.

"What? No smile? You're not happy to see me today?"

"Fuck you," she growled.

"Maybe later," he said and readjusted his hips to aid retrieval of a bag of walnuts from his pocket. "But first, you're going to tell me how you're feeling right now. I want you to be honest. I want to know what it feels like to be the American whore that you are. How does it feel to betray your friends and your principles for me?"

The girl reached up and wiped her nose with the back of her hand. He saw that her eyes were beginning to rim with tears.

"That's good, Amanda. Let it all out . . ."

"You make me feel dirty and cheap," she said, her American accent leaving much to be desired. "Worse than other men. Worse than all men."

He nodded and popped a walnut half into his mouth. "Go on . . ."

"I feel revulsion the moment you walk into the room. Especially here, in my chest," she said, pressing her right hand to her sternum between her small, shapely breasts. "It's like a black vine, strangling my heart, making it hard to breathe."

"And yet you want to please me?"

She nodded. "Yes, and that makes me ashamed."

"That's very good, Amanda. I know that was hard for you." He extended the open mouth of the bag toward her. "Walnut?"

She glared at it as if he'd just offered her dog food. "No, thank you."

"Stand up," he said. "I want to take a look at you."

She did as ordered, folding her arms across her chest to cover her nakedness.

"Turn in a circle."

She hesitated a beat, then did as instructed.

"You look thinner. Have you not been eating? And what are those bruises on your back and buttocks?"

She started to answer him; then her face contorted with sudden rage. "Fuck this shit," she cursed in Russian, then reached up, ripped the blonde wig off her head, and tossed it at him. "You're sick. This is not normal; I'm not doing it anymore."

The wig hit him in the chest and fell into his lap. He picked it up, then glared at her as she ran her fingers through her real hair, which was a dull auburn, cut short at his behest.

"You will do whatever I tell you, Veronika, because I am paying a king's ransom for the pleasure of your company." He tossed the wig back at her. "Now put that back on and never break character again. Do you understand me, you fucking whore?"

With seething ire only a real Russian woman was capable of, the prostitute he'd conscripted for the role of Amanda Allen glared at him. Given the chance, this one would slit his throat.

Hmmm, maybe there is a place for Veronika in Zeta. We need women like her. Corrupted, yet incorruptible.

She was already in the right line of work; maybe she'd simply fallen in with the wrong master.

His mobile phone vibrated in his pocket. With a sigh, he got to his feet and fished out the infernal device to check the caller ID. He knew the number.

"Yes," he said, taking the call.

"You're not alone," said the familiar baritone Russian voice on the line. The voice belonged to his boss, Arkady Zhukov, the brainchild and director of Spetsgruppa Zeta.

"Correct."

"We talked about this," the old spymaster said, the disappointment evident in his voice. "It's not sustainable. You need to purge your obsession with this American woman. Do you understand me?"

"I understand," Valerian said. There was no point denying where he was or what he was doing. Every Zeta operative was tracked. Even Zeta Prime. It had taken him ten years to ascend to the top of the field operations hierarchy, and it was a distinction he would not forfeit no matter the personal cost. He was the best of all of them, feared and envied . . . Arkady's favored son. No Zeta would wrest the title of Prime from him, at least not while his heart beat inside his chest.

"I need you back in Moscow."

"When?"

"Now. There's a car waiting outside for you."

"Is there a *problem*?"

"*Da* . . . and I have a job for you."

He resisted the urge to sigh and simply said, "On my way."

Still holding the wig defiantly, Veronika looked at him expectantly. "You're leaving?"

He nodded.

"So, are we *never* going to fuck?" she asked, tugging the wig back on.

With a tight smile, he stepped up and grabbed her forcefully under the jaw. "I thought you found me revolting?"

"*Amanda* finds you revolting," she said.

"What about Veronika?"

"Veronika wants to see what you're made of," she said, jerking her chin free from his grip.

He looked her up and down. She was very attractive, for a prostitute. "Maybe next time," he said and turned to leave. At the door, he paused and tossed a crumpled 100 euro note on the floor. "Work on your American accent. It's terrible."

On the way out, the madam who ran Saint Petersburg's most expensive escort service trotted after him and stopped him with a hand on the shoulder. "How was your experience today, Mr. Malik? Did it live up to your expectations?"

"Veronika's accent is shit," he said, glowering at her. "And somebody is hitting her; find out who. Nobody hits Veronika but me. Is that understood?"

The madam nodded.

"In fact, cancel all her clients. From now on, she's mine and only mine."

The woman screwed up her face and started to laugh. "The only way I will agree to that is if you pay me up front for the lost revenue."

"I know."

"It will be very expensive."

"I understand."

"And her regulars . . . they're not going to like it. Several of them could be a problem for me. You're not the only gangster in Russia, Mr. Malik."

The madam was nervous. He could see she was contemplating how to manage the demand he had just made of her. Right now, she was probably thinking she would pare Veronika's client list to the bare minimum and then lie to him about those who were simply too dangerous to refuse.

"You just tell them that Veronika belongs to Anzor Malik and if they don't like it, they can come and talk to me," he said with a cool smile. "And you also tell them, if they touch one hair on either of your heads, they will end up like Jora Kuznetsov." At her blank expression, he added, "Trust me, they will know what you're talking about."

"All right, I will tell Veronika the news. When can we expect to see you again? I want to make sure she is prepared next time."

"Probably a week, maybe more. I don't know." Then he pushed his way out the doors and headed toward the black Mercedes sedan idling at the curb.

CHAPTER 5

1650 Tysons Boulevard
McLean, Virginia
June 11
0432 Local Time

The nightmare was a horror show—the sum of all his fears.

"Kelso, wake up," Petra said, rousing him. "Breathe, Kelso, breathe."

"Where am I?" Jarvis gasped, trying to clear his throat.

"You're at home, in bed. You're safe," she whispered. "Try to breathe; it's just a dream."

He found her hand on his chest and clasped his palm against the back of hers. Even through her hand, he could feel his heart pounding like a war drum. He tried to sit up and felt a stab of pain in his chest from the still-healing bullet wound he'd received in Istanbul only a month ago, when he and the President had been the targets of an assassination attempt. He had never been prone to nightmares—not as a young SEAL officer, not as the CSO of the Tier One, not even as director of Task Force Ember. Only now as the Director of National Intelligence, years removed from the thick of action and violence, did the nightmares come. But these nightmares were not the product of his warrior past; they were not sins relived. The dreams that haunted his nights were twisted things born from a different kind of fear—a malignancy growing inside him that no matter how hard he tried, he could not purge.

"Ow," he said, settling back down, the pain clearing away the fog of sleep and disorientation from the nightmare.

He turned and found her eyes in the dark.

"Do you want to talk about it?" she asked, her head and torso propped up by a wedge of three pillows beside him.

"No," he grumbled. "And . . . yes."

She didn't say anything else, just gave his left pectoral muscle a gentle little *whenever you're ready* squeeze.

"I was in the White House," he began, turning away from her to look up at the ceiling. "In the Oval Office, in fact, waiting to brief the President. The whole gang was there, SecDef, the Vice President, Secretary of State Barnes, the National Security Advisor, and so on, and then I realize that they're all looking at me, waiting for *me* to say something. I look around and they all have this terrible, worried look on their faces. Only then do I realize that I'm the one sitting at the *Resolute* desk. Then Catherine Morgan steps up. 'Mr. President, can you hear me?' she says, waving her hand in front of my face. 'Mr. President, are you okay?' I try to speak, but my lips and tongue aren't working properly. Drool starts running down my chin. I try to move, wipe my mouth, do something, anything, but my muscles are like jelly. I can't even support my own weight and I flop over in the chair, like . . . like an invalid . . . it felt so real, Petra."

She didn't comment, just tenderly rubbed his chest.

"I lost my balance yesterday, getting up after the national security brief," he said. "Fell right back into my chair. Did you see that?"

"Yes," she said. "But I don't think anybody else noticed."

"Secretary Baker did. He asked me if I'd been out partying too late the night before."

"It wasn't mean-spirited," she said.

"I know," Jarvis grumbled. "He was giving me an opportunity to save face, which is even worse."

She didn't take the bait, wisely not encouraging this particular tangent.

"Well, aren't you going to say something?" he finally asked, his irritation growing.

"We're going to beat this, Kelso," she said with a certainty and confidence that woke him up like a bucket of cold water to the face.

He turned to look at her. She'd said "we." It was a simple distinction, yet one with profound implications. "We" was a pledge. "We" was a promise. "We" was a statement of solidarity. By uttering that one little word, she'd proclaimed her intention to go to war at his side. And in doing so, she'd set the expectation that he man up and do the same.

"It's time," he said with newfound strength and determinism. "I need to know what's happening to me. These dreams I've been having are a subconscious call to action. A SEAL doesn't run from a fight. A SEAL doesn't hide from the enemy. I need to stop living in denial and develop a battle plan to beat this."

"I agree," she said without a hint of patronization or "it's about time-ism" in her voice. "Early intervention increases our treatment options and is more likely to slow the progression."

"Let's schedule that appointment with that neurologist at Walter Reed you've been bugging—er, I mean, encouraging me to see."

"Don't worry, I'll make sure it's handled discreetly. No one will find out who we don't want to find out," she said.

In that moment, Jarvis realized the confidence in her voice was far more soothing than the feel of her warm hand on his chest. Petra had been downrange with the Tier One as an analyst, back in the day. She had gathered specialized intelligence and conducted fieldwork with

Naval Special Warfare Group Ten and then later with the Office of Naval Intelligence. Women did not serve as SEALs, but her pedigree working in the community for two decades made her part of the brotherhood. She had served with the same warriors, helped plan the same operations, and hunted the same enemies side by side. She understood him better than any other woman ever could, and now they were teammates in this new and very different kind of fight.

He blew air through pursed lips and stared at her. There were so many things he wanted to say to her, strong and intimate things he could have, should have said, but what came out was: "Speaking of being discreet—we can't keep doing this, not like this anyway. It will get out and then—"

"I know," she said, without bitterness. "But it doesn't change the truth."

"And what truth is that?"

"That we need each other . . . more than either of us dares to admit except maybe here and now, in the vulnerable privacy of the dark."

He didn't argue with her, didn't even try, because she spoke the truth. He'd never needed anyone like he needed this woman, and not just because of whatever insidious condition was lurking inside him, eroding his central nervous system. No, it was so much more than that. This bold and brilliant woman had stepped into the line of fire to take a bullet for him. And that bullet, which had been on target to kill him, instead punched a hole through her lung and exited her back before hitting him, changing trajectory so that he might live. Her blood now ran forever in his veins, a reminder with every heartbeat of the debt he owed her.

It was macabre, beautiful poetry.

Petra's hospital stay had been three days longer than his, but her first night home she'd come to him. He'd let her into his apartment, and they'd wordlessly celebrated their victory over death and terror like two kindred souls—through embrace and togetherness. They'd not made love yet—neither of them was in a condition for that—but that glorious communion would happen when it happened. They were bonded now. Where before they had been two, now they were one.

"Do you want to hear a strange confession?" he said.

She nodded.

"Until this moment, I always believed I was incapable of love. My mind isn't wired like other people's minds. I don't feel and perceive things the same way normal people do. Sensory data gets entwined and layered and transmuted."

"Your synesthesia," she replied. "I know."

"I've never told you that."

"You didn't have to. It's obvious."

"Oh," he uttered, taken aback and impressed by her insight.

"Is that all you wanted to tell me?"

"No, it's just the tip of the iceberg. This is going to sound strange, but there's not just one Kelso Jarvis. I've never felt like I could be just one person. To fit in, to be effective as a leader and a strategist, I became a chameleon—a collection of characters and personas adapted to foster constructive interaction with the people around me. I've worn so many masks for so long, I worry that I've lost the original one." He turned to her and gave her an uncertain smile. "Lying here with you, I can't help but wonder which of my personas you've fallen for."

"Hmmm, then we might have a problem," she said, twirling his chest hair with her fingertips. "Because I didn't realize I had to choose just one."

He stared at her, dumbfounded, because while he had not intended his confession to be a test, she had passed it nonetheless, by saying the one and only thing that proved she understood him better than anyone else in the entire world.

When he couldn't find the words, she simply said, "Call me greedy, but I want all of you."

He reached for her hand. "You might come to regret that decision."

"I doubt it," she said with a little smile, "but you are right about one thing."

"Which is?"

"That we can't keep doing *this*. It's a violation of your own fraternization policy, and we can't let each other become hypocrites. I'll start looking for my replacement. Once I resign, we can pick up where we left off, but until then no more sleepovers. Agreed?"

"I don't want another Chief of Staff," he grumbled, "I want *you*."

"Then you can have me, but in that case, we have to put *this* on the back burner until you either get promoted or fired. We're together either way," she said. "I'll let you decide the nuance."

"I can't do the job without you," he said.

"Okay, then it's decided," she said and carefully, gingerly scooted up against him until her breasts were pressed against his left arm. "We work and we wait."

"And you're not upset?"

"I'm not going to lie, I want to be with you, but we have more important things to do than snuggle and make pillow talk. The country needs us, Director Jarvis. The world needs us . . ."

She was right; they both knew it.

"All right, we've made our decision." He wanted to lean in to kiss her but then stopped himself. She would let him do it, but it would be a mistake, a self-inflicted wound weakening their resolve in the months to come. So instead he said, "Let's talk about Russia."

"You know how I love it when you talk dirty," she said, deadpan.

A beat later, they both started laughing. "See," he said, "this is exactly why we're meant for each other."

Despite the dark, her eyes seem to brighten at this, and he took a mental snapshot of her to both document and commemorate this moment—the moment he unequivocally committed himself to a woman for the first time in his life.

"Russia . . . you were saying?" she prompted.

"Petrov is winning," he said, the muscles in his jaw tightening. "The Kremlin seems to be keeping one step ahead of us, and I'm not sure if the root cause is systemic or acute. After what happened in Turkey, I'm beginning to worry that we have a mole operating in the upper echelons of our government. We know from the debriefs with Amanda Allen that Russia was the puppet master pulling the strings behind the events in Ankara and Istanbul last month. But what I still don't understand is how they knew the President was coming to Turkey. That trip was a short-fuse decision—less than twenty-four hours from the moment Warner said he wanted to meet with Erodan, we were on the ground in Istanbul, but they were ready for us. That assassination attempt was planned and executed with the maximum amount of advanced notice."

"You're right, they were ready for us, but let me play devil's advocate for a moment. It doesn't necessarily imply we have a mole. You've heard of the term 'big data,' right?" she asked.

"Of course."

"I'm no data scientist, but it seems to me that we, as a nation, emote a tremendous amount of data these days. And I choose that word, 'emote,' quite intentionally. The Justice Department, the CIA, the FBI—all have Twitter accounts run by professional social media moderators. My concern is that, even without releasing confidential information, we telegraph our intentions . . . like a poker player with a tell that he's not aware of but that his opponent can recognize and reliably exploit. Our military-industrial complex is so open and integrated into our economy that the chatter itself is a vulnerability. Before mobile phones and social media, chatter was distributed across the system. It could not be aggregated or effectively captured. Chatter was just what its name implied—background noise that was always present and yet continuously fading out of existence. But not anymore. NSA is always collecting, and so are the Russians. What if Russia has figured out a way to use that data to make accurate predictions about all kinds of things— from things as broad as the capabilities of the Joint Strike Fighter to things as specific as President Warner's itinerary for an emergency trip to Turkey? Look at what Ian Baldwin does over at Ember with mathematical algorithms to interpret raw data. It's incredible, and we'd be delusional to think there is only one Ian Baldwin, or that all of the Baldwins out there work only for the good guys. We've suddenly found ourselves in the middle of Cold War 2.0, but we're still stuck in a Cold War 1.0 mentality. This isn't a Ludlum novel, Kelso. I think we need to worry less about some Russian superspy who might have infiltrated our ranks and more about the possibility that the US intelligence community in aggregate is unwittingly undermining itself in the course of conducting everyday business. All it would have taken was one White House staffer to post something to a social media channel about a trip to Istanbul and the Kremlin gets a predictive data point to add to dozens of others, which, when considered together, gives them prescient predictive power."

Jarvis considered her theory. "All right, let's assume everything you just said is true. From a tactical perspective, how do we defend against this phenomenon?"

"I don't know," she admitted. "There's no one-size-fits-all Band-Aid. We live in a digital world now, and America—with our democratic, capitalistic system—has chosen the path of open source. Russia and China have gone the other direction, compartmentalizing data and limiting the free flow of information. That's created an asymmetrical battle space in the war for information, but it's the reality we live in. Social media is here to stay. Email, texting, blogging, photo sharing—none of these things are going away."

"Well, we're not going to solve the problem in bed tonight, but I don't think we table it, either. I think we need to put a team on this. Maybe this is something Catherine Morgan, as Deputy Director of Intelligence Integration, can work on."

"No," Petra said sharply, and then after an awkward beat added, "What I mean is I was kind of hoping that this was something I could spearhead."

"Are you sure you want to take this on? Your plate is pretty full, in case you hadn't noticed."

"True, but my evenings are about to free up," she said with a coy smile, "now that you're breaking up with me."

"In that case, Miss Felsk, consider yourself officially tasked with figuring out how to stop Russia from slurping up all our critical data," he said. "We're going to make a damn good team together."

"Going to?" she said with playful sarcasm. "I think it's pretty damn obvious we already do."

"Thanks for being here for me," he said, his voice going serious as he pulled her in tight for a hug.

"You're welcome," she said, hugging him back. Then, with a smile on her face, she laid her head on his shoulder and drifted off to sleep.

CHAPTER 6

The Kremlin
Office of the President
Moscow, Russia
June 11
1410 Local Time

Petrov threw the book at him.

Not figuratively—literally.

Arkady Zhukov ducked as the latest unflattering hardcover biography written about the Russian President sailed over his head and slammed into the door behind him with a thud.

"I'm going to fucking kill this guy," Petrov said and began pacing behind his desk.

Arkady stooped and picked up the book. The title, *Cult of Personality—a Profile of Vladimir Petrov,* was printed in large block font, superimposed atop an unflattering photograph of the man. An incendiary subtitle read: *Strongman, Tactician, or Global Menace?* And below that, the author's name, an American Arkady did not recognize.

"That could probably be arranged," Arkady said, tucking the book under his arm and walking to one of two vacant chairs opposite the President's desk. "But we should wait awhile, until this is forgotten."

"Not that piece of shit," Petrov said, slamming his fist down on the desk. "I'm talking about President Warner. Have you heard the news?"

"You mean the new sanctions levied by Washington to stall the Nord Stream 2 pipeline?"

"Not to stall, to kill," Petrov said, red-faced. "He's trying to kill it."

"Germany won't let that happen. There's too much momentum."

"First, Warner tried to strong-arm Germany using the media. When that didn't work, he tried to prompt the EU to investigate Gazprom, hoping the EU would view Nord Stream 2 as cementing our unfair monopoly on natural gas. And now that's failed, so he's using sanctions and claiming that Nord Stream 2 is a threat to the stability of NATO. If he can't use the bankers to bully Chancellor Mercer, then he's going to use her generals to do it. At the same time, he's pushing American natural gas exports everywhere he can. The US has a piece of every natural gas terminal under development in Europe. Six are already in the works, and there are talks about six more. Warner needs to go, my friend. It's that simple."

"He's in his second term," Arkady said, setting the book on the corner of Petrov's desk with practiced nonchalance. "He'll be gone in eighteen months regardless of what we do. The Americans change leaders like socks—it is one of their weaknesses that we exploit. What we need to be focusing on is who we want to promote as his successor. We're laying the groundwork for the next election's cyber campaign right now. I don't like any of the candidates but one."

Petrov sat down, and as he did his normal coloring returned to his face, the hot anger giving way to his trademark icy malice. Petrov *permitted* himself to lose his temper only in the company of trusted advisors and members of his innermost circle. "And then there's Lithuania,"

Petrov said, either not listening to or not caring about Arkady's conversational lure.

"What about Lithuania?"

"Their state utility company signed a two-year import agreement with Lone Star Energy out of Texas. The Lithuanian President then signed a $300 million infrastructure improvement bill so they can reexport American gas to Latvia. Poland is building a gas terminal with the same aspirations, and Estonia is working with Finland on the Baltic-connector pipeline to cut us out completely. Moscow may be Russia's beating heart, but oil and gas exports are her blood. Our economy cannot survive if we cede our monopoly of the European gas market to foreign powers. Warner knows this, which is why he's hitting us where it hurts."

"I agree, so what do you want to do about it?"

Petrov glared at him, apparently not liking the subtext of this comment.

"Let me rephrase," Arkady said with a deferential smile. "What I meant to say is what do you want *me* to do about it?"

"I want you to make them all pay. I want you to make them think twice about the next time they try to poke the bear. And I want you to do it in such a way that Russia does not come out looking like we always do—the big bully on the block."

A knock sounded on the door to the President's office.

"Come," barked Petrov.

A very tall, and very fine-looking, young woman entered carrying a beverage tray. She paused just past the threshold, her body language alone asking the question.

"Yes, yes," Petrov said, waving her in. "Your timing is perfect as always, Tatia."

Arkady moved the offensive book from the corner of the President's desk to make room, and Tatia set the tray in that exact spot. "Tea, the way that you like it, Mr. President, and coffee for you, Minister Arkady."

Arkady smiled at her. He hated tea. "Ah, you remembered, thank you."

She nodded at him with a little look that said, *Of course I remembered; you think this is all I'm capable of?* Then she turned to Petrov. "Is there anything else, Mr. President?"

"No, not now," Petrov said, staring at her with equal parts judgment and lust.

She nodded, turned, and let herself out.

Arkady raised his eyebrows at Petrov once the door was shut.

"Of course I am," the President said, while taking zero pleasure in the gloating.

That is when you know a man has no soul left, Arkady thought, studying Petrov's eyes. *There's no pleasure left in life that sates him. He is a fire in a freezer, burning and consuming, yet providing no heat or light.*

"What?" Petrov snapped. "Why are you looking at me that way?"

"I have an idea," Arkady said, rubbing his chin. "As you know, Lithuania's entire natural gas operation is dependent upon the FSRU *Independence* at the port in Klaipėda. This one ship is everything: floating storage and regasification unit. It's quite brilliant, actually. All a country needs is a pier and voilà—instant LNG terminal. Carrier ships moor alongside the *Independence*, which receives liquefied natural gas, then evaporates it to its original form and supplies it to the main transmission system for distribution to the rest of the country."

"I'm not an idiot, Arkady," Petrov said through a sigh. "Take out the *Independence* and you take out Lithuania's entire ability to import gas."

The spymaster nodded. "That's right."

"I assume you're proposing a false-flag terrorist operation? Make it look like jihadists have attacked the *Independence* for reasons of their own."

"No, I think this time we go small. Industrial sabotage made to look like equipment failure, followed by human error leading to the sinking of the vessel at the pier."

Petrov nodded. "If you sink it, it can be repaired. Why not blow it up?"

"*Da*, it could be repaired, but at what cost? On what timeline? If we do this properly, the rehabilitation cost might exceed the cost of replacement. And remember, the *Independence* is being leased from the Swedes. Just think about the circus once the lawyers get involved. It will take a year minimum, maybe longer. And it will be an environmental nightmare. There's a good chance when this is all over, Klaipėda as a natural gas import terminal will be done forever."

Petrov nodded but said nothing, so Arkady kept talking, kept selling.

"In the beginning, right after the accident, Russia will step in and offer a new one-year emergency supply contract with Gazprom to help the Lithuanians deal with this terrible crisis. Gazprom agrees to lock in the price at a favorable rate, and Russia looks like the hero to the rescue."

"Yes, I like this," said Petrov. "We can even offer technical support and equipment to help with the cleanup. Better yet, we help with the investigation. We can send engineers, divers, system experts from Gazprom and the Russian Navy to help find the cause of the accident."

"Exactly," Arkady said.

"Okay, you have the green light, but don't fuck this up, Arkady. The Americans know it was us behind the assassination attempt in Turkey. That's why Warner is throwing everything he has at taking Russia down while he's still in power. There can be no traces back to us."

"Understood, Mr. President," he said, showing the deference Petrov craved.

"Is that all you have for me?" Petrov asked.

It wasn't all he had, not by a mile. There was the incident in Narva he'd purposely neglected to share, and there was the ever-growing paranoia he felt that the Americans were closing in on Spetsgruppa Zeta, the ultrasecret task force he commanded. In his last communication with Catherine Morgan, she'd assured him that neither DNI Jarvis nor Task Force Ember had pierced Malik's legend. More important, Arkady himself was still completely off their radars as they prowled for clues as to who had conducted the attacks in Turkey. But Ember: they were tenacious, smart—nearly as much so as Zeta—and operated with a virtually unlimited budget. It was only a matter of time before they came knocking on his door, something he needed to preemptively circumvent. Even now he was moving chess pieces on American soil. When the time came, he, not Kelso Jarvis, would have the assets in position to deliver a death strike. Only one king could rule the board, and that king was him.

Arkady met Petrov's blue-eyed gaze. "I have nothing else, Mr. President."

"Very well," Petrov said, signaling that the meeting was over.

Arkady drained the remainder of his coffee, stood, and, tucking the biography under his arm, turned to leave.

"Aht, aht," Petrov tsked. "That's my book."

"Oh, my apologies. I thought when you threw it at me, it was meant to be a gift," Arkady said with a brother's smile.

"It's autographed," Petrov said with a fox's smile. "It goes on the shelf with the others." Arkady chuckled and handed it back to the man he both loved and despised—a product of his tutelage and the worst and best thing to ever happen to Russia. As the book changed hands, Arkady's gaze lingered on the subtitle, *Strongman, Tactician, or Global Menace?*

The answer was all three, of course. Something everyone knew . . . including the man behind the desk.

CHAPTER 7

Neiburgs Hotel
Riga, Latvia
June 11
1915 Local Time

"It's a far cry from life in the Teams, that's all I'm saying, Dan," Dempsey grumbled, with no idea why he was so irritable. Back in the day he would have high-fived a brother for taking advantage of the opportunity Munn had.

"What's goin' on?" Grimes asked, kicking the door closed behind her, plastic bags hanging off both forearms. The two-room suite instantly filled with the smell of food—real, delicious, hot food, not just the kind that rubbed out the hole in one's gut. The smell should have cheered him up, but instead it irritated him even more.

"We're hunting the most dangerous man in the world, and Dan's making time for a day at the spa," he said with more venom than he intended.

"It was an hour—not a day. And it was a therapeutic massage, because I got shot in the fucking back because you thought it was a good idea to drag a dead Russian thug to the boat for interrogation."

"He wasn't dead, bro, he was only *mostly* dead," Dempsey said.

"There's a big difference between mostly dead and all dead," Munn quoted, grinning.

"That's right, mostly dead is slightly alive. Pump a little air in that Russian's lungs and I guarantee he would have talked," Dempsey said, chuckling now.

"What are you two jackasses talking about now?" Grimes said, setting the bags of food on the table where Dempsey and Munn sat.

"Get back, witch," Munn snapped at Grimes, modulating his voice to imitate Billy Crystal's character in *The Princess Bride*.

"Oh God," she moaned. "Are you guys quoting some stupid movie?"

"It's not a *stupid* movie," Munn said. "It's a classic."

"Whatever you say." She began pulling plastic to-go containers from the bags.

"Anyway, the point is, Munn's gone soft," Dempsey said, getting back to the jibe fest.

"Look, dude," Munn said, legitimately exasperated now. "Smith booked a room at the nicest hotel in Riga. It has a spa. I got shot in the fucking back, it's bruised and full of knots, and that shit hurts, so why not get it worked on? I'll sleep inside a fucking log all night when I need to, but why should I be miserable when I don't have to?"

"Girls, girls," Grimes said with an exaggerated eye roll. "You're both pretty. Can we please just eat? I'm friggin' starving."

Dempsey shot her a look that people with thinner skin than Grimes might consider a glare, but it didn't faze her.

"I got you the rack of lamb, extra rare, 'cause you're a steely-eyed killer. Got the slow-cooked boar for the lumberjack and the sea bass for me. If anyone wants some, there's a salad to share, a roasted octopus appetizer, and a couple baguettes." She slid into a chair and tore off a large chunk of bread. "Enjoy."

The aroma subdued his grumpy attitude, and Dempsey tore into the perfectly cooked, or rather *not* cooked, lamb.

"That good, huh?" she asked, making him aware of the guttural groans of carnivorous delight he was making.

"This shit literally melts in the mouth," Dempsey said, his mouth full of lamb. "Thanks, Lizzie."

"No problem," she said with a chuckle. "You good?"

He nodded. "Yeah, I'm just pissed off at myself. You were right—meeting Amarov like that was one of my worst plans ever. We should have brought a bigger team. If we had, we'd probably have him in a black site interrogating his ass right now instead of sitting around complaining about it while eating gourmet takeout."

"You really think Michael the Broker knows who we are and tipped off Amarov?" Munn asked, setting his fork down and fixing Dempsey with a serious stare. "I mean, if that douche can crack our borrowed NOCs, what does that say about CIA's OPSEC?"

Michael the Broker was a midlevel matchmaker and information broker who operated primarily out of Hamburg—connecting all permutations of buyers and sellers in the underground markets and on the dark web. Dempsey had never heard of the guy before this op, but that wasn't unusual. In his former life, he didn't hang out with bad guys, he shot them in the head, which meant his network when he joined Ember consisted of zero connections in the criminal and terrorist underground. Dead guys, go figure, don't do a lot of deals.

Adamo had made the connection—one of those "I know a guy who knows a guy" sorta deals from his pre-Ember days at Langley. The first meeting they'd had with the arms broker had been on Michael's home turf in Hamburg. The middle-aged German had come to the meet unarmed, with no backup, and dressed in workout clothes. Dempsey, in his guise as bodyguard, and Munn, in his NOC as the American, had met him at a sidewalk café. On their arrival, Michael had informed them that he had a yoga class and they needed to walk and talk at the same time. So, that's how it had gone down—with two of America's most lethal operators dressed like thugs, negotiating with a man in a tracksuit, outside a yoga studio, to set up a meeting with one of the most dangerous Russian Vory bosses in Europe.

Strange world.

Dempsey nodded and shoveled some salad onto a plate, then reached over and loaded a spoon with charred octopus.

"You know you really shouldn't eat octopus," Munn said, his brow furrowed.

"Why's that?" Dempsey said. "E. coli or some shit?"

"No," Munn said, shaking his head. "'Cause it's like eating bottle-nose dolphin or gorilla meat."

"You mean they're endangered species?" Grimes asked.

"No, but they're really friggin' smart—probably sentient. It just ain't right."

"You know what else is smart?" Dempsey said, spearing a hunk of charred boar meat from Munn's container. "Pigs. Pigs are really smart. Smarter than dogs, they say, which means pigs are probably sentient, and you're eating one right now. But you already knew that, and you're still eating it. And do you know why, doc?"

"Why?"

"Because pig is fucking delicious," Dempsey said, pulling the meat off his fork with a snarl. "And so is charred octopus, especially when it's dripping in garlic butter. So shut your yap."

"Is this what you guys were like downrange?" Grimes asked, looking back and forth between them.

"Yeah, pretty much, except downrange there was no delicious pig or octopus to eat," Dempsey said through a laugh.

"What *did* you guys eat, by the way?"

"Dirt," Munn said with a mouth full of boar.

"And sand," Dempsey added. "Dirt and sand, mmm, delicious."

"All right, all right, let's get back to Amarov and Michael the douche," she said and took a bite of her fish.

"Here's the thing," Munn said. "Michael has no incentive to burn a big buyer like the American. He's a broker. He gets paid when deals happen. From his perspective, the American was a new client, and every new client is a potential repeat client. I guarantee there is zero possibility Michael pierced our NOCs. You see where I'm going with this?"

"I'm apt to agree, but that doesn't mean Michael couldn't have had us photographed at our last meeting and gave the pics to Amarov."

"And Amarov gave the pictures to Malik?"

Dempsey nodded. "It's possible."

"It wouldn't even have to be directly," Grimes said, leaning in on her elbows. "Amarov or even Michael could be working with Russian Intelligence. There's more than one channel for the information to get back to Malik."

"Why would the Vory work with Russian Intelligence?" Munn said. "I thought the FSB was tasked with taking down those Mafia assholes."

Grimes shook her head. "I'm not so sure anymore. The lines between the Vory and the Russian government are getting blurry these days. I read this report by a Russian expert at Langley— Wilson, I think was his name—who maintains that after Petrov's accession to power, the Kremlin started using the Vory as a tool. In the beginning, the FSB hired the Vory as contract killers to do their dirty work, giving themselves one degree of separation. But over the past decade, the relationship has evolved to much more than that. Petrov uses the Vory to launder money, abduct rivals, and more. He even uses them as assassins. These guys are integrated now. Intelligence suggests there are Vory occupying organic positions in the Russian intelligence community, and worse, embedded within the government ranks."

Dempsey sighed and pushed the plate away, no longer hungry. "Which means we have to find out if 'the American' NOC is busted. We need to find out exactly what Amarov knows and if Russia knows about the existence of Ember."

"So how do we do that without getting killed?" Grimes asked.

Dempsey clenched his jaw. "We start with the only lead we have— we call Michael."

"Right now?" Munn said, surprised.

"Why not?" Dempsey said. "I'm sure word has gotten back to him about what happened. He's undoubtedly expecting our call."

"Yeah, and he's probably scared shitless," Munn said with a chuckle.

Dempsey pushed back his chair, fetched the laptop computer from his bag, and carried it back to the dining table. He opened Baldwin's super wham-a-dyne untraceable phone call program and from the menu of recent calls, he clicked on "Michael the Broker" and initiated the call. He turned up the speaker volume so they could all hear.

"*Guten Abend. Das ist Michael. Wie geht es Ihnen?*"

"Michael, do you know who this is?" Dempsey said, holding Munn's gaze.

"You are the American's bodyguard," the German said after a pause, his accent thick. "We met in Hamburg."

"I didn't think you'd take my call. In fact, I thought you'd be running for the mountains of the Hindu Kush to find a suitable cave in which to hide before I come for you and cut your eyes out."

"*Was ist los?* What is this threat?" the German said, flustered. "I don't understand."

"Your 'good friend' Amarov tried to have me and my boss killed yesterday," Dempsey said. "Do you understand that?"

"Yes . . . I mean, no. I have no idea about what you're telling me. I'm a businessman. Whatever Amarov did, I had nothing to do with it."

"So, it sounds like you're saying you take no responsibility for your clients' safety and well-being and are happy to give them false information and send them into a trap?"

"There must be some misunderstanding. I'm doing business with many, many clients for many years, including Mr. Amarov. Tell your boss, I am very sorry. I will make this right. Tell him I will find another supplier. Please."

"Tell him yourself. I'm going to hand him the phone."

Dempsey nodded to Munn, who waited a beat and then, the anger in his voice undoubtedly fueled by the very real pain in his back, said, "Give me one reason why I shouldn't kill you and your family. They live in one of the penthouse apartments in the Regierungsbezirk Oberbayern, do they not? I have many associates in München," he said, using the German word for Munich. "I could make a call right now."

"*Bitte schön,*" the man replied, the fear in his voice real. "I will make this right. Let me talk to Amarov and find out—"

"No," Munn snapped. "Talking to *Amarov* is the last thing you will do."

"Then what? What do you want me to do?"

"Meet me in Riga," Munn said, giving Dempsey a thumbs-up.

"Latvia? Why?"

"Because I fucking said so," Munn snapped and then exhaled a long breath, loud enough for the man on the other end to hear. "I'll give you the exact location two hours before the meeting. If you attempt to inform Amarov about our meeting, I'll know and I'll kill you. If you try to run, I'll know and I'll kill you. If you notify German Intelligence, Latvian State Police, or any other law enforcement agency, I will know and I'll kill you. And then, even if it is my last act on earth, I will personally hunt down and kill every member of your family. Do you understand, Michael?"

"*Ja,* I understand," the man answered, his voice trembling. "I will be there."

"See that you are," Munn said. "And in the meantime, find some-one else to sell me those fucking missiles."

Munn nodded at Dempsey, who severed the connection with a click of the laptop's trackpad. Dempsey looked at Grimes. "What's that look for? You don't think he'll come?"

"Oh, he'll come," she said, but then blew air through her teeth. "Provided the Russians don't get to him first."

CHAPTER 8

6602 Eames Way
Bethesda, Maryland
June 11
1830 Local Time

Catherine Morgan pulled her Volvo XC60 into her garage and closed the overhead door behind her. She was exhausted, hungry, and tired of the lack of sex and intimacy in her solitary existence. These were the things she was thinking about when she unlocked the house door and walked inside. She kicked her heels off and padded straight into the kitchen to scavenge for something—not an apple—to eat.

She went straight to the refrigerator and stopped.

Something was wrong.

I'm not alone . . .

She had a Glock 19 in the cabinet drawer beside the fridge. She swung the refrigerator door open with her right hand while opening the drawer to retrieve the Glock with her left. Deftly, she stepped behind the open fridge door and switched the Glock to her shooting hand.

Dropping to a tactical knee, she cautiously sighted around the door and into her living room.

"I have a gun," she called, loud and with conviction. "I know you're in there."

"Don't shoot me, please," a male voice said from the living room, a hint of laughter in the voice. He spoke American English with an accent imperceptible to all but a well-trained ear. Catherine immediately detected his Russian roots. "I'm going to step out now," he said.

Looking down the barrel, her sights trained at chest level, she watched as a stranger stepped into the doorway separating her kitchen from the living room. He was relatively young, clean-shaven, and of average height and build. The operator—and there was no doubt he was an operator—wore dark blue jeans and a gray Patagonia fleece. He was not holding a weapon.

"Who are you and what are you doing in my house?" she said, adjusting her aim as he stepped fully into view.

"Have you recently swept your residence for listening devices and cameras?" he asked.

"Yes," she said.

Fixing her with his granite-eyed gaze, he said, "The shortest boy in the class was named Simon."

The phrase was one of several challenge statements she'd been told to memorize for authentication protocol.

"And his best friend's name was Oscar," she replied.

The intruder smiled at her, but when she didn't lower her weapon he said, "Not satisfied? Want to do another?"

"You look like him," she said, studying the assassin's face. "When he was a younger man."

"You're not the first to say it," he said. "But less now that he started wearing a beard."

The resemblance was so uncanny, this Zeta could pass for Arkady's son, had the spymaster ever married. *I wonder . . . No, impossible,* she thought, pushing the idea from her mind. "What do you want?"

"I just came to talk," he said, then frowned. "Why are you still pointing that at me? We're on the same team, you and me."

"No one informed me you were coming," she said, shifting her gaze past him.

"Don't worry, I'm alone," he said, his accent slipping and sounding more Russian now.

"Maybe so, but you broke into my house."

"The old man said this was the best way. He warned me you were vigilant but also said this was the safest location for us to meet. He said if I jeopardized your cover he would cut my balls off."

All right—that sounds like Arkady.

She exhaled, stood, and lowered her weapon. She did not, however, put the Glock away. "What did you come to tell me?"

"All business, huh?" the Zeta said with a shrug. "Fine, fine. I need to know the location of the Task Force Ember operations facility."

"Why?" she said, taken aback by the question.

"That information is need to know only."

"Well, if you want me to tell you, then I need to know."

The operative gave her a closed-lip smile. "Arkady said you'd say that. How long have the two of you known each other?"

"Years," she said, watching him intently as her anxiety level crept back up. She'd not told Arkady about her visit to Ember's secret hangar in Newport News nearly a year ago. Spies were not supposed to be judicious with their reporting or withhold information. Spies were supposed to be honeybees, gathering informational pollen that was then flown back to the hive and surrendered to the collective without animus. She understood this perfectly—but she had also long ago recognized that disobedience was a prerequisite for self-preservation. Despite the hundreds of plundered secrets she'd delivered to the Kremlin over the years, she always kept a crown jewel or two in reserve. An insurance policy. And the location of Ember's facility was one of them.

"You seem very nervous, Catherine," he said. "Is something wrong?"

She repositioned her index finger from the trigger guard onto the trigger. "You tell me why you want to know the location of the Ember facility, and I'll tell you what's wrong."

He sighed like a man in the middle of enjoying a fine meal, only to have it spoiled by the waiter prematurely delivering the bill. "He told me you'd want to know. And he told me to tell you that the order to execute has not been decided, but he wants us ready. *If* it happens, he wants you to know that you have zero post-operation obligations."

Her legs went to jelly at this last statement. Something must have changed. She wasn't read into Ember's operations or activities, but after the events in Turkey, Jarvis had finally awoken to the Russian threat. Ember must be getting close or Arkady would not be considering such an attack. And if she read between the lines, it didn't bode well for her professionally. To ask her to leak such sensitive and compartmentalized information put her at risk of exposing herself.

So, this is it. He thinks I've outlived my usefulness. Deliver my Ninth Symphony and then I'm being retired.

She'd always known this day would come. And if she was being honest with herself, she'd felt it encroaching ever since Warner had named Jarvis DNI. Maybe Arkady had groomed a replacement for her. Maybe her replacement was already active and in position. Zetas, as a rule, worked in silos, rarely interacting or collaborating. Arkady could have had another mole inside ODNI, maybe for years, with her none the wiser. Her mind indexed through her colleagues and contemporaries serving across the intelligence community. Mental snapshots of names and faces populated her mind's eye until only one remained—the one who was, in some ways, the most like her. An ambitious woman groomed and situated to earn the trust of Kelso Jarvis. Petra Felsk.

I've been so blind. How could I have not seen this coming?

She sighed and set the Glock down on the counter. Resistance was futile. Sure, she could shoot this Zeta, but what would that accomplish? Arkady would just send another, and if she got the jump on that one, then he'd send another, and another, until the deed was done. Arkady couldn't risk her being arrested or defecting. This was the Russian mentality, captured succinctly in the immortal words of Joseph Stalin: *Death solves all problems—no man, no problem.*

Find your courage, she told herself and walked straight to the cabinet where she kept the liquor. "What do you want to drink?" she said, turning her back on him. "Vodka?"

"Nah, do you have American bourbon?" he asked.

She grabbed a bottle of Basil Hayden's and two rocks glasses and walked to the kitchen table. "Neat or on the rocks?" she asked.

"How do you like it?" he said.

"They say a bourbon like this should be sipped neat, but I prefer mine cold."

"Then I'll take it that way, too."

She fetched the ice bin from the freezer, dropped three cubes in each glass, and poured. He raised his glass to her in a toast. "To our American comrades, without whom life would be very boring."

She nodded, clinked glasses, and they both drank.

"When do you think it will happen?" she asked, looking at him over her glass.

"I told you, it's not decided."

"That's not an answer to my question."

He exhaled and held her gaze. "If I had to guess—it'll be soon."

"I presume you'll come here after to finish the job," she said, her voice dry leaves scraping over concrete.

He jerked his head back and looked at her, eyes wide. Then he started to chuckle. "Okay, now I understand. Don't worry, Catherine, it's not your time. You're much too valuable in your position."

She took another swallow and, while she stared at him, wondered why people drank bourbon. Even the expensive ones burned her throat, and the flavor did nothing for her.

"You don't believe me?" he said, cocking an eyebrow.

"It doesn't matter what I believe."

"You're untouchable, didn't you know that? It's not an order he would ever give. Were that day to come . . ."

She met the young operator's eyes and spoke the unsaid: "He would do it himself."

The Zeta nodded, and she knew he was telling the truth.

"So, Ember . . . what can you tell me?"

Her stomach felt heavy and hot, like she'd just been forced to swallow a glass of molten lead. Yes, she was a spy, but she had devoted most of her adult life in service to this country. She had spent more years in her American legend working in the intelligence community than she had in her homeland. In fact, Russia had become more of a dream than a memory for her. She *was* Catherine Morgan now. The naïve, self-important girl she'd once been, the one with the Russian name, she was the stranger. She was the foreigner. It was the natural consequence of accepting a lifelong mission to become an American. Ninety-five percent of her daily endeavors, her relationships, and her emotions concerned America and promoting an American agenda. Every betrayal was unpalatable, but this one felt particularly heinous. Was she even loyal to Russia anymore, or was her loyalty only to Arkady Zhukov?

She exhaled, steeling herself for what came next.

"Ember is located in a bunker beneath a private hangar at the Newport News/Williamsburg International Airport," she said robotically, ignoring the emotions. "I have only been inside once. The facility is heavily fortified. The primary and secondary doors are hardened with biometric security. The frames and slab looked blast resistant, so traditional breaching is probably impossible. Assuming you get inside the hangar, accessing the bunker is even more challenging. The entrance is hidden in plain sight, and unless you observed someone coming and going, you'd probably never find it."

"Can you describe it?"

"Underground access is via a secure elevator, but the elevator doors are inside what looks like an old metal supply locker. They have security cameras monitoring everything, and all access points require dual authentication—passcode and biometric. Even if you open the locker, you won't be able to call the elevator."

"Interesting," he said. "They must have a secondary entrance or emergency egress—a ladder or a stairwell?"

"I'm sure they do, but I didn't see it."

"Do you have access to the facility plans?"

"No."

"Can you get them?"

"Highly improbable, and any attempt to do so would raise red flags."

"Understood. What can you tell me about their security and lock-down protocols?"

"Nothing, beyond what I just described. And don't ask me for a roster of personnel or access to their current locations and operational tasking, because it's compartmentalized, and I don't know."

"This was our expectation," the assassin said with a nod. "Can you facilitate a meeting there tomorrow, gather specific intelligence, and provide me with a report?"

"Not if you want me to retain my cover," she said. "It would be highly unusual, and the timing would be of great interest after an attack."

"All right, we will conduct ISR and do the best we can." He finished off the rest of his liquor and pushed his chair back from the table. "Thank you for the bourbon."

"You're welcome," she said, getting to her feet. "Would you like me to let you out?"

"That would be fine," he said, leading the way.

"What's your name?"

He hesitated a moment, then said, "You can call me Gavriil."

"Are you the Prime?" she asked, her curiosity getting the better of her. She rarely met other Zetas, and this one carried himself with a self-assuredness that reminded her of Arkady.

"No," Gavriil said, the corner of his mouth tipping up. "Not yet . . ."

CHAPTER 9

Walter Reed National Military Medical Center (WRNMMC)
Bethesda, Maryland
June 12
0630 Local Time

Jarvis stepped out of the dressing room wearing only a pair of gray sweatpants, wool socks, and a thirty-year-old navy-blue US Naval Academy hoodie he'd last worn *exactly* thirty years ago before hoodies were hip. The sweatshirt smelled like cedar, having absorbed the olfactory signature of the closet where he kept all the clothes and uniforms he rarely wore but saved nonetheless. This sweatshirt was proof that somewhere, buried deep inside, there *was* a sentimental bone in his body. Maybe the docs would find it during his MRI.

"I've gotta take a picture of this," Petra said upon seeing him, grinning large and fetching her phone from her handbag.

"You most certainly will not, Miss Felsk," he said in his command voice, but he was unable to suppress a wry smile.

"Sorry, Director, too late. Now that's a keeper." She rotated the screen to show it to him—a full-body shot of him looking ridiculous.

"In that single picture, you've accomplished what thirty years of adversaries could not."

"What's that?"

"The complete and total emasculation of a Tier One Navy SEAL," he grumbled. "I can't believe you found and packed this sweatshirt."

"Don't worry," she teased, slipping her phone back into her handbag. "This pic is for me and me alone. I promise it will never see the light of day—provided, that is, you do everything and anything I say from now on."

"You know, blackmailing the DNI is a felony," he said, narrowing his eyes at her.

"I know," she said, "but I'm dangerous that way."

He picked up the plastic bag they'd given him for his personal belongings and handed it to her. "My suit is hanging up in the locker, but my ring, wallet, ID, and phone are in the bag. I'd rather that stuff stay with you. I powered my phone off so it won't be going off every five seconds bothering you while I'm in there."

"Roger that," she said, opening the mouth of the bag for a quick inventory peek and then looking back at him. "I blocked your calendar this morning and instructed your PA to forward all your calls to me."

He met her gaze and felt something difficult to articulate. Gratitude? Solidarity? Intimacy? "Thanks for tagging along with me."

"Are you nervous?" she asked, her chin tilting just a few degrees to the right—an endearing, inquisitive mannerism that only appeared in moments like this. "Not about the MRI, of course; I mean for the results?"

"Nah," he said, shaking his head. "I flipped that switch the other night. You know what this feels like to me? Like pre-mission ISR—I'm chomping at the bit to plan and execute the next offensive, but before I can do that I need to first identify and locate the enemy. That's what today is all about."

Before she could respond, a knock came on the closed door behind her. "Director Jarvis, is there anything I can help you with?" Radiology technician speak for *we're ready for you and tired of waiting,* he assumed.

"No thanks, Jenny, I'm changed and ready to go," he called back.

With a parting glance at Petra, Jarvis opened the door and followed the technician into the imaging room, where the ambient temperature was at least a dozen degrees cooler. He stared at the giant gray MRI machine that took up half the room.

"I know you already answered this question on the paperwork, but I'm required to ask you in person. Do you have any metallic implants? These can include but are not limited to things such as artificial joints, pins or screws used in the repair of broken bones, a pacemaker, metallic tooth fillings or orthodontia?"

"You'd think a guy with my service record would be full of metal, but believe it or not, I'm metal-free. Even the shrapnel I've taken has all been removed."

He followed her instructions and positioned himself on the cushion atop the machine's extended tray. She handed him some foam earplugs. "Go ahead and put those in and then I'll hand you your headphones. It can be pretty loud in there, so we use double hearing protection, and we can play music on the headphones if you like. There's a microphone attached so you can talk to me in the control room at any time during the procedure. If you need us to stop or pull you out, just ask. Otherwise, try to remain as still as possible during the session."

"Understood. If you could play Sergei Prokofiev that would be great."

She made a funny face and said, "I'm sorry, could you say that again? I don't think I know that group."

"Sergei Prokofiev," he said, then spelled the famous Russian composer's last name for her. "Or if you're using a streaming service, you can just type 'Dance of the Knights' and Prokofiev should come up."

"Got it."

She walked through a few additional steps, then pressed a button and the table he was on began to move, delivering him headfirst into the cylindrical MRI tunnel. A strange, macabre thought overwhelmed him as the machine enveloped him—that he was not in an MRI machine but rather a coffin being slid into an oven for cremation. The heavy warmth of the blanket swaddling him would soon become unbearable as the flames charred his flesh and then consumed him to ash—

His headphones came alive with static and then, "Director Jarvis, it's Jenny talking to you from the control room. Can you hear me?"

"Yes, Jenny. I can hear you," he said, snapping himself out of the gruesome daydream.

"The machine is going to run through some calibration sequences, then we'll get started with the first scan, which will last approximately eleven minutes. I'm going to go ahead and turn on some music for you now, and I'll check back in. All right?"

"That'll be fine," he said, and a beat later deafening banging sounds began in earnest as the gradient coils inside the machine began cycling. The first time he'd had an MRI, the clanking was so loud he was convinced the machine was tearing itself apart, but the noise was a normal by-product of generating and manipulating magnetic fields sixty thousand times greater than the earth's natural magnetic field. These powerful oscillating fields and radio waves were capable of imaging virtually any structure in his body in three dimensions. If he had a brain tumor, cancer, or spinal cord injury, the MRI would detect this. If he had multiple sclerosis, then the MRI would detect demyelination in his central nervous system. But if the scans revealed nothing abnormal, then his doctor would order a battery of blood work and other tests. Either way, in a couple of hours, he'd know a helluva lot more about what was going haywire inside him than he did now.

Orchestra music began to stream in his headphones, and Jarvis closed his eyes. With its brooding and ominous opening, Prokofiev's "Dance of the Knights" transported him from the MRI chamber across the world to Moscow. His synesthesia immediately ratcheted up, merging and mingling his senses, and he found himself immersed in a vivid and epic waking dream.

Heavy brass bass notes accompany booted footsteps as a lone figure wearing a black overcoat marches down a stately marble-tiled hall in the Kremlin. In this place, Jarvis is an invisible observer, a ghost watching a scene unfold from the past, or the future, or maybe from his imagination. Strings soar and fall, oscillating with the man's long, deliberate strides and the swinging of his arms. The man in the overcoat has been beckoned. Snare drum triplet. Snare drum triplet. He walks with confidence. His aura is red. He walks with malice. His aura is black. The man arrives at the Office of the Russian President, and members of Petrov's administrative staff stand in attention—French horns play a salute, a respectful acknowledgment for this legendary, dangerous figure.

The doors to the President's office swing open—double bass and tubas hit hard and low on the quarter beat—and he marches in to greet his master, who is standing at the window, his back turned to the man. Then, the music falls away. A lone trumpet plays. The President begins to talk, quiet and pensive. Strings emerge and soothe, but this is a deception. Petrov is angry and yet wears an ice-blue aura. The President reminisces about a glorious Russian past, but as he talks a feverish crescendo creeps into the music. His aura bleeds red at the edges, turning it purple. The violins begin to soar once again, announcing his aspiration. The tubas and double bass return, growling and angry. Trombones roar and the flutes scream. Dominion—Russia returned to its former might and glory. This is what Petrov desires—what he demands—and the man in the overcoat will give it to him. Must give it to him!

Prokofiev's masterpiece fades and Tchaikovsky begins to play. The scene changes.

Jarvis is at the Moscow Ballet, watching the stage from a private box. A male and female dancer glide onto the stage. This is "Arabian Dance," the most sensuous and technically difficult performance in The Nutcracker— an intricate duet performed on a darkened stage. Clarinets breathe, violas keep time, and a lone oboe sings melodically. Why is his mind showing him this? The male dancer lifts his partner. He is her support, but she is the performer—lithe and flexible, seductive and acrobatic. Her serpentine movements are hypnotizing, and Jarvis cannot pull his eyes from her. The partners draw together for a lift and a spin. They drift apart but dance in perfect synchronicity. Strength and beauty, power and seduction. They come together. They drift apart . . . but they are tethered. Always tethered.

The song ends.

The music changes, and a new drama begins . . .

"Director Jarvis, are you doing okay in there?" said the technician in his ears.

Disoriented, Jarvis opened his eyes and was greeted by curved gray plastic four inches from his face. *I'm still in the MRI tube,* he realized as his mind rebooted.

"I'm doing fine, Jenny," he said and cleared his throat. "I think I drifted off for a bit."

"No problem, sir. You've been perfectly still the last thirty minutes, so we got great images. I'm going to bring you out now."

"Roger that," he said, and fifteen seconds later he was out of the tube staring up at the ceiling.

As he changed back into his suit in the dressing room, he contemplated the surreal experience during the procedure. A knock came at the door—Petra's knock.

"Come in," he said, taking a seat to slip on and tie his shoes.

Petra entered the changing suite and shut the door behind her. "How'd it go?"

"Fine," he said, looking up at her. "I decided to just let my mind relax and think. But I closed my eyes, the music started playing, and then something strange happened."

"Go on."

"It was like a fever dream. Sound and color and images all twisting into a hallucinatory narrative. It was so powerful, Petra." He got to his feet, feeling more alive and energetic than he had in months. "I got inside the head of the enemy, took a tour inside the Russian mind. They are a cerebral people, and yet remarkably artistic; cold and calculating, and yet so fiery and passionate. They're nothing like the ideological terrorists I've hunted most of my life. They're like us, and yet so, so different. I've been wearing blinders for too long—refusing to recognize the enemy inside my body as well as the enemy in my own house."

She nodded but didn't interrupt him as he tried to articulate the conclusions his synesthetic mind had formulated without words.

"I'm convinced now that we have a Russian mole. A dancer who is always on her toes—adroit, experienced, and enchanting," he said, keeping his expression clinical as he studied her reaction. "Supported and guided by a spymaster in Petrov's inner circle."

"And you're convinced the mole is a woman?" she said, her expression dubious.

He nodded and then suddenly remembered their last night together and how she had so deftly redirected the conversation the first time he'd confessed this concern about a mole. At the time, he'd thought nothing of her playing devil's advocate, but now he was curious. What would she say now that he'd pushed the theory again?

"But you have no data," she continued, "just a gut feeling?"

Jarvis resisted the urge to roll his eyes. He was not a leader who relied on his "gut." What everyone liked to call a gut feeling was really just another name for the situational and survival machinations of the primitive limbic brain. In the heat of battle, ceding control to the limbic brain was prudent, but when it came to strategic and abstract problems, letting the limbic brain drive the bus was a terrible idea. Gut feelings didn't solve mathematical proofs, win chess matches, or put a man on the moon. For the entirety of his adult life, he'd made a habit of ignoring the ego-driven, emotion-laden chatter of his primitive mind, relying instead on logic, probability, and knowledge to inform his decisions.

Which now begged the question: Was what he experienced during the MRI nothing more than the search for easy answers that seemed to plague the rest of the world's "go with your gut" thinkers?

No. It was a thought exercise, a meditative state of higher concentration in which my mind correlated observational and probabilistic data that I've been assimilating for months.

"No hard data," he finally answered, not willing to admit or concede anything more.

"Okay then," Petra said with a cool smile. "I'm already looking for data leaks and vulnerabilities, so adding a mole hunt to my plate shouldn't be too difficult."

"Good," he said, getting to his feet. He watched her, still wondering . . . Then, looking at the plastic bag in her left hand, he said, "My things . . ."

"Is everything all right?" she asked, handing him the bag. "Did I do or say something to upset you?"

"No, everything's fine." He flashed her a practiced, easy smile. He needed a fresh set of eyes—someone with experience and expertise dealing with Russian Intelligence—and he had an idea of just who might be able to help. The man was days from retirement, but perhaps Jarvis could convince him to delay that plan. Then, slipping on his wristwatch, he said, "We've wasted enough time here. Let's get back to the office."

"I thought the plan was to stay until Dr. Aberle looked at the scans and briefed you on the results. We're scheduled to meet in his office at ten."

"Yeah, well, change of plans. I don't need any hand-holding. The neurologist can call me with the results. I've got bigger problems to worry about at the moment."

And with that, the Director of National Intelligence turned his back on his Chief of Staff and walked out of the room.

CHAPTER 10

Brevings Whiskey Bar & Pub
Old Town
Riga, Latvia
June 12
1211 Local Time

"Don't lie to me," Dempsey growled at the German arms broker sitting across the table from him. "People who lie to my face make me very angry, and when I'm very angry, I'm prone to violence. So, unless you want to be on the receiving end of that violence, Michael, then you better start telling me the truth."

Tourists and locals alike streamed past on the cobblestone street, smiling and chatting on the sunny late-spring day, completely oblivious to the team of armed American operators stationed around them in plain sight. Despite the cool breeze and his position under the shade of their table umbrella, the German mopped sweat from his forehead with the napkin from his lap.

"I came here as a show of good faith. Please hear me when I say that I had no idea what they were planning. If my objective was to betray you, then why would I agree to meet you face-to-face today? I'm a broker. My job is to connect buyers and sellers and arrange meetings. I only profit when a deal is made and funds are transferred, and so you can see that it does not serve my interests to double-cross either party . . ."

Dempsey's earbud crackled. "He makes a valid point," Munn said while the German continued pleading his case.

". . . happened in Narva has spread like lightning, and now everybody is questioning my integrity." Michael frowned. "They say you killed a dozen men and tried to kill Amarov. There is no one who has not heard of this. My business could be ruined as well—my livelihood. All I have is my reputation, okay? You see?"

"Ask him if Amarov has tried to contact him since our call. Tell him your boss wants to know what Amarov's next move is going to be," Munn said in his ear.

"I agree, Daniel," Baldwin chimed in. "We'd all love to hear what he says because the chatter we're picking up is that *the American* was the one who double-crossed Amarov. I think Amarov is running an underground smear campaign to hide the truth and make himself out to be the victim."

Dempsey sighed under his breath at the unsolicited commentary and narrowed his eyes at Michael. The man was terrified—if not for himself, then for his family. "Have Amarov or his people tried to contact you since we last spoke?"

"No."

"Ask him if he tried to contact Amarov," Munn interjected.

"And did you try to contact Amarov?" Dempsey asked.

"I followed your instructions precisely. I talked to no one and came here at the appointed time," the German said, his exasperation seeping through despite his fear. "But as a professional, I need to discover why I was deceived. If people think that I'm a pawn of Amarov or that I'm a guy who can be played, then no one will ever use me again. Tell your boss this. Let him know that I take responsibility for my part, but that I am not the responsible party."

Munn laughed in Dempsey's ear. "Oh, that's rich. Tell *mish-ay-el* that he was Amarov's pawn and that he did get played. Tell him if he doesn't start giving us some information we can use, then the only business he'll be conducting from now on will be from a wheelchair."

"I'll tell my boss, and he'll probably believe you, but then he'll start talking in my ear, and he'll talk and he'll talk and he won't stop talking. He'll tell me what to say and how to say it, and it will be like he didn't trust me to do my job," Dempsey said, hoping Munn and Baldwin got the not-so-subtle hint. He leaned back in his chair, holding the German's eyes. "But you and I can avoid that, right now, because this is your chance to give me something I can take back to my boss so that he'll be satisfied. You see, Michael, my instructions were very clear: either you prove yourself to be loyal and helpful, or you leave with extra orifices in your body that weren't there before. So, give me something I can use, or this day is about to get exponentially worse for you."

"Okay, okay. When you contacted me and asked me if I could arrange a meeting with Malik, I told you that I did not know him and had never done business with him. Then you told me you'd pay me a big bonus if I could figure out a way to get you a meeting with Malik, and I told you that I do a lot of business with Amarov and that I knew for a fact that Amarov does business with Malik. Do you remember that?"

"Of course."

"Okay, so what I did *not* tell you is that when I contacted Amarov to arrange your meeting with him, he was not so interested. I said you had a lot of money to spend and connections, and still he was not so interested. But when I told him that you would pay a bonus for an introduction to Malik, then he got very interested. I said I would give him half of whatever you paid me, because that's how I work. When everybody gets paid, everyone is happy."

Dempsey exhaled and leaned back in his seat. This was the confirmation they'd been looking for. Malik must have established a protocol with his network of contacts to notify him in the event of a query like this, knowing that Ember would be looking for him after Istanbul. It's what Dempsey would have done if he were in Malik's shoes. Perhaps Malik was even paying incentives to dealers and brokers, hoping to lure Dempsey into just such a trap.

"How long have you known Amarov? What else can you tell me about him?"

"Oh, I have known him for many years, over a decade for sure. He is very tough negotiator . . ."

As Michael talked, a woman walking up nearby Šķūņu Iela caught his attention. Dempsey had arrived at the eatery on Tirgoņu Iela before Michael and had taken a seat with his back to the building so he could scan both Tirgoņu and Šķūņu and watch pedestrian traffic going in and out of Dome Square—the most popular public space in Riga's Old Town district. The other two members of his team were similarly positioned—with Munn seated outside a restaurant across the street and Grimes on the long gun keeping overwatch from an empty fourth-story flat in a building located at the intersection of the two streets.

Dempsey's gaze flicked from the babbling arms broker to the young woman in the street. She wore blue jeans, dark sunglasses, a simple gray windbreaker, and nondescript trainers and had a small backpack slung over one shoulder. Something about the woman's build and gait was eerily familiar. He squinted—wishing he had a spotter scope—but at this distance he couldn't quite make out her features in profile. Then she glanced in his direction, and for a fleeting moment he got a good look at her before she disappeared across the intersection.

His breath caught in his throat.

The adrenaline dump that followed sent liquid lightning into every muscle fiber in his body. He squirmed in his chair, and it took all his willpower and discipline to keep from chasing down the woman he'd just seen.

A woman who was supposed to be dead.

A woman he'd left to die—shot in the back and bleeding to death on the floor of the Grand Bazaar in Tehran.

Elinor Jordan.

An Israeli Seventh Order double agent he'd partnered with on Operation Crusader, the most dangerous mission of his career. She'd led him into the heart of Iran and delivered him to the VEVAK mastermind behind the massacre that had wiped out his old Tier One unit and set him on the path to joining Ember. Or had it been the other way around—with her delivering her VEVAK boss to him? To this day, Dempsey still wasn't sure if she'd double-crossed him or double-crossed VEVAK. From their very first encounter, Elinor had been an enigma—deceiving him but confiding in him, seducing him while entrusting him with her life. And despite these crimes of passion and protocol, he'd cared for her, believed in her, and mourned her death.

But now here she was in Riga.

Alive.

The German arms broker abruptly stopped talking.

Dempsey's gaze flicked to the man across the table, whose eyes were staring at him, wide and confused.

"Gurgalaka . . . gur . . . ga," Michael slurred and reached up to touch the back of his head. He brought around his fingertips for inspection but collapsed face-first on the table before he could look at them. They were covered in blood.

"Zero, we got a shooter. Michael is down!" Dempsey said to Baldwin and was out of his chair and moving a heartbeat later. Like a tactical computer, his mind crunched the data—estimating the bullet's trajectory, muzzle angle, and the assassin's elevation to determine the most likely firing quadrant. "Two, watch yourself," he warned Munn. "The shooter is in your neighborhood. Watch your six."

"Check," Munn said, slipping from his chair into a tactical crouch. "I heard no shots fired."

"Me neither," Dempsey said as he closed on Munn. "The bullet didn't punch through. Shooter is probably using a twenty-two with a suppressor."

Like a firefighter running toward a burning building, Dempsey charged *toward* the threat. His calm focus and clarity were born from twenty years of combat experience, and all irrelevant peripheral information melted away into the background. He systematically scanned every person inside a thirty-degree arc. The threat identification process was automatic, his brain assessing posture, facial expression, eye contact, and physical appearance. *No, no, no* came the silent verdicts in rapid succession as he worked his way through the restaurant's lunchtime crowd—a crowd that was just beginning to wake up to the fact that something was terribly wrong.

There!

Fleeing in the commotion he saw her—gray windbreaker, small black backpack, blue jeans, sunglasses . . .

How the fuck did she get over there so fast?

The shot had come too soon after he'd seen her down the street for her to be the assassin, and yet he was certain her presence here was no coincidence.

"Elinor!" he hollered as he catapulted into pursuit.

She bolted immediately, dodging and weaving between the tables, umbrella stands, and oversize wooden planters that filled a dining patio in her way. Dempsey sprinted across the brick-lined street, arms churning, Sig Sauer in his right hand. The crowd went into panic mode, with men, women, and a handful of children either screaming or stampeding in response to the wild man charging toward them with a gun.

"One—God. Report the target," Grimes said in his ear, her voice as cool and calm as a glacier mountain lake.

"Female, gray jacket, black backpack, jeans, sunglasses—she has dark hair, almond skin, medium height and build," he said, juking his way through the crowd. "She was heading for Rozena Alley or whatever the fuck the next street to the west is called."

"I'll lose her behind the building if—hold on, I got her," Grimes came back. "She's heading north across the square, toward the Rīgas Birža art museum."

"That's fucking impossible, I just saw her vector west," Dempsey said.

"Wait, I see her," Munn chimed in, running nearly stride for stride with Dempsey now. "She's on the lawn in front of the Riga Cathedral."

"Not possible—I saw her turn down Rozena," Dempsey said, breathing hard as he rocketed out the other side of the dining patio and into the massive public square.

"Guys, I think we've got a serious problem," came Baldwin's calm voice. "Including your two tangos I count four—wait, make that five—girls matching Dempsey's description. They're coming out of the woodwork. I got another one on Tirgoņu Street . . . and two on Šķūņu—one heading northwest and another heading southeast away from me. Shit, they're everywhere."

Dempsey glanced right and saw Munn's female target walking leisurely, not running, across the cathedral lawn. To his dismay, this girl was a nearly perfect clone of the other girl he'd just taken his eyes off. "Damnation, we're being played," he barked and then shifted his gaze back down the alley to reacquire the girl he'd been chasing.

"What do you want to do?" Munn asked as Dempsey vectored south, splitting off from his teammate.

"I dunno. Just start checking them all until you find the one that's Elinor Jordan and tackle her."

"Elinor Jordan? What the hell are you talking about?" Grimes said in his ear.

"Yes, One, please elaborate. Everyone back here at home is equally curious," said Ember Director Shane Smith, hopping on the party line for the first time.

"I know it sounds crazy . . . but I saw her in the crowd . . . right before the German went down," Dempsey said in bursts, punctuated by heavy breaths as he sprinted down the alley after his target. To his irritation, the girl was blazing fast, and so far he was not closing the gap. "Mother, do you have eyes in the sky?"

"Negative, One," Smith replied with what could only be described as a defensive edge. "We weren't expecting your *lunch* chat to turn into this kind of operation."

"Check. Not your fault . . . neither did I."

Sirens began to wail somewhere behind him, and Dempsey heard a police whistle blow.

"Does local law enforcement know we're here?" Munn asked.

"Negative," Smith said. "We'll try to get on the horn with Riga police, but no guarantees I can make that happen. God, I recommend you stay put, and fellas, remember the rules of engagement for this op. Nonlethal defensive fire only."

Dempsey could hear Munn groan on the open channel at this, followed by a grudging "Check." Dempsey, for his part, said nothing and just kept running. At the end of the cobblestone alley, the woman turned left and disappeared from view. Dempsey pushed himself until his legs and lungs were burning. Without eyes in the sky, every second without visual contact increased the odds of him losing her into the crowd. A mental count ticked in his head as he closed the corner: three, four, five . . .

She had at least a six-second lead on him, which meant the odds of escape were high in her favor. Leading with his Sig, he rounded the corner and transitioned from the heavily shadowed narrow alley to looking straight into the bright midday sun. Squinting, he raised his left hand to his brow as he sighted down the street over his weapon. A woman in a nearby gaggle of tourists screamed, and the group cowered en masse against the windowed facade of a shop displaying Russian nesting dolls. With the path down the cobblestone street now clear in front of him, he spied a flash of gray windbreaker as his target ducked into a crowded outdoor market. Legs pumping like twin pistons, Dempsey tore after her. A jumble of shrub-filled planters, wheeled carts, and tent-covered booths created a virtually impenetrable thicket—with merchants, local shoppers, and tourists intermingling shoulder to shoulder. Instead of trying to barrel his way into the throng, Dempsey looped around to the right, peering sideways into the market for his target as he ran. Within seconds, he was already rounding the back perimeter.

"One, this is Two, I got a problem," said Munn, voice oozing with aggravation.

"Tell me," Dempsey said.

"Two is getting arrested," said Grimes, beating Munn to the punch.

"Yeah, I'm out of the op," Munn said, and that's when Dempsey registered the chorus of sirens echoing through Old Town. "I suggest you holster your weapon and make yourself disappear, or we're gonna end up cellmates."

"Check," Dempsey said, scanning left along the back of the market. Several white delivery vans were parked along the curb, with vendors unloading goods and merchandise. He paused at the four-way intersection, shifting his gaze to the other two options, straight ahead and right. When he was six years old, he'd made choices like this using the default playground selection tool—*eenie, meenie, miny, moe.* As an operator suddenly stuck without visual backup, this decision felt about the same. But instead of trying to *catch a tiger by the toe,* he defaulted to a nostalgic and superstitious rule that had always served him well in the Teams.

When in doubt, go left.

He went left, slipping past the first delivery van and dropping his Sig to a low-carry two-handed grip. He advanced along the driver's side, his head and torso motionless but his eyes constantly moving. A police siren wailed nearby, and he placed it on the other side of the market. Getting arrested would be unpleasant, but not being able to defend himself in a gunfight with a trained assassin was the greater of two evils. Of course, this begged the question: If he came muzzle-to-muzzle with Elinor Jordan, could he pull the trigger?

In Tehran, he hadn't been the one who'd shot her, but by abandoning her he'd violated the SEAL ethos and betrayed the sacred tenet of "leave no man behind." This time around, would he be the one shot in the back and left bleeding to death on the cobblestones? Just as the thought occurred to him, a young woman in a white tee, blue jeans, and trainers with a black backpack slung over her shoulder stepped out from behind the rear bumper of the second delivery van. She'd shed her gray windbreaker and donned a pale-blue sun visor, but this was the girl he'd been chasing. She looked right and they locked eyes. Time seemed to grind to a halt.

Though the resemblance was uncanny, this woman was *not* Elinor Jordan.

She bolted.

He charged after her.

For the first thirty seconds, as she fled down yet another narrow alley, he thought she might outrun him. But then—chalk it up to superior conditioning, natural athleticism, or maybe Dempsey's indomitable will—he began to close. And as he neared, she started to panic, looking over her shoulder repeatedly, sacrificing a half stride with each backward glance. The fear in her eyes told him this girl was not a threat to him. She was not the shooter. He'd been lured into following one of the decoys—the primary decoy, most likely, the fastest of the team and one positioned in the kill quadrant to distract him from the real Elinor hiding in plain sight.

"Stop!" he barked, the nature of the engagement already de-escalating in his mind.

She didn't stop, however, and instead summoned a burst of speed. Dempsey dug deep, finding that other gear of his own, and kept on her tail. Ten meters later, she blasted out of the alley. Tires squealed, a horn blared, and she narrowly missed being obliterated by a white-panel delivery van. She stumbled across the street, executed a quick dogleg maneuver, and ducked down a new alley. Dempsey hit the intersection in stride, gambling that traffic had come to a halt behind the van. The gamble paid off, and he shot the gap and followed the girl into the next alley.

"Hey," he hollered, coaxing fate to intervene. "I'm not stopping until you talk to me."

She glanced over her shoulder at him and this time paid dearly for it as the right toe of her trainer caught the lip of a cobblestone and sent her flying. She hit the street hard, only managing to partially roll out of the fall. Dempsey was hovering over her a beat later, the muzzle of his Sig pointed at her forehead. The pained expression on her face and the involuntary whimper she let out told him she was done. He gave it coin-flip odds she'd fractured something—if not multiple somethings—in the fall.

"What's your name?" he asked her.

"My name is fuck you," she hissed in heavily accented English.

"Who do you work for?"

She closed her eyes and let out a groan. Her right hand went up to clutch her left arm at the wrist, and she mumbled something in what he surmised was Latvian.

"Mother, can you translate that?" he said, assuming Baldwin and the gang were still online.

"She said, I think I broke my fucking arm," came Baldwin's reply a heartbeat later. "And that was in Russian incidentally. In case you're wondering."

"Where is Elinor Jordan?" he asked, adopting his *don't fuck with me* voice, but she didn't answer.

She didn't even open her eyes.

A police siren fired up behind him, disturbingly close. Without looking, he knew there was a cruiser parked at the alley entrance at his back.

"Talk to me," he growled. "Is Elinor Jordan alive?"

She finally opened her eyes, and they were wet with tears—the involuntary kind born from acute pain. "Fuck off, American asshole," she managed, glaring up at him from where she lay writhing on her back, her expression revealing nothing other than disdain.

Dempsey holstered his weapon, pulled out his mobile phone, and quickly snapped a picture of the young woman's face. Behind him a male voice shouted something.

"That's the police. They just ordered you to put your hands in the air. It appears you're under arrest, John," Baldwin said, followed immediately by the sound of him slurping a beverage. "One more thing . . . the Director has asked me to pass along a friendly piece of advice."

"Oh really, what's that?" he said as he slowly stepped away from Elinor Jordan's doppelgänger.

"Don't drop the soap."

"Very funny," Dempsey grumbled as he raised both hands over his head and turned around to face the two Riga Metro police officers pointing guns at his chest.

CHAPTER 11

Protopopovskiy Pereulok
Botanichesky Sad Mgu Filial Apartments
Moscow, Russia
June 12
1730 Local Time

When Valerian arrived at his Moscow apartment, he found Arkady in the kitchen, cooking an omelet.

"Would you like an omelet?" the spymaster said in greeting.

He glanced at his watch. "It is late in the day, but how can I refuse? You're in my kitchen, cooking it as we speak." Valerian glanced at the single grocery bag on the counter; his boss had known Valerian's refrigerator would be spartan and bare.

"You know why the omelet is the perfect entrée?" Arkady asked.

"Nyet."

"Because it can be served for breakfast, lunch, or dinner, and it is not only satisfying but sating. You know what I mean?"

Valerian shrugged.

"If I offered you stroganoff for breakfast, it would be sating but not satisfying," Arkady said as he used a spatula to expertly fold the omelet. "If I offered you a Danish and coffee for dinner, it would be satisfying but not sating. The omelet is always both. A very rare occurrence in a life ruled by the collision of routine and uncertainty."

Valerian withheld comment and walked to the refrigerator. He opened the door and fetched the one thing he knew he had in abundant supply with no expiration date—a bottle of water—as he pondered what his mentor was trying to tell him. Always there was allegory or metaphor buried in the old man's theatrics. Before, when he was still young and learning from the man he had come to idolize, he had yearned for such lessons. But that was many years ago, and today he was a blooded Zeta. More than that, he was the Prime. He was, in many ways, more expert than his mentor in the means and ways of modern field operations. Today such a lesson was irritating, though he knew it should not be, and that annoyance reflected a weakness he'd best quickly get under control.

"Do you want a water?" he asked Arkady.

"No, thank you," Arkady said. "I had one when I arrived."

"Water is also something that is both sating and satisfying," Valerian said thoughtfully, unscrewing the cap.

"Only when one is very thirsty," Arkady said.

"Okay, so what is your point?" He leaned against the wall opposite Arkady, looking at the man's back as he cooked on the ancient gas range. "Because I have learned long ago, you always have one, *Uchitel.*"

"My point is that there is an important distinction between the two. With regard to your little project in Saint Petersburg, are you sating or satisfying this infatuation that you have with Amanda Allen?"

Valerian swallowed the resurging irritation the accusation brought and forced himself to consider the question for a moment. "I don't know. I fear, maybe neither," he answered honestly. And why not be honest? His boss was a walking lie detector—one he could never fool.

Arkady turned off the gas to the burner, then used a spatula to deposit an exquisite omelet onto a plate. He split the omelet perfectly in two, sliding one half onto a second plate and then setting both on the table. "I think that's right," he said, handing the plate to Valerian. "I think this appetite of yours cannot be sated. Cannot be satisfied. Even if you had the real woman in your possession, you would devour her, consume her, and in the act, maybe attain some pleasure, but when it was over, you would be neither sated nor satisfied. It's time to stop, Valerian. It is an unhealthy pursuit, psychologically, emotionally, and professionally. Amanda Allen is the prize that got away, but while for you she may be the first, she's not likely to be the last. It is the way of things in our line of work."

The words stung, but Valerian released his emotions in a long, slow exhale and then sat down at his two-person dining table. He instantly felt better—more like himself. More like Zeta Prime. He looked at his plate. "When did you come up with all this shit about the omelet?"

"While I was cooking it," Arkady managed to say with a straight face. "What? My food metaphor is not working for you?"

Valerian broke first, and then they both laughed. It felt good; he couldn't remember the last time he'd laughed. "I know I have a problem," he said finally. "I do, but I assure you, it's not affecting my work."

"That's a lie," the spymaster said with a shake of his head. "And also, not for you to decide. That's my job. While you were in Saint Petersburg playing bondage games, the Americans were in Narva."

His chest tightened. "Was it Ember?"

"We still don't have personnel files on the members, but I have a high degree of confidence." Arkady pulled his mobile phone from his pocket and turned the screen to show Valerian a picture of two men—one holding an assault rifle and one dressed like a pimp.

Valerian felt his cheeks go hot. "That's them. The same two operators from Istanbul. I shot this one in the neck—but, obviously, he lived—and this one with the assault rifle . . . this is the devil I want to kill."

"You should have been there. Amarov brought more than a dozen men and still barely escaped with his life." Arkady shook his head. "The Vory are ruthless, brutal killers, but they are not operators. They are not equipped—mentally, physically, or tactically—to take on Ember. They are not Zetas."

"Fuck," Valerian blurted and pushed back from the table. "Fuck, fuck, fuck . . . I should have been there. I thought this 'American' character might be a legend. I *felt* it."

"*Da,* you should have been there, especially if your instincts told you so. Clearly, they were attempting to kindle a relationship with Amarov to get to Malik . . . to get to you. Maybe they should have sent Amanda Allen instead—*that* would have gotten your attention." Then, with a sigh, Arkady added, "The truth is we shouldn't be having this conversation. We both know you're my best operative. There's nobody in the ranks who can fill your shoes as Zeta Prime, which means I have no choice but to manage you and your deviant temptations. But if there was someone waiting in the wings to succeed you, I would cull you from our ranks for this and move on."

Valerian watched as the Russian spymaster forked omelet into his mouth and then rolled his eyes in apparent pleasure. Despite being furious with himself, this last comment touched a nerve. "You can climb down from your pedestal now. What about your own extracurricular activities? Hmmm? How many of my Zeta sisters have you taken to bed? When did you become so pious, old man?"

Arkady smiled, letting Valerian stew in anger while he finished chewing. The old man dabbed the corners of his mouth with a paper napkin. "I do not begrudge or condemn any of my people the pursuit of pleasure. If you must indulge this fantasy, then fine, request two weeks leave and indulge. As for my extracurricular activities, as you call them, the art of seduction is a critical component of the training pipeline. Not all our agents are throat cutters like you. Going forward, if you desire an obsession, then you should obsess about this covert American team that threatens to best you—again. The stakes are too high. We are the vanguard in Russia's silent war with the West. A spy who cannot attain and *maintain* mastery of his own mind is of no use to me." Then, looking at the omelet on Valerian's plate, he said. "Are you not going to eat it?"

"*Nyet,*" Valerian said, the disgust in his voice more salient than he'd intended. He no longer felt hungry, and the laughter they'd shared moments earlier now seemed mendacious and contrived. Classic Arkady, always fucking with people's heads. A kiss on one cheek, a slap to the other.

Arkady pulled Valerian's plate to his side of the table and began to eat the other half of the omelet. "I have a job for you," he continued, talking and chewing now.

Valerian tried to listen, but he was still wrangling with the American ghost taunting his psyche.

That's twice, my American brother in murder—twice that you have thwarted me now. First you took my prize away in Syria, and then you disrupted my mission in Turkey. But it will not happen a third time. When we next meet, I'll be the one dancing in your blood . . .

Arkady snapped his fingers. "Pay attention."

"Sorry, go on . . ."

"The target is the FSRU ship *Independence* in Klaipėda. I want you to sink it, but it must look like an accident—equipment failure, operator error, or a combination of the two."

"What is an FSRU ship?"

"Floating storage and regasification unit," Arkady explained. "It receives liquid natural gas from tankers and then stores and processes it for distribution. This particular ship processes all of Lithuania's natural gas supply."

"Why can't I just blow it up?"

"Because that does not achieve the desired end result," Arkady said, putting his fork down loudly on the table. "Your place is not to question the big picture. You're not the Director; that's my role. You are a weapon—my sharpest blade—but nothing more. An instrument, that is what you are. What the hell is wrong with you today?"

"I'm sorry," Valerian said. What the hell *was* wrong with him?

It's the American ghost. I must not let him distract my attention from my work until I can make him my work . . .

"As I was saying," Arkady said, the ire draining from his face, "the objective is to make the sinking look like an industrial accident. This job *cannot* be traced back to Russia."

"I'll do it, but I don't know anything about this kind of ship, its design, operating procedures, crew, et cetera."

"I have a red team working the problem to help you as we speak."

"Who's running it?"

"Sylvie."

"Okay, she's good. I trust her." Sylvie had been in his ear on more than one operation. She had no delusions about her role, and that made her the best in the business. "What is the schedule?"

Arkady, having finished the omelet, pushed himself back from the table. "There is a new tanker delivering in three days. It would be preferable to execute before that happens. If you're not ready, you're not ready, and we do it after. Mission success trumps timetable."

He would be ready. He would do what Arkady trusted him to do—what no other Zeta did as well. Without his work, life meant nothing. He let out a long, cleansing breath and felt his clarity of mind begin to sharpen.

"I will see it done. But after, our focus must be finding the American operator," he said, still burning inside from the news that Amarov had been outplayed in Narva. "We need to set another trap, and this time I'll be the bait. If he wants to find Malik, we'll give him Malik."

Arkady said nothing, stood, and patted Valerian's shoulder. "Thank you for your service, my son," the old fox said and then let himself out of the apartment.

With Arkady gone, Valerian closed his eyes and slowed his breathing as he searched for, and found, his center.

I am stillness.

I am focus.

I am a blade, honed for a single purpose.

I am Zeta Prime.

He opened his eyes, his breathing barely a whisper and his heart rate in the low forties. He smiled. He would make the American operator pay for all his sins: foiling his mission in Turkey, ruining the operation in Narva, but most of all, for taking Amanda Allen away from him.

CHAPTER 12

115 Dewberry Court
Broyhill-McLean Estates Neighborhood
1.5 Miles West-Southwest of CIA Headquarters
McLean, Virginia
June 12
2030 Local Time

It had been a long while since Buz Wilson had felt excited about anything besides his wife and kids, but he was excited about this move. It was a new beginning, something he desperately needed. He grabbed the box of dishware and a few pots and pans—a box that would have been wise to split into two loads—and grunted shamelessly as he hefted it up into the air. It was an old-man grunt, born of stiff joints, bad posture, and a weak core. It was a sound he'd completely given up trying to suppress, even in mixed company—that's how old he felt.

"Oh, shit," he groaned as he shuffled toward the front door, his lower back protesting and grip slipping. Thankfully, the door opened on its own, ending his dilemma of how to work the handle without setting the box down and being forced to pick it up again.

"You okay, baby?" Bonnie asked, grinning. She was carrying take-out, a white plastic bag looped around each wrist. She had *told* him to split the kitchen load into two boxes, but had he listened? No, no he had not.

"Yeah, I'm fine," he lied. "Was just figuring out how to open the door, but you saved me."

"As usual," his wife chuckled. She kissed him on the cheek and then mercifully let him pass. "I think we should eat on the patio table, okay?"

"'Kay," he said, keeping the strain out of his voice. "What did ya get? McLean's?" he asked, meaning the family restaurant around the corner.

"Fahrenheit," she called after him.

Buz smiled. He was expecting McLean's because his wife, despite serving twelve years in the FBI and then following her CIA officer hus-band around the world for another fifteen, was not adventurous when it came to food.

"You hate Asian fusion," he called back as he slid the heavy box into the open back of their Chevy Suburban.

"But you love it," she hollered back. "I got a salad and those pastry things I do."

He chuckled to himself. *Pot stickers, not pastries. Why can't she remember pot stickers?*

It was the little things like that which kept him deeply in love with his childhood sweetheart—the only woman he'd had eyes for since the eighth grade . . . like getting their last dinner in Northern Virginia from *his* favorite restaurant, even though she hated it.

He arched his back and looked up in surprise at the sound of a vehi-cle pulling along the front curb. The black Lincoln Navigator screamed government wheels, and the driver's chiseled jaw and dark suit were the exclamation point. Buz waited while the VIP in back gave instructions to his driver before stepping out. He recognized his unannounced visi-tor immediately, but he was not completely prepared for the *presence* of the man. He had no idea how old the Director of National Intelligence was—a man with that kind of résumé would have to be close to sixty—but Kelso Jarvis carried himself like a man half that age. Buz knew Jarvis was one of the most decorated Navy SEALs in history, having led the legendary Tier One SEAL Team in almost every role possible, from operator, to squadron leader, to Operations Officer and eventually as the CSO. Jarvis's hands hung casually at his sides, but his body nonetheless gave the impression of a tightened coil, ready to spring. Powerful.

The driver stayed behind the wheel, leaving the engine running, while a broad-shouldered bodyguard escorted the DNI up the driveway. The young centurion in a suit was little more than a prop, because it was obvious to anyone encountering this duo which man to fear. He'd heard how Jarvis had saved the president in Turkey and taken a bullet in the chest, but the DNI did not look like someone recovering from a gunshot wound.

"Norman Wilson?" Jarvis said.

"I go by Buz," he answered with a grimace. "No one calls me Norman. Not even my mother."

Jarvis strode toward him, his right hand extended.

"Kelso Jarvis," the DNI said and gave Buz's hand only a brief squeeze before clasping his hands in front of him.

"Yes, sir," Buz said. "I know who you are, sir."

The Director nodded. "I spent most of my career in the shadows, so being recognized still takes a little getting used to. Is there somewhere we can talk?"

"Of course. I'm so sorry," Buz said, shaking his head as if coming out of a trance. "Please come inside."

Jarvis turned to his bodyguard. "Wait out here, please, Nick."

The Secret Service man began to protest, but the DNI stopped him with a simple raising of his right hand. "Yes, sir," the man acknowledged with a tone that said he had recited these lines too many times—and hated it.

Buz led the DNI into what had once been the living room. Now it was just a room with a sofa and stacks of mostly packed boxes.

"Sweetheart, we have company," Buz announced.

"Company?" Bonnie called from the kitchen with a laugh. "Who in the hell would drop by when everyone knows we're in the middle of . . . Oh my God." His wife brushed the wrinkles from the front of the sweatshirt she was wearing over grubby jeans—as if that was sufficient to make her presentable for the chief of all US intelligence operations and member of the National Security Council. "I'm so sorry. Sir, it's an honor to meet you."

Jarvis smiled disarmingly. "The honor is mine. Thank you both for your service. I was hoping I could speak to your husband for a few moments, and I apologize that my timing couldn't be worse. When do you guys head out?"

Bonnie hesitated. "Umm . . ." For a moment, Buz thought she was so gobsmacked by their surreal houseguest that she'd completely blanked on the answer. He was about to reply for her when she said, "We head to Williamsburg tomorrow. It took us two years to find the perfect house, and now we're finally going to make the leap."

"Beautiful little tourist town," Jarvis said, as if they were talking over coffee after church. "I have a home there myself. When I finally retire, we'll be neighbors."

"Well, won't that be nice" was all Bonnie could manage.

"Sir, would you like to chat on the back porch?" Buz asked, gesturing through the kitchen.

"No, no, please use the kitchen," Bonnie said. "I'll wait on the porch. Or go upstairs."

"Not at all," Jarvis said. The man was nothing like Buz expected. Where was the swagger and arrogance? Where was the air of entitlement that a presidential cabinet member inevitably became accustomed to? "It's nice out tonight. The porch sounds great."

"We were just about to sit down for dinner, so there's wine," Bonnie said, gesturing at the two glasses of chardonnay on the counter. "You take these," she said, distributing them to the men. "The good wineglasses are packed, so these plastic picnic goblets will have to do."

"Thank you," Jarvis said, accepting the plastic cup with two hands and a polite nod.

"This way," Buz said, leading the DNI through the maze of boxes to the porch. He held Bonnie's eyes on the way by. She raised her eyebrows, and he shrugged in reply.

Jarvis took a seat on the wicker sofa on the "porch"—which they'd converted into a four-season sunroom last year. The DNI set his wine on the little round end table and propped his left ankle atop his right knee. "Not exactly a SCIF out here," Jarvis said and smiled, but his hard gray eyes told Buz the man was holding something back. "From what I hear, Bonnie was quite the signals expert back in the day."

"Would you rather talk in your Navigator?" Buz replied, picking up on the DNI's subtext.

"That probably came out wrong," Jarvis said, shaking his head. "It wasn't meant to be an accusation."

"No offense, sir, but we cut our teeth in a different era. When I met Bonnie, her job title was fingerprint clerk, but in reality she was running signals for the Bureau in Berlin. We don't keep secrets from each other unless it's . . . well, what I'm trying to say is, when you've been playing this game as long as we have, you're either partners or you're not. We're partners."

He watched the DNI carefully, but the other man's face was a mask, giving up nothing.

"Congratulations on your retirement, Buz," Jarvis said, pivoting. "Thirty years, right?"

"Almost thirty-two."

"Not a lot of people serve for a lifetime these days."

"I love my country, sir. If I had to do it over again, I'd still sign up."

"I hear you're Langley's outgoing expert on Russian organized crime and the FSB."

Unable to help himself, Buz laughed out loud. "Yeah, well, after 9/11 that's like being the shortest kid at basketball camp, you know?"

"I can imagine," Jarvis said.

Buz felt like the man's eyes were a CT scanner, probing deep inside him. The funny thing was, he didn't have anything to hide, which made the feeling all the more disconcerting. "I probably would have been more help to the country if I'd been an expert in Islamic extremism, sir. That's all I meant," Buz said, resisting the urge to cross his arms across his chest.

Jarvis reached for his wine goblet but stopped short. Buz couldn't be certain, but for a fleeting instant he thought he might have seen the DNI's hand tremble. Jarvis immediately rotated his torso, stretching his back, and said, "I tweaked my back the other day; it's still giving me trouble."

"Yeah, I know the feeling," Buz said, arching his own in a gesture of solidarity. "Carrying all these boxes will put me in traction if I'm not careful. Bonnie says I'm a cheap ass for not hiring movers to do it, but damn it, if I can't carry boxes to my truck, then they might as well just bury me in the backyard."

Jarvis laughed at this, a real laugh, and said, "Amen, brother."

Buz chuckled, took a long sip of wine, and then after a pause said, "As enjoyable and surreal as it is to be drinking wine with the DNI, I know you didn't come here to chat about our aching backs, so if you don't mind me asking, what can I do for you, sir, on this fine, fine evening?"

"Indeed," Jarvis said, and his smile faded. "The problem with 9/11 was that the intelligence community didn't recognize the Islamic jihadist threat looming over the next hill. When we finally ran into it, we devoted all our energy and attention to managing it. Unfortunately, in the process, we forgot to keep an eye on the rearview mirror, on old adversaries, like Russia . . . The Russian threat never went away, did it, Buz."

"No, sir, it did not," Buz said, shaking his head. "To use your driving analogy, Russia had a blowout, ran off the road, and crashed into a ditch. But while we were driving away, they changed the tire, repaired the damage, and got their tractor trailer back on the road. They're back on our tail, and they're trying to run us off the road now. I would argue that in many ways Russia is more dangerous today than they were at the height of the Cold War. I think that Russia is the greatest threat to America at present."

"Interesting to hear you say that, because not many people recognize this. Why do you think that is?"

"Partly because of that sentiment," Buz said. He couldn't help himself; he stood and began to pace. "They've excelled at legitimizing themselves with the Western world, but in fact their motives and actions are scarcely different than when Berlin was still a divided city. Russia has always had an inferiority complex, but it has become far worse since their failed experiment with Communism and equally abysmal attempt at oligarch-driven capitalism. What Washington and the media fail to recognize is that the Russians don't think like us. Russians don't wear rose-colored glasses. You see, in America, we teach our children that life is a competition, and in that competition, whichever squad trains and prepares the best, plays the hardest on the field, and works best as a team will win. The idea that both teams will play by the rules is taken for granted. Cheating is frowned upon. We use referees to ensure fair play. In America, the winners elevate everyone around them—the strong carry the weak on their backs. Of course, this is an idealized version of the truth, but it is the American paradigm. The Russians don't view the world that way." Buz realized he had launched into a much longer soliloquy than he intended and gave a chuckle and looked at his hands. "Sorry, sir. I'm sure you didn't come over here to listen to me spouting off from my soapbox."

"On the contrary, this is exactly what I came for. Please, go on." The DNI recrossed his legs and leaned back, his hands in his lap. He apparently wanted to know, for some damn reason.

Buz sighed. "Do you remember where you were on 9/11, sir?"

"Absolutely, in vivid detail," the DNI said, but he didn't elaborate. "It's like the day Kennedy was shot for our parents. Or knowing what you were doing on December 7, 1941, for our grandparents. What were you doing that day, Buz?"

Something in the DNI's voice said he already knew, but Buz jumped in with both feet. He had never been given the opportunity to share his frustration with how his professional life changed that day. When so many had suffered and died, his own personal impact felt small and self-centered. Bonnie knew the truth, of course, but he'd always resisted complaining to her about it.

"I was in Bremerhaven, Germany," he said, retaking his seat. Despite his best efforts, he felt himself drawn back into that day—a day that should have launched his career instead of tanking it. "I was stationed in Berlin. I'd been there a couple years, collecting intel to support my theory that the Russian intelligence community was fostering a symbiotic relationship with the Vory. At the time, no one was fully buying into the idea." He took a sip—a pull, really—of his wine. "On 9/11, I was running a joint operation to capture an FSB operator and a rising Vory boss. The objective of the op was to prove that instead of working to cull the Vory ranks, the FSB was instead doing the opposite and cultivating certain actors. We'd tracked the Russian agent and his team to a meeting with a Vory boss in Bremerhaven named Sergein Kutslik. Kutslik was a well-known purveyor of stolen arms, drugs . . . people—women, some of them just children—for the sex trade." He paused, acutely aware of how intently Jarvis was watching him. "Anyway, we had a joint operation—at least as joint as we got back then. I was working with an FBI task force and some great Ground Branch guys from the Agency. We were able to confirm the meet at Kaiserhafen II shipyard."

Buz felt the excitement rise inside him at the telling, almost as real as the day he had been there and everything he had believed had been proven true.

"Go on," Jarvis said, nodding.

But Buz couldn't have stopped even if he wanted to.

"The real surprise was who was present in the FSB entourage. That day, I came a breath away from taking Vladimir Petrov off the street in Bremerhaven. You see, Petrov was a rising star in the FSB, but he still hadn't made the pivot to the political track. That would come six months later." Buz leaned back and felt the cool breeze of the evening lick the sweat that had formed on his neck and forehead.

"What happened?" the DNI asked, his face still a mask.

"We boxed in their convoy, but there was a firefight—a blood-bath really. It only lasted a few seconds, but we lost men—two good men, including one old friend . . ." Buz fought back the emotion as he remembered the smiling face of his friend Carl Logan who was dropped by a Russian sniper's bullet. He let out a rattling sigh. "We killed a bunch of their guys, but Petrov and the FSB spymaster got away. We could have grabbed them, but . . ."

He let his voice trail off and sighed.

"But what?" the DNI pressed.

Buz shrugged. "The towers fell, the Pentagon got hit, and we lost all those brave people on Flight 93. Word went out and we were immedi-ately recalled—Omega protocol was implemented, and we were ordered to the embassy." Buz took a long swig and finished the wine in his cup, which he suddenly wished had been bourbon. "After that, the pivot was hard and immediate. The CIA Director shifted focus where it needed to be—to finding bin Laden and prosecuting Islamic terrorists. All of a sudden, I found myself on the outside looking in. I became the 'Russia guy' in an agency focused on the War on Terror. Al-Qaeda, ISIS, Boko Haram, Hezbollah, Hamas . . . they became the enemy that needed hunting."

"But the Russian threat never went away, did it?" Jarvis said.

"No. While we were distracted, they got busy."

Even when the rest of the Agency had shifted focus, he'd kept his attention locked on Russia. He'd recognized what was going on and continued to collect intelligence, even when nobody else seemed to care. He knew what the hot runners called him behind his back—Cold War Wilson—but he didn't care. Accolades and recognition had never been his motivators. Love of country was the fuel that drove him.

"They have a new playbook, and they're a bigger threat than ever," he continued. "With Petrov, everything is a zero-sum game—for Russia to rise, America must fall. Everything he's done over the past decade has been an effort to sully and tarnish the reputation of Western democracies. Promoting Brexit, actively trying to break up the EU and NATO, turning Italy against France, stoking the fires of partisanship in the United States. And while we turn inward, trying to tame and manage the chaos Russia unleashed in our house, Petrov is systematically moving his chess pieces all over the board."

"Like in the Baltics?" Jarvis said, leaning in.

The thrill of having the DNI's captive ear rekindled a fiery passion in Buz he hadn't felt in years. "Exactly. Kaliningrad has been armed to the teeth with Iskander M ballistic missiles, a battery of land-based antiship missiles whose range covers the Baltic Sea, and a growing number of antiaircraft missile systems. Shit, half the Russian military is mobilized along the Belarusian and Ukrainian borders. There was a no-fly zone around Cyprus last week because the Russian Navy was launching cruise missiles and sorties into Syria testing new weapons systems. They're expanding their presence, and it's formidable. Meanwhile, Russian Intelligence is orchestrating false-flag operations throughout the Middle East and the Caucasus. Moscow is actively trying to destabilize the United States' relationship with Turkey. If Petrov can gain power and influence over Erodan, he'll have a puppet he can use to subvert NATO. Hell, I'd bet my retirement that it was Russia, not a PKK splinter cell, that was behind the assassination attempt on President Warner and yourself in Istanbul . . ." Buz got up and walked to the railing. He gripped the handrail and stared out into his backyard, probably for the last time, before finally turning back to face the DNI. "I'm going to stop talking now. This is how I get myself in trouble."

Jarvis rose, leaving his wine untouched on the end table, and strode over to him. The man moved with a fluidity and grace Buz had only ever seen in seasoned SOF operators. An old memory, a snapshot image of Carl Logan grinning at him in the back of a van in Bremerhaven, came to him. Logan had moved like that, before the Russian sniper ended his life.

"I would never ask you to bet your retirement, Buz, but it is an interesting way for you to have phrased it . . . under the circumstances," Jarvis said, staring out into the yard beside him.

Buz waited silently, studying the man in profile.

Jarvis turned to him and smiled. "Your country needs you, Buz. Hell, scratch that—I need you. There's an operation underway, one in which your expertise could prove incredibly valuable."

Buz felt his face flush and couldn't resist the urge to look past the DNI at Bonnie, who was working diligently to pack for the next season of their lives. She'd sacrificed so much already.

"Sir, there are literally dozens of CIA officers you could tap for help."

"There aren't any others who made the connection in the Turkey attacks just on instinct," Jarvis said, all but confirming Buz's guess. "And no others who nearly nabbed Petrov before his rise to absolute power—when he was still rank and file in the FSB."

"The keyword is 'almost.' We didn't get him."

"You would have. I read the report, Buz. I'm a man who does his homework. The timing of your operation was just rotten luck. If the op had been on September 10 instead of September 11—well, let's just say the world would be a very different place today. Have you ever thought about that?"

"Every damn day of my life," Buz said on an exhale. "But to delay my retirement when the Agency has plenty of other guys . . ."

"I don't want one of those guys. I can't say more without reading you in, but you're the man for this assignment and you're the guy I want. And anyway, there's no need to delay your retirement. The type of work I need you for—well, it's actually better if you retire first."

"What? You want me to retire but stay on at CIA as a consultant?"

"No, not at CIA. You'd be working directly for me. I have a task force—highly compartmentalized, very black—and right now they're waist-deep in an operation where your knowledge and experience could prove the difference between success and failure. The men and women of this task force are the best covert operators I've ever worked with, but they're experts in Islamic counterterrorism. They need someone with your particular expertise to help them pivot to the Russian threat."

Buz thought about being the odd man out on one more joint operation with a bunch of terrorism experts. He thought about trying to sell his "Arkady Zhukov is a Russia puppet master" theory to one more group of skeptics. But mostly he thought about the look of disappointment he would see in Bonnie's face when he told her, "Hey, remember that retirement thing we talked about? Just kidding. Alice called, and she needs me back down the bunny hole." He sighed. They were both so excited to start this next chapter in their lives—*their* chapter. With their youngest out of college, they were now really on their own. They were going to travel—see places as tourists instead of government agents. Most important, they were going to spend time getting to know each other again.

"You said you did your homework, sir, and if that's the case, then you know that not all my theories panned out to be true. I led the Agency on some wild-goose chases over the years."

"Which theories? You mean like the one where Russia was building a new, highly secret covert operations unit to rival, if not eclipse, the CIA's SAD?"

"That one didn't really pan out, did it?"

"Oh, it did all right."

Buz felt the air sucked from his lungs. "What?"

Jarvis nodded. "We've confirmed the Russians have a secret, highly autonomous direct-action unit. It operates covertly outside normal channels. It's not SVR, FSB, or GRU. We've been unable to identify their personnel, and we don't know who's calling the shots. It might even operate outside of Petrov's direct control for all we know . . ."

"Well, that's fucking scary," Buz interjected.

"Scary as hell. This group eschews traditional cloak-and-dagger boundaries. The assassination attempt on the President and myself in Turkey is proof of that. We don't know what they're capable of or what they're planning next."

Buz stroked his chin. If this was true, then he had been right all along. There was only one person he knew who could possibly be pulling the strings. But that man had disappeared from the face of the earth over a decade ago. Still, if he could close the loop on everything he had ever done, every hour he had ever spent away from Bonnie and the kids, it would, maybe, all have been worth it.

"What was his name?"

Buz looked up, brought back to the real world. "Who?"

"The FSB officer you said was with Petrov. The man running the operation in Bremerhaven that night."

"Zhukov," Buz said absently. "Arkady Zhukov. But he disappeared a long time ago. Most of my colleagues are pretty sure he's dead—another casualty of a Russian transfer of power under Petrov." But he wasn't dead. Buz was sure of it. And if the DNI was right—that there was some shadow intelligence operation on the fringes of the existing Russian power structure—then who other than Arkady could possibly run it? It all made perfect sense. It answered almost every question that had haunted him the last ten years. But how could he suggest such a wild-ass theory to the DNI—on his porch on the eve of his retirement?

"But you don't believe that, do you, Buz?"

He held Jarvis's eyes. "No, I don't."

"Then, this is the chance you've been waiting for, Buz, waiting for your entire career."

The DNI's words stoked a fire in his heart he hadn't felt in a very, very long time. He knew his answer, but the strength of his conviction took him by surprise. Was it hubris, revenge, or patriotism driving him now? If he took down the man responsible for Vladimir Petrov's rise to power, did it even matter?

"What would I need to do?" he said.

Jarvis smiled.

"You'll finish your move to Williamsburg, since, by providence, it's the perfect location for you to start your consulting job at Ember."

"Ember? What the hell is that?"

"To the world at large, it's a security consulting company, but that's a NOC. In reality, Ember is America's most lethal covert operations task force."

Buz rubbed at the stubble on his chin. They all suspected that deep, dark task forces existed, but to hear the DNI speak so openly about it, and recruit him in the same breath no less, was surreal.

"Can I talk to my wife before I give you an answer?"

Jarvis nodded. "Perhaps we can talk to your wife together. Because if you're in, I need you tonight."

"Tonight? You've got to be kidding me. Bonnie will kill me. She'll have to do this move alone. We have to be out of this house no later than the day after tomorrow."

Jarvis laughed. "No, she won't, because you'll be working for a very successful private-sector company. Relocation service is one of the many perks, as is the sizable signing bonus. Just say the word and Bonnie won't need to lift a finger."

Buz gritted his teeth. He knew what his wife would say. She would hug him and tell him to go for it, that she would hold down the fort. It's what she always said.

"Assuming we do say yes, where are you shipping me off to?"

"Riga. To meet your team."

"Oh boy, the Baltics," Buz said, shaking his head. "I'm almost afraid to ask . . . what kind of mess has the team gotten themselves into?"

"The kind that landed my best two operators in jail," Jarvis said as he reached for the patio door and then, with a wry grin over his shoulder, added, "And your first assignment is to bail them out."

CHAPTER 13

Office of the Director of National Intelligence (ODNI)
Department of Intelligence Integration
McLean, Virginia
June 13
1130 Local Time

Catherine shook her head and reread the same paragraph for the third time. Her body was present, but her mind was elsewhere—trying to wrangle a stampede of angry, paranoid thoughts racing a hundred miles an hour in a hundred different directions. Zeta was planning to hit Ember. When that happened, her life would be upended. Task Force Ember was the intelligence community's most closely guarded secret—a covert-action unit with a direct line to the President. The number of people who knew of its existence was so small that everyone inside the circle would be investigated with laser beam–focused intensity. She would not escape the inquisition unscathed.

Strand by strand, her legend would be unraveled, and the charade would be over. Best-case scenario, she would be prosecuted, incarcerated, and eventually traded back to Russia. Worst-case scenario,

Catherine Morgan would "die" in a well-publicized car accident while *she* was whisked away to a black site to be interrogated and tortured until she expired or went mad. Given her high-profile career and the embarrassment her infiltration would cause the Warner administration and the nation, she gave higher odds to the latter scenario. Whoever had authorized the Ember strike had to know this . . . had to know that to do so was a choice between her continued existence as a deep-cover asset and mitigating the Ember threat.

Only one person understood the stakes of this decision, and he was in Moscow.

She felt the tug in her mind. Like an undertow in the surf, it was always there—trying to pull her under and away. Like an invisible force, it tried to drag her heart home to Russia and to him. Instead of resisting, she closed her eyes and let it have its way with her, pulling her back in time and space.

"What's that look for?" Arkady asked her, tracing a fingertip across her naked shoulder as they lay facing each other. Outside, the first snow of winter was falling on the streets of Moscow. This was their last night together, and she was full of both excitement and trepidation for the journey ahead of her.

"I'm just happy," she said, instead of "I love you," which she was feeling but dared not say.

He responded with a lazy, happy smile but said nothing in reply. She knew he didn't love her, not in the way she loved him, but she saw genuine adoration in his eyes. She understood how men thought, how they felt and how they didn't. Seduction and intimacy had been part of her training, and besides, she'd never been naïve about such matters. They'd spoken openly and at great length about games of the heart. As her instructor, he wasn't supposed to sleep with her. He hadn't slept with the other recruits; she was positive of this. She was special. She'd tried to seduce him and succeeded, and yet despite this, she would always be nothing more than a mistress.

His fidelity lay with another woman—Mother Russia.

"Have I ever told you about my father?" he said.

"No," she said. "You've never told me anything about your family."

"Hrrrmmm . . ." He let out a long exhale and said, "My father was an intellectual, consumed by the Stalin regime and forced to become a creature of the state. And yet, he never broke—resisting subtly and stubbornly to the end. He made me read every book he could get his hands on. I used to hate him for it, because I was always so fucking hungry. We had no food back then, and my father spent every damn ruble he had on books. He'd come home with a small package wrapped in paper, and I'd think it was meat, but no, it was always a book hidden in butcher paper."

"Did he have a favorite?"

"Of course, he claimed to admire Tolstoy most, but I think Boris Pasternak was his favorite. He was an aspiring poet himself . . ."

She listened while he recited verse from memory:

"I chase each dawn, but time runs swift
Heart pounding, breath aching, I'm left adrift
My hopes and dreams and fears collected
In a soul box keyed but not protected
This treasure I give to you my dear
Your love eternal quells my fear
My only regret is bittersweet
That Death must take two 'fore again we meet."

"It's from the last poem my father wrote before he died," he said. "I memorized it . . . I'm not sure why."

"It's pretty," she said with a wan smile. "And sad."

He fixed his slate-blue eyes on her. "Listen to me. I want you to have an affair with America. I want you to get to know her, appreciate her beauty and strength, and fall in love with her . . ."

"I don't understand," she said, the contentedness she'd been feeling suddenly draining from her like the warm water at the end of a bath.

111

"I want you to be like my father. I want you to be a poet spy. To do your job well, you must love your enemy. I'm not talking about the men you're going to manipulate; I'm talking about the country. I'm giving you permission to break your vows, to cheat on Russia, to love another. Let America enchant you. Let her seduce you. I want you conflicted. I want you to want to protect and safeguard her interests. I want each and every activity I task you with to feel like a betrayal, not of Russia, but of America. Only then will you truly become one of them. Only then will you be a compelling spy. Do you understand?"

She nodded slowly. "Da, I think I do, but it will be difficult."

"Indeed, but not for the reason you are thinking," he said and leaned over to kiss her . . .

A knock at her office door ripped her from her thoughts, and she heard herself gasp. She shook her head, clearing it of the past.

"Come in," she said, glancing at the wall clock and surprised that fifteen minutes had slipped away in reminiscence.

The door opened and Petra Felsk stepped in. "Director Morgan," the DNI's Chief of Staff said with a curt nod.

"Petra," Catherine said, forcing a smile. "Come on in and have a seat." She studied the other woman's features: high, chiseled cheekbones, thin lips, heavy brow ridges, and a strong, angular jawline. The woman was quite attractive, despite her androgynous haircut and decision to eschew makeup. "Felsk is a Prussian surname if I'm not mistaken?" she asked, her subconscious getting the better of her.

"My family roots are in Königsberg," Petra said. "But I've never visited."

"Königsberg," Catherine echoed. "Not many people probably know that name anymore. The Russians renamed it Kaliningrad after World War II."

"And now Vladimir Petrov is trying to turn it into an arsenal enclave for when he decides to retake the Baltics."

Catherine nodded. "Sometimes I think he'd rather see Eastern Europe burn to the ground than prosper outside of Russia's grip."

"That's because the concept of win-win doesn't exist in the Russian lexicon. It's zero-sum politics or no politics at all."

"Yes, I think you may be right," Catherine said, before shifting gears. "You called this meeting. What can I help you with?"

"A couple of things. Does the name Matvei Amarov mean anything to you?"

Catherine searched her memory. The name was familiar, but she couldn't quite place it. "No . . . Should it?"

"Not necessarily."

"Who is he?"

"A Russian Vory boss who operates out of the Baltics. He's active in Klaipėda, Riga, Tallinn, and Saint Petersburg and has his fingers in all sorts of pies. I was wondering if you could put out feelers across the IC and see if you can find analysts who are currently working, or previously worked, with him and his network?"

"Sure. What else?"

"As the Director of Intelligence Integration, how do you manage interdepartmental counterintelligence vulnerabilities? Do you have separate and specific monitoring systems in place?"

Catherine felt a flutter in her stomach at the question. "Well, as you know, every shop has its own CI team that monitors for both active and passive leaks, including unusual communication and behavior patterns. And here in my office, I have a six-person team that I stood up to interface with the CI teams at all the other shops. When Director Jarvis created this position for me, it was one of my first acts."

"So your CI team acts as an aggregator and watchdog for the other teams? Is that what you're saying?"

"That and more. We run red-team scenarios once a quarter to stress-test potential vulnerabilities, always rotating the department or division. Last quarter was CIA DS&T; this quarter we hit NCTC with a real doozy, and next quarter is the Pentagon's budget and forecasting group—the event is confidential by the way, so please don't tip them off. Beside stress tests, we also collect, evaluate, and share best practices from the different shops. I'm also standing up a training program, so instead of just spitting out a quarterly newsletter of dos and don'ts, my team will travel and provide instruction. Why do you ask?"

"I'm looking into a potential vulnerability that's of particular interest to the DNI," Petra said, scribbling a note in her notebook before looking up to make eye contact.

"Can you be any more specific?" Catherine asked. The butterflies in her stomach were beating their wings now with fury.

"I'm not at liberty to say. This is one the DNI has decided to hold close to the vest." Petra smiled a half smile. "You, if anyone, understand the importance of discretion."

Catherine felt heat rising to her cheeks, and she silently cursed herself for letting Jarvis's seductress and acolyte push her buttons.

But is that what this is? Petra pushing my buttons? Or is there something else going on here? Could she be testing me—her version of cat and mouse? Or does she already know, and there's something deeper and darker at play?

Not waiting for a reply, Petra stood and headed toward the door.

"My only regret is bittersweet," Catherine said as the other woman reached with her long, lithe fingers for the doorknob. Although it wasn't an official Zeta challenge-response pairing, it served the same intimate purpose. Was it possible? Could Petra be another Zeta?

"Excuse me?" Petra said, turning back to face her.

"Oh, it's nothing," Catherine said, regretting the foolish impulse. "Just talking to myself."

Petra cocked her head, a distinctive mannerism Catherine had observed before in briefs and meetings. "Hmmm . . . And what regret is that?"

She met the other woman's gaze, and the space between them felt thick with unspoken animus. Instead of answering she said, "Is there anything else, Petra?"

"Come to think of it, there is one more thing. Does the name Anne Parsons mean anything to you?"

A cold bead of sweat dripped from her armpit and chased down along her ribs into her bra. Keeping her voice and expression placid, she said, "It doesn't ring a bell. Do you want me to put out feelers on her at the same time I do for Amarov?"

"Oh no, that won't be necessary, Catherine," Petra said as she turned to go. "I already know what happened to her."

CHAPTER 14

Curonian Spit National Park
Klaipėda Municipality, Lithuania
June 14
0245 Local Time

"Whatever happens, don't kill anyone . . ."

Those were Arkady's final instructions in Moscow before Valerian left for the airport and his two-hour nonstop flight to Kaliningrad. Valerian had tried to get away with a nod; as Zeta Prime he had implicit flexibility and authority to conduct his missions as circumstance required to achieve the objective. And yet Arkady had made him repeat the order. Blame it on conditioning or respect for the old man, saying the words shouldn't have mattered, but it did.

It just did.

Tonight, he was working alone in the field, which was both a blessing and a curse—the former because the mission could not be bungled by the incompetence or cowardice of a lesser operative, but the latter because teamwork was a force multiplier when facing daunting odds. And, although he'd never admit it, when an op did go bad, it was nice to have a sacrificial lamb to offer the enemy. He understood how the game was played. Counterterrorism operations did not happen in a vacuum; after an incident, political and media pressure might demand a neck for the gallows. Sometimes, the most expedient means to putting an end to the hunt was to hand the hunters a trophy.

Tonight's mission was to flood and thereby sink the *Independence* at her mooring in the middle of the channel at the northernmost end of the Curonian Lagoon. The lagoon was a long, narrow gulf spanning 625 square miles and separated from the Baltic Sea by a dune-covered spit of land. The northern half of the waterway was Lithuanian territorial waters, while the southern half was claimed by Russia as it bordered Kaliningrad. A two-lane highway ran the length of the peninsula from the mainland in the south to the tip of the spit and the harbor entrance at Klaipėda in the north, where his target awaited.

After arriving in Kaliningrad, Valerian had driven to the coastal resort town of Zelenogradsk and then headed north onto the spit. He cleared the border checkpoint without incident and continued into Lithuania, driving until he reached a dirt road that took him nearly to the water's edge on the lagoon side of the spit. From there he could see the FSRU *Independence* at her mooring.

At 150 feet wide and 965 feet long, the *Independence* was a monster of a ship. Although she did not transport oil, she had a double hull constructed of steel to minimize the risk of a catastrophic breach and environmental disaster in the event of an accidental grounding or collision. *Independence* had a storage volume of 170,000 cubic meters, equating to seventy thousand tons of chilled natural gas stored at -162 degrees Celsius. Contrary to popular misconception, in liquefied form, natural gas was not explosive. Only when the flashpoint concentration was reached would the vapor become an explosion. This was explained during the mission planning session to rebuff Valerian's suggestion that he simply stick an explosive charge on the hull, swim away, and watch the ship go boom from the shore.

The mission planners had cooked up an entirely different kind of offensive. Valerian would sneak aboard, install malware into the ship's computer, and let Sylvie and her team of cyberwarfare technicians back in Vyborg do the rest. Once inside the ship's computer, the hackers planned to sink the ship by venting the LNG storage tanks while simultaneously flooding seawater into the massive internal ballast tanks used for buoyancy control. He had to admit, provided the scheme worked, it was an ingenious plan. The only trouble was gaining access to the vessel.

The planners' original scenario had him hiding in plain sight as a member of a fictional safety inspection team, but he had rejected this out of hand. Bringing an inspection team aboard, real or otherwise, would put the crew on edge and increase their vigilance. Moreover, the company operating the vessel would most likely respond to the inspection notification by sending an experienced senior representative to act as liaison—aka a watchdog—for the duration of the event. Valerian didn't want to mess with any of that. His preference was to sneak aboard at night and exploit a sleepy, apathetic night shift. Assuming he got aboard undetected, executing the mission would be exponentially easier.

The *Independence* was moored in the middle of the channel. Routine access to the ship required delivery by water taxi, ferry, or helicopter. None of these options were viable in the middle of the night without drawing attention, so his plan was to scuba in and covertly climb up onto the docking platform at the forward end of the jetty. From there, he would sneak aboard, install the malware, and then sneak away with no one the wiser. The cyberwarfare team could then execute the sinking operation remotely once he was safely back ashore—

The wireless earbud in his left ear canal crackled, then came to life.

"Spire, this is Cornerstone. Do you copy?" came Sylvie's voice.

"I copy you."

"We have you on satellite infrared in a clearing between two groves of trees and forty meters from the shoreline."

"Check," he said, trying to hide his irritation at being forced to engage in this pointless conversation. When he didn't say anything else, Sylvie spoke again.

"Don't you want a report on ship traffic in the bay and thermal signatures of concern near your location?"

"*Nyet,*" he answered. "If there is a problem, I trust you to inform me."

"What about the positions and movements of the topside personnel on the *Independence*?"

"Pointless. By the time I get there, they will have repositioned." He sighed. "Let's keep the chatter at a minimum, Cornerstone. If there's a problem, report it; otherwise I work best with silence."

"Copy all, Spire. Cornerstone out," she said, her reply hard and clipped.

Message received, thank God.

Valerian gritted his teeth as he worked his dry suit over the pant legs of the orange *Independence* crew coveralls he'd donned. He didn't know and nor did he care how the crewman's uniform had been obtained, so long as it was genuine. As a rule, he didn't concern himself with the minutiae of an operation; those details were for the planners to worry about.

Does a blade concern itself with the scabbard? No. A blade's only care should be where to strike and how deep to cut.

Tonight, he was the blade, and everything else was just noise.

Threads popped as he yanked the dry suit over his hips, and he hoped it was a seam on the coveralls and not one on the dry suit that had torn. He grimaced with irritation, and the expression stretched the skin along his scar. After pulling the diagonal zipper across his chest to his left hip to seal the dry suit, he set to work quickly assembling his Dive Propulsion Unit, a military-grade variant of the torpedo-shaped sea scooter that divers used to extend their range and overcome ocean currents.

The DPU, powered by a lithium-ion battery, was about the size of his thigh and equipped with two handles, two gear brackets, and a ducted propeller. Instead of messing with a full-size scuba tank, Valerian fastened a pony tank and regulator to the DPU, then fastened on weights to offset the tank's added buoyancy. The trip from the spit to the mooring structure was approximately five hundred meters, but he didn't intend to go deep, so the pony bottle would be sufficient. He pressurized the rig, checked the gauge, then positioned his dive mask up on his forehead.

"Cornerstone, Spire is set," he said.

"There's zero lagoon traffic, and we have eyes on the lone topside patrol walking the *Independence*," Sylvie reported. "All clear."

"Copy, Cornerstone," he said.

With a grunt, Valerian picked up the DPU rig and hoisted it onto his shoulder. He walked toward the shoreline, his oversize dive booties crunching twigs as he weaved through tree trunks toward the sand and gravel beach that ran the length of the spit. Before stepping out of the tree line, he scanned for threats and boat traffic in the lagoon, verifying Sylvie's report. Finding the area clear, he advanced onto the beach and headed straight into the water. He waded until he was waist-deep, lowered the DPU into the water, and then submerged himself up to his neck. He felt gentle pressure as the water compressed the dry suit against his body. He paused, one hand holding the DPU, to conduct a quick leak check on his suit. He counted down from ten, but he didn't feel any cold water leak in. Test complete, he lowered his mask into position and adjusted the straps until he had a good seal.

"Cornerstone, Spire. Report set and drift."

"Winds are 9 kilometers per hour from bearing 323. Tide is ebbing. We calculate your set and drift to be negligible: 155 at 0.2 knots," came the reply.

He popped the regulator into his mouth, oriented the rig, and then squeezed the trigger on the right pistol grip of the DPU and pulsed the propeller, which made a nearly silent *vrrrruuuum* sound in the water and tugged against his grip. With a final scan of the horizon, he pointed the nose of the DPU just north of the bow of the *Independence* and submerged into the black. Within thirty seconds he was cruising at 1.7 knots at a depth of 4 meters. His visibility was effectively zero, which meant he would need to rely on the DPU's rudimentary GPS to guide his approach.

As the lagoon bottom sloped away from the spit, he increased his depth to 6.5 meters and cruised all the way to the *Independence*'s mooring structure in just under seventeen minutes. When the GPS held him within 5 meters of the jetty's concrete pylons, he slowed to a half knot, just enough to maintain steerage and ease into position directly under the docking platform. Considered in total, the jetty was a massive mooring structure with multiple piers and multilevel platforms, but only the front platform had a landing at water level designed to receive water taxis, tugs, or ferries. In addition to serving as a landing, the docking platform also functioned as a pumping station, with its own control room one level up, and served as the connection point to the gas pipeline that ran to the mainland for off-loading operations.

As he closed inside the GPS's two-meter circle of uncertainty, he eased off the throttle altogether and let his body settle into a vertical hover. He resisted the urge to flip on the DPU's headlight—worried it might be visible from the surface above—and instead reached out with his left hand into the inky, swirling black. Like a blind man feeling his way, he cautiously advanced using short pulses from the DPU.

Less than a minute later, his palm contacted a mussel-encrusted concrete pylon and he maneuvered around it to the opposite side. He glanced at the DPU control screen, checked his depth, then pointed the nose of the DPU toward the surface and made a slow, controlled ascent. At a depth of one meter, he took a final breath from his regulator and released the DPU, letting the entire rig drift slowly down toward the bottom of the lagoon. He kicked up the rest of the way and silently breached the surface.

Valerian quickly assessed his surroundings and confirmed that, yes, he had surfaced as planned under the docking platform. He glided over to the inside of the dock, which had a landing two feet above the waterline. As expected, the landing was deserted, but it was better lit than he'd hoped. With this much light, he would be noticed if someone was looking in that direction.

He scanned for other options but found nothing he could climb onto. *Oh well, I don't have a choice.*

With a fatalistic grin, he removed and sunk his dive mask, then hoisted himself out of the water into a seated position on the landing platform, facing the understructure. He quickly stripped off the dry suit, only getting hung up when trying to pull the oversize dive booties over the actual boots he wore underneath. This little logistical nightmare had caused the planners serious heartburn and required a last-minute custom modification to the dry suit to accommodate footwear that met the FSRU *Independence*'s safety standards.

"I will not risk my life on this mission only to be undone by my shoes," he'd argued with Sylvie. "Safety shoes are mission critical."

He tossed his dry suit into the water and then whispered, "Report."

"I have you. We hold a single warm body inside the pump station control room; otherwise the jetty is deserted," came Sylvie's reply. "Topside on the *Independence* we have one roving watch, but there's too much thermal interference to give an accurate count on the heat signatures inside the superstructure of the vessel."

He clicked his tongue twice in acknowledgment, then advanced to the metal staircase leading from the landing up to the platform level. The staircase would place him on the northwest corner of the docking platform, but to get to the stair tower that led onto the ship, he'd have to walk past the pump station control room and take the jetty walkway to an adjacent platform located twenty meters to the south.

Being observed and questioned during this onboarding sequence was arguably the greatest risk. Which is why, as he climbed the staircase, he flipped the switch in his mind from being someone who was sneaking aboard to someone who was "already" aboard. Instead of trying to slip past the pump control room undetected, Valerian went straight to the door and walked inside.

"How's it going?" he said in Lithuanian, dropping his voice a half octave. He walked with purpose and the gruff surety of a seasoned crewman while expertly scanning the room—his brain assimilating information as fast as his gaze could cross the space.

The control room night supervisor startled in his chair and quickly closed the laptop screen he'd been looking at. "Fine, fine, good," the man said, red-faced. Then, sitting up straight and reclaiming his composure, he said, "What are you doing here?"

"I came for coffee," Valerian said, walking toward the doorway to the right of the desk, which he predicted and hoped was the break room.

"I don't think we've met," the man said as Valerian passed him.

"What are you talking about, Pärn?" Valerian called over his shoulder. He'd read the guy's name tag immediately upon entering, anticipating this very exchange. "We talked on the water taxi a couple of times. I'm Eero from Vilnius, remember?"

"No."

"I told you about my kids—Mari and Andreus. Andreus is playing soccer," Valerian replied, resisting the compulsion to frown. The encounter wasn't going as well as he'd hoped. This guy Pärn oozed skepticism and might turn out to be a problem. Valerian fantasized briefly about snapping the man's neck as he said, "You really don't remember?"

"I'm sorry, I really don't," Pärn said, now standing in the break room doorway watching Valerian from behind.

"Well, that's okay. I know my kids aren't as interesting to other people as they are to me," Valerian said with a self-deprecating laugh as he rummaged for a coffee pod in the cupboard above the machine. He grabbed a sleeve of the black-label espresso variety and turned with a smile. "Ahh, this is what I was looking for."

"Are you the new maintenance technician?" Pärn asked, narrowing his eyes.

Valerian recognized verbal quicksand when he heard it. There was no way for him to verify the veracity of the question. Had a new maintenance technician *actually* joined the night shift, or was Pärn simply fishing?

"I'm not new," he said, screwing up his face as he walked out of the break room. Instead of leaving, he went over to where Pärn's laptop was resting and gave it a tap. "What you got on here? Some good pictures?"

"It's nothing," Pärn said, his cheeks going crimson again. "Just work."

"Ahhh, I saw the look on your face when I came in," Valerian said with a wink and opened the lid of the computer. "Does she have some nice titties? Show me. I promise I won't tell."

Pärn shoved past him and snapped the lid closed. "I told you, it's nothing."

"Relax, relax," Valerian said. "I won't tell. Everybody does it." He walked around the other side of the desk. Reaching the control room door, he turned and tapped the cardboard sleeve of espresso pods he was clutching in his other hand. "Anyway, thanks for the coffee. See you at shift change."

"Yeah, okay," the other man said just before the door closed.

The transceiver in Valerian's ear came alive as he strode down the interconnecting walkway between mooring platforms. "What was that about?" Sylvie asked, an unmistakable hint of chastisement in her voice.

Valerian didn't justify the question with a response; he made a mental note that when this was over, he would remind Sylvie that her role was support, not oversight.

A minute later, he was at the metal stair tower, a three-story open-air structure that provided access to and from the *Independence*'s main deck. Feeling suddenly energized, he took the treads two at a time and made the ascent in no time. Upon reaching the main deck level, he stepped off the platform, down the ramp resting against the gunwale, and onto the *Independence*'s port-side walkway, which ran from the bow to the bridge tower at the stern. He glanced left, then right, looking for any patrols. Seeing no one, he headed toward the bridge tower, where he could gain access to the command and control spaces. So long as Pärn didn't try to stir up trouble for him, the rest of this op would be a walk in the park.

Upon reaching the bridge tower, Valerian spied an open hatch, the door dogged open against its stops. He stepped through the hatch and walked inside, self-assessing as he did. He felt nothing—no tension, no adrenaline, no exhilaration or fear. Since his encounter with the American operator in Istanbul, this had been his default state—like a nineteenth-century orchestra conductor unable to find joy in lesser works after conducting Tchaikovsky for the very first time. This mission was child's play. Mundane. Tedious.

As he walked down the passage, Valerian spied a wall placard with a diagram of the upper decks. Administration was on Level Two—a good place to access a computer—and so that's where he went. The cyber ops team had been unable to breach the ship's firewall, which indicated that the Distributed Command System—which functioned as the brain for all the ship's mechanical, electrical, and fuel-processing systems—ran on a secure local area network, a rarity these days. Once the malware was installed, the cyber team would be able to connect the LAN to a Zeta router back in Vyborg.

Humming to himself, he took the amidships staircase up one level and stepped out into the transverse passageway. The passage was deserted, but he noted two office lights on at the far starboard end. So, he turned left instead and stopped at the first dark unoccupied office he encountered. He tried the door handle—locked. He walked to the next door—locked. He walked to the next office, tried the handle, and it turned. The placard beside the door read: V. ELGIN—ELECTRICAL ENGINEER.

He stepped inside the small office and flipped on the light. A notebook computer sat on a desk strewn with papers, notebooks, dirty plates, and four different coffee cups all with different liquid levels. Taking a seat behind the desk, Valerian opened the computer's lid and it woke from sleep to present him with a log-in pop-up in the middle of the screen. He inserted a USB thumb drive into a port on the right side of the computer and then said, "Cornerstone, this is Spire, the package is delivered."

"Copy, Spire," came her reply. "Are you in a secure location?"

"Check."

"Request you hold position until we establish the tunnel."

"Check," he said, but he was already turning off the light and stepping out of the little office. Cyber ops would take care of business, he had no doubt, and so why risk getting caught somewhere he didn't belong? With casual nonchalance, he walked back to the stairwell. Taking care not to make unnecessary noise, he padded down the stairs to Level One and walked back to the placard with the diagram of the ship's spaces. He took a mental snapshot and committed it to memory.

"Spire, this is Cornerstone. We're in. Cyber is locking out the control room operators from the DCS and will begin the scuttling operation momentarily. Advise you head to the ferry landing."

He was about to reply when an earsplitting alarm reverberated throughout the superstructure, followed by a loudspeaker announcement. "Multiple casualties in the engineering and fuel-handling spaces," a panicked male voice announced. "Flooding in Engineering lower level and the Auxiliary Pump Room. Bilge flooding alarms at frames two, seven, eight, eleven, fifteen, eighteen, twenty-two, twenty-three, twenty-five, thirty-three, and thirty-seven. LNG storage tank overpressurization alarms on tanks one through twelve. Automatic venting has been initiated."

A Cheshire grin spread across Valerian's face as he executed an about-face and headed for the exit. Before he could reach the hatch, however, multiple doors flew open along the passage. Like angry bees from a molested hive, crewmen in orange coveralls charged for the Damage Control Room, which was located on the port side of the passage. A powerful hand grabbed a handful of fabric just above Valerian's right elbow and jerked him toward the other end of the passage.

"C'mon, let's go," a burly Estonian barked. "We need to suit up."

"Didn't you hear what he said? LNG storage tanks are venting!" Valerian shouted, ripping his arm free from the other man's grip. "We need to evacuate."

"No, I just talked to the roving watch. Local pressure gauges read normal. They've been in range all night. This is a computer malfunction. We need to isolate the relief valves on the storage tanks. And at the same time, we need to stop the flooding. If we don't we'll lose the ship!" the man shouted back over the wail of the General Alarm that had resumed blaring.

"You're crazy; we'll asphyxiate long before then," Valerian countered.

"Not if we suit up and don our EBEs."

By now, two of the first responders were already sprinting out of the DC room dressed in flame-retardant coveralls, gauntlet-style gloves, and face masks connected to Emergency Breathing Equipment rigs they wore like backpacks. "We're going to isolate the overpressure reliefs. You guys stop the flooding," one of the two men called, looking down the passage at them.

Valerian clenched his jaw. *Why does everybody have to try to be a hero?*

"Make sure to inform the control room as you isolate each valve in case DCS shows conflicting indications," the crewman in front of Valerian called back.

"Good idea, Ludwig. We're using channel two on the radio."

"Spire, this is Cornerstone. We didn't see you exit on thermal. Report status," said Sylvie in his ear, her voice tense and ripe with concern.

"It's a suicide mission, Ludwig," Valerian said, ignoring Sylvie. "Be smart. We need to evacuate."

"Don't be a coward. This is what they pay us for," Ludwig shouted back, taking him by the arm for a second time. "Let's go."

Shaking his head, Valerian let the other man pull him for a stride until grudgingly setting off toward the DC room together.

"Spire, this is Cornerstone. What the hell are you doing?" said Sylvie.

"Improvising," he murmured, wondering if she could even hear him over the din of sirens and chaos that was the FSRU *Independence*.

"I highly recommend you abandon the ship," came her reply a heartbeat later.

"Then the mission will fail," he said, answering in Russian while shadowing Ludwig's every move as he donned the unfamiliar damage control gear.

"What was that?" Ludwig asked, looking up.

"I was cursing your name and your courage," Valerian replied with a soldier's bravado.

"That's what I thought," the big man said with a crooked smile, his Lithuanian now tinged with German undertones in the stress of the moment. Already dressed out, the German reached over and helped Valerian don his EBE rig and then turned on air to Valerian's face mask. "Okay, you're ready to go."

"Thanks," Valerian said, then in German said, "Now, let's go save this bitch."

Ludwig nodded approvingly, then turned to two other men in the DC locker who were also just finishing dressing out. "Everybody ready to go?" he asked. When he got three nods back, he shouted. "Okay, follow me."

Ludwig charged out of the DC locker like a mad footballer with a vendetta to mete. Valerian followed, moving stride for stride with the German down stairwells and ladders into the bowels of the ship, with the two other *Independence* crewmen hot on his heels. When they reached the lower level, Valerian noted pooling water in the bilge, but there were no water jets or spraying pipes anywhere to be seen. He was no sailor, but his quick and capable mind made sense of the situation while the other three men looked around bewildered. The *Independence* was not flooding because of a *real* casualty, like a hull breach or pipe rupture. The Zeta cyber ops team was subverting the ship's ballast and dewatering system to flood the vessel.

Ludwig had already demonstrated he was both vigilant and courageous; Valerian strongly suspected he could add intelligent to that list. It wouldn't be long before the big German figured out what was going on, which meant that unfortunately, the time had come for him to break the promise he'd made to Arkady.

Valerian flipped the switch in his mind, changing his skin from cautious crewmember to lethal assassin. With lightning speed, he hit Ludwig in the throat with a knife-hand strike, crushing the man's trachea with the outside edge of his hand. Ludwig, who had been barking orders, collapsed to his knees clutching his throat with both hands, his eyes going wide with shock. Valerian followed the strike by ripping the EBE mask off Ludwig's face and knocking him over with a kick to the chest. Evaporated natural gas vapor venting from the ship's cryogenic storage tanks was already displacing the breathable air on the lower decks. Valerian could smell it leaking in around the edges of the imperfect seal between his EBE mask and his right cheek. Ludwig would be dead in less than two minutes.

"What the hell are you doing?" one of the remaining two crewmen said, looking on with astonished bewilderment.

Valerian didn't reply, just charged the man and dispatched him with a deft combination of incapacitating strikes—a kick to the solar plexus, a crossing elbow to the temple, and lastly a downward driving elbow to the base of the skull, intended to fracture the spinal column at the atlantoaxial joint. The target of his malice collapsed in a lifeless heap at his feet. In his peripheral vision, Valerian saw a shadow closing on him. He ducked just in time to avoid the swinging arc of a large crescent wrench that had somehow materialized in the hand of the final crewman of their DC party. Valerian whirled to face him and was surprised to recognize that the coverall-clad crewman was a woman. Her androgynous face and build had thrown him. No matter—he didn't discriminate when it came to killing.

The god of murder was gender agnostic.

He tried to taunt her into swinging the wrench again with a *come-hither* double curl of his fingers, but she didn't take the bait and instead took a cautious step back. He shifted his gaze beyond her to the middle distance, as if spotting something of concern. This distracted her for a beat, which he exploited by feigning a lunge at her, stopping just short of her reach. She swung reflexively and wildly, missing him by a foot, and he capitalized on the mistake. He closed the gap in a flash and sent her flying with a shoulder tackle to her midsection. He felt her ribs crack on impact and heard the crescent wrench clang against the metal grating as it tumbled from her grip. A split second after they hit the deck, he scrambled up and punched her in the gut from a kneeling position. She buckled at the waist, wailed, and rolled onto her side, clutching her midsection. He ripped her mask off her face and then jerked it hard enough to tear the flexible rubber hose free from its attachment point. He tossed it into the bilge, then picked up the crescent wrench and swung.

Arkady is not going to be happy with me, he thought, wiping blood spatter from the back of his hand as he retraced the route they'd taken down to this level. Sirens wailed and echoed throughout the engineering spaces. With a scowl, he made his way up the ladders, ready to get out of there, when a loudspeaker announcement cut out the alarms.

"All personnel evacuate ship. I repeat, all personnel engaged in damage control efforts stop immediately and evacuate ship."

Valerian's mouth curled into a grin, and he set the crescent wrench down on top of an electrical control cabinet. When he reached the main deck and stepped outside, he resisted the compulsion to rip the sweaty, stinky face mask off and instead kept breathing from his compressed air supply.

"Cornerstone, Spire. Egressing now," he reported, his voice strange and metallic sounding in his mask.

"Copy, Spire, we were beginning to worry," Sylvie said in his ear.

"Touching," he murmured, picking up speed as he ran forward along the gunwale toward the tower staircase amidships—the same staircase he'd used to board the ship not thirty minutes ago. When he reached the third-level landing, three more crew members, two dressed out in DC gear with EBEs and a third just wearing coveralls, ran up behind him.

"Everyone get to the ferry platform," the man bringing up the rear said. "There's a rescue boat en route to pick us up."

Valerian followed the leader's instructions and descended the metal-rung ladder to the ferry landing. The white bow wave of a rapidly approaching rescue boat immediately stole the group's attention, and a nervous, palpable excitement washed over them—that almost inappropriately euphoric feeling that comes from cheating death even in the presence of others who have not. It was a feeling that Valerian knew all too intimately.

Everyone scurried to the dock's edge as the small watercraft pulled up to the landing. Valerian smiled tightly to himself and moved to the left, intent on one more minor defiance of Arkady's instructions, one that he hoped would immediately begin his next priority—baiting the trap that would bring the Americans to him.

Valerian looked up into the corner of the overhang where the security camera should be. The images, he knew, would be reviewed in great detail from the servers that stored the feeds remotely. They would get into the right hands quickly, since there would be an urgent desire to rule out terrorism as the cause of the devastating loss he had set in motion. He looked up, staring hard and straight into the camera, stepping back to be sure his face was not in shadows from the overhang.

Come, my American ghost. It's time to meet again. I'm waiting for you.

He moved to join the group at the edge of the landing, where the rescue ferry was decelerating to pull even with them. Before it was even secure, everyone began scrambling aboard. The *Independence* was a ticking time bomb, and everyone knew it.

As Valerian watched the FSRU *Independence* shrink behind in the ferry's wake, he popped a piece of nicotine gum in his mouth and began to chew.

"Do you think everyone got off?" Pärn said, stepping up beside him.

"Doesn't matter," Valerian said.

"Why not?"

"Because, anyone who didn't make this ferry," Valerian said as a fireball the size of a football stadium erupted in Klaipėda's harbor, "is already dead."

PART II

The battle line between good and evil runs through the
heart of every man.

—Aleksandr Solzhenitsyn, Russian novelist, moralist,
and gulag survivor

CHAPTER 15

"Dude, you gotta stop," Munn said with exasperation.

Dempsey turned to glare at the man he'd called his friend, confidant, and team member. Now, he could officially add "cellmate" to that list. Munn, for his part, didn't see the glare because he was lying on the room's only cot with his eyes closed.

"I thought you were asleep," Dempsey said without breaking stride as he paced their detention suite. The present space was several steps up from their original accommodations—the Latvian equivalent of DC Metro lockup—after they'd been hauled in for the "incident" in Old Town. Swift interaction by Smith, or more likely by the Office of the DNI, had resulted in the upgrade. Dempsey was proud of himself. He had not punched a single person since being arrested, including the young, hot-tempered detective who'd questioned them in turn . . . and he'd *really* wanted to punch that guy.

"I was asleep until the incessant shuffle of those size-thirteen gunboats you call boots woke my ass up," Munn said, pressing up onto his elbows. "Why don't you take a seat, kick your feet up on that table, and relax. Or if it'll help, you can have my cot. I don't really care, so long as you chill the fuck out."

Dempsey stopped pacing, shot more daggers at Munn with his eyes, then started to laugh.

"Now see, that wasn't so hard, was it?" Munn said with a chuckle. He sat up and began to scratch in earnest at the four days' growth of scruff along his jawline. "Why does this shit itch so much?"

"It was her, Dan," Dempsey said, ignoring the small talk and venting about what was really bothering him. "The way she walked, how she held her shoulders, and that look when she turned . . . I swear to God it was Elinor."

"Aw, c'mon, dude, don't tell me you're going to start with this shit again. Why do you gotta torture yourself like that?"

"I'm not torturing myself. You know me as well as anyone left in this world knows me. Have I ever been a bullshitter?"

"Well, no, but—"

"Exactly. I'm not creative enough to make up stuff. I'm a door kicker, Dan. I go where they tell me, shoot who they tell me, and report back the details."

"That's who you used to be," Munn said, getting to his feet and stretching. "You haven't been that guy since you pulled my sorry drunk ass out of that bar in Key West. And neither am I. If you think that going from SEAL operator to covert spook—or whatever the hell we are—didn't change both of us, then you are completely lacking in situational awareness, bro. That's who we were—not who we are."

Dempsey shook his head. "Whatever. That's not the point. Yes, we're different, but does that mean I'm now someone who invents shit?"

He felt anger—displaced, but hot and real—swelling up and tried his best to swallow it down. Getting pissed at his best friend and teammate helped no one.

"Of course not," Munn said softly, starting to pace himself. "But we see a million shades of gray now that in our old lives we never even knew existed. That's all I'm saying."

Dempsey grumbled at this, but he didn't argue. Instead, he just met Munn's gaze and said, "Why would I make something this crazy up?"

"I'm not saying you made it up. I'm just sayin' it sounds to me like your subconscious at work. You're still carrying around all that Persian love 'em and leave 'em guilt, and it manifests as operational paranoia."

Dempsey made a *pffitt* sound and swatted away the comment. "You sound like Grimes, you know that? Since when did you trade in your MD for a PhD in head shrinking?"

"Now that's a low blow," Munn said and was about to say something else when his gaze ticked over Dempsey's shoulder to the cell door.

Dempsey spun around and locked eyes with a late-middle-aged suit staring at them through the drilled Plexiglas window in the door. Though the man hadn't uttered a single word, Dempsey pegged him for an American. "You here for us?"

"That depends," the guy said.

"On what?"

"On whether you two ladies are done bickering," the spook said with the swagger of a big brother sent by Dad to pick up his belligerent younger brothers from after-school detention.

"Now see, that's the sorta comment that'll get you in trouble," Dempsey said, taking a step toward the door. "We don't even know each other, and already you're talkin' shit."

"Ahh, give it a rest, JD," Munn said with a good-natured chuckle. "It was funny."

"The DNI sent me to help expedite your release," the suit said and theatrically checked his watch. A beat later, a buzzer sounded and the detention cell door unlocked.

Munn trotted toward the door. "I like this guy," he said, grinning ear to ear. "He's got style."

"Style?" Dempsey grumbled. "His suit is thirty years out of date, and so is his mustache."

"Maybe so, but he's old-school cool." Munn extended his fist for a bump.

The spook looked at Munn's fist and then shoved his hands in his pockets with a bored expression.

"Or . . . maybe not," Munn said with a shrug.

Dempsey, along with his sour mood, wordlessly trailed them out of the detention center. Jarvis's errand boy, who'd yet to introduce himself, did all the talking during their out-processing. To Dempsey's delight, he even got their sidearms returned along with their Kevlar vests, passports, and micro earbud transceivers without picking a fight or ruffling feathers. The "prisoner release" took all of five minutes and ended with what Dempsey surmised to be an apology followed by a genuinely cordial handshake. The spook led them to a parked Volkswagen Touareg and climbed into the driver's seat. Dempsey and Munn both hopped in the back seat, happy to let Jarvis's errand boy play chauffeur.

"You got a name, fella?" Munn said once they were underway.

"You can call me Buz," the spook said, glancing at, of all things, a paper map he had unfolded and spread out on his lap.

"Good to meet you, Buz," Munn said. "I'm Dan Munn, and you can call my grumpy, brooding friend here—"

"Patrick," Dempsey interjected, referencing the NOC on his passport and glaring at Munn.

"He knows who we are, dude," Munn said, shaking his head.

"No he doesn't," Dempsey said. "Have you not learned anything over the past year?"

"Jesus, the two of you are worse than my kids in the back seat on family vacations," Buz said.

Dempsey fixed his gaze on the rearview mirror, intent on giving Buz a look to put him in his place, but the spook was too busy looking at the map. Dempsey waited a few moments, but the man continued to stare at the map in his lap, glancing up and out the windshield only occasionally.

"Hey, dude," Dempsey finally said. "You think you oughta keep your eyes on the road a little?" He realized he was more annoyed than he was actually worried about his safety.

Buz looked up long enough to roll his eyes, then looked back at the map in his lap, folded it with one hand, and tossed it on the passenger seat. "I was driving lights out in the backstreets of Eastern Europe before you got your fingers inside your first set of panties. Keep on bickering with your girlfriend back there, and I'll take care of getting us where we need to be."

Dempsey tried to think of something clever to say but came up with nothing. The remainder of the ride to the airport took ten minutes, with Dempsey staring out the window lost in thought. Buz drove them to a private corporate hangar, where the Boeing was waiting for them on the tarmac. Just seeing Ember's flying tactical palace was like a Xanax for Dempsey's ill temper. He suddenly couldn't wait to collapse in one of the leather executive chairs around the conference table, even if it meant listening to Baldwin drone on and on about the latest signals intelligence. Whatever it took to put the embarrassment of Riga behind him and move on to the next mission to ensnare the Russian bastard who never left his thoughts.

Buz pulled the Touareg right up beside the aircraft and parked.

"Thanks for the ride, brother," Munn said.

"You're welcome," Buz said, unclipping his seat belt and opening his door.

Dempsey robotically climbed out of the SUV. He walked around the back of the VW to join Munn, who was already heading up the air-stair. In his peripheral vision, he noticed the spook trailing behind as if intent on boarding with them. Dempsey stopped halfway up the metal staircase and turned around.

"We said thanks for the ride, bro."

"And I said you're welcome," Buz said, continuing up the steps until he was standing just below Dempsey.

"Yeah, well, this is where we part ways, my friend," Dempsey said, his irritation beginning to simmer. "Why don't you head back to the embassy and grab yourself a sandwich. You've earned it."

"As tempting as that sounds," Buz said, the side of his mouth curling up into a satisfied grin beneath his Tom Selleck mustache, "I don't work at the embassy."

Dempsey was about to inform this annoying spook, whoever the hell he was, that he certainly didn't work here, when Grimes appeared on the landing at the top of the air-stair, smiling at Buz.

"I told you he'd be grumpy," she said.

"You did indeed," Buz said. "I presume that's the reason you declined my offer to come along on the pickup?"

Grimes touched her index finger to her nose and then pointed at Buz: *we have a winner.*

"Well if I'm such a pain in the ass, then why not just leave me in jail?" Dempsey growled, turning around and resuming his climb up the staircase.

"Because we love you," Grimes said playfully and reached out and pinched his cheek.

Scowling, he let her do it and then ducked around her and into the Boeing. He made his way straight to the conference room, where three other Ember teammates were gathered, having just arrived to round out whatever mission was undoubtedly coming next.

"Hey, JD," Richard Wang said with annoying exuberance from his chair. Ember's tech guru was a genius at his job, but sometimes Dempsey wasn't up for his schoolboy personality. This was one of those times.

"Richard," he said gruffly.

Reading his mood, Wang checked his usual banter and kept any follow-on comments to himself. The more savvy Special Activities Division members, former Marine Luca Martin and one-time Green Beret June Latif, read his mood and greeted him with silent nods, although Latif was wearing a shit-eating grin on his face that said he was dying to take a shot about their stint in jail. Dempsey's scowl kept the joke unspoken, and he collapsed in the middle chair directly opposite the large monitor.

On-screen was Ember's Operations Officer, Simon Adamo, glasses off and massaging the bridge of his nose. Noticing Dempsey, Adamo slipped his eyeglasses back on, adjusted their tilt, and said, deadpan, "Hi, John. How was your incarceration?"

"Restful," Dempsey said. "And how is your transition from real person to on-screen avatar going?"

Adamo broke first, smiling at the dig.

Since the Amanda Allen rescue, things had been better between Dempsey and the former CIA officer filling Ember's number-two role. He wasn't sure exactly when they'd turned the corner, but he suspected it was something they both felt. Dempsey's wisecrack was the latest in a running thread they had going, after he'd joked that the only place he ever saw Adamo was on a monitor.

It wasn't much, but it was something.

When Jarvis left Ember to become DNI and Shane Smith took over as Director, the organization changed to mirror the shift in character at the top. With Jarvis at the helm, Ember felt like a precision machine, operating at peak efficiency all the time. Under Smith, it felt more human, reflecting his fluid approach to problem solving and crisis management. Where Jarvis took the "we're getting to the top of Everest even if I have to carry half the expedition team on my back" approach, Smith employed inspiration and motivation to get every team member to the summit using the power of their own two feet. And while Jarvis's style resonated more closely with Dempsey's own, if forced to choose he would grudgingly admit that Smith was better at managing the collective Ember personalities than Jarvis ever could be. This current incarnation of Ember was happy—a family with all members pulling their weight.

Munn set a cup of black coffee in front of Dempsey and slid into the chair on his left just as Smith joined Adamo on-screen. "Hey, guys, welcome back," Smith said, his mood upbeat as usual.

"Hey, Shane," Dempsey said. "Now about what happened—"

Smith waved a hand, stopping him. "Shit happens; it comes with the territory. We were just fortunate it happened in Riga. We have a good working relationship with the Latvians, and nobody died, so they're happy."

"Except for Michael the Broker who was assassinated two feet away from me," Dempsey replied.

"Yeah, well, he doesn't count," Smith said through a chuckle. "The Latvians have no love for arms brokers. So, they consider that us doing them a favor."

"We weren't the ones who killed him," Munn chimed in.

"I know that, Dan," Smith said. Grimes and Buz walked into the conference room. "Looks like the gang's all here. I see you've all met Buz Wilson, resident Russia expert and Ember's newest member."

Munn sat up and Dempsey arched his eyebrows.

"Did you say 'newest member'?" Dempsey asked, irritated this was the first he was hearing about it. Technically, Dempsey was only in charge of personnel recruitment for Ember's Special Activities Division, but in the past Smith had consulted him on all key personnel considerations across the organization. In the case of Amanda Allen, it had been Dempsey's vote of confidence that had ultimately swayed Smith's decision to bring her on as their foreign affairs analyst. But nobody had consulted him regarding this Wilson guy.

"Yes, John, Buz is officially part of the team."

"Officially as of when?"

"As of yesterday," Smith said with just the slightest hint of irritation creeping into his voice. "Buz has one helluva pedigree at the CIA, where he's been on the Russia desk for two decades. He was handpicked and recruited by the DNI, and we're lucky to have him on board."

Dempsey silently translated the subtext: *This call is above your pay grade. No further discussion is wanted or warranted.*

"Happy to be here," Buz said and gave a courteous nod to the room.

"He doesn't *look* happy to be here," Latif said softly. Martin grinned broadly but kept the laugh inside.

"Hey, guys," a familiar female voice said as Ember's second-newest member, another CIA transplant, stepped into frame on the screen. Amanda Allen's gaze scanned all the faces until it settled on Dempsey's. The girl had been through hell and back, and even though her physical injuries from her abduction and hostage ordeal in Syria had nearly healed, she had a long emotional and psychological road ahead. But she had her shoulders back and was wearing a smile on her face. She looked confident, almost cheerful.

Dempsey smiled at her and gave her a little nod.

"Hello everyone," said the disembodied voice belonging to Ember's Signals Chief, Ian Baldwin, who sounded like he was in the room but was nowhere to be seen.

"Where in the world are you today, Ian?" Grimes asked.

"In a SCIF at Fort Meade," Baldwin said.

"What the hell are you doing over there?" Latif asked.

"Groveling," came Baldwin's reply. "Young Richard"—at this, Wang rolled his eyes—"took it upon himself to borrow some information from our friends at the NSA, without permission I might add, and a few senior individuals were not happy about it. At Ember, we are black, but that does not mean we operate without accountability or integrity, which is why I came in person to make amends." He paused, probably giving Smith a chance to weigh in, but when the Ember Director said nothing, Baldwin continued. "Anyway, it's neither here nor there, because it's all been worked out and we're friends again. And as a gesture of good will, our friends at Fort Meade have generously provided us with an image I think everyone on this call will find stimulating."

The monitor in the Boeing switched to split screen, and a grainy photograph appeared on one side showing a man dressed in coveralls looking straight into the camera. He was handsome, with dark hair, a square jaw, and an uncanny resemblance to Dempsey.

"Malik," Dempsey growled.

"Or, as Amanda likes to say, the Man not Malik," Munn added.

"He's a Russian ghost, whoever he is," Grimes said.

Martin and Latif stopped smiling and sat up in their chairs, all business now.

Wang was tapping on the keyboard of a laptop and didn't even look up.

Dempsey saw Allen tense at the appearance of the image. Malik, or rather the Russian operative who had assumed the evergreen legend of the Chechen international arms dealer, had tortured and interrogated Allen in Syria. This bastard had gotten inside her head, and Dempsey was pretty damn sure she hadn't yet managed to get him out. The same could probably be said for Dempsey and his own fixation on catching the man who had slipped through his fingers once.

"That's right," Baldwin said, reclaiming Dempsey's attention. "This image was captured overnight on a security camera at an LNG storage and degasification facility in Lithuania. In this particular case, the facility happens to be a ship—the FSRU *Independence*."

"The *Independence*, which is moored at Klaipėda, receives and processes *all* of Lithuania's natural gas imports," Adamo said, capitalizing on Baldwin's pause. "Prior to its arrival, Lithuania was dependent on Gazprom—the Russian state gas monopoly. The ship's name is no coincidence. Bringing in the *Independence* was a shrewd and calculated move by the Lithuanian President—with the help of our current administration and our friends at the CIA—one that gave her nation energy independence and removed a powerful lever Moscow wielded over her."

"What does any of that have to do with Malik and arms dealing?" Munn asked, leaning back in his chair.

Adamo's expression darkened. "Minutes after this image was captured, the *Independence* exploded and sank at the pier. It's the top story in Europe this morning."

Dempsey shook his head. "Let me guess, the disaster is being called an industrial accident."

Smith and Adamo nodded in unison.

"Right now, this photograph is the only evidence contradicting that conclusion," Smith said. "We know Malik is a Russian agent, but the rest of the world does not."

"But even our conclusion is circumstantial," Munn said. "Unless you guys in the head shed are holding out on us, we still don't know this guy's real identity."

"No, we don't, and that's the primary reason we've brought Wilson aboard." Smith looked at Ember's newest member. "Buz, would you like to share your thoughts on the topic?"

Buz stroked his mustache with thumb and forefinger and said, "I don't know who this guy is, but I might have a pretty good idea who he works for. Can somebody throw up that pic of Arkady?" An image of a man, photographed in profile and at a distance, replaced Malik on the split screen. "I'm sorry it's such a shit picture, but it's literally the only photograph we have of the man. This picture was taken in 2001 during an op I was running in Bremerhaven. His name is Arkady Zhukov, and I would argue that he is the most powerful man in Russia who doesn't appear on any org chart. He's an old-timer who came up through the ranks of the KGB. When the Soviet Union imploded, no matter who you were in Russia, your world got turned on its head. With the unraveling of Communism, some institutions collapsed, some fragmented, and others downsized or rebranded. The KGB did the latter, changing its name to the FSB. Many of the rank and file left government service for the burgeoning private sector, but Arkady stayed the course through crippling budget cuts, an ambiguous charter, a fractured command and control hierarchy, and a leadership vacuum in Moscow. In such a scenario, what is a patriot and tactician like Arkady to do?" Buz looked around the room. "What would you have done?"

Dempsey studied Buz's eyes as he spoke. Just like his throwback style and mannerisms, the way this guy briefed was quite different from what Dempsey was accustomed to. The typical modern CI brief followed a simple three-step formula: Here's everything we know about, here's everything we don't know, and now that I've told you everything I do and don't know, do you have any questions that I may or may not choose to answer? With Buz, the brief had a completely different vibe—this felt like they were sitting in a college seminar.

"I'd capitalize on the chaos and confusion," Grimes said, not surprising Dempsey by being the first to answer. "I'd try to exploit first-move advantage and blaze a path at the new FSB to aggregate the resources and power I need to achieve the goals I want to see accomplished."

Buz nodded with approval. "Spoken like a true tactician. What else?"

"With the old lines of power and communication broken, I'd start building new relationships and forging new alliances," Grimes continued, not missing a beat. "If Arkady is an operations guy, he'd understand this and he'd take steps to quickly put in place a new ecosystem of assets, information brokers, and funding channels."

Dempsey looked over at Grimes and mouthed "teacher's pet," to which she gave a self-satisfied smirk and a middle finger.

"And that's exactly what he did," Buz said, sitting up straighter. "And the way he did it was very, very clever. The minute the Communist order imploded, a power vacuum was created. With the KGB in shambles, Russian organized crime rushed in to fill that void. It's important to understand that the Russian Mafia, aka the Vory, was one of the few Soviet-era institutions to survive the collapse unscathed. The Vory was already beginning to thrive in Europe and the United States, but in their home country, they had been kept in check by both the KGB and the economic realities of Communism. Practically overnight, Russia was transformed into a mafia state where government and organized crime commingled. Nowhere was this more true than in the intelligence arms of the Russian state. State assets, institutions, and enterprises were 'transitioned' to the most unscrupulous and corrupt men in the private sector, and the oligarchy rose. Arkady saw this happening, and he was no fool. He knew that the FSB had neither the funding, manpower, or support to challenge and manage the Russian Mafia like the KGB once did. So, what did he do?"

"He decided to start working *with* the Vory," Munn said.

"Bingo," Buz replied. "And one of the first guys he roped into his scheme was a young, charismatic, and thoroughly corrupted officer named Vladimir Petrov. At the time of the collapse, Petrov was a mid-level KGB guy in Saint Petersburg, supervising commerce in and out of Russia's busiest seaport. Wherever you find maritime activity, you are guaranteed to find the Mafia. Before the collapse, a man like Arkady probably hated guys like Petrov—KGB agents who were bought and paid for by the Vory. But after the collapse, a guy like Petrov, someone with long-established Mafia relationships and a detailed knowledge of Vory operations, would make an invaluable partner. Arkady befriended Petrov, promoted him, and began to mentor him. With Petrov's charisma and Vory contacts and Arkady's strategic prowess and experience, the two of them rapidly gained influence, personal wealth, and power. Arkady worked as the puppet master from the shadows while his acolyte slithered his way into the halls of the Kremlin. The rest of the story we know—Petrov's meteoric ascension through the ranks to become the Russian President."

"Are you saying the Russian President is an acolyte of some KGB spymaster?" Dempsey asked.

Buz nodded. "That's exactly what I'm saying."

"Then can somebody please explain how it's possible we didn't know about this fucking guy until now?"

"After Petrov's ascendance to the presidency, Arkady went dark, and by dark I mean he completely evaporated from our universe. Most of my colleagues at CIA believed him to be dead, the victim of power shifts within the Russian government."

"Then maybe he really is dead," Latif suggested.

"Yeah, maybe Petrov had him whacked because he knew too much," Munn chimed in.

"It's possible, but unlikely," Buz said. "Arkady made Petrov, but even if Petrov did not feel indebted to his mentor, he would be a fool to eliminate an ally with a strategic mind as creative and cunning as Arkady's."

"So you believe Arkady is still in the game?" Grimes asked.

Buz nodded. "Over the past decade, rumors have been percolating of a secret Russian black ops organization—an organization so compartmentalized that I believe even the leadership in FSB is unaware of its existence. This group is so buried in black that we didn't even have a name until very recently. I believe it's called Spetsgruppa Zeta, and I believe it's run by Arkady."

"That name sounds familiar. Are you talking about Vympel?" Allen asked, perking up.

"No, Vympel is Spetsgruppa Alpha. To use a relevant American comparison, Vympel is like Russia's Tier One, whereas Zeta would be analogous to your—I mean our—little Task Force Ember here."

"Hold on. Are you saying there's a Russian Ember out there right now actively working against us?" Dempsey said, leaning forward in his chair.

"Yes, there's a Russian Ember out there. Whether or not they are aware of our existence is another matter altogether. I wasn't aware of Ember's existence until yesterday, and I had Top Secret/SCI clearance."

Dempsey fixed his gaze on Buz. "Your brief about Arkady and his history with the Vory pulls everything into perspective. We had always assumed the Malik legend was similar to 'the American' legend Dan borrowed from CIA for the Amarov meet. But if Malik is a Zeta operative, then that means everything that happened in Turkey, Narva, and Klaipėda was the brainchild of this Arkady guy."

Buz gave him a solemn nod. "He's a brilliant, cunning, and devious sonuvabitch. If I were a betting man, I'd put all my chips on that theory."

"So what's our next move?" Grimes asked, looking from Dempsey to Buz to Smith.

"I'll tell you what our next move is," Munn interrupted, his right fist balling up. "We find this Arkady bastard and we take him out."

"Were you even listening, Dan?" Grimes said. "Nobody knows where he is. The last sighting of him was in 2001."

"Then we need to fucking find him, Elizabeth."

"All right, all right, everybody simmer down. Connecting the dots and finding bad guys is what we do best," Smith said. "It took us a year to get Amir Modiri, and we knew where he lived and worked. We're not going to find Arkady overnight, but you have my word that finding him and piercing the Zeta veil of anonymity is my top priority. In the meantime, I want you guys to head to Klaipėda and see what else we can learn about what happened to the *Independence*. The global stakes here are huge, and Buz thinks the incident has Arkady's fingerprints all over it. If we can prove this was a sanctioned Russian operation and not an industrial accident, then we give the DNI and the President powerful ammunition to use against Petrov. The sabotage and sinking of the FSRU *Independence* would be considered an act of war. Lithuania is a NATO member; an attack on Lithuania is an attack on NATO. We want to stay a step ahead of everyone else on this one. The DNI was explicit that he wants the President to be able to control the narrative."

"What's our NOC?" Dempsey asked.

"You'll be going in as an FBI Counterterrorism Division investigation team that specializes in augmenting international terrorism investigations in host countries with FBI legal attaché offices," Smith said. "FBI opened an office in Riga in 2011 serving the Baltic nations. Adamo and Allen have begun a dialogue with the attaché, and Miss Felsk at ODNI has Ambassador Bulle talking with the Lithuanian President, who is, as you can imagine, more than happy to have us involved."

"I thought FBI CTD was a domestic entity?" Martin asked. "Won't this raise some eyebrows, us poking around where we don't belong?"

"As it turns out, Lone Star Energy, a US oil and gas company, signed an import contract with Lithuania's state-owned gas supply company, which imports all its gas via the *Independence*. Even without the contract, a request from the Lithuanian government is all that it would take to justify a US augment to the local investigation."

"If our NOC is FBI CTD, then can we get a Tactical Mobility Team flown in?" Munn asked. "I mean as much as I love having Buz chauffer me around in the Touareg, it wouldn't hurt to have some backup and some wheels . . . just sayin'."

"I'll see what I can do," Smith said. "We'll schedule another brief as soon as your NOCs are finalized and work out all the details. Any other questions or comments before we break?"

"Yeaaaah," Dempsey said with incredulity. Was it possible that Smith was going to close the briefing without even mentioning what weighed on him the most? "Were you not planning to debrief what happened in Riga yesterday?"

"Oh yeah, sorry, John. While you and Dan were relaxing in detention, the rest of us spent that time reconstructing the events in Old Town," Smith said. "Obviously, it was a targeted hit on Michael."

"Obviously," Dempsey parroted.

"And Michael was clearly the only sanctioned target, because nobody took a shot at you or Munn. Which means we can rule out Malik and his people. We can probably also rule out Amarov and the Vory for the same reason."

"I hear you, but it can't be a coincidence that the hit was ordered immediately after the Narva debacle."

"We don't have a viable explanation for that. A guy like Michael could have made dozens of enemies over the years. It's very possible the hit was related to other business we know nothing about. It could be any of a hundred things. We're still working on that," Smith said, with Adamo and Allen nodding in collective agreement.

Dempsey looked first to Munn and then to Grimes for backup, but neither of them stepped up to join his campaign. "C'mon, guys, you saw what happened. All those girls, dressed in the same exact clothes, arriving on scene at the same time. I mean that was some über-orchestrated *Thomas Crown Affair* shit. Did the Latvian State Police question the girl I chased into that alley? Did we get any IDs on any of them?"

"Director Smith assigned me the case," Allen said and held up a printed image of a young woman that Dempsey surmised had come from Grimes's scope. "I don't have anything yet, but you'll be the first to know when I do."

"Anything else?" Smith asked.

"Seriously, Shane, are you trying to get me spun up?" Dempsey said.

"I don't know what you're talking about, John."

"I'm talking about the big fucking white elephant in the room—Elinor Jordan. Why are we not discussing this? Have you informed the Seventh Order that she's alive? Has anybody talked to Levi Harel yet?"

151

Dempsey scanned the faces on the monitor and then looked around the room. No one was making eye contact with him except for the new guy, and Dempsey didn't give a shit what that old spook thought. "Oh, c'mon, guys, don't pull that 'Dempsey's losing his mind' shit and pretend I'm not here. I saw her with my own two eyes!"

Wang was staring at him. Latif and Martin were both staring at their hands.

"Hey, John, why don't we take this off-line, okay? In fact, if everyone could please give us the room, that would be great," Smith said.

On that cue, Buz and the rest of the team pushed their chairs back from the table and headed for the door. On his way out, Munn paused at the threshold and turned back to Dempsey. With a wry grin he said, "I'm a surgeon, not an ophthalmologist, but you know, I'd be happy to administer a vision exam."

Dempsey held up his middle finger. "Here's your vision test—how many fingers am I holding up?"

They both laughed, and Munn shut the door behind him. When Dempsey looked back at the monitor, the split screen was gone and only Smith remained in frame. The Ember Director opened his mouth, but Dempsey beat him to the punch.

"I know what I saw, Shane," he said. "It was her."

Smith pursed his lips and ran his fingers through his hair. He didn't say anything for a beat. When he finally did, all he said was, "Okay."

"Okay what?"

"Okay, I'll make the call."

"That's it?" Dempsey said, surprised. "What happened to telling me the whole thing was just a product of my imagination and that you're going to schedule an appointment with the headshrinker for me next time I'm back in Newport News?"

"Do you remember the night in Florida when you said goodbye to Jack Kemper and your old life and decided to join Ember?" Smith asked.

Dempsey nodded as his mind transported him back to the night he'd said goodbye to his ex-wife, Kate, and teenage son, Jake. That they thought he was dead—another murdered hero of Operation Crusader—was a knife in his heart even now.

He inhaled, imagining he could smell the salty tang in the air and feel the sea breeze on his face. "I remember."

"Do you remember what you said to me?"

"I believe it was 'Fuck off, Smith,'" Dempsey said.

Smith laughed. "Yeah, that was the first thing out of your mouth. Do you remember what you said next?"

"If memory serves, I gave you a bunch of shit about being Army and accused you of being afraid of getting wet."

"You did," Smith said, still grinning. "I'm talking about before that?"

"Sorry, man, I don't remember."

"You said you didn't trust me," Smith said, his smile fading. "And do you remember what I said?"

Dempsey nodded, his memory primed now. "You said that you didn't trust me, either. But that you trusted Jarvis, and Jarvis trusted me, so that's why we were having the conversation—or something to that effect."

"Exactly. A lot has changed since that night, John. We've walked plenty of miles in each other's shoes."

Dempsey nodded. "Are you trying to say you finally trust me, only going about sayin' it in a long-winded, convoluted, Army dude way?"

"Yeah, pretty much," Smith chuckled.

"I know I've got my demons to battle, but I've always had demons to battle. That's nothing new. When I step out into the field, I check that shit—lock it up tight. You don't ever have to worry about me losing my objectivity on a mission. I would hope, by now, you recognize that."

"I know that," Smith said. "Which brings me to my point. I do trust you. If you believe the assassin who whacked Michael the Broker was Elinor Jordan, then I believe you. We'll look into it, okay? But in the meantime, promise me you'll leave Persian ghosts for me to worry about while you guys focus on the Russian ones."

Dempsey stood up, signaling he was ready for this to be over. "Roger that. Thanks, Shane."

"One more thing, John, before we cut this off."

"Yeah?"

"This new guy—Buz—don't write him off so quickly. He knows his shit, and he brings a level of expertise to the team we don't have. Arkady Zhukov, and this black ops task force Zeta that we're starting to tangle with, they make me nervous. Even before Jarvis recruited Wilson, I could feel this malevolent force out there—a red specter—hunting us." Smith's gaze went to the middle distance. Then, shaking it off, he refocused on Dempsey and flashed him a *never mind* grin. "Anyway, my point is I think we need this guy, so don't write off what he has to say just because he's a spooky old-timer."

"Roger that," Dempsey said and then suddenly found himself craving a lip full of wintergreen snuff and wishing for the good old days with the Tier One in the Iraqi desert. He ran his tongue along the inside of his lower lip and flashed Smith a cocky smile. "Don't worry, Director Smith. I promise, I'll be nice to the new guy."

CHAPTER 16

Office of the Director of National Intelligence (ODNI)
McLean, Virginia
June 14
0945 Local Time

Jarvis looked at the flashing light on his desk phone.

This was the moment of truth; the neurologist from Walter Reed was holding on the line to give him the results of the second battery of tests. The MRI had *not* detected a brain tumor, nor had it indicated signs of central nervous system demyelination. On the one hand this was good news—they could rule out cancer and MS. On the other hand, with proper treatment many types of cancer could be eradicated. Similarly, a diagnosis of multiple sclerosis was not a death sentence. With holistic life changes, a significant percentage of patients put the disease into remission. Promising immunotherapies in the pipeline signaled that cures for cancer and MS could be on the horizon. The same could not be said for the diseases that had not been ruled out.

Jarvis steeled himself, exhaled, and picked up the phone.

"Go ahead, Doctor," he said and then listened as the doc walked him through the various test results. He felt a paradoxical calm as he waited for the only thing that mattered—the conclusion. When it finally came, the news hit like a punch to the gut, and everything else the doc said became background noise. He wasn't sure how long the neurologist talked before the sound of his name being spoken snapped him back.

"Director Jarvis . . . do you have any questions for me?"

"Not at this time."

"Eventually, you will," the doc said, "and when that time comes, I want you to know my door is always open. There are a myriad of treatment options that improve quality of life and lessen symptoms, and some new stuff on the horizon that promises to slow the progression of the disease. But that's a conversation for another time and something I don't want to burden you with today. I am familiar with your service record and your accomplishments. In the meantime, I suspect you'll do what your Navy SEAL brethren always do when faced with great adversity—harness your inner strength and never give up the fight."

"Thank you, Captain," Jarvis said to the Navy doc. "I'll see you in three months."

He hung up the phone and, like the times he'd been shot in combat, performed a quick self-assessment. Except this time, instead of patting himself down for puncture wounds, broken bones, and lacerations, this was a psychological assessment.

I'm still in the fight. I am the same man I was yesterday, only better informed. I know the enemy now, and I will adapt and overcome—

A knock came at the door: tap, tap . . . tap.

Petra's knock.

"Come in," he barked.

The door to his office opened and Petra stepped inside. She quietly shut the door behind her but made no move to approach him. Instead, she just leaned back against the doorframe, swallowed, and looked at him—her eyes asking the only question that mattered.

"The preliminary diagnosis is Parkinson's disease," Jarvis said. "But the EMG results were not definitive, so they want to repeat the test in three months to try to rule out ALS."

Petra knitted her fingers together as if in prayer and raised her clasped fists to rest against her lips. The expression on her face was strange and one he'd never seen before—vulnerable, anxious, and upset.

"Well," he said, staring at her. "Aren't you going to say something?"

"You think I'm the Russian mole, don't you?" she said.

The non sequitur caught him completely off guard, for quite possibly the first time in his life. When his composure returned, he said, "I just told you that I have Parkinson's disease, and *that* is your response?"

"Yes," she said, and now he could see that her bottom lip was quivering.

"I tell you I have an incurable, debilitating neurological disease and you're worried about self-preservation?" he said, pushing his chair back from his desk. When she didn't respond, he got angry. "Get out."

"No," she said, setting her jaw.

"Excuse me?" he said, his cheeks going crimson.

"I said *no*. Not until you answer my question."

In that moment, he wanted to grab the lamp on the corner of his desk and hurl it at her, but instead he stood, pressed his palms firmly against the desktop, and glared at her.

"Something happened while you were getting that MRI," she said. "You decided something—flipped a switch in your head—and ever since you've treated me . . . differently. Oh, it's subtle. You're very good at subtle, so good I'm sure no one else has even noticed, but I've noticed. I've felt it. I *see* it in the way you're looking at me right now."

"Give it a rest, Petra. We made the decision together, or have you already forgotten? So long as you're my Chief of Staff, we agreed to distance ourselves from each other."

"No," she said, shaking her head. "That is not what we agreed. We agreed not to pursue a romantic relationship; we did not agree to build a wall between us. Our relationship is built on a foundation of mutual respect and admiration, not lust and carnal desire. So, don't you fucking lie to me, Kelso Jarvis. Answer the question . . ."

He swallowed. "Yes," he said softly. He held her eyes. "I think you may be the mole."

She dropped her hands to her sides and stared at him, her lip still quivering, but from anger or fear he did not know. She held his gaze, not looking away, not blinking, and said, "What evidence are you using to support this accusation?"

"It's not an accusation, or you'd be in a very small room talking to very large people. It's a mathematical hypothesis, and one that fits—mathematically. The circle of people who know about Ember's existence is incredibly small. The circle of people with knowledge at the pre-operation and planning level is even smaller. You are one of the half dozen or so in the latter group. The Russian operational pivots started only after I brought you on board as my Chief of Staff. And . . ." He stopped, hesitating.

"And what?" she said, her gaze going frosty.

"And you compromised me emotionally." For one of the first times in his life, he'd hesitated. Because for the first time, he was unsure. Never had emotions leaked into the algorithms that made up his suppositions and conclusions. But now, they were wreaking havoc, like sand in the gears, grinding his faculties to a halt. To what extent had those emotions compromised his judgment? Were they compromising him now? In another setting—with anyone else—he would test his hypothesis with a full-on accusation, despite any uncertainty, and then read the response. But here, with Petra, he found he couldn't get himself to quite that level. "It's possible that you lured me into an untoward romantic relationship, to blind me to your true agenda and create a scenario where I would be complicit in your espionage activities."

"Is that all?" she asked.

"Yes."

"And that's your working hypothesis, Director?"

He cleared his throat and shifted his weight. How on God's green earth could this woman make him this uncomfortable and unsure? He hated the sensation with all of his being.

"It is one working hypothesis," he fudged.

Petra's face flushed and he watched her jaw twitch.

"First, let us be clear. *You* recruited *me*. I was working at ONI when you showed up out of the blue and invited me to lunch. The only reason I'm your Chief of Staff is because you asked me to be."

"I considered that," he said. "But, it doesn't rule out the possibility that you were already a well-placed mole working at ONI. In that case, your recruitment is just very bad luck for me and a remarkable turn of fortune for you. In such a scenario, your handlers would have encouraged you to accept the position and then carefully pursue a romantic relationship with me."

"I took a bullet for you," she said with her characteristic head tilt. "Do you really think I'd do that for a mark I was trying to exploit and compromise?"

"No," he heard himself say. None of this felt right to him. Even after the epiphany, it had never quite sat right with him, and yet the circumstantial evidence was just too significant to ignore . . .

"This is a vulnerable time for you," she said, taking a cautious step toward him. "I recognize that. You're under a tremendous amount of stress. When you started pursuing me—and let's be crystal clear on this point, it was *you* who took the first step toward intimacy—I should have rebuffed you. But I couldn't help myself. I'm . . ." She made a noise he was unfamiliar with—not quite a groan but more than a sigh—and wiped a tear from her cheek with angry irritation. "I'm drawn to you. There's no flowery metaphor to describe how it feels when I'm with you. It's like gravity—willpower alone is not enough to resist the earth's pull, and it's the same with you." When he didn't say anything, she continued. "After the MRI, as soon as you looked at me that way, the voice in my head whispered, 'He thinks you're the mole.' I considered confronting you about it, but when I played out that conversation in my mind, it always ended badly. So, I decided that instead of trying to convince you of my innocence, I would personally find the mole and deliver his or her head to you on a platter. But when you told me the news just now . . ." She shook her head. "The answer to your original question is a resounding no. When you told me you had an incurable neurological disease, I wasn't thinking about self-preservation. What I was thinking was, how can I be the woman he needs me to be if he doesn't believe in me anymore? *That* is what I was thinking, you fucking asshole."

They stared at each other, neither flinching, each measuring the other's strength and resolve. Jarvis spoke first.

"Will you take a polygraph?"

Petra gave a huffing laugh and shook her head, but he saw tears rim her eyes.

"Yes, I'll take it over, and over, and over again—as many times as it takes until you're satisfied. But we both know that it would be a waste of time. You're a better polygraph than the machine. And I learned to beat a fucking polygraph when I was a twenty-eight-year-old girl serving under *Commander* Jarvis at the Tier One, so what would be the point?"

He took a deep breath. "I've never willingly put myself in a professionally and emotionally vulnerable position like I have with you."

"I know. There is a part of you that equates intimacy with treason—not sovereign treason, but betrayal of self. You have spent your lifetime purging and eradicating vulnerabilities and personal insecurities. From the outside, Fort Jarvis is quite formidable and, to all the world, impenetrable. Our relationship is a threat to that paradigm. Your Parkinson's diagnosis is a threat to that paradigm. And yes, the mole is a threat to that paradigm. So, why not lump all three together, label us a common threat, and go about the business of expunging us with surgical precision; that way you can go back to the business of being you. Unfortunately, I have some bad news for you—your days as a citadel of one are over. There's a reason SEALs conduct operations as teams instead of individuals, or have you already forgotten? Didn't you used to *preach* that dogma, you fucking hypocrite?"

"I've not forgotten."

"Then do you think brotherhood only applies to combat or that it only applies to everyone but you?"

He shook his head. "Neither," he nearly whispered, feeling like a six-year-old being disciplined in front of the class.

"Good, because life *is* combat, my love. Never forget that."

His desk phone rang, interrupting the most important conversation of . . . well, of his life. He glanced at the phone and saw that the flashing light indicated a caller on his secure line—an Ember number. He looked back at Petra, the most resolute, intrepid woman he'd ever known, and in all her strength he saw profound beauty.

"You've given me a lot to think about," he said, but his eyes betrayed the true message: *I was wrong . . . forgive me.*

She nodded in acknowledgment, and her look softened. Turning to leave, she said, "This conversation is not finished."

He nodded again, hoping his eyes still sent her a message that would help.

He waited until she'd shut the door to pick up the receiver. "Hey, Shane," he said, pressing the phone to his ear. "How can I help?"

"Is everything all right, sir?" Smith said, as intuitive as ever. "You sound pressed."

"Just another day as DNI," Jarvis said. "Being pressed is business as usual."

"Roger that, sir. I'll try to keep it short. Something came up that I need to talk to you about, something with Dempsey in Riga."

"Fire away," Jarvis said and listened while Smith recounted recent events. He concluded by reporting Dempsey's Elinor sighting with an undertone of skepticism.

"What's your ask here, Shane?" Jarvis said, shifting the phone from one ear to the other. "Is the point of this call information, validation, or inquiry?"

"I suppose the point of the call, sir, is to find out if you know something that we don't know," Smith said.

His initial reaction was to interpret Smith's comment as an accusation, but that was just his bad mood talking. Smith was a straight shooter and didn't play games or hold petty grudges. If Jarvis had decided to withhold sensitive information from Smith—like new details regarding Elinor Jordan's fate in Tehran—then Smith would accept that decision without animus. Such was the nature of their business.

"The last brief on Elinor Jordan's fate that I can recall was the Crusader after-action debrief. She's been off my radar ever since," Jarvis said. "But since you're calling me about it, then I assume you're putting weight into Dempsey's conviction that he saw her in Riga?"

"You know how Dempsey is on an op, boss. He's like a heat-seeking missile. For him to get distracted, or more accurately, for him to *let* himself get distracted in the field by something like this would be, well, not Dempsey-like."

"I agree. Unlike most people, John has never suffered from the 'chase the shiny object' syndrome," Jarvis replied. "That being said, we've all been under tremendous pressure since Istanbul."

"That's true, but . . ."

"You'd like me to call Harel and confirm?" Jarvis said, verbalizing the unspoken ask.

"Yes, sir."

"All right, Shane. Consider it repayment for the hell I put you guys through in Turkey," Jarvis said.

"Thank you, sir. Please give Director Harel my best."

"Will do," Jarvis said and ended the call.

He checked his watch. Tel Aviv was seven hours ahead of DC, which put the time at late afternoon. It had been three weeks since they'd spoken—his friend and confidant, the Israeli Mossad Chief, had called to check on Jarvis after he'd been shot. The call had been brief, an expected formality between peers, but Harel's expression of concern had been genuine. In the hierarchy of opinions in the world that mattered to Jarvis, Harel's was at the top along with President Warner's and . . . *Petra's*.

Focusing his mind, Jarvis dialed Harel's desk office from memory and imagined the glass cage Harel called an office overlooking the Intelligence Ops Center in the basement of Mossad headquarters. The line picked up on the third ring.

"Hello, my friend," Harel answered, his voice hoarse but his demeanor as collegial as ever. "How are you today?"

"I've had better mornings. I was diagnosed with Parkinson's disease today," Jarvis said, wondering what in the world had prompted him to open with that.

"Ah, shit," Harel said. "That's terrible news, Kelso. How many people have you told?"

"Two—you and my Chief of Staff."

"How many people do you plan to tell?"

"Two, at least for the foreseeable future."

"I think that's smart. Keep the circle small," Harel said as a matter of fact. "You need to be the one to manage the transition on your own timetable. The minute the sharks smell blood in the water, they'll start circling and they'll never leave you alone. You're very healthy and strong; I suspect you'll have many more years of service before they ship you off on the ice floe."

"Thanks for the vote of confidence," Jarvis chuckled. "I knew I could count on you to cheer me up." He heard the flick of a cigarette lighter and pictured Harel lighting up a Noblesse in his glass-walled office for everyone to see in the explicitly smoke-free building. During the pause while Harel took his first drag, Jarvis added, "Anyway, that's not the real reason I called."

"No?" the Israeli spymaster said, his voice ripe with sarcasm. "What other happy news do you have for me today, Kelso? Let me guess, someone stole your pickup truck, you lost your guitar, and your dog died? Oh, wait, that's a country music song."

"This is not the reaction I expected from my best friend and ally on the other side of the world," Jarvis said.

"I know, I know. What's the American expression—I'm just busting your chops? The way I see it, the last thing you need from me is pity. You'll get plenty of that from everyone else later, and I want you to remember me this way."

"That's a strange thing to say, Levi," Jarvis said, holding up his right hand and watching it tremble like a leaf in the breeze.

"Well, since today is apparently bad news day, I might as well come clean and tell you my dirty little secret."

"Go on, I'm listening."

Harel exhaled loud enough that Jarvis could hear it on the line and then said, "I have stage-four lung cancer. The doctors tell me I have three months to live. Tops."

The news hit Jarvis harder than his own diagnosis. "Then why the fuck are you still smoking? I've been telling you for years that shit was going to kill you, but did you listen?"

This comment made Harel laugh, which sent him into a terrible coughing fit. When he finally recovered, he managed to say, "If I was still married, that's exactly what Chana would say. You're like my work wife, you know that?" When Jarvis didn't answer, Harel added, "Listen, I know it's not good news, but I've had one helluva run. Unfortunately, I don't have much time to get my house in order. It's a fucking circus over here right now, and the PM is on my ass every day."

"You still haven't told him?"

"Unlike most people, I follow my own advice. I kept the circle small. In fact, you're the first person I've told. But . . . it's time. The PM and his wife invited me to their house for dinner on Friday. I'm planning to tell him then."

Jarvis shook his head. "What the hell happened to us, Levi?"

"We got old," Harel said through a cough. "Men like us either go out in a bang before our time, or it's death by a thousand cuts. Either way, the Reaper always gets his man, and my number is up."

Jarvis was about to tell Harel he was sorry, but he stopped himself and instead said, "In that case, I hope you can stay alive long enough for me to make good on our last bet. I believe I owe you a six-pack."

"That's right, that's right you lost. But don't forget the terms of the deal—you have to come to Tel Aviv to drink it with me."

"I'll start looking at my calendar and plan a trip."

"All right, enough of this morbid shit. What did you *really* call me about, Kelso?"

"Two things. The first concerns Elinor Jordan . . ."

"What about her?"

The slight change in Harel's voice was something perhaps only Jarvis would have noticed. The dying Israeli spymaster knew something. *Son of a bitch. What a fucking day.*

"One of my operatives swears he saw her in Riga, but I was under the very distinct impression that she was KIA. Do you have any intelligence to the contrary?"

Harel met the question with a very long silence. When he finally spoke, he said, "You know how fond I was of Elinor."

"Yes, I remember."

"Despite everything, she was like a daughter to me. A prodigal daughter, but a daughter nonetheless. I never had one of my own . . . Anyway, I digress. After the Modiri hit at the Grand Bazaar, we tasked the Seventh Order spotters working the op to confirm Elinor's death.

She was observed being taken from the scene by paramedics on a gurney. Modiri and his wife were taken away in body bags."

"So Elinor survived?"

"Yes, she survived."

"And you decided to withhold this information from me why?"

"She was one of *mine*, not yours. I'm under no such obligation."

"Fair enough," Jarvis said, his curiosity piqued. "So, what happened to her?"

"VEVAK happened to her," Harel said through a sigh. "She spent three days in hospital, and then they disappeared her. I tried like hell to get her out, but we couldn't find her. I just assumed that when they were done interrogating her, they shot her in the head and dumped her body, but maybe not. Do you have a picture from Riga?"

"No."

"Who saw her?"

"Dempsey."

"Ahhh, of course," Harel said, and Jarvis could practically hear the smile on his friend's face. "This is the best news I've had in months. It almost makes up for all the shit."

"Well, if she's not with you, and VEVAK didn't kill her, then that must mean she's working for them."

"Maybe . . . maybe not," Harel said, a strangely ambiguous answer.

"Are you going to try to find her?"

"Of course I am. I'm a selfish man, Kelso. I want to say goodbye."

"Please let me know what you discover. I'm afraid there's more here than just curiosity and concern for the effect her death had on my best operator. If it was her in Riga, she's on mission for someone. So, if not you . . ."

"I will see what I can find out. And as for John Dempsey, he should find peace. He did the right thing no matter what truth may have followed. I would have done the same thing in his shoes. So would you. Former SEAL or not, it's the job—his job, now," Harel said with a hint of melancholy, and then asked, "You said you called about two things. What's the other one?"

Jarvis transferred the phone receiver to his other hand, because the arm holding it was already tiring. "Does the name Arkady Zhukov mean anything to you?"

"Now that's a name I haven't heard in a long time," Harel said, and Jarvis could picture him taking a drag during the pause. "He was very active during the Cold War and a five-year period after, then he disappeared off our radar. Why do you ask?"

"We have reason to believe he is running a covert Russian task force similar to Ember and the Seventh Order, called Spetsgruppa Zeta."

"Interesting . . . but it's no surprise. Great minds think alike. Apparently, he came to the same conclusions that we did—to be effective and avoid the scourge of political oversight, you have to go small and go black."

"It appears Arkady has set his crosshairs on me and my team, because we've traced the events in Turkey, including my assassination attempt, to a Russian false-flag operation. We don't have hard evidence that Arkady and his task force are responsible, but that's our working theory."

"Kelso, this is very bad news. This guy is like us. He's smart, devious, and plays the long game. If what you're saying is true and Arkady Zhukov is indeed alive and running his version of Ember and Seventh Order, then he has pegged you as his adversary. If so, then you need to elevate your thinking."

"In what way?"

"You've been fighting Islamic terrorists and immersed in Middle Eastern politics your entire career. The Russian mind doesn't think like the terrorist mind. First of all, a guy like Arkady is not constrained by dogma or ideology. Nor is he worried about American drones circling overhead. Today's terrorist spends most of his time on the move, managing his own survival. Not Arkady. It may be a tired analogy, but it is the best one—this guy is a chess master, and you just realized he's been moving pieces in a game you didn't even know you were playing. He is several steps ahead of you, and to win, you will be forced to take chances and make sacrifices. You will lose pieces on the board. This will be a problem for you. The modern American wartime strategy is governed by a zero-friendly-casualty premise. I can assure you, your Russian counterpart has no such illusions or constraints. You've never faced an enemy like Arkady Zhukov before, my friend. Amir Modiri was good, but he was only a shadow of the man you're up against now."

They talked for several more minutes before Jarvis thanked Harel for the advice and ended the call. Slumping back into his chair, he looked at the ceiling and murmured, "Could this day possibly get any worse?" On that cue, his desk phone rang. He glanced at the caller ID and recognized it as belonging to the office of Secretary of State Baker, who was undoubtedly calling to talk about what was left of the FSRU *Independence* and what it meant for American gas exports to the Baltics from the President's home state of Texas.

"I guess the answer is yes," he said through a weary sigh, picking up the phone, "it apparently can."

CHAPTER 17

Jarvis watched President Warner's face turn from placid pale to angry crimson as he briefed the Commander in Chief on the sinking of the FSRU *Independence* in Klaipėda. Secretary of State Baker, the President's Chief of Staff, Deputy Director Catherine Morgan, and Petra were also in attendance, but so far it had been a decidedly one-sided conversation. Jarvis concluded by explaining that the event was not an industrial accident but rather a covert Russian operation to take down Lithuania's ability to import natural gas from any other source but Russian state-owned Gazprom.

When Jarvis finished, the President asked through gritted teeth, "Was the operation executed by the same Russian cell that tried to assassinate me in Istanbul last month?"

"We believe so, Mr. President," Jarvis said. "They're known internally as Spetsgruppa Zeta and operate in the black, very much like our own Task Force Ember."

Wordlessly, Warner reached for the highball glass on the coffee table containing his signature drink—a diet Arnold Palmer—and Jarvis wasn't sure if the President meant to take a sip or hurl the heavy crystal tumbler across the room. He'd expected the news to antagonize the President, but Warner was so angry he looked like he could have a stroke. This was not the response Jarvis had expected from the man he'd come to think of as the world's best political poker player. He glanced sideways at Secretary of State Baker, and the man's open-mouthed stare confirmed Jarvis was not the only one taken aback by the President's uncharacteristic ire. Beside him, Petra shifted in her seat, and in the corner of his eye, he saw the President's Chief of Staff visibly tense.

"Blowing up a gas terminal on Lithuanian soil—a *civilian* facility no less—is nothing short of an act of war." Warner's words were a buzz saw ripping the uncomfortable silence to shreds. "Who the fuck does Petrov think he is?"

"I think this might be quid pro quo for our recent sanctions to stop the Nord Stream 2," Secretary Baker said after a moment's hesitation, choosing to ignore the obvious rhetorical nature of the President's comment. "Petrov is sending us a message."

"Yes, he is," Warner said, clutching the highball glass so tightly the knuckles of his right hand looked like four miniature snowcaps. "And the message is that he believes himself untouchable and me feckless. He's operating without restraint, without fear of consequence or retribution . . . but that's a grave miscalculation." Warner's gaze went to the painting of General George Washington hanging over the fireplace mantel. "In April 1793, Washington issued the Proclamation of Neutrality, declaring the United States a neutral party in the escalating conflict between England and France during the French Revolutionary Wars. The Proclamation threatened legal action against any American

170

who provided assistance to a foreign power at war. This single act by Washington became the philosophical bedrock of American foreign policy until World War II. So powerful was this legacy that despite the obvious and murderous aspirations of Nazi Germany and Imperial Japan, FDR resisted intervention until bombs fell on American soil." Warner shifted his gaze from the painting back to Secretary Baker. "Most people assume the portrait hangs in my Oval Office as a matter of tradition, but that's not the reason. This portrait reminds me that my duty is to keep this nation on course and to steer her rudder with a steady hand. I am no isolationist, but during my tenure as President I've adhered to Washington's vision as my default position. In *this* administration, overt foreign intervention is always the option of last resort."

Warner, finally, took a sip of his iced tea and lemonade and set the glass back down on the coffee table. As Jarvis contemplated the President's words, he noticed that despite the calm delivery and controlled diction, Warner's face still simmered red with anger.

"So, are you saying we take a measured approach in our response to these moves by Petrov?" Baker asked, seemingly confused by Warner's mixed signals.

"No. The time for measured responses has passed. I may be a lame duck, but I'll be damned if I hand over the reins of an emasculated America to the next Commander in Chief. And I'll be damned if I let Petrov think he can turn the clock back to 1988. There's only one superpower in this world, and it's the United States of America. The Cold War is over. We won. They lost. It's time for Petrov to be reminded of that."

"What are you suggesting, Mr. President?" Baker pressed.

"Lithuania is a NATO member. An attack on one NATO member is an attack on NATO," Warner replied and let the pregnant pause that followed serve as his unspoken exclamation point.

Jarvis watched the Secretary go pale. "But that would mean, uh, certainly you're not suggesting . . ."

"Yes, Ted, that is exactly what I am suggesting," the President replied. "It's time to give Petrov a bloody nose."

"Mr. President, if I may," Catherine Morgan interjected. "If NATO responds to the Russian provocation with overt force, the Kremlin will cry foul and brand the United States as the aggressor. The sinking of the *Independence* was executed in such a way as to give the Kremlin plausible deniability. If Petrov can send Russian troops in unmarked uniforms into Ukraine, force a fake election, and annex Crimea at gunpoint without sparking a NATO response, then we certainly cannot move against Russia over an operation that took place in the dead of night with none of their men anywhere in sight."

"Ukraine is not a NATO member," Petra said quickly. "Lithuania is."

"I realize that, Petra," Morgan fired back. "But it doesn't change the fact that the way the operation was carried out leaves us no evidential capital to justify retaliation."

"That's not true," Petra replied, glancing at Jarvis. "The Lithuanian government has already requested US and Norwegian support as they conduct their postmortem investigation of the event. If the findings of that investigation conclude that the sinking was an act of sabotage, then NATO will have a compelling multinational case to act."

"Wait a minute," Baker interjected. "You just said Lithuania requested the United States and Norway to assist with the investigation. Why Norway?"

"Because the *Independence* is owned by a Norwegian shipping and trading company. The vessel is leased by Lithuania—which means the attack on the facility technically constitutes an attack on not just one but two NATO member countries."

"Be that as it may," Baker said, "I can't help but agree with Director Morgan. We'd need a video of Petrov himself placing the explosives and lighting the fuse before we could rally a NATO response. NATO is a consensus decision-making body. All it takes is one dissenting member and any offensive you're contemplating will be dead in the water."

"The Secretary is right," Morgan said, nodding. "Relations with Turkey are at an all-time low. I think we can count on Erodan to undermine any attempt by NATO to move against Russia. Our best course of action at this point is to inform the other Baltic states to step up their security at similar installations in case the Kremlin has other targets."

Jarvis, who had been quiet during the debate, shifted his gaze from Morgan to the President and found Warner's eyes coming up to meet his. The President's color had returned to normal, and his poker face was back.

"I stand by what I said before. Petrov has wreaked havoc for too long without being held accountable. That ends today." The President turned to his Chief of Staff. "David, I want you to call an emergency meeting of the National Security Council. I want all the key players in my cabinet to be aware of what's going on."

"Yes, Mr. President."

"And Kelso, I want you to lead that meeting and give the same brief you just gave me."

"Yes, Mr. President," Jarvis said, but he shot the President a look that said he had more to discuss with the Commander in Chief.

"Everyone, please give me the room," Warner said, surveying the group gathered on the facing sofas.

Everyone nodded deferentially and stood, including Jarvis.

"Not you, Kelso. I have a few more questions," the President said.

"Yes, sir," Jarvis said, retaking his seat and giving Petra a nod to do the same.

"Hold on a second," Secretary Baker said, his hands going to his hips. "I'm the one who called this meeting, but now I'm getting the boot and his secretary gets to stay?"

"Commander Felsk is the DNI's Chief of Staff," Warner said, narrowing his eyes at Baker. "She's *not* a secretary, Mr. . . . . Secretary."

Morgan, who had also gotten up to leave, now stood frozen in place looking at Jarvis for an invitation to stay. He gave a subtle shake of the head, to which she responded with a deferential nod. Jarvis did notice, however, that she waited for the indignant Secretary of State to move toward the door before following suit. He also noticed her whisper something in Baker's ear just before the President's Chief of Staff closed the door behind them.

"Do you have Ember in country looking at this?" Warner asked, not wasting any time.

"Yes, sir. They're posing as an FBI counterterrorism investigation team. We have a security camera image of a high-level Russian covert operative dressed as a maintenance technician leaving the *Independence* only moments before it exploded. There is no doubt the Russians are responsible and this is a willful act of sabotage."

"I believe you, but unfortunately, a photograph won't cut it. Global tolerance for malfeasance is at an all-time high. Crimes and scandals that would have ended careers and toppled governments just a decade ago are now paraded in front of the populace by their perpetrators with impunity. Secretary Baker and Deputy Director Morgan were correct when they said that any accusation we levy against Moscow will be met with staunch and blustery denial. Any action we take will be dubbed not as retaliation but as instigation by the Russian propaganda machine," Warner said, shaking his head. "That conniving bastard really has us hog-tied this time."

"Should I presume that you asking me to stay behind means that covert retaliation is on the table?" Jarvis asked, choosing his words carefully.

Warner nodded.

"In that case, do you have something particular in mind, or would you like us to work up a list of options?"

"Oh, I definitely have something *particular* in mind, Kelso," Warner said, getting to his feet and walking over to look up at the picture of George Washington hanging over the fireplace. "I want you to find this Russian version of Ember . . ."

"Spetsgruppa Zeta," Petra said, filling the pause.

"That's right," Warner continued, his back still facing them. "I want you to find them, and I want you to take them out. Do you understand me? I want you to hunt down every last one of those bastards and put them in the ground. Until the mission is completed or I say otherwise, this is Ember's new charter."

The President's words sent a shot of adrenaline through his veins the likes of which Jarvis hadn't felt since his last combat mission as a Tier One SEAL. He felt electric, and alive, and strangely vindicated.

Taking great care to keep his expression neutral, he said, "And if that new charter requires us to operate on Russian soil?"

Warner turned around and met Jarvis with eyes on fire, "Then, Director Jarvis, you operate on Russian soil . . ."

CHAPTER 18

National Hotel, Room 408
Žvejų Gatvė 21
Klaipėda, Lithuania
June 15
1730 Local Time

Valerian resisted the urge to rise from his chair and pace.

Doing so took far more effort and control than it should have. He was unbalanced and wrangling to control his impulses. His gaze ticked to the cup of tea on the small round table beside the window. His body wanted the caffeine—craved it. The impulse to grab the tea-cup was overpowering. He imagined reaching for it, visualized bringing the white china to his lips, taking a long, slow sip. He imagined the warmth, the flavor, and the little metabolic uptick as the caffeine did its work. He actualized the act of drinking the tea, without indulging. The craving slayed, he let out his breath through pursed lips.

His body, deprived of caffeine, manifested a new craving immediately.

An image of the pack of nicotine gum popped into his mind. Without looking, his mind knew exactly where he'd left it—sitting on the nightstand beside the bed. Brains are meticulous record keepers when it comes to vices. His body wanted the nicotine, craved it. He imagined chewing the gum . . . a cigarette would be better, but he'd not packed any. The impulse to walk to the nightstand and pop a piece of gum into his mouth was overpowering.

Do you know the difference between a free man and a slave? Arkady had once asked him. *A free man is master of his impulses, whereas a slave lives to serve them. In times of stress and urgency, will you let your impulses rule your behavior, or will your wits prevail? The ability to maintain physical control and mental discipline can be the difference between life and death.*

The words came to him from the past, from the campus where his mentor trained Zeta operatives—a sadistic boot camp for would-be killers. Old imagery flooded his mind and brought a curl to his lips—more snarl than smile. Arkady paced behind him and the other recruits, both teacher and torturer. His words of instruction were drowned out by erratic gunfire, sudden and unexpected, close to the backs of their heads. Television monitors on the opposite wall streamed horrifying imagery—scenes of torture, rape, and dismemberment—while Valerian and his compeers stood naked and shivering in a cold, wet concrete room.

Slaps of wet leather on the backs of thighs.

Words, gunfire, imagery, pain . . . words, gunfire, imagery, pain.

The impulses were strong in that place—carnal and overpowering.

Run, scream, fight, hide . . .

But to succumb was weakness; to succumb was failure. Only those who mastered their primitive and bodily impulses prevailed. By the end of his training, he could remain perfectly still in the cold, in the horror, unflinching in the noise, unflinching in the pain. With practice, he gained control of his heart rate, slowing his pulse to as low as forty—a sleeping man awake—in control, no matter how intense and unpleasant the stimulus.

Valerian opened his eyes and looked at the teacup and its matching saucer. "I am in control, not you," he murmured, then looked at the package of nicotine gum. "And not you." He shifted his gaze out the window, across the canal and the bridge at Pilies Gatvė. He swept his eyes over the intersecting street and then southwest to the ferry pier. A new impulse bubbled up to his conscious—the desire to glance at the Bremont Waterman timepiece on his left wrist. He denied it. Amarov's men would contact him when there was something to report.

Convincing Amarov to participate in this operation had not required any inducements. A mere mention that the Americans who'd murdered his top lieutenants and made a fool of him in Narva would be in Klaipėda was all it had taken. The Vory kingpin had jumped at the opportunity to mete revenge. This time, however, Amarov understood the enemy he was facing. Valerian had read him in, at least partially, so Amarov would be prepared.

He'd not told Arkady about the security camera image or his certainty that the Americans would come in response, and a twinge of guilt—no, not guilt, a twinge of well-intentioned disobedience— needled his subconscious. It wasn't that Arkady was above taking risks. To the contrary, the old fox had hatched the insane operation to target a B61 nuke cache in Turkey and the failed assassination attempt on President Warner. But Arkady's operations followed a very particular paradigm. Valerian wasn't sure if it even had a name, but if forced to give it one he'd call it big risk/big reward. Arkady loved taking big risks for big perceived rewards but despised taking small risks for small rewards. Despite all his professorial philosophy, strategic bluster, and chess metaphors, Arkady was a gambler who refused to give up his seat at the high-roller table.

Setting a trap and taking the American ghosts out in Klaipėda would not hold any appeal for Arkady, because it didn't achieve a strategic geopolitical objective, just a tactical one. Yet, despite Arkady expressing a loss of confidence in him, Valerian was still Zeta Prime. As Prime, he had the authority and autonomy to plan and execute a mission of this caliber. Was that not the very purpose and charter of the Zeta program? Arkady had agreed—or at least not *dis*agreed—that the destruction of the American black team was to be the next mission, had he not?

The problem with Arkady was that the old fox had been too long from the field. He was no longer an operator; he was a manager now. The Director of the Zeta program should leave the operational details to those best suited to them—and no one was better suited to them than Valerian. His record of success was perfect. Well, nearly so. Had it not been for the interference of that American operator on the last mission . . .

Picturing the man who'd been the architect of his only failure sparked an impulse to pace that he could not quell, an unbearable itch that could only be scratched with a finger dipped in the blood of the dead American—the only man ever to have bested him.

Disgusted with himself, he stood.

His mobile phone rang. Valerian walked to the desk and checked the cable connecting it to the silver box—encryption hardware for both incoming and outgoing data—as well as the cable connecting it to the laptop computer. Next, he entered a six-digit code and the connection was made. He waited a moment before speaking, watching the two lines at the bottom of the screen that squiggled like an EEG monitoring a seizure—neither showing anything but background noise.

Satisfied the call was secure, he answered. "Yes?"

"I have them," said a male voice, which he recognized as Amarov's second.

"Where?"

"They're at Vivalavita dining with an Interpol team."

"And?"

"They checked in at the National. Three men and a woman. We have indication they are FBI."

"They're not FBI here, just like they were not arms traffickers in Narva."

He had baited the trap and they had come, just like he'd known they would. Vivalavita was one of the finest restaurants in town—a suitable place for their last meal.

"What are your instructions? We can easily take them en route to the hotel after their dinner. Or we can hit them at the restaurant and make a statement—but there will be high collateral damage. Also easy."

He resisted the urge to laugh. Taking the Americans would be anything but easy. This was not so simple as a drive-by shooting. It was complicated by the fact he wanted to take the American operator from Istanbul, his black ops doppelgänger, alive. It was important to deliver a prize to Arkady. Arkady had always been explicit on that point, which was why Amarov's first attempt had gone so wrong. A snatch and grab was orders of magnitude more complicated and dangerous than a hit. No, the operation had to be executed inside the hotel, where he could control the variables and box in his prey. But when Arkady's interrogation was finished, he would give Valerian his reward—the honor of killing his prize and killing him in his own way.

Now he indulged in a smile.

"Well?" Amarov's man said with impatience.

Valerian exhaled and regained his focus.

"No. I told you, the big one in the photograph taken at Narva must be taken alive. He has information we need. It will be here—at the hotel—as we planned."

"Very well. We will trail them, but not too closely."

Valerian's pulse ticked up. This may have been the only part of the plan that could result in failure. All Zeta work was black, but this was a fully autonomous operation, and the risk would be considerably more. He'd drafted Sylvie for this op but otherwise was forced to use outside assets—cultivated over time and paid for with personal funds he had acquired over the years.

"No. Leave Three and Five in place where we agreed. Have all of team two in position here at the hotel. Let the Americans come to us. They are experienced, dangerous, and highly adaptive. Our advantage will evaporate if we tip our hand, and you saw what happened the last time they turned the tables on you."

"Very well. We will notify you on arrival."

"Just before."

"Yes, yes," the man said, annoyed now. "As we discussed."

Valerian severed the connection.

He would have preferred to be on the street, trailing the Americans himself, but that was no longer possible. Networked security cameras were being deployed throughout Europe at an astounding rate. Facial-recognition software was far more sophisticated now, and they would be searching for him. He'd not left this room since the night of the *Independence* operation for that very reason. He forced himself to stop pacing and sit down in his chair. Then, finding his center, he visualized every element of the operation—from the moment the Americans arrived at the hotel until he was driving away with his adversary hogtied in the trunk of his car.

Tonight, he would be the victor and eliminate any doubt in Arkady's mind as to who should wear the crown of Zeta Prime.

CHAPTER 19

Vivalavita Restaurant
Naujojo Sodom Gatvė 1A
Klaipėda, Lithuania
June 15
1915 Local Time

Since becoming head of Ember's Special Activities Division, Dempsey had slowly, grudgingly, and painfully become competent at stepping in and out of NOCs and legends. But he hated it, he really did. Every time he was forced to slip into someone else's skin and become somebody new, it reminded him of who he wasn't. He wasn't Jack Kemper, Tier One Navy SEAL. And it made his yearning for the simplicity of those days all the more palpable. Hit the target, accomplish the mission, then come home to the FOB and throw steaks on the grill. Simple and straightforward; none of this sneaking around in someone else's shoes.

"This guy," Grimes said, tapping the printed image of the Zeta operative who'd let himself be photographed just minutes before the *Independence* blew up. "This is the man we are interested in."

"I understand," said the gray-haired man from Lithuanian State Police. "But, like you, we don't know who he is."

She turned to the two Interpol agents at the table, who offered nothing and instead were chatting in French quietly between themselves. When they didn't notice her stare, she cleared her throat.

"I'm sorry, were you talking to us?" one of the men said.

"Same question," Grimes—or Special Agent Deborah Tillis, as her FBI identification suggested—said, showing them the picture. "This man was on the *Independence* the night of the incident. Have you run a facial recognition search in the Interpol databases?"

"Yes, yes, of course. That was the first thing we did when you submitted the photo. We would have told you immediately if we'd had a match."

"Okay," she sighed. "I'm sorry, I just can't believe we have no information at all on this man."

"We have some information," the other Interpol agent said. "We requisitioned personnel files from the company operating the *Independence*. We know this man is not a member of the operations or maintenance staff. The Norwegians are arriving tomorrow morning. Maybe they can tell us more."

Grimes turned to Dempsey and shot him a look that he could not precisely decipher but took to mean roughly *feel free to jump in anytime.*

"If it's not in progress already," he said, "we should run a search of archived city security camera data, including traffic cameras, ATM cams, as well as hotel and storefront surveillance feeds. And I'd like to interview the survivors from the ship that night, the folks that got off on the rescue ship."

"Francois and I have already been working on the camera data search. Tomorrow I will instruct my office to bring all survivors into the central city station for questioning. Does this work for you?" the Lithuanian officer said, looking from Dempsey to Grimes.

"That would be excellent," Grimes said. "Thank you."

"Do you really think this was terrorism?" The Interpol agent called Francois leaned in on his elbows. "It is a strange choice of target, no? I have talked with my colleagues at RAID, and they tell me there was no chatter in the cells they are monitoring for the days leading up to the event."

"We're not ready to rule out anything at this point, although we think industrial sabotage is the most likely driver," Grimes said.

"But who would do such a thing?"

"I'm telling you it was the Russians," the Lithuanian agent said, leaning in and speaking in a hard whisper. "It's no coincidence this happened two weeks after our President announced that Lithuania intended to double re-exports and agreed to build a pipeline into Poland."

"That is crazy," Francois said through a laugh. "Petrov is an asshole, but he would never blow up your LNG terminal."

"Just like he would never invade Ukraine to annex Crimea, or use chemical agents in the UK to assassinate his critics in broad daylight, or conduct cyberwarfare campaigns to corrupt elections in the US," the Lithuanian fired back. "No, no, he would never do anything crazy like trying to punish my country for refusing to buy Russian gas. We're not like France; we don't have nuclear-powered energy independence—the *Independence* was our independence."

"Gentlemen," Grimes said with a forced smile. "I know this is a sensitive, important topic. That's why we're here to help." She turned to the Lithuanian officer. "Lithuania is an important partner to America. The responsible party will be held accountable. I promise you that."

This comment earned her conciliatory nods from everyone around the table, while Dempsey slyly snagged the check from the waiter who had been hovering just out of earshot.

"Oh no, no, no," the Lithuanian said as Dempsey surrendered his credit card. "You should not be doing this. You are my guests. Please, let me pay."

Dempsey winked at Grimes, then said, "You can get the next one. Consider this a thank-you for letting us crash your investigation and all the hoops we're going to ask your people to jump through."

Their host smiled and nodded. "Okay, but I get the dinner on the last night, when we celebrate catching the bastards who did this terrible, cowardly thing."

"To catching the bastards responsible," Munn said, raising his glass.

The group toasted, and the dinner wound to a rapid close. Latif and Martin, sitting in the same dark-gray golf shirts and khaki cargo pants as Dempsey, Munn, and Grimes, tipped back the last of their beers while the Interpol agents finished their wine.

"Allow us to give you a ride to your hotel?" the Lithuanian asked.

"No, thank you," Grimes said, answering for all of them. She was the senior agent in charge according to their NOC. "It's only a few blocks, and it's a nice night for a walk."

"Sure, I'm up for a walk. If anyone cares," Munn said. His "Agent Dutton" was still bitter about working for a woman younger than him—at least according to the legends they had rehearsed.

"No one does," Latif said, and they all laughed and then said their goodbyes to their European counterparts.

They walked in a tactical formation meant to look like a loose group, Dempsey at the rear, clearing their six, while Munn and Latif took point ahead of Martin and Grimes. A half block later, they turned south onto Jūros Gatvė, which would take them across the two-lane bridge over the canal on their way to the National Hotel, where they were already registered under their FBI NOCs.

"Nothing suspicious between you and the hotel. No ticks in trail—though I half expected that Lithuanian dude to try to tag along so he could hit on Grimes," Wang said in their ears from his room in a bed and breakfast two blocks southeast of their upscale hotel.

Wang was serving as eyes and ears locally, though Dempsey knew that Baldwin and the boys were probably listening and watching from back in Virginia as well. As they strode over the bridge, Dempsey tensed. If he were a bad guy, this is where he would hit them—drive by in a van with open doors, mow them down when they had no cover and no avenue of escape. Without reaching for it, he became acutely aware of the feel of the Sig Sauer in the uncomfortable high carry on his right hip—worn like the FBI agent he was pretending to be would wear it. But no van accelerated toward them, no group of armed men emerged from the shadows, and a few minutes later they'd crossed the cobblestone intersection across from the festive and brightly lit Theatre Square, kitty-corner from the hotel.

And yet, when they walked through the double oak-and-glass doors into the lobby, something felt off. Dempsey had learned long ago never to ignore *feelings*—no matter how paranoid or ill timed when they consumed him. Munn had them, too, and called it his sixth sense. His former Tier One teammates had called it their "spidey sense," and Dempsey's was tingling like hell.

He reached out and grabbed Munn by the sleeve.

"See something?" Munn asked, his voice parlaying his concern but his expression unalarmed.

The team wordlessly picked up on Dempsey's hesitation and instinctively began to fan out. He felt Grimes's eyes on him as he scanned the lobby. An older woman sat in the white-and-gold French-style chair against the wall, fingering a bangle on her left wrist. Beside her a man stood, hunched over, his hand on her shoulder. An apology while she played the injured bird? He tuned out the background noise to focus on the man's words. German? Yes, German. His gaze ticked to a middle-aged man at reception. He wore a wrinkled suit, and a worn leather satchel hung from his shoulder by a strap. The young blonde behind the dark wood counter, the attendant who'd checked them in hours earlier, handed the man his room key and gestured to the elevator bank. The man nodded, mumbled his thanks, and turned toward the business center in lieu of the elevators. The attendant caught Dempsey's attention, smiled at him with eyes expectant and ready to help. He smiled back at her.

"Spidey sense," he said, finally turning back to answer Munn.

Munn nodded and moved left to peek into the alcove that held the two elevators.

Dempsey moved casually through the lobby, his hands clasped behind his back. He checked the hall past the older couple. Clear. Beyond the hallway sat two vacant chairs beside a wood-and-glass display case holding antique china below a large mirror. Clear. The mirror showed him the corner of the elevator alcove—also clear. Sheer curtains hung over the double French doors leading into a small business center across from them; through them he spied the middle-aged man from check-in a moment ago taking a seat at a computer. The businessman didn't glance up.

Dempsey turned to Munn.

Well? Munn asked with his eyes.

Dempsey shrugged and then shook his head. "You guys heading to the rooms or wanna grab a drink?" he said, the question casually conveying that he saw nothing of concern.

But still . . .

"Rooms," Grimes said, and her tone—as the Special Agent in Charge—suggested they should all do the same.

Latif shrugged. "You're the boss," he said in a tone that hinted he might rather have a drink. Dempsey knew it was all part of the NOC—none of Ember's SAD team would be in a bar drinking on mission unless the NOC demanded it.

Dempsey forced himself to relax, but he took point nonetheless as they moved to the elevators. His peripheral vision caught motion, and he glanced through the sheer curtains to see the man at the computer pull something from inside his jacket—something black. Dempsey angled between Grimes and the corner, repositioning . . . it was a phone, which the man speed-dialed and put to his ear. The businessman gestured in frustration at his computer screen, then began a diatribe in what sounded like Lithuanian.

Dempsey felt a hand on his arm and turned to look at Grimes.

"Are we good?" she asked.

"Yeah," he said and forced a smile. "We're good."

And they were, right? What the hell was wrong with him?

It's Malik. Just knowing the Russian ghost was in Klaipėda is making me hypersensitive.

Dempsey knew the odds that Malik was still in Klaipėda were practically zero, but the way the Russian had grinned into that fucking security feed had gotten into Dempsey's head. The Russian *wanted* them to know he had been here. He wanted them to know he was the one who'd sunk the *Independence.* Dempsey had told Smith as much, but the Ember Director had only given a skeptical frown and mumbled a grudging "maybe." But why else would the Russian do something so brash and reckless? Because it was a message, a taunt, an invitation—an invitation meant specifically for Dempsey.

I know you're incapable of finding me, so here I am . . .

Come and get me if you dare.

The ding of the arriving elevator snapped him back to the moment. He felt Grimes's hand back on his arm. "You good?" she asked again.

"Yeah, boss," he said, playing his role. "Just tired. Long-ass flight, and I just need some Zs to shake the jet lag."

"We'll all get some sleep and hit it hard in the morning," she said to the group as the doors to the elevator slid open.

Dempsey stepped aside as the elevator's two male occupants exited, jostling for space politely between the five of them. Dempsey let the others in his party step into the elevator first, while he turned ninety degrees to watch the duo go. The larger of the pair hadn't taken two strides before he suddenly patted his black overcoat and pants pockets in the universal *oh shit, I forgot my . . .* gesture. He barked something at his travel companion, who rolled his eyes and crossed his arms over his chest, chastising his partner in . . . *Polish, perhaps?* The big man turned back toward the elevator and reached his arm out.

"Escuse for me, please," he said in thickly accented broken English. Munn, who was holding the door open for Dempsey, nodded. The man joined them, squeezing into the middle of the group. "I am forgetting my . . . um, it be calling my . . . um . . ." He made a gesture like opening a small book.

"Your wallet?" Martin offered.

"Yes," the man said, delighted to be understood. "I am forgetting my walad."

He leaned in front of Dempsey and mashed the button for the second floor. Munn had already pressed the button for the third floor. Dempsey's "spidey sense" went from a tingle to electrifying as the broad-shouldered man pushed back toward the rear of the elevator.

But he's getting off first . . .

Dempsey pulled his room key from his pocket, fumbled with it, and let it drop. "Shit," he said and squatted to pick it up, rotating inward as he did and glancing up at the lone stranger in their midst.

He watched the man's right hand slip inside the left flap of the unseasonably long winter coat he was wearing . . . in June.

Take him now, said the SEAL inside.

Dempsey exploded from his stance, a swimmer off the blocks, left hand shooting up and catching the man open palmed under the chin. The man's head snapped backward into the mirrored rear wall of the elevator. Instead of surprise, the man's face twisted into a snarl as his own NOC dissolved away. Dempsey felt the hard metal of a short-barreled machine pistol trying to come up between them from under the heavy overcoat, and he pounded the man's head a second time into the rear wall, shattering the mirror and stunning the assassin as he drew his pistol and drove it up under the man's chin.

Munn hit the emergency stop, reading Dempsey's mind, and quickly silenced the alarm.

Dempsey stared hard into the assassin's raging gray eyes.

"How many?" he demanded, pressing the barrel hard into the soft flesh. Peeking out beneath the open collar of the man's shirt was the top of an eight-pointed star—a Vory tattoo inked high on the man's chest.

Amarov . . .

"Fuck you," the man seethed in what Dempsey now decided was Russian-accented English.

It was enough. He drove a hard left elbow into the man's temple, and the assassin slumped.

"This guy's Vory," Dempsey said as he snapped out a pocketknife and cut away the sling holding the Pindad PM2 submachine pistol to the man's chest and pulled it free.

"It's like Narva all over again," Munn groaned.

"Get ready for them to hose us down when the doors open on the second floor. Everyone get tight in the corners. Next stop we make our stand." He looked around to find everyone already in tactical crouches with their weapons drawn, backs pressed against the walls. "Get us moving, Dan."

Munn released the emergency stop and the elevator jerked upward as Dempsey hoisted the dazed thug to his feet. The assassin swayed but stood, leaning against the shattered mirrored wall on unsteady legs, his glassy gaze confirming the concussion dealt by Dempsey's crippling blow.

The elevator slowed.

"Be ready for a flash-bang," Dempsey said. "If it's a live grenade, we have to get it out and get those doors shut."

Munn grabbed Martin by the arm and pointed to the close-door button. Martin nodded, and Munn moved to the left side of the elevator, bookending the swaying Russian next to Dempsey.

The elevator stopped.

The Ember team bunched into the front corners, weapons at the ready.

As the doors eased open, Dempsey released the incoherent thug and pressed himself against the wall behind Martin and Latif. He glanced over at Grimes, pressed into the corner in front of Munn. She nodded at him with fire, not fear, in her eyes.

He aimed the short barrel of the 9 mm machine gun at the expanding gap between the elevator doors, cool metal pressed against his cheek. On the other side, four men were waiting in military-style tactical crouches, assault rifles at the ready. As a group, they peered perplexed into an elevator that—upon first glance—appeared to have only a single rider. The ruse had worked, buying them the half second they needed and allowing Dempsey to fire first.

He squeezed the trigger and unleashed a barrage of 9 mm rounds from the compact machine gun. Trading his usual precision for shock and awe, he hosed down the hallway, holding the trigger against the backstop and not letting go. Two shooters dropped to the ground, pitching face-forward, and the other two backpedaled furiously while returning fire into the elevator cabin. In Dempsey's peripheral vision, he saw muzzle flashes from Munn's and Grimes's pistols on his left and Martin pressing the door-close button on his right. The stunned Russian who'd tried to kick off this murder party jerked and wiggled as the fusillade of bullets from his teammates pinned him against the back wall and his chest and face spit blood from the wounds opening like blossoming flowers.

After what felt like an eternity, the doors began to slide shut, and Dempsey's weapon coughed out the last of its thirty rounds. He heard hollering from the hallway, and then everything went silent.

The doors shut with a paradoxically soft click.

But if the assaulters thought to hit the call button . . .

A heartbeat later, the maelstrom of gunfire resumed as the assassination team peppered the elevator doors with assault rifle fire. The rounds didn't fully penetrate the thick double-skinned doors, and the elevator jerked upward. Dempsey blew air through his teeth.

"Everyone okay?" he barked, ditching the machine gun for his Sig.

"All good," Grimes replied, her voice clear and relaxed. After Jerusalem, Adana, and Syria, she was as blooded as any operator he knew.

"Good," Martin and Latif replied in unison.

"I saw four," Dempsey said. "Were there more?"

"Yeah, I counted at least three more down the hall on your side," Grimes said.

"And I saw a second pair on the left," Martin said.

"Now what?" Munn asked.

"Get ready to do it again on three," Dempsey said. "Wang, you up?"

"Yeah," the tech genius replied. "What are you guys doing? Is someone, like, shooting at you?"

"Yes, Dick," Munn said sarcastically. "Lots of someones are, like, shooting at us."

"Listen, we're coming to the third floor. Anybody waiting to hose us down?" Dempsey barked.

"Wait one, I'm pulling up thermals . . ."

"Hurry," Dempsey said, his voice a hard line as they pressed back into their respective corners.

"I know, I know, I'm trying . . ."

The elevator began to slow.

"Richaaaard . . ."

"Hallway is clear," Wang blurted, "but you have two sets of tangos. One storming the north stairwell and one coming up the south. They're going to hit you from both ends, put you in a crossfire."

"Then tell us where to go," Dempsey growled. "You gotta guide us out of here, bro."

"One second. One second."

The elevator jerked to a halt and chimed.

"Wang we need an exfil now."

The doors began to open.

"Where is that picture I took of the fucking floor diagram?" Wang murmured. "Okay, got it. When you exit the elevator, across the hall you should see a small alcove with an ice machine and vending machines. There's a door at the back. Go through it."

"We can't get trapped in a fucking closet, Wang." Dempsey pressed the "1" button to send the elevator back to the lobby before stepping out into the hall. He cleared left as Munn crossed behind him and cleared right.

"You won't," Wang said, his voice rising in pitch. "Hurry up. You got a shitload of guys coming up the stairs on both sides of you."

Dempsey charged across the deserted hallway and cleared the vending alcove. Just as Wang said, there was a door in the back wall. He grabbed the handle, which was locked of course, and dropped a hard left elbow down on the handle, shearing it off at the stem. He then used his fingertip to slide the plunger for the simple lock mechanism and pulled the door open.

Footsteps pounded behind him as the other four members of the Ember SAD team joined him. He led them into a dark, cramped space, picking up the sheared knob as he went. A wooden shelf crammed with tools and paint buckets lined the right wall, and two rolling buckets with mops beside them sat on his left. Footsteps and voices echoed in the third-floor corridor now as the Russians stormed out of the stairwells. Dempsey watched Martin ease the door silently shut, the only light now a cone of yellow from the missing doorknob that he prayed would be overlooked by the Vory hit squad when they searched the floor. Hopefully, the elevator doors would be closed and the car would already be moving by the time the Russians got to it. And if they were really lucky, the bastards would chase it back down to the lobby.

But when had he ever been *that* lucky?

Even in the dark, Dempsey felt four sets of eyes looking to him for direction inside what now definitely appeared to be a closet.

So, this is how Ember ends. In hell, I'll forever be known as the guy who—in his final act on earth—listened to Dick Wang and led his team to their death . . . in a mop closet.

CHAPTER 20

Valerian's victory smile faded as he listened to the exchange of gunfire two floors below. Something about the way the assault rifle fire was preceded and drowned out by an insanely long burst of 9 mm automatic fire sent an ominous chill down his spine. He didn't need a call from Amarov's assault team leader to tell him that something had gone wrong. Instead of the Vory surprising the American team, his intuition told him, the opposite had happened. And when the gunfire abruptly stopped, his chest tightened at the realization he should have led the assault on the second floor himself.

This American operator is a fucking magician.

Valerian grabbed the HK416 from the steel suitcase at the foot of the bed and slipped the sling over his neck. He flipped the selector with his thumb to single shot, dropped the short rifle beneath his right armpit, and shrugged on a thigh-length leather coat. With his jaw set and eyes burning he made for the door.

"Victory, this is Bastion," a gruff male voice said in Valerian's ear-bud. "They were ready for us."

"What happened?" he said.

"Firefight on the second floor. I've lost four men and have one wounded. They took the elevator to the third floor. We're pursuing."

"I'm coming down. Don't fucking shoot me."

"Use the north stairwell," Amarov's lieutenant said.

"Spire, do you have eyes?" Valerian asked, querying Sylvie, who was providing cyber and comms support from a room at a nearby inn.

"I have eyes on the building with satellite but no thermal."

"I need close coverage of the exits—all exits, including the courtyard. The target is attempting to exfil."

"Check," she said simply.

"Can you kill their comms?"

"I can try."

"Whatever it takes, just fucking do it," he snapped, turning right and moving at a fast walk for the north end of the hall.

The instant he entered the stairwell, he dropped into a combat crouch and pulled his weapon up from beneath the leather coat. He descended cautiously. On the landing below, he spied six Vory shooters pressed into the wall on either side of the steel door. Amarov's team leader glanced up at him, nodded, then ordered his men into the corridor. The door flew open and the shooters swarmed the hall like angry hornets.

The absence of immediate gunfire told Valerian the hall was clear. He dashed down the steps and entered the corridor behind the hit squad, which was moving toward the elevator. At the far end of the hallway, the second half of the Vory assassination force poured out of the south stairwell, assault rifles at the ready. Thankfully, the morons didn't open fire on each other.

"Elevator," Amarov's team leader barked, and both squads converged on the elevator bank in the middle of the hall.

Valerian followed with a five-meter setback, visualizing the layout of the hotel in his mind.

"Shit, we're too late. It's moving back down," the lead Vory said, turning to look at Valerian.

"Send five men to the lobby," Valerian barked. "Five to the basement, and the rest search this floor. Time was short. It's fifty-fifty whether they got off."

"Where do you want me?" the team leader asked.

"Lobby. Go!"

The Vory barked out the assignments, and the assassination force split up as Valerian had commanded, leaving four assaulters with him.

"The Americans were booked in rooms 308, 309, 311, 312, and 315," Sylvie said in his ear with perfect timing.

"You two clear 308 and 309. And you two, hit 311 and 312. I'll take 315," he said.

"You want us to kick the doors in?" one of the men asked.

"Of course, you fucking idiot. Go."

Valerian shook his head and started moving toward 315, then abruptly stopped. He narrowed his eyes and scanned the hall, his gaze settling on a vending machine alcove across from the elevator with a door on the back wall—a door he'd not noticed at first because the slab was wallpapered to match the walls.

A vulpine grin curled his lips.

I wonder . . .

CHAPTER 21

"What are you guys waiting for?" Wang said in Dempsey's ear.

"You led us into a mop closet," Dempsey whispered with profound acrimony. "If we survive this, I'm going to kill you."

"Dude, it's not a closet—there should be a service elevator behind you," Wang said.

"He's right," Munn whispered as Martin and Latif forced the single sliding elevator door open, which Dempsey's dark-adjusting eyes could now just make out. "It's painted the same color as the wall."

Dempsey shook his head. *I guess the boy genius earned himself a beer instead of death.*

"The car is on the fourth floor," Munn said in hushed tones as he shined the beam of a compact LED flashlight up the shaft while Martin wedged the door open with a mop handle. "You want me to call it?"

"No," Dempsey said. "They might hear it. Can we climb down the shaft?"

"Yeah, I think so. The shaft is pretty narrow."

"Get moving," Dempsey said and prayed that some maid with a laundry cart didn't call the damn thing while they were shimmying down.

Munn went first while the rest of them took tactical knees with their weapons trained on the door to the vending alcove. Dempsey closed his eyes, diverting all his focus to listening for the converging Vory threat. Pounding footsteps echoed in the hall, and then . . . the soda machine's chiller compressor kicked on. The entire vending machine vibrated something terrible as the compressor came up to speed and hummed so loud he couldn't hear anything else.

Motherfucker.

"Hurry, we gotta move, people," he whispered over his shoulder.

Dempsey kept his Sig Sauer pistol leveled at the dark door until he was last man. With a deep breath, he holstered his pistol and ducked under the angled broomstick to climb into the shaft. He looked down to see how the others were making the descent. Martin, who was second to last, had his back pressed to the side wall of the shaft and his legs out ninety degrees, his feet pressed against the opposite wall. The elevator shaft was wider in one direction than the other, so despite having a hell of a wingspan, Martin's arms couldn't reach wall to wall. Instead, he'd grabbed the elevator's counterweight track, working hand over hand to steady himself as he descended.

Getting himself into position was the tricky part, but once Dempsey had wedged his back against one wall of the shaft and his feet against the other, he felt solid . . . well, sort of. Thirty-five feet was a long way down.

He looked back at the propped-open door.

Now, how the hell am I supposed to get the mop out of the door?

Supporting himself with just his legs, he worked the stupid mop handle free and barely managed to slide it through the gap before door slid shut. With the door shut, the elevator shaft went completely dark. Munn had pocketed his light and probably would not retrieve it until he reached the bottom. In the pitch black, listening to the sound of his teammates' panting and their soles dragging on concrete, he found a rhythm and shimmied his way down. By the time he reached the bottom, his quads were on fire. A tap on his hip let him know he'd arrived, and as he dropped to the ground, his elbow smashed into something bony.

"Ow, shit," Munn hissed. "That was my collarbone, dude."

He was about to apologize when a motor kicked on somewhere above and an unmistakable sound reverberated in the elevator shaft.

"Shit, the elevator's coming," Latif hissed, pointing out the obvious.

"Get the fucking door open," Dempsey said.

"Hurry," Grimes said. "It's coming fast!"

"We got it," Martin said, light flooding the shaft as he and Latif pulled the outer door open.

"The elevator opens into a pantry behind the kitchen, in case you're interested," Wang said in Dempsey's ear, followed immediately by a slurping sound. Dempsey silently cursed Wang and the foo-foo coffee beverage he was undoubtedly drinking with a straw.

He rolled out of the shaft, clearing over his Sig. "Clear," he said, but the others were already pouring out of the impending death trap.

"I think it's coming here," Grimes said, staring up at the floor indicator above the door, the numbers illuminating and going dark in sequence as the elevator descended.

Dempsey quickly assessed the space around them. To his left, an aluminum swing door with a porthole window separated the pantry from the kitchen. He could hear the clatter and clamor of a busy kitchen staff working beyond. To his right were racks of canned and box goods. Directly across from him were two doors, both ajar—one leading to a tiny office and the other to a dirty restroom for the staff. Satisfied they weren't about to be flanked, he whirled and took a tactical knee at a forty-five degree offset and sighted on the elevator door. The rest of the team followed his lead, splitting into two fire teams, leaving a gap in the middle between them.

"Ready," Dempsey said as the number 1 illuminated.

Ding.

The door slid open . . .

"Clear," Dempsey and Grimes said in unison as he eased his finger off the trigger and back onto the trigger guard.

"Wang, you need to get us out of here," Dempsey said. "There are at least a dozen assholes with assault rifles still in this hotel trying to hunt us down and kill us."

"The FBI TMT is en route with two SUVs. But I should warn you, they are all kind of pissed that they didn't know what was going on."

"I thought Buz was keeping those guys company?"

"Yeah, well, I'm not sure if that's a good thing or a bad thing for us," Wang said.

"I heard that," Buz said, talking on the party line for the first time. "Where do you want the pickup, John?"

"Split the convoy. I want one at the rear where the alley meets Mesininku. That's our primary; we'll egress via the courtyard and take the alley. I want the other—"

A shrill howl interrupted comms, followed by a blast of loud static and then wailing electric guitar, heavy drumbeats, and a man shouting, "I can't breathe . . . I can't breathe . . . I can't breathe."

"You hear that?" Dempsey said, looking at Munn and wincing.

"Yeah, what the hell is it?" Munn said, tugging at his left ear.

"Sounds like a heavy metal track, playing in a loop," Martin said.

"Wang, turn that shit off," Dempsey barked. "Wang? Wang . . . do you copy?"

"John, it's not Wang," Grimes said. "Someone hijacked our comms."

"Well, that confirms this ain't just Amarov's guys coming after us. Malik is pulling the strings tonight," Dempsey said, his jaw hard set. "He's here, in Klaipéda. I can feel it."

"Which means we should assume that in addition to the Vory shooters Malik has cyber, spotters, and snipers in place," Grimes said, the pained look on her face telling him the raging rock in her left ear was as distracting for her as it was for him. "Also, if they can broadcast

200

on our party line, then we should assume they've been listening in. We can't exfil to Mesininku anymore; that's blown."

"True, but the alternative is walking out the front door," Dempsey said.

"There's that door that opens out onto Teatro," Munn said.

"That door is only like thirty feet from the main entrance on the corner," Grimes said. "That whole intersection is no-man's-land. It's completely wide open, and there's a half-dozen sniper options with great sight lines and wide targeting arcs. Also, there's street parking everywhere. I counted five minivans parked out there on the walk back. Amarov could have guys waiting in any of those."

"Exiting through the front forces us to cross the lobby," Dempsey said, shaking his head. "I guarantee he has a fire team camped out in front of that damn elevator bank. It's what I'd do."

"Both options suck. We're just gonna have to shoot our way through," Grimes said.

"We don't have a single rifle among us, Lizzie," Munn said, practically yelling now to hear his own voice over the heavy metal. "I think we should hunker down here."

"Here? In the pantry with no exit?" Dempsey said, screwing up his face at Munn. The noise in his earbud was really starting to piss him off.

"Yeah. Malik blew it, man. Amarov's guys fucked their first attempt to kill us in the elevator, and now they're out of time. Klaipėda SWAT has gotta be en route, if they're not here already. The Vory shooters aren't going to stick around to get shredded and arrested. We just need to wait here until the good guys secure the building."

"I don't know, Dan, these Vory are highly motivated. The Russians must be paying them a ton. It won't take Malik much longer to figure out we're down here. One grenade lobbed in and we're finished," Grimes said.

"You're right . . . God, this is a fucking shit show," Munn cursed, shaking his head.

Dempsey was about to weigh in when a commotion erupted on the other side of the door separating the pantry from the kitchen. He gestured for everyone to get low as he crept forward in a tactical crouch. The team fell in behind him using staggered offsets, like muscle memory—with Munn behind him on the left, then Grimes, then Martin, then Latif. He peeked through the crack between the edge of the swinging door and the frame and saw two Vory shooters with assault rifles scanning the kitchen.

Dempsey eased back onto his haunches and gritted his teeth.

Shit, they found us . . .

CHAPTER 22

Fourth Floor
National Hotel

"So, this is your game—cat and mouse? I expected more," Valerian murmured, talking aloud to the American operator who continued to move a step ahead of him at every turn.

"Say again," said the Vory killer beside him.

"I wasn't talking to you," Valerian said, fixing the gunman with a glare. "Get ready. We go again."

The Russian nodded and brought his assault rifle up to the ready. Valerian and his two Vory shooters had cleared nine rooms and were in position to breach number ten. It was exhausting, nerve-fraying work—knowing that each new door kicked in could be your last.

He had the mettle for it.

His hired gangster muscle did not.

Just minutes earlier, he'd been standing outside the third-floor elevator bank when he'd noticed the missing knob on the door in the vending alcove almost immediately. He'd ordered these same two Vory shooters to clear the maid's closet—happy to let them be the sacrificial bullet cushions for the American team he'd been certain was hiding inside. But when they pulled open the door, the closet had been empty. He'd flipped on the light, saw the service elevator and the indicator light glowing amber for the fourth floor, and knew how they'd escaped. No magic, no miracles; just luck and tactical prowess.

The American ghost was clever, and he'd correctly predicted that Valerian would redeploy his shooters to the lobby level to block their escape, so against conventional wisdom, the American had decided to go up. There were twenty-two rooms on the fourth floor to hide in. Valerian was playing the odds, hoping the Americans had decided to wait it out long enough for Lithuanian police to arrive en masse at the hotel before being forced into another engagement with a hit squad that had them greatly outnumbered and outgunned.

"Victory, this is Spire. You're out of time," Sylvie said in his right ear, her voice soft but insistent. She knew her place. She was talking to him on a private comms circuit separate from the channel shared with the Vory. "I jammed the Americans' comms, but I don't know how much longer it'll be until they defeat my exploit. They have tactical backup five minutes out, and Klaipėda SWAT is only a few minutes behind them."

"I'm not leaving without him," he seethed.

She didn't speak for several seconds, finally saying, "My recommendation is you egress via the courtyard to the back alley onto Mesininku Street. There's a vehicle parked a half block down Kurpiu with keys under the seat. I'll stay on with you as long as I can."

A geyser of anger erupted inside Valerian and a flurry of curses flooded his mind, but he controlled the impulse to verbalize any of them. Sylvie was right, damn it. The American's plan had worked— Valerian was out of time. He looked at the number placard on the door in front of him: 422.

One more, he told himself. *One more room, then I go . . .*

He looked at the Vory shooters, nodded, and counted them down, "Three, two, one, breach."

The bigger of the two thugs kicked the door in, splintering the wooden jamb and sending the slab flying into the doorstop. The three-man team swept into the room, scanning over their weapons, clearing left and right. After multiple dry runs they had developed marginal proficiency, clearing the bedroom first, then bathroom and closet.

"Clear," said the bigger of the Vory shooters.

"Clear," said the other.

"Fuck," Valerian cursed and whirled to leave.

"We clear the next one?" the first guy asked.

"Yes, and I want you to clear the rest," Valerian said.

"Where are you going?"

"Down to talk to Yuri," he said, referring to Amarov's second. "I'll be back."

The big gangster grumbled his displeasure at this development, but Valerian didn't care. The American had beaten him . . . again. He walked with angry strides to the east stairwell and descended. While he did, he slipped on a pair of large tinted eyeglasses. The thick lenses were specially designed to distort the lines of his cheeks and block any view of his eyes from cameras that would be recording everywhere outside the hotel. The Lithuanians would give the Americans access to everything, and they would use their fucking facial-recognition software to track him down in real time.

Without talking to Yuri or calling Amarov on the radio, he slipped out the rear of the hotel into the courtyard. Without a backward glance, he walked down the alley and then turned right onto Mesininku. A half block down on the left, he spied the car Sylvie had reported. Once he got out of Klaipėda, exfiltration from Lithuania would be simple. Russian soil was only fifty kilometers away. In an hour, he would be back in Kaliningrad. Hopefully, Sylvie made it out. She was a Zeta, but not a *real* Zeta. There were operators and support, and she was support.

He liked her and she was good at her job, but he wasn't willing to risk his life or the mission for her. She'd understood this when she'd agreed to participate in the op. These things were implicit, weren't they?

As he slipped into the driver's seat, he thought about his next conversation with Arkady. It would be terrible, that much he was certain of. There was no way Arkady wouldn't learn of tonight's events. The old fox would probably summon him to Vyborg for a compulsory "reeducation" training module. Or maybe he would have a sniper put a bullet in Valerian's brain. Either way, it would be unpleasant. Maybe it was time to start thinking about life after Zeta. Nobody talked about it, but Primes didn't retire . . . they were retired. There was a difference.

I'm not going out that way, he told himself as he shoved his HK under the driver's seat. *When it's my time, it's going to be on my terms.*

CHAPTER 23

The Otto Restaurant Pantry
National Hotel

Dempsey watched the two Vory shooters through the gap between the pantry door and the wall. The closer of the two Russians pointed at the pantry and said something to his partner, who looked at least ten years older and appeared to be in charge. The senior Vory gunman nodded and gave a flippant *then go check it out* wave of his left hand.

"You're gonna have to take that guy," Munn whispered in Dempsey's ear, peering over his shoulder.

"I know," Dempsey said and sighted over his Sig through the gap, which was just wide enough for the muzzle. Just when he was about to pull the trigger, he thought better of it. "Get back," he whispered and waved his team toward the bathroom and office.

"What are we doing?" Munn asked as he backpedaled.

"Too many collaterals," Dempsey whispered. "And if I miss, he'll cut us all to pieces through the swing door."

"Then don't miss," Munn said with a crooked grin. "Or let Lizzie take the shot."

Dempsey shook his head as he crabbed backward into the office—which was little more than a cubby—and took a tactical knee next to Munn. As he did, the rock music in his ear abruptly stopped, followed by a burst of static and then Wang's voice: "Motherfuckers think they can hijack my shit? Hell, no! I'm going to own their asses now."

"Glad to have you back," Dempsey said. "Default call sign protocol now. I'm One."

"Two," Munn said, followed by Grimes, Martin, and Latif numbering off in that order.

"Check," Wang said. "I'm Zero, Big Brother is at home, and Papa is riding with the TMT."

"Check," Dempsey whispered. Through the gap, he watched one of the Russian mobsters question the chef and the other raise his rifle to the ready and start scanning. "Zero, we have a big problem. Looks like we're going to have to shoot our way outta here. Do you still have thermal?"

"Check."

"Report possible tango snipers and any perimeter shooters that could fuck our exfil."

"Stand by . . ."

Dempsey glanced right at the wall separating the office from the kitchen and noted that it was brick, which would fare much better against the inevitable strafe from the second shooter than the flimsy aluminum swing door. He counted steps in his head, visualizing the Russian mobster closing on the pantry door.

He's going to come through that door in three . . . two . . . one . . .

A heartbeat later, the swing door slowly drifted open and the muzzle of an assault rifle poked in.

Dempsey adjusted his firing elevation a tad and put tension on the trigger . . .

The Russian's AK-12 barrel slid into view, then the shooter's lead hand gripping the handguard, then his other hand on the pistol grip, then the tip of his nose and—

Dempsey pulled the trigger.

His round found its mark and drilled a hole through the Vory shooter's left temple and splattered blood and gray matter all over the opposite wall. The mobster's body crumpled in the doorway, half in, half out of the pantry. A split second later, a prolonged, uncontrolled volley from the second Vory ripped a dozen holes in the aluminum swing door. Dempsey held up a closed fist, holding his team. Screams erupted on the other side of the door as pandemonium ensued among the kitchen staff.

Wait . . . wait . . .

Dempsey fired two rounds into the back of the swing door, and the Vory shooter returned fire with another prolonged volley, setting off a new chorus of screams. Dempsey's gaze went to the AK-12 assault rifle four feet away, still clutched in the dead shooter's hands.

"He's not coming," Munn said.

"Nope, he's sitting back in a covered position, waiting for us to come out."

"We need that rifle," Munn said.

"Yep."

"Want me to cover you so you can go get it?"

"Only if we both want to die," Dempsey said with a sideways look. "Unless of course you're feeling like a lucky lumberjack today."

"Zero, this is three," Grimes said. "We're boxed in. Need a SITREP. How far out is Papa and our wheels?"

"Papa is five mikes out," Buz said, beating Wang to the punch. "You want us to split, or both vehicles up front?"

"Depends on what Zero is seeing outside," Dempsey said.

"I hold no rooftop shooters," Wang reported, "but I have one possible in a third-floor apartment on Mesininku in line with the alley exit from the courtyard. I've got two idling vehicles on the west side. One parked down Zveju and one at the intersection of Zveju and Teatro kitty-corner to the hotel entrance. Don't know if they're shitheads or not, but I'll interrogate their comms and try to find out."

"Check," Dempsey said and fired two more rounds at the door, but this time the Vory asshole in the kitchen did not return fire.

"Looks like he done learned that trick," Munn said.

"Yeah," Dempsey grumbled. "I gotta get that AK."

He fixed his gaze on the dead Russian slumped over his rifle a mere four feet away. The urgency in his gut was at a crescendo because he knew—with absolute certainty—that the shooter in the kitchen had radioed for help and enemy backup was on the way. Before Munn or anyone else could object, Dempsey slid on his belly across the filthy cement floor to where the dead Vory lay crumpled in the doorway. With explosive power, he propped up the dead man's torso as a shield and grabbed the grip of the AK with his other hand. Automatic weapon fire reverberated as the Vory shooter peppered the door and the body with bullets. Time slowed, and Dempsey entered the slipstream of combat clarity—where his muscles, reflexes, senses, and mind became hyper-connected and attuned.

He brought the iron sights of the AK-12 up and, as if the gun were guiding him and not the other way around, the muzzle found the enemy shooter crouched behind the corner of a food prep island. He squeezed the trigger and turned the top of the Vory hitman's head into a canoe. His mind was like a computer targeting system sorting threat from friendly as he scanned bodies in the kitchen. Female, nonthreat, cowering behind a shelf at his three o'clock. Male, nonthreat, curled on the floor in front of stoves at two o'clock. Female, shot in the chest, bleeding out at his twelve o'clock. Male, head chef, dead in a pool of blood at his ten o'clock . . .

Rage at the carnage of innocents lit a fire in his chest, and the engine of war—that thing that propelled him to fight, defend, and protect—supercharged his body. He was up and charging into the kitchen, sighting over his AK. Just as he predicted, Vory backup arrived an instant later, four men entering the kitchen in a diamond formation from the door on the opposite wall. But Dempsey was in the slipstream, and they weren't prepared for *him*.

Pop pop.

Sidestep, *pop*.

Duck, pivot—*pop pop*.

And it was over.

"Damn, bro—how you do that is beyond me," Munn said, falling in on his right shoulder and shaking his head in disbelief at the body count.

"Guys, I think I found him," Wang said in Dempsey's ear.

"Who?" Dempsey said, sighting at the kitchen door in case the Vory had a second squad held back.

"Malik. Eighty-five percent confident he's observing from an idling SUV on Zveju. He's in the back seat with a driver and front passenger." Wang's voice was frenetic with excitement. "Boo-yah. He doesn't have any idea who he's dealing with. I triangulated his ass, and now I'm going to find the assholes running his cyber so you can hit them next."

"Good work, Zero," Dempsey said. "Current threat SITREP?"

"The guys you just took out came from the lobby, which means you have a clean egress if you go now. You've still got two shooters on the third floor and two more dudes on the fourth. They're clearing rooms, presumably looking for you guys, but I don't know how much longer you have before they wise up and head down."

"Check. Papa, this is One. To take Malik we're gonna need your help," Dempsey said.

"One, this is Papa," came Buz's voice, ripe with irritation on the open channel. "Do you want him dead or alive?"

"Alive."

"Shit . . . that's what I was afraid of." Dempsey heard him talking to the FBI TMT driver for a moment before he said, "Zero, which vehicle is Malik in?"

"A black Mercedes SUV parked on the corner of Karlskronos and Zveju, nose out," Wang answered.

"All right. We'll box him in. One hits the car, grabs Malik, and then we all egress together."

"One, you've got three mikes to get it done before Lithuanian SWAT arrives on scene," Wang said.

"Check," Dempsey said and turned to his team, who now were all armed with the assault rifles that only seconds ago had been in the hands of the four dead Russians at Dempsey's feet. They quickly checked their magazines, with only Munn refreshing his with a spare off one of the dead guys. "Y'all ready?" he asked, sweeping eyes across the group.

"One quick thing," Munn said, looking at Martin and Latif. "This guy thinks and shoots like JD. He schooled my ass in Turkey, so be ready for anything."

"Hooyah, old man," said Latif with a shit-eating grin. "Army has your back."

"Munn's right, Malik is extremely dangerous," Dempsey said. "Stay focused. Assignments: One and Two are on the HVT, Three kills the driver, Four takes out the passenger, and Five, you get the engine and the tires. We hit at the same time TMT arrives to capitalize on the confusion." Seeing no questions or concerns on their faces, he chopped a hand forward. "Let's move."

"When you exit the kitchen, take the door on your left that leads into the dining room," Wang said in Dempsey's ear.

"Check."

"Move straight across the dining room toward the double doors on the opposite wall. After you exit the restaurant you'll be in a short hallway that dumps you out into the lobby in front of the elevator, but I'd take the west-side exit instead of charging out the front."

"Two mikes," Buz reported as Dempsey barreled through the restaurant, which was completely abandoned. Multiple tables still had plates of food and half-full wineglasses, proof it had been busy before the shooting started.

Dempsey pulled up short at the double doors leading from the restaurant into the hallway off the lobby. He took a tactical knee and sighted around the corner.

"Clear."

A heartbeat later he was on the move again. He glanced at the elevator bank, and the indicator showed the car was on the third floor. He paused at the edge of the wall where the short hall intersected the lobby and sighted around the corner. Like the restaurant, the lobby was deserted. He glanced at the tiny business center on the opposite wall—also deserted.

"Clear," Dempsey barked and chopped a hand straight.

"One mike out," Buz said in his ear. "Be ready."

Legs churning, Dempsey sprinted past the elevator, across the back of the lobby, past the business center, and into another short hallway that led to the exit onto Teatro Street. He put on the brakes at the door and scanned the street outside through the glass in the door.

"One is at the door. Zero—report," Dempsey said, wanting a threat assessment before he led his team into the wide-open intersection. If Malik had shooters in another vehicle or a sniper had repositioned, they would take casualties. Headlights on his left caught his attention. "That vehicle screaming north on Teatro, is that us?"

"Yes, that's Papa Two," Wang said. "Papa One is westbound on Zveju."

"Fifteen seconds . . ." Buz said.

"One, the lane is clear. Go now," Wang said.

Dempsey pushed the door open and sprinted into the night just as a black Suburban hurtled past, tires roaring over the cobblestone street. With Munn moving stride for stride on his right, Dempsey sprinted after the big SUV, cursing silently that his team would be late hitting the X. Not by much, only seconds, but seconds mattered. Brakes squealed and tires skidded as the two black Chevys slid into place, bookending Malik's Mercedes SUV. Malik's driver noticed the converging Suburbans and tried to accelerate clear but was too late and crashed into the passenger side of Papa Two.

Legs pumping, rifle up, Dempsey closed the forty yards to the Mercedes fast, but not faster than Grimes's first round, which sailed past him on the left and hit the driver just above the right ear as he was looking over his left shoulder trying to execute a reversing maneuver. The big Benz's engine roared momentarily, lurching the SUV backward five yards before it fell still. Latif fired two controlled bursts into the Mercedes's grill and left front tire.

Sirens wailed in the distance and were getting louder by the second, which meant Lithuanian State Police would be on the scene shortly. The countdown timer in Dempsey's mind was at ninety seconds and ticking. As he and Munn arced around to assault the passenger compartment, the Mercedes's windshield suddenly exploded in a torrent of flying glass and bullets. The Russian operative in the front passenger seat unloaded a prolonged burst with an automatic weapon. Dempsey and Munn dropped to the ground as bullets whistled by overhead. Grimes and Martin ended the short-lived counteroffensive a second later with sequential kill shots. Dempsey guessed that Grimes's bullet hit first.

"Your HVT is huddled low in the back passenger side," Wang reported, reading Dempsey's mind. The kid was on fire today.

Must be cruising in the same slipstream, Dempsey thought as he closed the final ten feet toward the Mercedes. He loathed extracting an HVT from inside a vehicle. It was fucking dangerous and he hated it. Open the door and take a round in the face—no thank you. The only safe way was to—

"Flush or chase?" Munn said, also reading his mind.

"Chase," Dempsey said and without waiting for Munn's reply rounded the rear bumper of the SUV in a hunched shuffle.

A prolonged up-angled burst from Munn's AK blew out the rear passenger window and punched holes in the roof. The volley did its job, and the rear passenger door flew open and a man bolted out, running low and fast into the expansive green space across from the hotel. The dude was fast, but Dempsey was faster. He took Malik down with a lunging tackle, landing hard on the Russian's back. The impact drove all the air from Malik's lungs, and Dempsey heard him immediately begin to hyperventilate. With a triumphant snarl, Dempsey rolled the bastard onto his back and drove his right fist into the other man's nose—flattening it with a sickening crunch.

The Russian raised both his hands defensively, shielding his face from a second blow as he gasped for air. Dempsey froze. This man behaved nothing like him, fought nothing like him . . . looked nothing like him.

"What the fuck?" he seethed. "You're not Malik."

This comment elicited a sputtering cackle as the still-hyperventilating Russian tried to breathe and laugh at the same time while blood poured into his mouth.

Fuming, Dempsey patted the Russian down for weapons, pulled a Makarov from a shoulder holster, and stuffed it in his waistband at the small of his back. "Get up," he barked, tugging at the Russian's arm. "I said get up, you motherfucker!"

"That's not Malik," Munn said, trotting up behind him.

"I know."

"Then who is he?"

"Matvei Amarov," the Russian said through a cough, pressing to his feet. "And you have just made the biggest mistake of your—"

Dempsey cut Amarov off with a punch to the solar plexus, buckling the Russian Mafia don at the waist. "Shuuuut up."

Blue and red lights flashed in Dempsey's peripheral vision. One of the black Chevys was tearing across the grass toward them.

"Get in," Buz said in Dempsey's ear as the Suburban braked to a rolling stop beside them. "We're leaving."

The rear passenger door flew open and Dempsey and Munn together hurled Amarov headfirst into the back seat, where an FBI dude kitted up in body armor dragged him into the third row, making room for the rest of them. Munn went first; Dempsey followed and slammed the door shut as the big Chevy ripped tracks in the lawn as the driver exfiltrated them at ludicrous speed.

Dempsey felt eyes on him and looked up to see Buz turned around in the front passenger seat staring at him.

"What?" he said, full of piss and vinegar.

"You're a one-man wrecking ball, aren't cha?" the former CIA man asked.

"You have no idea," Dempsey said and then turned to look at his prize in the back seat. Amarov looked like he was about to say something but then thought better of it. Dempsey said to the FBI man, "You got flex-cuffs?"

"Yeah." The operator retrieved a pair of heavy nylon restraints from a pouch on his thigh and deftly cuffed the Russian gangster.

"Keep an eye on that one," Dempsey said. "He'll slit your throat when you're not looking." Then he turned back to look out the front.

"Where to now? The Boeing?" Buz asked over his shoulder.

"Yeah, and send Papa Two to pick up boy wonder."

"Ain't nobody picking up my caffeinated ass yet," Wang said on the still-open channel.

"And why is that?" Dempsey said.

"Because, beeyotch, I told you—nobody hijacks my shit and gets away with it." This was accompanied by a shuffling sound that Dempsey was certain was Wang dancing.

"You found him?" Dempsey asked, his pulse rate ticking up.

"I found his cyber crew; whether Malik is there playing mother or not I don't know. Sending you the GPS coordinates now."

Dempsey turned to Munn. "You up for another one?"

Munn shrugged with a *take it or leave it* expression. "And if I say no?"

"Before I dragged you out of that bar in Key West, I made a standing agreement with that VD clinic where you worked that you could have your old job back anytime, no questions asked . . . so there's that."

"You're such an asshole, you know that?" Munn said through a laugh.

"I know, but it's not my fault."

"Then whose fault is it?"

"Smith's."

"Smith? Why's it his fault?"

"Because, he wrote 'asshole' into the personality profile of my NOC," Dempsey said with a smug chuckle. "And you know I take the authenticity of my NOC very seriously."

CHAPTER 24

Dempsey could feel Amarov's eyes drilling a hole in the back of his head, but he resisted the urge to turn around and look at the Vory boss.

"He's going to hunt you down," the Russian said, his accented English and broken nose making him sound like an ominous Russian Rudolph the Red-Nosed Reindeer. "One by one, he'll find you and gut each and every last member of your team."

Why assholes in Amarov's position felt compelled to taunt their captors and make hollow threats Dempsey would never understand. It was just a stupid, stupid thing to do. He turned around and looked at the FBI guy sitting next to the mobster. "You got a gag?"

The FBI man shook his head. "Nope. I don't carry those."

"How about a bottle of chloroform?"

The FBI agent raised his eyebrows in disbelief; then his expression turned to disapproval.

"Relax, he's kidding," Munn said.

Dempsey shifted his gaze to Amarov, who was sneering at him, a fool comforted by the fallacy of his delusion that he was somehow still in control of his world.

"How long have you worked for Malik?" he asked the Russian.

"I don't *work* for Malik," the mob boss said through a laugh. "We are business partners."

"Did Arkady know about this hit tonight?" Buz interjected from the front passenger seat.

If Dempsey hadn't been staring straight at the Russian, ready with a pointless quip, he would have missed the flicker of emotion in Amarov's eyes. Dempsey knew that critical interrogations were filmed not just to document the exchange but also so that trained interrogators could slow down the recording and look for microexpressions exhibited by the subject being questioned. Unlike regular facial expressions, which could be controlled, microexpressions were involuntary, subconscious, and impossible to prevent or hide. Amarov's expression had been *surprise*. Dempsey had seen it an instant before the Russian adopted a look of smug indifference.

"I have no idea what you're talking about," Amarov said.

Dempsey turned and looked at Buz and saw a spark in the former CIA man's eyes. Apparently, this was the confirmation he'd been waiting for—waiting for over a decade. The Russian spymaster Buz had been chasing his whole career, Arkady Zhukov, was alive and still pulling the puppet strings. Buz turned around in his seat to look out the windshield, but Dempsey could see in profile that he was smiling.

"All right, people," Wang said in Dempsey's ear, as giddy as a schoolboy about to get laid. "This is Zero and I got Big Brother on the line helping out now with some augmented processing power and imagery. Big Brother?"

"Your target is a single individual on the second floor of the Preliudija Bed and Breakfast," Baldwin chimed in from the other side of the world. "It's a rather small establishment at the coordinates that Richard—I mean Zero—gave you. Subject is seated at a desk on the north wall, second floor, southwest corner room. The boutique hotel has a single point of entry front and a rear entry from a courtyard with a seating area."

"So the target is alone in the house, or do we have civilians to worry about?" Dempsey asked.

"I hold a single signature on the ground floor, probably the owner of the inn or night manager. Appears to be male, working at a desk. And I have another thermal signature in the bedroom on the northeast corner . . . Oh my."

"What?" Dempsey said, shaking his head.

"The signature appears to be two individuals—overlapping thermal images, one is sitting on the other's lap . . . confirming—yes, it is a couple, and they are . . . um, coupling. And most vigorously, I might add . . . Regardless, your target is still stationary working at a desk in the room on the southwest corner. Also, I am tying the FBI in to our comms network."

"We're going to loop you guys in to our comms," Dempsey said, patting the driver gently on the right shoulder before turning to look at the shooter in back.

"What channel?" the FBI operator asked.

"No need to change anything," Baldwin said. "I've set up with your command and control to handle everything from here."

The FBI man screwed up his face in amazement at Dempsey, because he had apparently just heard that.

"How the hell did he do that so fast?" the FBI operator asked, eyebrows up.

Dempsey laughed. "Hell if I know, man, but he does it all the time."

"That's some James Bond Q-level shit right there."

"You're telling me."

"Tango One is broadcasting again," Wang said suddenly.

"Yes, I see that, Zero. Very interesting. Different mobile device this time."

"Who's he calling?" Munn asked.

"Well, of course I'm not psychic, but we'll find out," Baldwin said with a hint of bemusement. "Not nearly in time for it to help you with your current decision tree, however."

"There's no decision tree, here," Dempsey said. "We're hitting it, no question." He turned to see the FBI operator in the back bent over doing something at Amarov's feet. "Whatcha doing, brother?" Dempsey asked.

"Zip-tying our friend's ankles to the seat support bracket," the FBI shooter said, and when he sat up he dropped a black hood over Amarov's head. "Less this dude sees the better, right?"

A smile curled Dempsey's lips. "You read my mind," he said, and when the operator slipped on a pair of gloves and a helmet he said, "Looks like you're planning on coming with us?"

The FBI man didn't answer right away, just reached over his seat into the back of the vehicle and then passed forward two black tactical vests for Dempsey and Munn, followed by a far better gift—two SOPMOD M4 assault rifles with forward grips, EOTech holographic sights, and both white and IR tactical lights on the Picatinny rails. Dempsey handed a gun and vest to Munn, slipped the vest and then the gun sling over his head, and then gratefully accepted six extra magazines from the assaulter, three of which he handed to Munn.

"Yeah, I'd like to join this party," the operator finally said. "Assuming y'all don't mind having a third wheel."

"Thought you'd never ask," Dempsey said.

"Before we do this, you mind telling me who the fuck you guys are exactly?"

"Yeah, sure . . . we're a covert counterterrorism task force," Dempsey said and couldn't quite seem to wipe the grin from his face. "Does that help clear things up?"

"So, it's a 'I need to have my boss talk to your boss' sorta thing?" the operator said.

Dempsey pointed a finger pistol at him and clicked with his tongue.

"Three minutes out," Grimes said in his ear from the other SUV.

"Us, too," the driver said from the front of Dempsey's Suburban.

"Check," Dempsey said.

"What's the plan, One?" Grimes said.

"Three, Four, and Five, you're Bravo team. Alpha team just added a pinch hitter," Dempsey said and then to the FBI operator added, "You're Six."

"Check," the FBI shooter said.

"We've got two more eager and willing players over here in Papa Two looking to join the game," Grimes said. "You want another augment?"

"Yes, that would be helpful," Dempsey said. "They're Seven and Eight."

"Check. How do you want this to play out?"

"Bravo team will make a rear approach and Alpha team will breach through the front. Four and Five will secure the lobby, Seven and Eight will secure the courtyard and perimeter respectively. Three, you'll hold at the corner to cover the front approach," he said.

"Check."

"Alpha team will go up the stairs and take the target. Assuming no interference, Alpha will exfil through the front, but—and this is important, people—I want to keep our HVTs separated. I mean no contact between them, period. Which means Tango One is going to be riding in Papa Two. Both teams are swapping rides. Bravo team is exfilling in Papa One and Alpha team in Papa Two. Then we haul ass to the jet. In and out in sixty to ninety seconds. Questions?"

There were none.

A minute later, Grimes said, "Dropping off Bravo team now."

Dempsey watched Papa Two stop at the corner and kill its headlights. His driver did the same and pulled up in front of the B&B.

"Bravo in position," said Grimes, her voice liquid calm. "On your mark."

Dempsey's SUV rolled to a stop.

"If it's possible to get in and out with no rounds fired, that would be ideal," Dempsey said on the open channel. "We're two and half blocks from the National Hotel; let's try to avoid another possible run-in with Klaipėda Police."

He got a double-click back.

Dempsey felt Buz looking at him and realized Ember's newest member had been incredibly quiet. "You good with all this?" he asked.

Buz nodded. "Yeah."

"And you good babysitting this asshole?" he said, jerking a thumb at Amarov in the back seat.

"Easy day," Buz said, borrowing the ever-popular SEAL euphemism.

Dempsey grinned broadly. Maybe Buz was going to fit in at Ember after all. He turned to Munn and their FBI augment. "Let's go. Bravo, hold for my call. We're on the approach."

Dempsey pressed open the door and slid out of the Suburban into the night. He felt Munn a step behind to his right and the FBI operator behind Munn as they moved across the street. He moved swiftly and silently up the brick approach and onto the inn's front porch. Dempsey didn't see anyone in the large bay windows beside an ornate front door made of stained wood and inlayed glass. The door looked old and expensive—the type of craftsmanship that was impossible to find these days—and he hated to put a boot through it. Shaking his head, he grabbed the knob, which to his surprised turned.

"Bravo, go," he said, then pushed the door open and entered the inn leading with his SOPMOD M4.

A young man, with long unkempt hair wearing a hipster gray suit, raised his hands and opened his mouth as if to scream but then stopped, somehow reassured by the large yellow FBI letters stenciled on the front of the vests of the three killers who had just entered his lobby. From the rear of the inn, Dempsey heard Martin and Latif breach.

"What is going on?" the man said in heavily accented English. "Are there being bad guys here? Are you finding terrorists?" The young man seemed more excited than frightened, and Dempsey half expected him to ask for a selfie with the team.

He heard Martin bark "Clear" and in a moment, Martin was beside Dempsey while Latif played sentry at the back door.

"Watch this guy," Dempsey said to the FBI operator, nodding at the inn manager. "Four, you're with us," he said, preferring to have Martin as his third. He chopped a hand forward and he and Munn ascended the wood staircase with Martin bringing up the rear.

"Left at the top of the stairs," Wang said in his ear. "The two people in the room at the end are still shagging and definitely not a threat. Tango One appears to have heard you, however, and he's packing up really quickly."

Dempsey moved past the target door, taking a position that was usually Munn's, and Munn and Martin held at the other side.

"His back is to the door," Wang said, his voice brimming with excitement. Wang was like a kid playing Fortnite, only his players would not respawn if this went bad, Dempsey thought.

Dempsey gave Munn a nod and promptly smashed his booted foot into the door right below the handle, smashing the bolt for the lock out of the doorframe. Then Dempsey tapped Munn's right shoulder and the SEAL-surgeon moved through the door and then to the left. Dempsey followed closely and moved right. He shouted no warning—Malik would only turn such a warning to his advantage, just as Dempsey would in his position. As he cross-stepped right, Dempsey kept his rifle low, intent on shooting the Russian, certain he would need to.

The room's only occupant froze in mid-action—stuffing a computer half in and half out of a silver metal case. Despite the dark, Dempsey instantly identified Tango One as a woman. Instead of going for a weapon, she put her hands up in the air. She wore an oversize red sweater with a thick roll collar and had short hair, cropped severely below her ears.

"Turn around," Dempsey barked. "Slowly," he added, raising his rifle to center mass.

She did, slowly, her arms now straight up in the air, her fingers reaching for the ceiling. She wore a thin boom mike, extending to within a half inch of her lips, and looked genuinely terrified.

"What is this?" she asked, her voice trembling. "Who are you?"

Dempsey wasn't buying it. He moved forward, snatched the earpiece and boom mike from her head, and shoved her down by the shoulder. Instead of going to her knees, however, she bent at the waist awkwardly, her hands still up. Dempsey crushed the mike and earpiece under his boot. It took Munn and Martin only seconds to clear the rest of the room, the small adjoining sitting room, and the bathroom.

"On your knees," he commanded and took a step back. Once she'd complied, he said, "Where's Malik?" but when she didn't answer, he tilted her face by her chin with the toe of his boot. "Tell me right now, and we'll let you go."

He saw a flash of something—another telling microexpression—but it disappeared too quickly for him to register it.

"I don't know what you mean," she sobbed, and her eyes no longer looked as frightened. She had trained for this scenario. "I'm Olga Deveren. I'm here on business from Frankfurt. I work for Odero Pharmaceuticals. Please, put away your guns. You are scaring me. You have the wrong room."

"The couple going at it down the hall have stopped," Wang said in his ear. "They appear to be getting dressed."

"Watch their door," Dempsey said, gesturing to Munn and then to Martin. "Clear the other bedroom just to be sure."

Munn and Martin both nodded, and they disappeared into the hall.

Dempsey raised the rifle, putting the red dot in the center of the woman's forehead.

"Last chance," he growled. "We know you're working with Malik. Tell me right now where he is or I'll shoot you."

"I'm a German citizen—the marketing director for Odero," she repeated, but her trembling bottom lip betrayed what he decided was genuine fear. He tried to imagine how Chip or Dale would react in a similar situation. Probably worse. Facing the business end of an assault rifle in the hands of a bastard who clearly knows how to use it is no easy proposition.

Even for spooks.

"Other room is clear," Martin said, poking his head in the doorway.

Damn . . . the Russian ghost outplayed me again.

"Make a decision, One," said Buz from the SUV, the last voice Dempsey expected to hear on the channel. "You're outta time."

But instead of it irritating him, Dempsey appreciated that the former CIA man was checked in and paying attention to the op. Besides, Buz was right. They needed to go.

"Take her," Dempsey said to Martin. "In the SUVs in fifteen seconds."

Dempsey shoved the computer into the silver case, slammed the lid, and grabbed the woman's other duffel on the floor. Then he turned and followed Martin out as the former Marine shepherded the woman down the hall toward the stairs.

"Exfil. Exfil. Papa Two, pick up Zero en route to the airport. Big Brother, let the aircrew at the Boeing know we need to be wheels up in forty-five minutes."

"Destination?" Baldwin's calm, professorial voice asked.

"Home," Dempsey growled. "We have two very clever crows, and I have lots of questions."

CHAPTER 25

Ember Hangar
Newport News/Williamsburg International Airport
Newport News, Virginia
June 16
2030 Local Time

"Fuck," Grimes said and paced away from the group. "So, I have to be bad cop?"

Smith nodded. "Two interrogation teams, one for our female and one for our male guest. I want you with Amanda on the female. I need Munn and Buz together in the room with our male prisoner."

Grimes nodded but clenched her jaw.

Munn shifted uncomfortably beside her. "You sure about this, boss?" He scratched the three-day stubble on his chin. "After everything Amanda's been through, it's just . . . it's kind of cruel—deceiving her like this. I mean, can she handle this?"

Grimes felt her chest tighten at the angst they were about to cause Amanda Allen. She'd grown close to the analyst, despite her initial reluctance at her joining Ember. But Munn was underestimating

Allen—maybe because she was a woman, maybe not. "I get your res-
ervations, but this is the nature of the profession we've all chosen, and
Allen is much tougher than you think. It'll sting, but she can take it.
Once she understands what we did and why, she'll be fine."

God, I hope that's true. This is gonna more than sting.

"All right, now that that's settled—do the two of you understand
what you're supposed to do?" Smith's heavy gaze went back and forth
between her and Munn.

In that moment, she became acutely aware of the two faces of
Ember represented in this four-person huddle. On one side stood her
and Munn—a pair of operators ragged from the field, still wearing
the same clothes as yesterday, bathed in deodorant in lieu of a shower,
and both sporting three days of stubble . . . his face, her legs. Opposite
were Smith and Adamo—clean-shaven, hands unmarred, and wearing wrinkle-resistant button-down shirts, clean trousers, and unscuffed
shoes. And yet despite the stark difference in their outward appearances, the mental burden that Ember's two ranking members carried
was unmistakable. As an operator, if the plan went awry, she had the
luxury of blaming the architect behind the plan. Smith and Adamo
could not, and they wore that responsibility like invisible ox yokes she
noticed now for the first time.

She and Munn both nodded.

Adamo handed each of them a tablet computer. "Your interrogation
objectives and respective scripts . . . in case you need them. You'll be on
open mikes the entire time, so if you need something, just say so. We'll
have bidirectional live feeds streaming between the rooms, but monitor
control is at your discretion. Any questions?"

"No," she said, with Munn echoing her in unison.

"Remember, we only have one shot at this. I want you both to take
full advantage of the situation. This is a no-holds-barred interrogation,"
Smith said. "I will not intervene under any circumstance."

Grimes took a deep cleansing breath and steeled herself for what was about to come. When she was ready, she said, "Okay, let's do this."

Munn's expression darkened as he slipped into character. She watched him don a pair of black tactical gloves, flexing his fingers and then balling them up into fists. It was Munn—and his symbiotic relationship with Dempsey—that had made the team complete. "See you on the other side, Mother," he said, using one of her sniper call signs, his voice hard and cold as granite.

Mother—that's what I am on the team, isn't it? Making sure my team is safe and comes home. This is the same. This is a necessary evil.

She nodded and followed him out of Smith's office into the Tactical Operations Center—the heart of Ember's underground complex. Latif, Martin, Baldwin, Baldwin's two analysts, Chip and Dale, Allen, and Buz Wilson were all gathered and waiting in the Ember TOC. Everyone was standing—driven by nerves, caffeine, and anticipation—everyone, that is, except for Martin. The Marine sat reclined in a chair with his legs up on the conference table, feet crossed at the ankle, asleep. She smiled. That was just Martin—had been from the first op together in Ankara, Turkey. Even in his screening training—where they pressured the trainees to the point of failure—he had stayed chill, always a smile and a joke. She loved that he had so quickly become a part of the team. The only lone and noteworthy absentee was Wang, but that was understandable considering the key role he had to play.

And Dempsey, of course.

A palpable tension hung in the air, and all eyes went expectantly to her and Munn. If everything went according to plan, it was going to be a helluva show and they all knew it.

"Amanda you're with me," she said, looking at Ember's only other female member.

"And Buz, you're with me," Munn said, his voice all business.

"Good luck, guys," said Latif as the pair of interrogation teams headed off to do their work.

Since their capture, Amarov and the female prisoner, whom they felt certain was a Zeta version of Wang, were kept isolated from each other—first in the SUVs and then aboard the Boeing. That protocol continued after their arrival at the Ember hangar, with both captives being unloaded separately from each other. The Ember facility was large, but it hadn't been conceived as a detention or interrogation facility. To manage two detainees, certain accommodations had to be made. The SCIF was being used to house the woman, and the bunkroom had been transformed into an interrogation suite housing Amarov, the Russian Vory boss. The woman's identity was one of the things they were seeking.

Grimes led Amanda to the SCIF but paused outside the door. "Have you ever led an interrogation before?" she asked.

"No . . . but, as you know, I've been a participant in one," Allen said, referring to the brutal ordeal she'd experienced after being kidnapped in Turkey only a month ago. Her position as the Chief of Staff to the American Ambassador had been her first field assignment and high-profile NOC working undercover for CIA Clandestine Services. Her placement in such a high-profile assignment, one in the nexus of Middle East politics no less, had been a testimony to both her wits and work ethic. Her trajectory at the Agency had looked meteoric until Malik's operation sent her career careening off course. The ordeal that followed would have broken most people, even battle-tested operators, but Allen had persevered. She'd been stripped bare, robbed of her dreams and innocence, and emerged as Ember material. "I guess what I'm trying to say is, you don't have to worry about me. I think I have a pretty good idea what to expect."

Grimes winced, but she was committed to her role. "Are you sure you're ready for this?"

Allen nodded.

"Do you have any questions?"

"Just one," Allen said, the muscles in her jaw visibly tensing. "Can you tell me . . . is it him in the other room? Malik? You got him—didn't you?"

Grimes pressed her lips into a hard line. "Are you sure you want me to answer that?"

Allen nodded.

"Yes, we got him." She watched as an involuntary shiver washed over the other woman, and again she felt a wave of guilt at the pain their deception might cause her. But she'd meant what she'd told Munn— Amanda was tough. She was capable. She deserved to be on this team, and she'd make it through the challenge she was about to face. "Are you okay, Amanda?"

"Yeah. It's just weird to know that he's here, in this building," Allen said, her eyes belying the silent battle of emotions that Grimes knew must be raging inside. "I didn't expect to ever see him again. I feel . . . I don't know what I feel . . . Fear. Vindication. The desire to hurt him and to watch him be hurt. And yet at the same time, I also feel pity . . . and a weird, perverse yearning to go in there and be near him. I want to look him in the eyes and ask him if he's thought about me since . . ." She clenched her jaw and then turned and held Grimes's eyes. "And then I'd like to drive a knife into his face. What does that say about what I've become?"

Grimes reached out and put a hand on her shoulder. "It says that you're human."

Allen took a deep breath, exhaled, and nodded.

"Before we go in there, let's just recap our roles and objectives," Grimes said. "This is a tag team interrogation, but I'm the lead. Feel free to ask questions of the captive, but your role is to be the dedicated observer. A significant portion of my attention will be focused on my performance, and so it's invaluable to have a second set of eyes on her during the exchange looking for tells, tics, and slips that I'm apt to miss.

If things get rough, you'll also put on the good cop hat later. If we get to the point where she needs a friend, that will be you."

"Okay, but I'm not a trained interrogator. You guys get that, right?"

"It's okay. Your experience as a captive means you bring some special insights that can't be trained. Your input will be invaluable, I promise. Whenever you have two or more detainees as we do, as an interrogator you gain powerful additional leverage over the subject. Our girl knows we have another member of her team, but she has no idea what or how much information he's given up. We're going to use this to our advantage. Have you ever heard of the prisoner's dilemma?" Grimes asked.

"Yes, it's a thought exercise and well-understood example of game theory which basically says that when two actors are faced with the choice whether to cooperate or defect but cannot communicate, the rational actor will assume the other person will defect and therefore they'll choose to defect themselves," Allen said.

Grimes nodded. "That's exactly right. So, when we have two detainees, the default starting point is always the prisoner's dilemma scenario. Hopefully she'll defect, tell us what we want to know, and make life easy. But if she's loyal and strong and won't cooperate, then we'll have to escalate to more upsetting and persuasive tactics."

"I understand," Allen said, looking away. "But if she works with Malik, I can promise you, she will never give him up." She looked back at Grimes with wet eyes. "She'll be more afraid of him than of us."

Grimes shuddered a moment and then shrugged into the person *she* had become. Smith was right—Amanda's visceral reactions would validate everything they needed the subject to believe. Authenticity trumps role-playing every time.

"Okay, let's do this." She turned and pressed her thumb against the biometric security device mounted on the wall. A green LED flashed and the magnetic door lock clicked open. She grabbed the handle, opened the door, and led Allen into the room.

The Ember SCIF was a typical example of its kind—a spartan, windowless room, with both physical and electromagnetic shielding incorporated into its construction to prevent snooping. The only decoration was a framed picture of the President of the United States hanging on the wall opposite the one with the bank of monitors. All the room's regular furniture—a conference table and comfortable leather executive chairs—had been removed and replaced with a folding table and three hard plastic chairs. The Russian female they'd snatched in Klaipėda was bound with plastic flex-cuffs—wrists behind her back and ankles to the chair legs. She sat unmoving, body slumped and her hooded head bowed. To her credit, the woman did not flinch or tense at their entry.

Grimes stole a last look at Allen, whose face was now a mask—hard and fearless.

Without a word, Grimes walked over and removed the hood. With clinical detachment, she studied the girl who was now squinting against the brightly lit room. She was altogether unremarkable in appearance and presentation, with short-cropped chestnut hair, hazel-gray eyes, and average looks. Grimes pegged her at twenty-five or twenty-six, and with the exception of the tiny diamond stud piercing in her left nostril, she had no memorable characteristics. From her slight build and lack of muscle mass, the girl was not an operator and unlikely to be a physical threat, but Grimes was certain she was trained to resist interrogation.

"What is your name?" Grimes asked, walking around behind the girl. Baldwin and the boys had been unsuccessful in their efforts to identify her through any Five Eyes or Interpol databases. Discovering her name was Grimes's first objective.

The girl did not answer.

"We're going to be having many conversations," Grimes said, circling the table. "You can call me Virginia. What shall I call you?"

The girl sniffed but said nothing. Her face was stoic, but her eyes held fear.

"I know you speak English," Grimes continued, watching closely for her reactions to what she was about to say next. "I know you are a member of Spetsgruppa Zeta. I know your boss is Arkady Zhukov. I know you are a signals technician and communications specialist. Your partner has told us these things already."

Upon mention of Arkady's name, the girl flinched.

Hiding her satisfaction at this tiny victory, Grimes walked behind their guest and took a knee, inspecting the girl's hands for signs of loss of circulation from the bindings. Color was good, no swelling, skin not too cold to the touch. Everything Grimes had rattled off was educated conjecture based on the Zeta profile Ember had been building since enlisting Buz Wilson. Unfortunately, they knew little else, and time was of the essence. After learning of this agent's fate, Arkady would initiate defensive protocols—the same kind of protocols Ember had in place in the event their veil of anonymity was somehow pierced. They had a limited window of opportunity to extract actionable intelligence from this girl and hit Zeta where it mattered, before the elite Russian task force scattered like leaves in the wind.

"Would you like something to drink?" Grimes asked. "Water? Coffee . . ."

"Water please," the girl said in accented English after a long beat.

Without having to be told, Allen poured water from a pitcher on the table into a paper cup and helped the Russian drink.

"I know your organization has trained you on what to expect in this situation and how to resist interrogation and torture," Grimes said, walking around to the other side of the table to face the girl. "My colleague and I are similarly trained. We're both experienced in interrogation and being interrogated. I suspect you are less capable than the man you were running signals for, but we found ways to penetrate his armor. It required chemicals, which I'm afraid, typically results in irreparable damage. We'd hate to have to resort to similar methods with you."

The girl looked at her lap and said nothing.

"Look, we're all professionals here, so let's cut to the chase. Everybody breaks. It's not a matter of *if*, it's a matter of *when*." Out of the corner of her eye Grimes noticed Allen stiffen. "Now I know what you're thinking. You're thinking, 'Fuck this bitch, because there is nothing she can do to me that my people won't do to me tenfold when they find out what I confessed.' But I want you to put that idea completely out of your head, because they're not going to find you. Your people don't know about this place. No one knows about this place . . . not even *our* people know about this place. And if you don't talk to me here, we're going to move you to another place—a terrible place, where I promise you don't want to go. A place you can't come back from—not ever."

She watched the girl's lips purse ever so slightly, but with anger or anxiety she could not tell. Grimes turned to look at Allen and sensed that her collaborator had something to say. She nodded, and Allen sat down in one of the two vacant chairs across the table from the prisoner.

"I was once in your situation," Allen began, knitting her fingers together and placing her hands in her lap. "Quite recently in fact, but I didn't have the luxuries that you do now—like a chair . . . or clothes," she said, her voice flat but strong. "My interrogator said something I'll never forget for as long as I live . . . he said I had only one choice to make: I could either pick the hard way, or the easy way. We're offering you the same choice now. The easy way is simple—you answer our questions truthfully, tell us what we need to know, and the interrogation ends without further pain, humiliation, and deprivation. You will survive this. You are young, and if you choose this way, you even have an opportunity for a life beyond your situation. If you pick the hard way, choose not to cooperate with us, then the only thing you have to look forward to is misery and suffering."

To Grimes's surprise, the Russian girl looked up, met Allen's gaze, and said, "Which one did you pick?"

"What do you think?" Allen asked with a hard smile.

"Your face is unmarked, you don't walk with a limp, you seem to have your teeth—so you want me to believe you picked the easy way." Grimes saw Allen nodding. Then, taking them both by surprise, the girl began to laugh, "But I know that's not true, Amanda Allen, because he told me about you. Oh, yes . . . I know all about you. He told me everything. After that, I looked you up online. I wanted to know what you looked like—the American angel who enchanted the devil. But seeing you in person, I don't understand . . . I don't understand why—"

Grimes slammed her palm against the table with a resounding crack. To her surprise, Allen's strategy had backfired. The Russian had flipped the exchange and gained the upper hand, and in doing so, despite her unimposing physique, had proven she had mettle. Both the Russian and Allen flinched and turned to look at her. "Tell us your name," Grimes said, her voice as hard and baritone as she could muster.

"My name is *girl*," the Russian said.

"Where is the Zeta Operations Center?" Grimes said, unaffected by her belligerence.

"In Russia," the girl said.

"I'm going to give you one more chance to cooperate. If you don't answer my questions, I'm going to have to change interrogation strategies," she said. "It's a very simple question: What is your name?"

"Fuck you, American whore," the girl growled with defiance.

Message received.

"New York, are you listening?" Grimes said aloud.

"To every word," came Smith's reply over her earbud on the open channel with Munn. "Texas, are you ready?"

"Standing by," Munn answered.

Grimes glanced at Allen, then fixed her gaze on the Russian girl. "I think it's time we check in on your colleague so you can compare his experience to yours."

After she spoke, the bank of four monitors on the wall opposite the girl powered up, each showing a different live feed from the Ember locker room where an entirely different kind of interrogation was taking place. The upper-left monitor was a bird's-eye view from a ceiling-mounted camera. The camera was aimed down on a hulking male figure, bound to an armchair positioned in the middle of a heavy-duty plastic tarp spread out on the floor. The upper-right camera feed was zoomed in on a small table shrouded with a medical drape, which was splattered with copious amounts of blood. The table held sundry hand tools—hammer, pliers, heavy-duty pruning shears—and a polished metal tray with medical implements—syringes, vials of various liquids, scalpels, clamps, rubber tubing, and little piles of blood-soaked gauze. The bottom-left monitor showed a chest-level view of the scene from behind the captive, and the bottom-right monitor streamed footage from a camera positioned in the back corner.

Grimes watched the Russian girl's eyes tick from monitor to monitor to monitor, her gaze lingering on the feed showing the tools of torture the longest, before finally settling on the bird's-eye-view feed. In addition to the captive, two other people were present in the room—Munn and Wilson. The former was standing in front of the seated Russian, chest heaving, heavily muscled arms hanging at his sides, his black tactical gloves slick with blood. Wilson, who was dressed in slacks and a suit coat, was pacing the room talking.

"Can you turn up the audio, please?" Grimes said, and an instant later streaming audio accompanied the video feed.

Wilson was speaking in Russian, which neither Grimes nor Allen spoke, but that didn't matter because Baldwin gave them the play-by-play.

"He's asking the prisoner to report on when he last was present in the Zeta Operations Center," said Baldwin's voice on the open channel.

Grimes looked from the Russian girl to Allen and back again. Both women's eyes were transfixed on the bird's-eye-view camera feed, which, she had to admit, was a surprisingly intimidating and effective perspective—evoking a very similar sensation to what it felt like behind her sniper scope from a rooftop. It was the perspective of the high ground, the perspective of judgment and superiority . . .

The perspective of God.

The Russian man in the chair didn't answer, just sat slumped forward, his powerful shoulders rising and falling with each breath.

Buz said something in Russian, which Baldwin translated: "I couldn't hear you, comrade. Please speak up."

Munn looked over his shoulder at Buz, who responded with a nod. This nod earned the Russian a right hook to the side of the head. The blow snapped the man's head around ninety degrees, and something small and white flew out of his mouth and landed on the plastic sheet. Buz walked over to the white thing, picked it up between thumb and index finger, and dropped it onto the metal tray with a clink. The camera zoomed in, and Grimes saw that it was a tooth and noticed that there were two other teeth already on the tray.

Grimes looked at the Russian girl and saw that she'd gone a shade or two paler than she'd been moments ago. Then she stole a glance at Allen, who shivered, then closed her gaping mouth, shook her head, and regained control after the shock. She thought she was seeing her former tormentor. She thought she was watching Malik being tortured.

"How . . . how did you capture him?" The Russian girl shook her head from side to side and closed her eyes. "No, no, no. It can't be."

"It's him."

Grimes and the Russian girl both looked over at Allen. She'd folded her arms across her chest as if fighting off a chill. Her eyes remained hard, but her lower lip quivered.

"I want to go in the other room," Allen said, her voice a stiletto blade cutting through soft butter. "I want to help them with the work in the other room."

"Later," Grimes said. "You'll have your chance."

The Russian girl was staring at Allen, whose eyes remained transfixed on the monitors, unmoving, almost not breathing. Grimes walked over and took a seat on the corner of the table closest to the Russian girl. "This is what happens when you don't cooperate. Like you, your colleague has decided to be difficult. We gave him some special medicine to help loosen his tongue and, for a little while, he answered some of our questions. It was through this we learned not only that Arkady Zhukov is still very much alive but that he is the head of Zeta. He's told us other things, too, but those things must be confirmed. Unfortunately for your colleague, we can't give him any more drugs or we risk inducing a coma. His resistance to the chemical and enhanced interrogation stimuli has been remarkable. Normally, we don't get this aggressive so fast, but like I said, the situation is quite urgent. We need answers, and we need them now."

The girl said nothing, just stared at the screen.

"When were you last at the Zeta Operations Center?" Buz asked on camera, this time in English, but the question garnered no response from the captive.

"Tell me where I can find Arkady Zhukov?"

No response.

"Tell me the details of your next planned operation?"

No response.

"Last chance . . ."

No response.

Buz put his hands on his hips, and his expression turned grave. Munn looked at him for instruction, and the former CIA officer said, "Take his left thumb."

In the corner of her eye, Grimes saw Allen tense, but not so much as the Russian girl in front of her. She wondered what conflicting thoughts and feelings were coursing through her teammate's mind right now. A fresh wave of guilt swept over her, but she shrugged it off.

Munn walked to the table with the tools and surgical implements. He picked up the pruning shears and walked back over to the Russian. "Which thumb?" he asked.

"Start with the left thumb," Buz said.

"Nyet!" the Russian girl shouted, then fixed Grimes with a desperate glare. "Stop this, please. Don't do it."

The male prisoner's wrists were lashed to the arms of the chair, but when Munn tried to angle the pruning shears into position, the big Russian balled his fists and bounced wildly. The man's face remained in shadows, and Grimes watched as Allen shifted her position, as if trying get a better angle on the Russian's face. The chair tipped over and crashed onto its side. Munn kicked the captive in the stomach multiple times, then knelt and worked the open jaws of the pruning shears around the knuckle of the man's left thumb.

"Last chance, Malik," Buz said. The Russian spat a series of curses at his tormentor but apparently didn't give up any information because Buz shook his head and said, "Do it."

The mike in the room picked up a nauseating crunching sound as the pruning shears cut through bone and cartilage a split second before being drowned out by an inhuman wail of pain. Munn held up the thumb for inspection before walking callously over to deposit the amputated digit next to the pile of teeth.

"You're fucking animals," the Russian girl shouted, looking back and forth between Grimes and Allen. "Animals," she repeated, her eyes flooding with tears.

"You're not powerless in this situation," Grimes said to her. "You can make his suffering stop. You're a team. You can help your teammate by telling us what we need to know."

Next to her, Allen murmured something. Grimes turned. Allen's expression was braided with both sadistic satisfaction and revulsion, but the look in her eyes told Grimes that her teammate was close to breaking. She could practically hear the thoughts echoing in Allen's head, because they were the same thoughts she'd be thinking: *This is wrong; this isn't how Ember operates; this isn't who we are supposed to be.* She needed to close the deal before it all fell apart.

A guttural scream interrupted Grimes's thoughts and all eyes went to the monitors, where Munn, using the pliers, was crushing the Russian's right thumb knuckle in lieu of amputating it this time around.

"Stop it! Please stop it!" the Russian girl screamed.

"Will you answer my questions?" Grimes said. When she didn't answer, Grimes repeated herself, this time emphasizing each word: "Will . . . you . . . answer . . . my . . . questions?"

Panic consumed the girl as, on-screen, Buz pulled a subcompact from a chest holster and marched over to the captive lying on the floor, still bound to the chair. He waved Munn back and then looked up at the ceiling camera.

"This is a waste of time; he won't talk. Tell your girl she has five seconds to save his life." Buz pressed the muzzle of the pistol into the man's temple and started counting, "Five . . ."

"No!" Allen shouted, her eyes darting back and forth between the monitor, Grimes, and the girl. "You can't do this!"

"Four . . ."

"Give me something. Anything . . ." Grimes said, ignoring Allen and putting her hand on the girl's shoulder.

"Three . . ."

"I . . . I . . ." the girl stammered. "I can't . . ."

"Two . . ." Buz's voice echoed over the speakers, and in theatrical fashion the camera slowly zoomed in on the gun.

"It's in Vyborg," the Russian girl shouted.

"Vyborg?" Buz screwed up his face and looked up at the camera. "That doesn't make any sense. You're lying," he said and pressed the muzzle hard into the big Russian's temple.

"No, no, I promise," the girl said. "Arkady wanted a location away from Moscow. Somewhere convenient, but overlooked. Muscovites never go to Vyborg, and no one in America has ever heard of this place . . . and yet, it is nice place. Only 130 kilometers from Saint Petersburg and 30 kilometers from the Finnish border. Good infrastructure. A high-speed train. But you need to understand, most of the Zeta are in the field. You will find nobody there, except for analysts and support—people like me. That's all."

"Where in Vyborg? I want the address," Buz said.

"Please. There is no address. It is a compound south of Vyborg that I can show you on map."

Buz shook his head and placed the pistol against the side of the man's head again.

"It is the truth." The girl was sobbing now. "Please believe me. If he has told you otherwise, it is he who lied. His ability to resist is remarkable. Now will you stop his torture? Please."

"What is your next target?" Grimes asked, grabbing the girl by the chin and pulling her jaw until they were staring eye to eye.

"I don't know," the girl said. "Everything is compartmentalized. I work on one operation at a time."

"Tell me your name, or he dies," Grimes said, her voice hard as steel.

"Sylvie," she said quietly, looking down at her lap. "Sylvie Bessonov."

Grimes turned toward the ceiling camera in the SCIF with a look that said, *I believe her.*

Buz lowered his weapon.

"Okay, Sylvie. Your honesty won your comrade a stay of execution," Grimes said, looking back at the girl. "But we're not done here. Not even close."

"Cut the feed," Buz said, and the four monitors streaming video from the other interrogation room went dark.

Grimes glanced at Allen. "Let's go," she said and headed toward the door.

Wordlessly, Allen followed, but as soon as they were outside and the sound-insulated SCIF door was locked shut, her junior teammate erupted. "What the fuck was that, Elizabeth?"

"Follow me," Grimes said and turned down the hall, but Allen grabbed her upper arm. Grimes resisted the reflex to spin the hand on her arm and crack the wrist. Instead she let herself be pushed back into the wall by Allen.

"I had no idea," Allen growled. "When you recruited me for Ember, I thought I was joining America's best—the highest-caliber people, doing the highest-caliber work, for the highest-caliber reasons. Never in a million years did I think that the organization that rescued me from an enemy that kidnaps, tortures, and kills field agents would operate by the same barbaric code. My God, for a moment there I actually *enjoyed* what I was watching. What the hell are you turning me into?"

"Please, Amanda," Grimes said, taking her by the hand. "It's not what you think. Please just come with me."

She led her teammate down the hall, saying nothing until they were standing outside the door to the bunkroom. Then, and only then, did she turn to face Allen. "There's something you need to see," she said, reaching for the door handle.

"I'm serious, I don't want to see him. I mean, a part of me does, but it's not a good idea." A sob escaped her, but she held her head up. "I shouldn't go in."

"Trust me," Grimes said, opening the door and then ushering Allen inside with an arm around the shoulder. "You should."

They stepped inside. Munn was behind the chair, his back to them, cutting the plasti-cuffs binding the big Russian's ankles and wrists.

"Is that really a good idea?" Allen said, screwing up her face at him.

Munn, hearing the comment, turned to them and flashed Allen his best shit-eating grin. The Russian, now freed from his bindings, rolled his left wrist and then his right wrist, getting loud cracks from each. Next, he twisted his shoulders, earning a series of joint-popping cracks up and down his spine. With a weary groan, he got to his feet and turned to face them.

"Dempsey?" Allen said, her mouth agape, seeing his face out of shadow for the first time. "But I thought . . ."

"Yeah, well," he said, showing her both hands and wiggling his intact thumbs. "You thought wrong."

Allen's relief quickly turned to ire, and that ire was directed at Grimes.

"Why didn't you tell me?" she demanded. "Why would you do that to me? My God, that was . . ." She shook her head and walked across the room, staring at the wall.

"Cruel?" Grimes said, finishing Allen's sentence.

"I was going to say 'unprofessional,' but I'll take 'cruel' instead. Yeah—'cruel' works." The analyst wiped tears from her face with the back of a trembling hand.

"I know," Grimes said, bowing her head in apology. "And I'm sorry about that, but we needed this little charade to work. What I said back there about this being time critical was the truth. We needed Sylvie to talk and talk quickly before the window of opportunity to hit Zeta is lost. We didn't have time for a protracted interrogation. We needed to scare the shit out of that girl and do it in a way that didn't violate Ember's code of ethics."

"So was this your idea?" Allen asked.

"No. But it was a brilliant idea that I agreed with."

"But I saw Munn cut off your thumb and your tooth fly out," Allen said, looking back at Dempsey.

"It's called CGI, baby." Wang stood in the doorway separating the bunkroom from the adjacent locker room, holding a coffee cup in one hand and his laptop tucked under his other arm. "Computer-generated imagery, like special effects in a movie. We used the same software they use in Hollywood to generate the *effect* of the tooth flying out, the thumbs getting amputated, all the good stuff."

"We prerecorded most of the sequences," Dempsey explained.

"But you don't speak Russian, and I swear that was Malik's voice I heard."

"I had some voice intercepts from the failed hit on us in Klaipėda," Wang said, looking entirely too pleased with himself. "Enough data to reproduce the unique characteristics of Malik's voice and synthesize those simple exchanges convincingly."

Allen began to nod but then shook her head. "But I *saw* him. How could you reproduce his face?"

"What you saw were CGI overlays," Wang said. "And it didn't take much. The facial structure, jawline, physique—all of that is so similar between JD and Malik that all I had to do was give you just enough detail for your mind to fill in the blanks. You wanted to believe we had Malik bound to the chair, and so that's the picture we painted."

"We even have an execution sequence recorded and ready to use if necessary," Dempsey said, walking over to Allen. With a crooked grin, he threw an arm around her shoulder. "But don't worry, I survived it."

"But why?" Allen said, shrugging him off. "Why would you not tell me?"

Grimes felt her chest tighten as Allen's eyes bore into hers. She wasn't talking to the team but to *her*. Clearly, Allen felt betrayed by her most of all, for violating that which was sacrosanct in their relationship.

Must I say it? Isn't it obvious? Because the ends justified the means, dear girl. Because I'm a cold-hearted killer who can turn my heart on and off like a light switch . . . just like when I'm up on a rooftop.

But instead of saying these things, she walked over and took Allen by the hands. Her teammate tensed but didn't pull away. "I'm sorry, Amanda. More than you know. But if we had read you in to what we were doing, then you would not have reacted like you did. It was the authenticity of your reactions that tipped Sylvie into believing that she, too, was watching the real Malik getting tortured."

"And that was the only way?" Allen asked, sniffing and looking up at her.

"Yes," Grimes said with projected certainty. "At least we believed it was the best chance of success."

Allen nodded and pulled away. Then, she turned and walked over to Dempsey, where she gently touched an angry red welt on the side of his face.

"That looks real. And painful."

"Yeah, I have Captain Interrogation over there to thank for that," Dempsey said, jerking a thumb at Munn. "Apparently, lumberjacks don't know how to pull their punches."

"Buuuuullshit," Munn said drawing out the word, "That *was* me pulling a punch. The real problem is a particular retired, over-the-hill SEAL forgot to turn his head."

This garnered a laugh from everyone, even Dempsey.

"One last question," Allen said, eyeing Dempsey. "If you're Malik, then who is the hooded guy I saw you escorting off the plane in the hangar?"

"A Vory boss named Amarov," Dempsey said. "We've got plenty of questions for him, too, but breaking the Zeta girl was priority one."

"As much fun as this Hollywood production has been," said Smith over the intercom, "let's muster in the TOC and debrief this thing so we can start planning. We've got a lot of work to do and very little time to do it."

"Roger that, Skipper," Munn said and slapped Dempsey on the back on his way by. "Sorry about your face, bro."

"It's okay, Dan," Grimes said with a backward wink to Dempsey as she followed the doc out. "He wasn't so pretty to begin with."

CHAPTER 26

Zeta Compound (Bright Falcon)
South of Vyborg, Russia
June 19
0945 Local Time

"Get up," Valerian barked at the man bleeding at his feet.

The recruit, a powerfully built Spetsnaz operator who was down on hands and knees, shook his head trying to clear the stars undoubtedly swirling in his vision from Valerian's last blow.

"You're weak . . . and slow . . . and stupid. Get up."

The recruit grunted and pressed to his feet. Valerian contemplated three different strikes he could have used to end the session, but he showed restraint and waited for his adversary to get into a fighting stance.

"You fight dirty," the recruit said and spat a glob of bloody mucus on the ground. Valerian had jumped the recruit while the man was walking to the range, and the operator had not been ready. This was one of Arkady's favorite drills—one he called *watch your back*—and it was a lesson all commissioned Zeta operatives never forgot. Situational awareness and omnipresent distrust were the qualities that kept an operative alive in the field.

Yes, *every* situation was potentially dangerous.

Yes, *everyone* was a threat . . . including one's allies.

Maybe this bull would learn, or maybe he would be slaughtered. Valerian didn't care. He wasn't mentor material. He'd picked this fight because he was angry about the botched hit in Riga and what happened to Sylvie, not for training purposes. He hated Vyborg. He hated this compound. The only reason he ever came here was when he was ordered here or when he wanted to hurt someone without professional, legal, or civil repercussions. He'd hurt a lot of people at Bright Falcon over the years.

Hurting people felt good.

"Well, aren't you going to say something?" the former Spetsnaz man said, glaring at Valerian, his fists up.

"And on the fourth day, the wicked sisters became so jealous of Maryushka that they fixed knives to the sill outside her bedroom window and locked it shut," Valerian said, reciting from memory his favorite passage from the Russian folk story after which Arkady had named this facility. "That night when Finest, the Bright Falcon, appeared at the cottage to visit his beloved, he found the window shut. He fluttered, flapped, and beat against the panes trying to get in, but the wicked sisters' blades cut his powerful breasts to ribbons. Poor, clueless Maryushka slept through it all—oblivious to her magical lover's suffering. Finally, unable to enter and to transform from falcon into a man, Finest decried, 'If you love me, you can find me, but not without pain.' Then, the Bright Falcon, flew far, far away, leaving behind nothing but his blood on the window . . ."

"You're fucking crazy, you know that," the recruit said. "But I'm going to kick your ass anyway."

A malevolent grin spread across Valerian's face. "Now that's the spirit, my little Maryushka. Do your worst."

The remainder of the sparring match did not go well for the recruit. Despite the other man's determination, he was ill equipped to challenge a Prime. Rather than doing any permanent and lasting damage, he finished off his adversary with a choke hold, leaving the Zeta recruit lying passed out in the dirt.

"And I had such high hopes for that one," Arkady lamented from where he stood several meters away, staring down at the pile of unconscious muscle at Valerian's feet.

Valerian had observed the spymaster's stealth approach in his peripheral vision and had kept an eye on Arkady during the sparring lest he fall victim to the same "watch your back" training lesson he was imparting. Arkady had a penchant for untelegraphed blows to the kidney and solar plexus. He'd belted Valerian once while they were celebrating a win with a bottle of vodka. The old man was such a dick.

"I wouldn't count him out yet," Valerian replied, dusting his clothes off. "He bit a chunk out of my forearm while we were grappling."

Arkady's gaze flicked to the blood running down Valerian's left arm and dripping off the back of his hand. "I would clean that immediately or you're going to get an infection. The human mouth is disgusting. If people knew the truth, there would be no kissing in the world."

Valerian dismissed the comment with a smile and got straight to the point. "Are you revoking my status as Prime?"

"It's what you deserve, but unfortunately I don't have a suitable replacement," Arkady said plainly before turning and waving Valerian to follow him. "Walk with me."

Valerian hesitated a second, then did as he was told, catching up to his boss and accompanying him on the short walk to the admin building.

"Tell me, did you hit your head, Valerian? Because I want to know what is going on with you. Ever since Istanbul, your judgment has been terrible. We both know what type of operations our Vory partners are suited for and what type of operations they are not. I appreciate the fact that you are trying to be proactive against the enemy while masking our presence, but the Americans are not fooled. Why would you think that after failing in Narva, you could use Vory knuckle-draggers to take the Ember team in Klaipėda? It wasn't an accident the Americans were there. They know we sunk the *Independence*. They know we run the Malik legend, and they know we were behind the operations in Turkey." Arkady sighed and then turned to face him. "As Prime, you need to be thinking at my level. That's the point of our system. If I was a young man, I'd be in the field doing these things myself, but I'm not, which is why I need to be able to count on you to act as my proxy."

"If the hit had succeeded, you'd be singing my praises right now. Hindsight is perfect vision, but at the time I was thanking fate for my good fortune. They came to me, to the same hotel! I had their location and I had the assets at my disposal to make the hit. Frankly, it would have been irresponsible of me *not* to try. I took a calculated risk, and it didn't work out in my favor. I don't think it is a question of my judgment but rather a question of outcome."

Valerian followed Arkady into a room and shut the door behind them. A series of A4-size photographs were spread out on a table. Without asking, Valerian began to leaf through the lot.

"I'm sorry, Valerian, but in the spy business, operatives are defined by the outcomes they achieve. The best operative is the one who bends fate to his will. Make no mistake, what you orchestrated at the hotel in Klaipėda was a disaster. The world thinks the American FBI was targeted as retaliation for the investigation of the sinking of the *Independence*; they don't know about Task Force Ember and they never will. But that won't stop the media from running stories speculating that Russia was behind the sinking—the exact opposite of what we wanted." Arkady shook his head in frustration. "And on top of that, Amarov was taken—one of our oldest and most loyal partners, Valerian! The other Vory bosses have heard what happened and now they're talking—not to me, but to each other. In three days, you've managed to walk back two decades of a carefully cultivated partnership with the Vory!"

"That's ridiculous."

"Is it?" Arkady said, rubbing his heavy beard. "The hit has drawn Lithuanian State Police scrutiny and Interpol's attention, and it's given them the excuse they needed to root out and prosecute not only what's left of Amarov's operation but every other Vory cell operating in country."

Valerian averted his gaze. "I'm sorry."

"Sorry doesn't fix this mess," Arkady growled, the baritone of approaching thunder. "Sorry doesn't change the fact that the Americans took Sylvie!"

"What are you talking about? We aborted. I was talking to her all the way to the car."

"And did you pick her up? Did you take her with you to Kaliningrad?"

"No, but that was never the plan. We had separate exfils. It's much safer that way. You taught me that."

"She's Zeta cyber, not an operator," Arkady said, his expression hard. "You drafted her for the op and then you left her—left her to die. But instead, the Americans took her. Make no mistake, they will break her, and when they do, Ember will harvest reams of damaging information about our operation."

"Then I'll just have to put a bullet in her head before that happens. Is this the compound where the Americans are holding her?" Valerian said, tapping one of the photographs.

Arkady nodded.

"Where is it?"

"Newport News, Virginia."

"Shit," Valerian murmured his bravado tempered.

"This aircraft hangar is where the Ember Operations Center is located," Arkady said, tapping his index finger on the building in one of the photographs. "And I believe it is where Sylvie is being held."

"But this looks like a civilian airport," Valerian said, flipping through the spy satellite photos. "Why is it not on a military base? I don't understand. It's vulnerable here. Completely unprotected."

"Kelso Jarvis decided to hide the crown jewel in plain sight," Arkady said. "A strategy I have employed many times myself. In fact, I chose this location for similar reasons. Who would think to look in Vyborg for us, and more importantly, it is far away from Moscow."

"Yes, but Bright Falcon is secure and very difficult to access."

"I think Jarvis has a trick or two up his sleeve. My source tells me the facility is underground in a hardened bunker. I think you will find the mission a greater challenge than you think."

"That's why you summoned me here. You want me to get Sylvie out?"

Arkady shook his head. "She knows too much. I can't let them harvest information from her indefinitely. If you can get her out alive, that's good; I can find out what she's told them. But a bullet in the head will achieve the goal, too."

"And the facility?"

"Blow it up. Kill everyone. We need to strike now before Sylvie breaks and Jarvis decides to attack our operations," Arkady said.

"This is no small endeavor." Valerian blew air through his teeth. "First, I need to put a team together. Second, we need to get into the US, which is not as easy as it used to be. Once we're in country, we'll need to conduct ISR, develop a tactical plan, task and reposition Zeta assets, and figure out how to egress."

"It's all done," Arkady said with a harsh smile.

"What?" Valerian said, taken aback. "I don't understand. What are you talking about?"

"While you were fucking things up in Klaipėda, what do you think I've been doing?" Arkady slid a hip over the edge of the table to sit on the corner. "Everything has been arranged. Gavriil is in Virginia with

Franco and Yukov. You leave first thing tomorrow on a flight from Helsinki to Washington. Kostya is going with you from here."

Valerian kept his face a mask as his mind processed everything the old fox had said and everything he hadn't. Something didn't feel right. Kostya was past his prime and head of training at Vyborg; it had been at least five years since he'd been in the field. Gavriil operated out of Moscow, not America. Arkady was clearly grooming him to become a Prime, and Valerian had pegged him long ago as the old man's first choice for his successor. Franco and Yukov were both experienced field agents, but since Zetas generally worked alone, he'd not met either of them. This operation would be the largest gathering of veteran Zeta principals in one place since Valerian had joined the organization. The whole thing had a very fatalistic aura to it; it suddenly felt like a compulsory suicide mission.

Every Zeta knew he had an expiration date.

Maybe the old fox intends this to be a one-way trip for me? Well, if only one Zeta is meant to walk away from this operation, then that Zeta is going to be me.

"What's that look for?" Arkady said with a paternal half smile.

"I don't need a babysitter. Kostya can stay behind."

"*Nyet.* Five is the minimum required for this assault," Arkady said. "Some of you won't be coming home. That I can almost guarantee."

There was no point in arguing with the spymaster. This was Arkady's chess match, and he didn't take counsel from the pieces on the board.

"In that case, I need to go to Saint Petersburg and set my affairs in order," Valerian said with fatalistic determinism, turning to look at his once friend and mentor.

"Of course. Let me drive you," Arkady said with a smile. "I have a car."

"Thank you, old friend," Valerian said and clasped the man on the shoulder. "But I think I can handle this alone."

"Very well," the spymaster said and pulled Valerian in for a powerful hug. "Good luck, my son. And don't fail me again."

CHAPTER 27

Ember Tactical Operations Center
Beneath the Ember Hangar
Newport News/Williamsburg International Airport
Newport News, Virginia
June 20
0615 Local Time

When Kelso Jarvis stepped into the Ember conference room, Dempsey popped to his feet. He hadn't been active duty for two years, but it didn't matter. Old habits die hard . . . and Jarvis had that effect on people. Everyone else was on their feet, too.

"Hey, John," Jarvis said, greeting Dempsey before anybody else in the room. "Been a while, hasn't it?"

"If you don't count Istanbul, then yeah, it's been almost a year," Dempsey said. "How you doing, Skipper?"

"Sharp as I've ever been," Jarvis said, but then with a wan smile he gestured to himself below the neck. "But sitting behind a desk all day every day isn't doing the rest of me any good. I'm drinking so much coffee these days, I've got the shakes half the time."

Dempsey tried to think of something to say back to this strange comment, but the DNI had already moved on to greeting Grimes.

"Elizabeth," Jarvis said with a nod. "I'm hearing only good things from Director Smith about your performance in your new role as overwatch and team sniper. Helluva job you did in Adana, by the way. Not sure if you heard, but the President, SecDef, and the Joint Chiefs watched you in action on that one from the Situation Room."

"Thank you, sir," she said with an easy yet respectful formality that Dempsey took to mean that the contentiousness in their relationship from the early days in Ember was water under the bridge, or at least for now. For the briefest of moments, he could have sworn he saw her cheeks rosy up with the compliment.

When Jarvis got to Munn, the doc made a point of walking over to shake Jarvis's hand, an awkward evolution that Dempsey decided was deliberate on Munn's part, but to what end Dempsey wasn't sure. Jarvis asked Munn why he wasn't decked out like a proper lumberjack, and Munn quipped that he'd had to retire his Woolworth plaids because they made Smith and the other Army guys insecure. Jarvis chuckled at the old inside joke about Munn's ever-present backwoods appearance on the job. Whether working as a surgeon or a SEAL, Munn always looked like a walking L.L.Bean advertisement. Jarvis then quickly greeted the rest of the gang before walking over to Smith, who asked everyone to take a seat around the conference table.

Jarvis whispered with his Chief of Staff, a woman Dempsey had not met in person but remembered well as one of the best intelligence analysts and counterintelligence officers ever to serve at the Tier One back in the day. He'd known her only by her impeccable reputation—one that had continued to grow in her new role. In Istanbul, Petra

Felsk had taken a bullet for Jarvis—something even Dempsey could not claim with his pedigree. A moment later, they both sat down, with Jarvis eschewing the podium for a seat at the table.

"When President Warner tapped me to assume the Office of the DNI, the primary factor in my decision to accept the appointment was the confidence and esteem I held for the people in this room. I knew that when I handed the reins over to Shane, the combination of his leadership style and my absence would allow Ember to grow and evolve into something even more potent and capable than it was under my direct command." Jarvis looked around at the team. "In the beginning, before Ember found its footing, I was the right man for the job. But as with all organizations—from Silicon Valley start-ups to the White House—change is not only inevitable, it is necessary. The leadership team that's in place now has expanded Ember's charter, capabilities, and, dare I admit, effectiveness. I'm telling you these things because I want everyone to understand this is not an intervention . . . I'm here as a harbinger. Ember has been targeted by an organization that, up until a month ago, we didn't even know existed."

Jarvis waited for it to sink in—watched their stunned faces as they looked at one another. He waited until their eyes turned back to him.

"Make no mistake, Spetsgruppa Zeta is Russia's Ember—an evil twin with matching resources, capabilities, and autonomy. The characteristics that have made Ember so lethal and effective also apply to Zeta. When I informed the President that Zeta was behind the assassination effort in Istanbul last month, he took it personally. The sinking of the *Independence* in Klaipėda this week was the proverbial nail in the coffin. President Warner has directed me to revise Ember's charter. I informed Director Smith of the President's order over the phone, but I felt it was both important and necessary that I speak to all of you in person.

"Effective immediately," Jarvis said, "Task Force Ember will locate, prosecute, and eliminate Spetsgruppa Zeta and all her members. The murder squad that targeted us in Klaipėda was no coincidence, and taking one of their people will not go unnoticed. It will also not go unpunished. They will retaliate and they will escalate. Which is why we must act first. All other counterterrorism operations and intelligence-gathering missions are suspended until further notice. *This* is your single priority."

Dempsey leaned back in his chair and took the temperature of the room. After barely escaping Klaipėda with their lives, they'd been operating with both extreme caution and prejudice, but to have the official mandate delivered in person by the DNI made it real. The order to take out Zeta had come directly from the President of the United States. To give such an order, even when it was intended to stay buried in black, was symbolic—America and Russia were officially at war. Dempsey shifted his gaze to Buz, the only real Cold Warrior in the room, and found the man's expression had gone hard and grim. Dempsey knew that look; he'd worn it himself many, many times over the years. This change in charter represented a political pivot. The gloves were coming off, and things with America's old nemesis on the other side of the world were about to get much, much worse before they had any chance of getting better.

"Does anyone have any questions for the DNI?" Smith said expectantly. Normally, this was the part of the brief where Grimes would express her misgivings about the wisdom of the plan, Adamo would question the veracity or prudence of some element of the strategy, and Munn would whisper a wisecrack and demand a celebratory *let's get it on* fist bump from Dempsey. Today none of these things happened, and Dempsey understood why. This time, Ember and everyone in its chain of command, including the President of the United States, was being targeted. What was there to debate? What was there to argue about? This was a kill-or-be-killed scenario and everyone in the room recognized it.

When no one spoke, Smith turned to Adamo. "All right, Ops O, why don't you bring everyone up to speed on the plan you've been working on."

Adamo pushed his glasses up onto the bridge of his nose, a nervous habit that in other circumstances would have made Munn and Dempsey chuckle. Not today. "Our detainee stated that the Zeta Operations Center is located in Vyborg," he began. "Baldwin and his team have been working around the clock, revisiting all the SIGINT data collected during our recent ops in Narva, Riga, and Klaipėda. In the Narva and Klaipėda events, outgoing transmissions were traced to Vyborg. While that alone is not conclusive proof that Vyborg houses the Zeta command and control center, it is compelling evidence. Strategically speaking, while this location is preferable to, say, Moscow or some location in the heart of Russia, Vyborg does pose geographical, logistical, and tactical problems for an operation."

On this cue, Baldwin opened the notebook computer in front of him and began typing. The screensaver on the central monitor in the room refreshed to display a map of the Gulf of Finland with Finland to the north, Russia to the east, and Estonia to the south. Next, an overlay appeared showing the territorial waters claimed by each nation, dividing the waterway into three areas with a maritime traffic scheme highlighted in the middle. A red dot appeared at the far eastern end of the Gulf of Finland at the back of a bay sheltered and blockaded by dozens of islands.

"The red dot is Vyborg," Adamo continued. "It's located approximately twenty-five kilometers south of the Finnish border. I tasked Baldwin and his team to take a very hard look at Vyborg and the surrounding areas and give me possible locations for an operations and training center." He tapped a button on his laptop. "This is what they turned up."

The satellite aerial map zoomed in on a peninsular region south of the city, and Baldwin began to speak. "The west side of the peninsula presents access to Vyborg Bay and the eastern side to what appears to be a brackish, marshy inland lagoon. There's a small marina on the northern tip of the landmass and a two-lane road, Primorskoye Shosse, in good repair that runs north–south in the middle of the peninsula before turning east into Vyborg proper. What got my attention are the similarities between this area and our own Camp Peary up the road. If you look here, near the bottom of the peninsula, this is clearly a water treatment facility, but these structures to the north along the shoreline and nestled into the woods are more interesting. This cluster of buildings could be anything, but the layout does, again, remind me of Camp Peary. The easternmost building looks like a dormitory or dining hall, this building to the north could be admin and classrooms, and this building here to the west looks a lot like an armory and kill hall. This paved area here is meant to look like parking, but I've never seen a parking lot with a wind sock and touchdown and liftoff lights, which tells me it's a helo pad. Lastly, there's a hardened radio antenna north of the facility, and these here look like backup diesel generator sets. When considered in total, the empirical evidence makes a compelling case that this is not some Russian summer Camp Ivanhoe."

"Is that residential housing on the east side of the peninsula?" Munn asked.

"Yes, it appears so," Baldwin replied. "And if you look closely, you'll see fencing on the east side of Primorskoye Shosse, enclosing an area which we estimate to be around three hundred acres—further support that this is not a civilian facility. The last item of interest concerns a structure on this island about half a nautical mile offshore. Without better imagery, I can't tell you what it is or whether it is associated with the compound."

"Ian, why don't you tell them about the recent intercepts?" Adamo prompted.

"Ah yes. After identifying the antennae, I had a friend at the NSA reach out to Supo in Helsinki to see if they monitor communications from this antenna. As it turns out, we aren't the only ones interested in this facility. Finnish Intelligence monitors Vyborg traffic and was kind enough to provide us with logged data collected over the past forty-eight hours. In analyzing this data, Chip and Dale have determined that the overwhelming majority of the data traffic processed by this tower is civilian GSM traffic encrypted with 64-bit A5/1 protocol and LTE traffic encrypted with standard 128-bit EPS integrity algorithms. However, a small percentage of the traffic is 128 bit with novel military-grade ciphering. I believe this is by design. I think this antenna primarily serves civilian and commercial traffic from Vyborg, and the hard-encrypted traffic from the compound is sprinkled in below a threshold that would draw attention from snooping ears to the north."

Dempsey rolled his eyes at Baldwin's encryption mumbo jumbo and said, "And your point?"

"My point is that we managed to decrypt one of these transmissions and we have a high degree of confidence that it is a conversation between Arkady Zhukov himself and Vladimir Petrov in the Kremlin."

"Well, holy shit, why didn't you lead with that?" Munn looked heavenward with a *God help me* expression.

Baldwin was about to answer when Smith held up his hand.

"I think the point is that we have strong confirming evidence to support our Zeta detainee's admission that Vyborg is home to a secret Zeta command and control facility and that the head of the organization, Arkady Zhukov, is there as we speak. As of twenty minutes ago, satellite IR showed nineteen warm bodies at the compound. This is it, people. We found the Russian Ember."

"I agree with what Baldwin said earlier about this compound resembling a poor man's Camp Peary," Dempsey said. "And let's assume for a moment we're convinced this is the Zeta HQ. I think we need to discuss whether hitting this target is realistic. Access is hard enough, but once the shit hits the fan they're going to send a QRF after us, and I don't see how we're going to egress without ending up dead."

"Agreed," Adamo said. "That's my concern as well."

Dempsey pushed his chair back from the table, looking from Jarvis to the monitor and back again. "If I may, sir?"

"By all means, John. Talk us through what you're thinking."

Dempsey nodded and walked up to the monitor so he could point and talk at the same time. "Ian, if you could zoom us out a bit, to say one-nautical-mile-per-inch scale . . . yeah like that. So if you look at this overlay you can see how far we have to go to make a stealth approach. Now, can you measure from the line marking the edge of Russian territorial waters to Vyborg?" A cursor appeared on the screen and Ian deposited a waypoint on the Zeta compound and then stretched a line west until it reached the demarcation between Russian and Finnish territorial waters. "Yeah, like that. So we're looking at around forty nautical miles as the crow flies, make that forty-five by the time you dodge all these islands and pass through this strait here at Vysotsk, or however the hell you pronounce it. That's a ninety-mile round trip minimum. There's no way we can make that in a submarine."

"And even if you could, where are you going to find a submarine skipper crazy enough to drive his boat into the Gulf of Finland? Can't be more than thirty meters deep here," Munn chimed in.

"I've already spoken to COMSUBLANT, Vice Admiral Rousselot, about sending one of his SSNs into the Baltic, and he politely informed me that such a request was a nonstarter," Jarvis said. "Access to the Baltic requires a surfaced transit, because it's too shallow to navigate submerged around Denmark. Moreover, the Admiral feels strongly that the Baltic Sea is simply too shallow to risk SSN operations. Once you're in, there's no escape to deep water, which means nowhere to run and nowhere to hide if things go bad. I looked at the bathymetry and the Admiral is right: most of the Baltic Sea is shallower than a *Virginia*-class submarine is long."

"The Swedes have three AIP subs, if I'm not mistaken. *Gotland* class," Grimes said, speaking up for the first time. "And the Germans have their Type 212 diesel-electric boats. The *Gotland* and the 212 are about half the length of one of our SSNs, and they're experienced at operating in the Baltic. Maybe they can help us out."

"Not in this political climate," Jarvis said. "The German Chancellor is furious with the Warner administration over the Nord Stream 2 sanctions, so we can't count on Berlin for help. And the Swedes are still digesting the sinking of the *Independence* in Klaipėda. They want to conduct their own investigation before placing blame on the Kremlin and poking the bear. Which means, unfortunately, hitching a ride on a *Gotland* is also a nonstarter."

"We can't take a small boat, " Dempsey said. "It's too far to travel undetected. This ain't Al Wadi Thar Thar during Operation Dagger. Instead of goat herders scanning from shore, we'll have Russian air assets protecting the approach and their satellite net watching from above. And I think we can all agree that an air infil and egress is not an option. Nowhere to jump that's not a long-ass hike, some of it through neighborhoods—not cool for dudes with guns."

"What about the Proteus?" Munn said, sitting up straight in his chair. "I've never ridden on it, but from what I hear it has plenty of range."

Dempsey rubbed his chin. "Not a bad idea, Dan. That could work."

"What's the Proteus?" Latif asked.

"The Proteus is a badass prototype minisub," Dempsey answered. "It's like an SDV but on steroids—better equipped and super stealthy, with a faster cruising speed, longer range, and room for six SEALs, ten when you strip it down and limit what you bring. It's new and I haven't seen it, but the rumor is it can deliver payload to the seafloor and operate autonomously like a drone." What Dempsey didn't say was that the Proteus was not a dry-delivery solution. Like an SDV, when submerged the internal compartment of the Proteus flooded and equalized pressure with the ocean at depth. Anyone who participated on this mission needed to be an experienced diver prepared for a period of nitrogen decompression. The stakes were too high for on-the-job training. The truth was, by incorporating the Proteus, this was no longer an Ember mission; it became a Tier One SEAL mission. To pull this off, he needed more than a shit-hot tac team. He needed more than the world's most lethal counterterrorism task force. He needed Thiel and Spaz, Rousch and Gator—he needed his old teammates, but they were all dead and buried.

He shook off the sudden wave of melancholy and looked at Munn, who nodded, reading his mind. The old team was gone, but thankfully, they knew a guy . . .

"Proteus sounds like the solution we need. I'll find out where it is and when we can get our hands on it," Adamo said and then turned to Jarvis. "That is assuming we have the green light to use this asset, sir?"

"You do, Mr. Adamo," Jarvis said with a note of finality in his voice.

Dempsey cleared his throat and knew his next statement was going to piss off some people—most notably Grimes.

"Sir, the only other concern regards personnel for the op. If we infil using a long-range submersible, that's going to limit us to experienced SEALs with significant dive training. We'll need the SDV pilots assigned to work with Proteus, but I suggest we also augment with a small team of operators from the newly stood-up Tier One SEAL Team."

In his peripheral vision, he saw Grimes lean forward to object, but Jarvis cut her off.

"I agree completely. We need a team experienced in this sort of infil and comfortable in submersibles. I'll take care of that for you immediately." Grimes crossed her arms, and Dempsey felt her glare on his back. "I think this is a good place to break. You all have a lot of homework to do. Once you have a viable plan, Director Smith can brief me on the details. As for now, I'd like to have a quick chat with just the principals for a moment." The DNI rose, ending the meeting. "Thank you."

Dempsey felt Grimes's eyes on him, and he turned to look at her as she slid back from the table and stood. No words were necessary—he knew her well enough to read in her eyes that she'd reached the same conclusions he had. The risk-reward balance was skewed heavily to the risk side of the equation. The geopolitical stakes from a failed mission were sphincter-clenchingly bad. And if the team were captured—an abnormally high probability given the five-hour, ten-knot egress back to Finnish water—the horrors that awaited them in the basement of Lubyanka prison were unimaginable.

He nodded at her—*it'll all work out.*

Munn gave him a pat on the shoulder before filing out of the conference room with the others. When the door finally shut, only Smith, Adamo, Baldwin, and Dempsey remained behind with the DNI and his Chief of Staff. Jarvis, who had been talking quietly with Petra, turned to face the group. With a tight smile, he knitted his fingers together and rested his clasped hands on the table. "All right, gents, this is your chance to tell me what you really think, so don't pull your punches."

"I thought the operation to snatch Modiri in Tehran was a suicide mission, but Dempsey walked away from that," said Smith, taking the lead. "This mission has higher geopolitical stakes, but provided the team can get back into the water before the Russian QRF arrives on-site, I think a stealth exfil in the Proteus is doable, but only if our goal is to take out their command and control. If the objective is to disappear Arkady and harvest hard drives, forget it. So, I want to be crystal clear that *if* we do this, it has to be get in fast, kill everyone, blow up the facility, and then disappear back into the water. The Russians won't be looking for a submersible because SDVs are range limited, and as it was pointed out, it's too shallow for an SSN in the Gulf of Finland."

Dempsey nodded. "I agree with Shane, but I've been thinking, even with the Proteus, delivery is still a problem. Assuming we can get our hands on it, how in God's name do we deploy it?"

"Petra and I were just talking about that, and I think we might have a solution," Jarvis said.

"In my previous life, I worked at the Office of Naval Intelligence," Petra said. "And during my tenure, I ran across all kinds of interesting tech. A couple of months before I left, my counterpart in the UK told me about some very interesting work he was doing involving a mother ship—disguised as a civilian vessel—to deploy unmanned underwater vehicles. I think that could be the golden ticket for this operation, but I need to give him a call."

Smart thinking, Dempsey acknowledged with a nod.

"Simon, what's on your mind?" Jarvis said. "I can see something is bothering you."

"We're rushing this," Adamo said through an exhale. "If you had ordered us to hit a target on Russian soil a year ago, I would have called you insane. But then we pulled off Operation Crusader, which recalibrated my thinking. And then Ankara and Istanbul happened . . . and we all know how that story ended. I recognize the urgency of this operation. Zeta is a clear and present danger to everyone in this compound. I know these bastards have to be stopped, but this op feels like forcing a square peg into a round hole. Yes, we have SIGINT indicating Arkady is on-site, and satellite imagery supports a paramilitary presence, but wouldn't it be nice to know exactly what we're hitting? There has to be a better option than rushing this op without all the data."

"I agree with you, and in a perfect world I would give you all the time and resources you need to plan the perfect op. But we're on the clock, locked in a match to the death with a chess master who's been consistently one step ahead of us. Arkady knows we took one of his people. He knows we're going to break her and that she's going to talk. I promise you, he's prepping his next move; that is, if he hasn't set the wheels in motion already. If I were in his shoes, I'd already be looking for a new home base and would vacate the Vyborg facility as soon as possible. We're never going to get another shot at this. Can I guarantee this op will drive a stake through the heart of Zeta? No, I can't, but if we bag Arkady Zhukov, decimate their command and control infrastructure, and take out nineteen Zeta personnel, well . . . let's just say that what's left of Spetsgruppa Zeta will be on life support."

Adamo nodded, sniffed, and pushed his glasses up onto the bridge of his nose with a finger pistol. "You can count on me, Director Jarvis."

"I know," Jarvis said, then turned to Dempsey. "What about you, John? Comments or concerns?"

Dempsey flashed his former CO a crooked grin. "Truth is, I've got nothing better to do, Skipper. You can count me in."

"Hooyah, frogman," Jarvis said through a chuckle, then leaned back in his chair comfortably and dropped his hands into his lap. "All right, y'all are dismissed. I need to talk to Shane for a few minutes."

Dempsey pressed to his feet. He nodded at Petra and then met Jarvis's gaze. "I'll see you on the other side, Skipper."

"Good luck, John," Jarvis said, and then like the SEAL Dempsey had once served under, he added, "Be the night."

CHAPTER 28

The Atlantic Zeus
Secret British SBS Mother Ship and SIGINT Platform Operating
as a Garbage Ship
Gulf of Finland, Twenty Nautical Miles South of Kotka, Finland
June 22
2040 Local Time

Dempsey sighed.

"Whatcha thinkin' about?" Munn asked from the narrow bunk across from him in the visitors' quarters.

Oh, I'm just thinking about the Iranian double agent who I slept with, left to die, and who has haunted my dreams for the past year—a woman who has since apparently risen from the dead to stalk me, infiltrate our top-secret operations, and assassinate my sources in broad daylight. That's what I'm thinkin' about, dude.

But he didn't want to go there; he really didn't. He'd not shared his conflicted feelings about Elinor with anyone, despite Munn's and Grimes's repeated attempts to play headshrinker with him. This was the problem with *the waiting*—the worst part of an operator's job. It left you with abundant time to think about things best left alone.

"I'm thinking about Jake," he lied, turning his head to look at his friend. Munn knew that Dempsey's son had begun the long journey to earn a trident. Dempsey had mixed feelings about his son following in his footsteps as a Navy SEAL recruit. No, not in his footsteps, in Jack Kemper's footsteps—the father Jake thought was dead. There were so many things Jack Kemper would have told his son. He would have told him that he had nothing to prove, that his death had been avenged and that was not Jake's responsibility now, and that choosing the life of a SEAL came with a high price . . .

"He's in Great Lakes, right?" Munn said.

"Yeah."

"Anything noteworthy on Kate's Facebook?"

"Nah."

The truth was there'd been plenty on Kate's Facebook account the last time he'd checked. Pictures of the happy couple, now that she had remarried. It was painful to see. Even before he'd "died" she'd been in the process of moving on. *But still* . . . A strange pang of guilt blossomed in his gut. Here he was obsessing over Elinor when he *should* be obsessing over Jake and Kate.

I wonder what the headshrinkers would have to say about that?

Munn gave him a little grace and thankfully didn't press.

The ship rocked gently back and forth, and Dempsey stared up at the bottom of the bunk above him. Someone had scratched the words "Bitch don't cry" into the paint on the underside of the bed pan. Dempsey gave a weary smile. Sage advice from another shadow soldier like him, no doubt—someone familiar with the headspace trap every operator fell into when he should have been sleeping.

A sharp rap on the door snapped him from his thoughts. He turned as the hatch swung open, creaking on rusty hinges corroded by the omnipresent salt air.

"They're here," Grimes said, sticking her head in through the gap. The wafting smell of putrid garbage accompanied her from the hall. The smell had been even worse when they'd approached the ship south of Helsinki, and despite being on board for over twelve hours, his nose had yet to completely acclimate to it. But for the calm seas, even his iron stomach would be roiling right now.

Dempsey swung his legs off the bunk and a middle-aged grunt escaped him as he sat up, surprising him. Munn cocked an eyebrow at him but wisely said nothing. They followed Grimes a short distance to the ship's TOC—a stark contrast to the rest of the vessel with its clean high-tech design, computer equipment, and furnishings. Even the air inside smelled fresher, and Dempsey suspected the space was equipped with its own air-filtration system.

As he looked around the superslick TOC, he couldn't help but think what a true marvel the *Atlantic Zeus* was. From all outward appearances, it was a garbage ship—ferrying around and handling real garbage—but hidden beneath the rust, the trash, and the stench was a state-of-the-art multipurpose platform designed to covertly collect signals intelligence *and* transport British Special Boat Service operators.

Colloquially known as a "mother ship," the *Atlantic Zeus* was outfitted with a camouflaged antennae array that would make the NSA jealous and a submersible delivery bay that was one of the coolest things Dempsey had ever seen. The ship's modified hull and propulsor station systems were hidden from view below the waterline, permitting total stealth for submersible launch and recovery operations. During their tour, the ship's skipper had explained why the ship didn't flood when they opened the bay doors. The principle was the same as why an inner tube didn't sink despite having a hole in the middle. A series of ballast tanks gave the ship sufficient surplus buoyancy so that opening the underwater bay doors didn't flood the vessel.

Upon entering the TOC, Dempsey's gaze immediately went to the four men dressed in 5.11 Tactical blue jeans and plaid shirts talking quietly in a huddle. They wore their hair long and their faces in full beards. Two of the operators had full-sleeve tattoos, visible beneath rolled-up shirtsleeves. At present, three of them were laughing at what was clearly the fourth man's expense. A smile crept across Dempsey's face, their laughter and camaraderie infectious. He had once been one of these men, these Tier One SEALs.

The team leader, a solidly built and handsome man despite his best efforts to appear otherwise, looked up. He wore a dirty ball cap over his unkempt hair while dribbling brown tobacco spit into an empty plastic soda bottle. "Well, well, well—I think this proves that once again you can't do shit without me, can you, Mr. Dempsey?" Lieutenant Commander Keith "Chunk" Redman said, flashing Dempsey a tobacco-stained grin. "What kind of a mess did you get yourself into this time?"

"The 'we're all probably going to die' kind," Dempsey said, grinning back. "You know—same old, same old."

"John, I gotta tell you, this boat fucking stinks," Chunk said, shaking his head and rolling his eyes at his bearded brothers. "I mean it *really* smells like ass."

Despite trying to suppress a chuckle, Dempsey laughed and said, "Hey, man, we're crashing this party barge just like you. This is an SBS boat, and you know how the Brits like it dirty."

"I fookin' 'erd that," a voice behind him said with a pronounced Scottish lilt.

Dempsey looked over his shoulder at the two British commandoes standing in the doorway. The taller of the two wore a thick red beard and had broad, square shoulders. He nudged his stout dark-haired companion and said, "Now that be the pot callin' the kettle black, if I've ever 'erd it."

Dempsey smiled and walked over to shake hands with the SBS commander. "You wanna hang out while I read these guys in, or would you rather bask in the glory of plausible deniability?"

"I'd rather stay, mate, if it's ahl the same to ya," Commander Frazier said. "Before I send my boys in to rescue yer Yankee arses, ah'll be needin' to know what we're rescuing you from."

Dempsey laughed. He'd served beside SBS warriors—the UK's version of Navy SEALs—more than once in his years in the Teams, and these boys were the real deal. It was the Ember way to keep the circle of knowledge as small as possible, but Frazier and his commandos would be risking their lives as Ember's QRF if things went bad.

"We really appreciate your help. There's no way in hell we could pull this op off without you, but I'll trust you to share only what you and your men need to know to support us. Cool?"

Frazier's red beard split in a toothy grin. "Understood, mate."

Dempsey turned back to Chunk. The SEAL stepped up and wrapped Dempsey in a tight—almost painful—bear hug.

"How are you, Chunk?" Dempsey said, slapping his brother on the back.

"Living the dream, bruh," the SEAL said, letting go. "Y'all helped me get the best damn job in the Teams. My squadron is top notch, and we're fucking up the bad guys. What's not to like?" Chunk looked past Dempsey at Munn and Grimes. "What's up, Doc?" he said, extending a hand and shaking it. Then he looked at Grimes and shot his best frat boy smile at her. "Elizabeth."

"Chunk," she said, bemused.

"You look amazing," he said. "And friggin' ripped. You been hitting the CrossFit circuit or something?"

"Or something," she said as Chunk pulled her in for a hug.

Dropping the frat boy routine, Chunk said, "So, JD, I haven't heard from you since that silly shit in Cyprus almost a year ago. Thought maybe you was retired, since I know you can't do much without me and my boys."

Dempsey laughed. "Oh, man, if you only knew the half of it. How's Buddha? I haven't seen him in a while."

"Buddha's good. He's going through screening now, otherwise he'd probably be here with us. But let me introduce you to these guys." Chunk turned to his three teammates. "This here is Riker, Saw, and Trip. Brought my two best assaulters, and the Sawman is the best damn sniper in all of JSOC."

Dempsey, Munn, and Grimes shook hands all around, and then everyone took a seat around the conference table so Dempsey could kick off the brief.

"First off, let me begin by thanking you guys for the augment. As you can see, the DNI makes sure our little task force only travels in the world's finest accommodations," he began. Everyone laughed. "Seriously, though, the *Zeus* is an important part of the NOC and a believable explanation why the ship has to loiter in the Gulf of Finland so close to the Russian border. The Swedes and Norwegians have been exporting their garbage for years, but it's getting harder to do, even with what they pay. Garbage ships are regularly refused docking privileges and forced to loiter and turn donuts off the coast, something our spooky British friends noticed and decided to exploit. And the *Zeus*, here, has another trick up her sleeve. She's got a submersible bay belowdecks."

"No shit?" Chunk said, scraping his index finger along the inside of his lower lip to claw out a wad of spent tobacco. "That's fucking cool."

"Yeah, it's slick. We'll do a tour after the brief," Dempsey said. "As I was saying, our NOC is that *Zeus* was 'refused' port in Finland and has nowhere to go while diplomats supposedly negotiate where she can off-load her trash."

Chunk held Dempsey's eyes, his boyish face all business now. "Guess I can figure out where y'all are taking us then," he said.

Dempsey nodded.

"Aw shit," Chunk said and blew air through pursed lips. "You really are fucking crazy, you know that?"

Dempsey's only answer was a tight smile while he waited for Grimes to open an oversize laptop and key up several satellite images. "This is

Vyborg, a town catering mostly to tourists, located about a hundred miles north of Saint Petersburg and less than twenty miles southeast of the Finnish border."

"How quaint, but I'm guessing we ain't taking a Thomas Cook tour," Chunk said. The thick man beside him tapped Chunk twice on the arm, and Chunk handed his teammate his tin of Copenhagen while he leaned in to study the satellite image more carefully. "Looks mostly residential. Pretty good hunting to the west of the highway it looks like—nothing but forest. Betcha could bag a nice eight point in there."

"Look closer at the forest," Dempsey said, pointing to the northwest quarter of the peninsula.

Grimes zoomed in on the satellite images, showing a cluster of four buildings in the dense woods.

Chunk looked skeptical. There were no vehicles except one out-of-date open-bed truck and an oversize jeep-looking vehicle beside it. There were no people in the static image, either.

"Y'all gonna blow up some trees and rough up a few park rangers or what?" Chunk said, but he looked quite serious now, and his teammates were studying the images intently, already plotting distances and approaches in their heads, Dempsey knew.

"Gonna be hard to be spooky coming in on the road from Vyborg," said the SEAL called Saw.

"Which is why we're not coming in from Vyborg," Dempsey said.

"Wanna tell us what we're hitting, JD?" Chunk asked, anxiety in his voice for the first time.

Dempsey took a deep breath and then spent the next few minutes summarizing what they knew—and what they thought they knew—about the Russian covert team known as Spetsgruppa Zeta. He ended by reading them into the failed assassination attack on the DNI and the President in Istanbul, the sinking of the *Independence*, and the two hit attempts on Dempsey and his team in Narva and Klaipėda.

"Holy shit," the SEAL called Trip said. "That's some real Cold War shit. I knew about the Russians' operations in Syria, of course, and we all know about Crimea, but, I mean, just holy shit."

"Holy shit is right," Munn said. "The plan is to cut off the head of the snake, take whatever intel off the X we can, eliminate the Zeta threat, and get the President the hard intelligence he needs to prove to the world that Russia is behind these attacks."

"Us operating on Russian soil is big, bro—like nukes-in-Cuba big," Saw said. The SEAL grabbed the plastic bottle from Chunk and added his own brown dribble to the collection. "If we get caught there ain't no coming back."

"No different than anything else we do," Trip said.

"Yeah, man, but this is fuckin' Russia we're talking about hitting, not some goat herder's hut in the 'Stan," Saw fired back.

"Which is exactly why we need you guys," Dempsey said. "This is the type of mission the Tier One was created for."

Saw let out a whistle and said, "Hooyah, boys. Looks like we're going to Russia."

"Infil by helo or fast boat are obviously out of the question," Chunk said, concentrating on the satellite images. "And there's no way seven of us are going to HALO in undetected—"

"Six," Dempsey corrected and saw Grimes's jaw tighten. As much as he'd love to have her on the long gun, her inexperience as a diver ruled her and the other non-SEAL SAD members out of this op. "Grimes is going to stay behind to run comms in the TOC and coordinate with our other assets, like Frazier's SBS operators who are our QRF if things go bad."

"But what if somebody tries to steal the garbage?" Munn said with a wink at Frazier. "Who will protect the *Zeus* while you're gone?"

"Don't worry," the red-bearded SBS commander said, "if yer arses need rescuing, this fookin' tub'll float on its own till we get back."

Dempsey grinned at the Scot before turning back to Chunk and the question the SEAL officer was dying to ask.

"So how *are* we getting in? It's too far for SDV infil."

A malevolent smile spread across Dempsey's face.

"Oh no, I know that look," Chunk said. "That's the same look you gave me just before you decided to drive two inflatable boats up the Sirwan River in Iran with the entire Republican Guard hunting our asses."

"Don't worry," Dempsey said, "I promise we're not taking inflatable boats."

"Then what is it this time? We gonna dress up in red suits and fly in on a sleigh pulled by reindeer?"

"What do you know about the Proteus?"

"Ah, shit," Riker and Saw said together, and Chunk dropped his head to the table with a thunk.

"God, no," the SEAL officer said, his forehead still pressed against the table.

"What? It'll be fun," Dempsey said, his voice ripe with sarcasm.

Chunk sat back up and held Dempsey's eyes. "I probably shouldn't admit this, but we've completed a full training module on the Proteus. It's an amazing beast, but the problem is, she's so damn capable that you can be Spam in a can for six or seven hours straight."

"Yep, the air will run out before the batteries," Dempsey said with a nod.

He got it. No one *liked* infiltration by minisub. Known as SDVs, or SEAL Delivery Vehicles, minisubs were scaled down, bare-bones versions of their larger, more capable submarine cousins. Unlike the Navy's conventional submarine force, SDVs were wet subs, which meant sitting on a bench in full scuba while cruising at four to five knots, barely enough speed to overcome ocean currents. The Proteus was the Navy's prototype *next-gen* SDV—still wet inside, but technologically advanced and capable of holding up to ten SEALs in the back with two SDV operators in the cockpit. The Proteus's advanced propulsion system was capable of cruising at speeds up to ten knots and had an astounding potential range of seven hundred nautical miles with the right battery configuration, but it still meant slow speeds in a confined space.

"We think this disgusting garbage scow can get us within fifty or sixty miles of the target under the NOC we're using. That means an infil of only six hours or so."

Chunk nodded, but the look on his face said he was not enthused by the prospect of what lay in store for them. He looked back at the satellite images, this time studying the Gulf of Finland and Vyborg Bay. "These images don't have bathymetry overlays, but looking at the color swaths you can tell the water gets mighty damn shallow once you get past Vysotsk. My issue is getting spotted from the air. We're going to be cruising in at thirty feet deep and they're going to see us."

"We'll infil under the cover of darkness for that very reason," Dempsey said.

"Gives us a kind of narrow window for the hit, doesn't it?" Saw asked. "Six-plus hours in, then the swim to shore, then the hump to the target—I mean, shit, we got like minutes on the X if we want darkness for the exfil. And even then, at this latitude, we're hitting daylight on the ride out. Same issue applies."

"Yep, on the exfil they'll be looking for us since we just blew up their base," Trip added.

Chunk leaned back in his chair. "So we're going to loiter. Is that your plan?"

Dempsey nodded.

Chunk let out a whistle. "Jesus, JD, that's a lot of daytime to hole up on Russian soil. They're going to have security patrols, and surveillance tech, and probably satellite coverage on this location. Just what do you have in mind for that?"

Munn grinned and then Dempsey did as well.

"You won't believe it," Munn said. "It's wicked cool."

"We're going camping in an invisible tent," Dempsey said, stealing Munn's thunder.

"An invisible tent, huh?" Trip asked, his voice ripe with skepticism. He turned to Chunk and folded his arms across his chest. "Who the hell did you say these guys are, Chunk?"

"I didn't," Chunk said, his eyes on Dempsey. "But if they say they have a tent that'll make us invisible in the woods, you can bet your ass they got one."

"Nah," Munn said. "We're not camping on land, we're camping underwater."

"What? How the hell does that work?" Riker asked.

"Let's go over an assault plan first," Dempsey said. "Then we'll give you a brief on the Stealth Underwater Campsite."

"The SUC?" Chunk pronounced with a chuckle. "I'm betting that it's appropriately named."

"Haven't tried it yet, but the specs on this thing are ridiculous," Dempsey said and ran his tongue along the inside of his bottom lip.

Chunk noticed and tossed him the tin of Copenhagen, which Dempsey caught in midair. "Well, it can't be any worse than that Russian helo we crashed in Iraq."

"Exactly—an experience I plan never to repeat." With a satisfied grin, Dempsey packed himself a big fat lipper and savored the taste of being in the ranks of a Tier One SEAL Team once again.

CHAPTER 29

Proteus SDV
Vyborgsky Zaliv (Vyborg Bay)
Two Miles Southwest of Vyborg, Russia
June 24
0345 Local Time

Dempsey felt the minisub slow for the first time in hours, a hopeful indicator that this leg of the infil was almost over. He rolled his neck and then stretched his aching back. He'd underestimated his physical tolerance for sitting in the cramped SDV, underwater and shoulder to shoulder with his fellow assaulters, for nearly six hours. Thank God the tides had favored them, cutting nearly forty-five minutes off the ride inland from the Gulf of Finland, because he doubted he could have made it another thirty minutes. Now that he'd crept past the forty-year-old line toward senescence—or was it obsolescence—he was becoming increasingly aware of how his chronology was impacting his biology. All the injuries he'd accumulated in two decades as an operator screamed in unison, but none so loudly as the bones in his back that had been knitted together with stainless steel. He was as strong as he'd ever been in his career, but he didn't bounce back like he used to. He was living proof of the classic Harrison Ford line from *Raiders of the Lost Ark*: "It's not the years, honey. It's the mileage."

A red light flashed in the cabin. As the SDV came to a silent stop, Dempsey turned to the station on the wall beside him and secured the regulator delivering air to him from the Proteus's generous internal stores. He pulled off the full-face mask, which had allowed for easy comms and dry face during the transit, and put the regulator from the low-profile dive tank on his back into his mouth. He purged the regulator of cold water with a heavy puff of air, then took two long, slow breaths before slipping on his mask and purging the water out. Once he was all set, he turned to Munn, who was seated on the bench beside him, and gave his teammate a thumbs-up.

"Attention, comrades," came the voice from the pilot in the cockpit forward of them, and yes, the dude was talking with a Russian accent. "This is your stop. Please mind the gap as you exit the bus, and be sure you take all your personal items with you. Thank you for riding the Vyborg Express and have a nice day."

It's the little things that make this job bearable, Dempsey thought as he watched a rectangular section of the hull swing upward and away to reveal the ocean. Dempsey and Munn pushed up from their bench seat and finned out through the generous opening. Chunk, Saw, Trip, and Riker fell in behind, the latter two towing a large gray bag between them. Dempsey waited beside the SDV, looking up at the surface thirty feet above. His breathing produced no bubbles, thanks to the mixed gas rebreathing system they used for covert operations. Once the two SEALs swam past with their cargo, Dempsey and Munn retrieved two special black cargo boxes designed for neutral buoyancy to compensate for their heavy internal loads. They finned behind Trip and Riker's green-gray shadows while Chunk and Saw grabbed two additional boxes from the Proteus.

They swam east, fifty yards over the rocky bottom, with Dempsey checking his depth gauge as they went. Upon reaching their GPS mark, he gave Trip and Riker a thumbs-up. The SEALs pulled opposing handles on the bulky gray bag, which immediately expanded outward, trickling bubbles from each of the four corners. Dempsey watched with atypical curiosity as the SEALs deployed the underwater shelter, working as deftly as if they'd done it a thousand times, despite this being the first time any of them had worked with the new technology. Like watching underwater origami unfold, the auto-inflating structure took shape, transforming a 2 x 3 x 4–foot bag into a 6 x 9 x 12–foot polyhedron. As it expanded, the enclosure took on the appearance of a large mountain tent, but with strange bends and angles along the sides and an oval top. Chunk finned underneath the rectangular bottom of the shelter and pulled down on a rigging box affixed to the base. As he descended with the rigging box in hand, he pulled the slack out of black nylon lines secured from the box to each corner of the structure. Once the lines were taut, he jerked another black nylon rope—the anchor line—out the bottom of the box and promptly finned to the seabed ten feet below. From what Dempsey could make out, Chunk then used a pistol-shaped tool to drive primary and secondary stainless-steel anchors into the rocky bottom.

Dempsey looked up to inspect their temporary home, which was now fully assembled. He finned over and then swam up to the access slit in the floor. He slipped his hands through the overlapping elastic flaps that sealed the opening and wiggled his way upward until his torso was inside the air-pressurized, water-purged environment.

I'm in a friggin' underwater tent! How messed up is that?

He looked around for a handhold to pull himself the rest of the way in and found convenient strap handles tied off to the hard-plastic foldable interlocking grates that made up the floor. The engineers had apparently thought of everything. Dempsey quickly doffed his dive gear, took a test breath, and then slid the gear into a corner. Next, he

scooted back to the access flap and began pulling up the cargo boxes—
which went from weightless to heavy as shit—as his teammates pressed
them up. He slid one box into each corner of the SUC to keep the
weight evenly distributed but heard the subtle hiss as the shelter auto-
matically adjusted buoyancy for the changes in weight distribution,
keeping itself perfectly level.

Amazing.

Moments later his five teammates were inside with him, the Tier
One boys slipping through the opening with the fluidity of actual seals
shooting through a hole in the ice. The enclosure hummed and hissed
for several seconds after each entry and then settled into an eerie quiet.
The operators wasted no time shedding their dive gear, dry suits, and
boots, with each man stuffing his wet gear into waterproof rucksacks.
Chunk pulled a can of Copenhagen out of the cargo pocket of his black
BDUs—stored inside a Ziploc bag in case he had a leak in his suit—and
stuffed a generous pinch in his lower lip.

"Okay, now this," he said quietly, gesturing all around, "is cool as
shit. When do we get some at the command?"

"What I don't understand is, why aren't we sitting in a puddle of
water?" Trip asked, looking down at the floor.

"Because we're on a plastic grate, you dumbass," the normally quiet
Riker fired back. "You can see the little bit of water at the bottom."

"Obviously we're on a grate, but you'd think every time one of us
moves, water would be coming in. That fucking slit in the floor isn't
watertight."

"I think it works the same as purging a dive mask," Munn said.
"I've heard it go through a couple purge cycles to blow the water out
the corners."

"Like I said, cool as shit," Chunk said in hushed tones. "Dempsey,
you guys get all the best toys."

"Y'all don't have to whisper," Munn said. "The acoustic characteristics—both the material and the shape—are designed to prevent

281

detection by passive and active sonar, among other things. We were told this thing is all but soundproof from the inside, so we can relax and shoot the shit without counterdetection risk."

"Where'd you guys get this damn thing?" Saw asked, waving his hand to pass on the can of tobacco offered to him by Chunk.

"It's a prototype finishing trials with DARPA," Dempsey said. "Our Director is good at finding us shit like this. We'll make sure your shop is the next stop in the testing circuit."

"Who'd you say you guys were, exactly?"

Chunk shot the younger SEAL a look of admonition. "They didn't," he said. "Is it me, or is it getting a little warm in here?"

"Hot flashes," Riker laughed. "You're going through *the change*, boss."

Chunk flipped the middle finger.

Dempsey chuckled. "It's equipped with chemical heaters up to sixty degrees. Above that, our thermal signatures would be detectable."

He accepted a towel from Riker, who was pulling them from the black boxes and handing them out. Dempsey dried his hair and beard, then wrapped the towel around his neck and damp collar of his black BDU-style shirt.

"I don't know, man," Saw said, pulling on dry socks and passing out pairs to the rest of the team. "We're like—what—fifteen feet beneath the surface? We gotta get through an entire daylight cycle before we can even infil for the op. Even with the thermal masking, I'm worried about some asshole seeing us in a boat driving by or a plane flying over."

"Like we mentioned in the brief," Munn said patiently, taking a pair of socks, "this thing is special. The shape and materials make us invisible to radar, sonar, and thermal. As far as visual goes, there are microcameras all over the bottom of this thing, videoing the seabed beneath us and then projecting the images onto the surface above us in real time. The roof is like a movie screen. Just like a chameleon or an octopus, this thing uses active color camouflage so that anyone who sees us from above sees nothing but the uninterrupted seabed."

"What are you talking about, octopus?" Trip said

"Octopi are amazing creatures; they have the best active camouflage adaptation in nature," Munn said.

"Dude, don't get him started on octopuses," Dempsey said, shaking his head, "or we're all going to have to listen to him go on and on about how fucking smart they are, and how they have feelings, and can recognize themselves in a mirror. Yada, yada, yada . . ."

Munn threw a balled-up pair of socks at Dempsey's head, which he caught and chucked back at the Doc at double speed.

"How much air?" Riker asked. "Twelve hours?"

"With just six of us, probably more like thirty," Munn said and crawled past Dempsey to pull a tablet out of the box in their corner. He handed it wordlessly to Dempsey and kept talking to the SEAL. "Air isn't the amazing thing. Did you see the two gray boxes near the access slit? CO_2 scrubbers. Six of us in here, breathing oxygen in but CO_2 out. Our captive respiration would raise the carbon dioxide in here to danger levels in just a couple of hours without those scrubbers. Those things will keep the carbon dioxide normal for twelve hours with six guys in here."

"And after that?" Riker asked.

Munn laughed. "We swap out the scrubber cartridges. Think of this as a giant communal rebreather. Once inflated, the CO_2 exhaled by our bodies gets absorbed by chemical scrubbers and the ATCOM computer bleeds pure O_2 in from pony tanks to replace the oxygen we've consumed. When the tanks run out, we can burn O_2 candles. Disciplined, steely-eyed frogmen like us could probably hang out for three or four days."

Dempsey pulled a USB cable from a white box labeled "aux" and plugged it in to his tablet, connecting it to the antennae array at the top of the shelter. He tapped a button on the screen that said "Deploy" and waited while a silent unseen electric motor unspooled the buoyant antenna overhead. The bars in the upper-left corner of the screen went from no signal to full strength, indicating he was now linked to the secure comms satellite.

"The other benefit of this baby is after six miserable hours in that damn tuna can, we got a nice place to decompress so we don't get the bends when we infil to the surface," Munn said, stretching out now on a sleeping bag that had somehow expanded to full size after being pulled from a compression bag the size of a soup can. "We're blowing off our nitrogen at like twenty feet, lying here at the bottom of this thing. We'll levitate up to ten feet after nightfall and fully decompress before we swim ashore."

Dempsey tapped a message into the box that appeared on the screen.

Spear One. Buccaneers. Alpha.

He waited for the reply as his message routed from low space orbit back to Grimes on board the *Atlantic Zeus*, who would see it seconds before Baldwin and Adamo back at Ember headquarters in Virginia. The mission call sign was Spear, and Dempsey was Spear One. "Buccaneers" meant they'd reached the first checkpoint—where they would stage, decompress, and hopefully rest until it was time for them to depart for the final leg of the infil. When they reached dry land, he would call "Redskins," and then "Chiefs" when they were in position for the assault. Of course, by then Ember—and Grimes with her QRF on the *Zeus*—would be watching them from above in real time. The final code word of his message, "Alpha," meant all was well—they were on time and on target.

A reply appeared on his tablet.

Mother. Check. Alpha here as well.

Dempsey smiled, picturing Grimes rubbing her hands through her hair and pacing back and forth. Mother was the perfect call sign for her on this op, just like God suited her when she was overwatch on the long gun.

Clubhouse. Check. Fair winds.

Dempsey nodded at Adamo's acknowledgment from Ember HQ and set the tablet down beside him. He would check in again in four hours. For now, he tapped the red button in the comms box on the side of the shelter. Although he couldn't hear it, the antenna must have retracted, because the signal went to two bars, then one, then flashed a red exclamation point. He crawled over to the sleeping bag Munn had pulled out for him. The other SEALs were already in their own bags. Rest was a weapon, and these men—the new generation of Tier One SEALs—knew that.

Chunk had his ball cap on, pulled low over his eyes. "Does this thing scrub gasses other than carbon dioxide, Doc?" the SEAL officer mumbled from beneath his cap.

"Don't think so," Munn said. "Why?"

A grin spread out on Chunk's face.

"If it don't scrub methane, then no MREs for Riker," he said. "Or we're all going to asphyxiate."

The SEALs laughed, Dempsey and Munn with them.

"Seriously, boys," Chunk said. "No cracking ass."

"Hooyah," Trip said and let one rip.

Dempsey wondered what his life would have been like if he were still with men like this instead of signing on as a damn spook at Ember. Four people in the whole world knew his true identity—Jarvis, Munn, Smith, and Grimes—and only two of those people had known him before Ember. He sighed. Did it even matter anymore? Was it a man's name that mattered or his deeds? The name Jack Kemper meant something to people because Jack Kemper followed a code of conduct that meant he was reliable, competent, and courageous. John Dempsey followed that same code. Which meant that the same people who had put their faith and lives in Kemper's hands would just as readily put their faith and lives in Dempsey's. The ethos of what he was had survived, or rather transcended, the death of his name. But his ethos couldn't wrap his son up in a bear hug. In that respect, ethos was a poor substitute for identity.

He let his thoughts drift to Jake. What kind of dad let his son grow up believing the lie that his father had died in an attack in Yemen? What kind of dad let his son pursue a war-torn existence, in the mistaken belief that doing so would satisfy some debt he felt to the SEAL father he had lost? And what kind of dad watched from the shadows, like a coward, when he should have been actively mentoring his son for a life in the Teams?

He mouthed a silent prayer that his only son would find himself in the company of SEALs like the men sharing the shelter with him now, but as he did a strange and provocative thought occurred to him: the people who wanted Jack Kemper dead were gone.

No one is hunting me anymore, at least not the old me. The reason for becoming Dempsey was to protect my family, and that reason is no longer valid. Maybe I have it all wrong. Maybe it's time to say goodbye to John Dempsey and take my old life back?

Munn nudged his shoulder, snapping Dempsey out of his thoughts.

"Hey, what do you want to do if Arkady Zhukov is there?" Munn asked. "We didn't ever officially decide."

"It's not like we can stick a HEEDs bottle in his mouth, throw a bag over his head, and take him with us," Dempsey said. "No way he makes the swim back to the SUC."

"Yeah," Munn said with a grim-faced nod. "But think of the intelligence in that old man's head. I mean can you fucking imagine?"

"I know," Dempsey said, "but we didn't come here for that."

"So, a bullet in the brain—that's the order."

Dempsey hesitated, trying to imagine another option before finally making the call.

"Yeah, that's the order. Shoot on sight."

CHAPTER 30

Dempsey pulled the curved fins off his boots, snapped them onto the carabiner on his kit, and slipped his legs underneath him, transitioning from prone swimmer to a wading assaulter in the shallow surf. Slowly, and in near unison with the other five SEAL assaulters, he rose silently from the dark water into a tactical crouch, scanning through his mask over the water and along the dark and rocky beach. With the beach clear, he rose the rest of the way, covering the approach as Munn, Trip, and Riker slipped their dive gear off and moved forward. He continued scanning while they banded the gear together and left it in a depression between the rocks at the edge of the surf. The three operators raised their rifles and moved forward, covering Dempsey, Saw, and Chunk as they repeated the maneuver, hiding their dive gear in the same pile of rocks. Ready to move, Dempsey raised a hand and chopped it forward, and together the team left the beach, spreading out as they moved inland.

Despite the assessment of Baldwin and his boys that the Russians had no visible surveillance or detection systems monitoring the coast, Dempsey assumed there had to be something. Perhaps not here, but certainly before they reached the target a kilometer and a half away, which meant the chances of arriving at the objective undetected were practically zero. It wasn't like they were assaulting some cave in the Hindu Kush—the Russians had all the same tech that the US had. The only comfort he took in their situation was that Baldwin, Smith, and Grimes were watching them in real time from space, which meant he had an active detection/counterdetection system of his own relaying data directly into his left ear.

"Clubhouse, Spear One—Redskins," he said, creeping over the rocky terrain.

"I have you, Spear One. No changes. The target compound is one-point-six kilometers northeast of your position. I hold four tangoes in what appears to be a loose roving patrol around the edges of the compound. I will alert you if their behavior changes indicating you have been detected. As a reminder, the westernmost building of the horseshoe arrangement is likely the operations center due to the antennae array and a heat signature that resembles server room architecture. There're two tangoes inside and what looks to be a single sentry by the entrance at the south side of the building. Just east of that, the small building across the open courtyard holds four tangoes, all inside, but we don't know what that building is. That leaves the two southern-most buildings—the one to the east has nine tangoes, all stationary and horizontal, indicating this is a dormitory. The other building is empty except for a single tango in the northwest corner—we assume this to be the cafeteria and the tango is the unlucky one who has what we used to call KP duty."

Dempsey listened to Baldwin drone on, selecting the tidbits of relevant information from the soliloquy. He imagined this was jaw-clenchingly annoying for the Tier One guys, who were accustomed to minimal chatter—just quick bullets of information, and only when necessary. But he no longer hated Baldwin's long-winded descriptions and instead found his mind painting a picture in cadence with Baldwin's bloviating, yet surprisingly useful, narrative.

He imagined the team spreading out as briefed, with Chunk, Saw, and Riker bending north around the top of the compound as he, Munn, and Trip arced south. They would all seek opportunities to silently eliminate the four roving shooters before the melee kicked off. Once in position, Dempsey would call "Chiefs" and the assault would begin. Dempsey would eliminate the single tango in the chow hall while Chunk's team hit the operations building, killing the occupants and securing any relevant intel before setting explosives to vaporize the facility. By this time, site alarms would be wailing and the dormitory and the unidentified building with four tangoes would empty. That's where Munn and Trip came in, having gotten into position with sight lines to take out as many Zetas as possible as they streamed out of the buildings to mount a defense. Once the operations center was gutted, Chunk's team would join the assault on the dormitory, setting up a crossfire on any Zetas left trying to join the fight. Saw, the top sniper in the new-generation Tier One, would find a high-ground position to provide cover fire. Once they had killed everyone, they would search the dead for Arkady and Malik, rig the dormitory to blow, and exfil back to the water, where they'd hide in stealth until the Proteus could come back to pick them up. The destruction would slow Zeta's capabilities to a crawl—that was the hope, though Dempsey felt uneasy believing that. Eliminating Arkady, if he was here, would be the crowning achievement. He wasn't convinced they had that kind of luck these days.

The plan assumed that any Russian QRF was more than fifteen minutes away and a security breach alarm didn't sound until they began the assault. A lot of assumptions. Back home in Virginia, you couldn't land a Sunfish sailboat on Camp Peary's side of Queen's Creek without being engaged by armed security in under two minutes. Of course,

Camp Peary was an enormous compound hidden in plain sight, and this was a tiny cluster of unimpressive buildings. Dempsey hoped that the Zetas' security strategy for this facility was to maintain a minimum footprint so as not to attract attention. Imagery suggested they would not encounter significant resistance, but in Dempsey's experience imagery never told the whole story.

The minutes ticked by, and the only sound Dempsey heard was his breathing and that of his teammates from their open mikes in his left ear. He took a knee, just outside where the tree line met the open space between the buildings, and surveyed the area. Just like the satellite pictures suggested, he noted a series of chunky floodlight boxes atop light poles. Some of the lenses were aimed to illuminate the green space and others to light a narrow gravel path that snaked between the buildings and terminated at a spot occupied by a few vacant picnic tables and a dilapidated BBQ grill. When those big halogens came on—and they *would* come on—the luminosity would turn night into day, washing out their NVGs and trashing their night eyes.

Dempsey pointed them out to Munn and Trip, who both nodded their silent understanding.

"Spear Three, Spear One—in position," Dempsey whispered.

"Gotcha, Spear One," came Chunk's hushed reply. "Forty-five seconds."

Dempsey frowned. Total time on target from the "go" was only eight minutes. He could use that forty-five seconds to dispatch the lone occupant in the chow hall, but if he was detected, then Chunk's team would lose their element of surprise.

"Check," he replied and held a closed fist up for Munn and Trip. They would wait.

Then, as fate would have it, Baldwin found something to kill the time.

"Roving sentry approaching your position from the east, One," Baldwin said. "At your three o'clock, fifteen yards, other side of that small finger of trees extending into the quad."

Dempsey looked at Munn and Trip, pointed to himself, then pointed two fingers at them and raised a closed fist.

I'll take him. You two hold here.

Munn nodded and Dempsey skirted right, low and completely silent. His fingers found the hilt of the SOG knife on the front of his kit, and he slipped it from the scabbard. As he moved, his perception sharpened and his legs primed for the strike. The Russian sentry slipped into view. Dempsey could make out every detail in the green-gray world of night vision—the Zeta was turning away, perhaps to pace east again on his back-and-forth perimeter patrol. The guard had his own night vision, but the tubes were flipped up on top of his head . . . maybe because he found the lights from the compound to be too bright, or maybe because NVGs were uncomfortable to wear continuously on a six-hour watch where nothing *ever* happened. Regardless of the reason, it was a mistake. Just like it was a mistake not to be patrolling in shadows just inside the tree line, where it would have made Dempsey's approach more difficult. The Russian had chosen to be lazy, and laziness was a killer—something this man was about to learn in a most brutal and inconvenient way.

Three, two, one . . .

Dempsey closed the gap in a heartbeat. The sentry turned, but too late. Dempsey was already on him, his left arm whipping around the man's neck. With the speed and power of a bear trap snapping shut, his forearm crushed the man's throat in a choke. The guard threw his arms up and attempted to squat—a self-defense technique to counter a stranglehold—but the maneuver was futile. Dempsey drove his blade deep into the man's brainstem through the opening at the base of his skull. The body slumped into Dempsey's arms, and he dragged it several yards back into the woods before lowering the corpse quietly, face-first, onto the forest floor. He crouched beside the body, searched for a radio, found it, and turned it off. Then he wiped his blade on the back of the man's black utility pants. He scanned left and right for threats as he slipped the SOG back into its scabbard.

"Your six is clear, Spear One," said Baldwin's voice in his ear.

"Check," he said, and a few seconds later he was taking a knee back beside Munn.

The doc raised an eyebrow at him. Dempsey simply nodded.

Done.

"One, Three—in position," Chunk said in his ear.

Dempsey double-clicked and then added: "Clubhouse, Spear One—Chiefs."

"Go, Spear," said Smith's voice this time. As Ember Director, this was his call to make.

"Check. Go, Three," Dempsey acknowledged and released Chunk's squad.

Dempsey sprinted north toward the chow hall, knowing Munn and Trip were moving to the southeast corner, ready to engage the targets who would momentarily pour from the dormitory. Dempsey rounded the corner, pulling his Sig Sauer P226 from his thigh holster with his right hand and the suppressor from its pouch with his left. He threaded the suppressor onto the muzzle, scanning the deserted courtyard space as he moved.

"I have you, One," Baldwin said in his ear. "Inside the door move left down the hall. Solitary thermal image at the end of the hall that opens into what appears to be the kitchen. Looks like we were right about the absence of a robust security system. I suppose it's lucky they didn't see you on a routine satellite pass."

Dempsey smiled tightly.

Lucky indeed. The luck of the operator.

He double-clicked and scanned over his pistol as he moved through the door and then swiftly down the hall. To his right, two swinging doors were blocked open, and inside he saw rows of cafeteria-style seating and a serving line beyond; it reminded him of the KBR hall at

Korean Village, the Marine FOB in western Iraq near Ar Rutbah. The door to the kitchen hung partially open a few yards beyond. He paused and flipped up his NVGs against the light streaming from the gap.

"Target is across the room. He may be obstructed—about fifteen degrees to the right of your sight line."

Dempsey slipped through the gap and into the room, advancing quickly and quietly. He slinked past two commercial-size stainless-steel refrigerators, two eight-burner cooking stations, and a short row of prep stations—pots and pans flipped upside down on top to dry. His oblivious target stepped into view, pushing a mop. Dempsey put his iron sight on the man's temple, pulled the two yellow dots at the rear sight in line with the single center dot on the front of the barrel, and squeezed. The man never looked up as the pistol made a dull burp. The round impacted the side of the Russian's head just behind his temple, and he crumpled to the floor.

Dempsey moved left and pulled two canvas bags from the satchel behind his left hip. He jammed one beside what looked like the gas line coming into the stoves, opened the top of the bag, and depressed the green button on the cell phone–size box inside. A yellow indicator light illuminated and the word "armed" appeared on the detonator's tiny LCD screen. He headed back toward the exit with the other bag in his left hand, lowering his NVGs.

"You have a roving sentry moving toward your building, One," Baldwin reported.

"One, Two—I have him," said Munn.

"One, Three—ops center secured. Three KIA. Negative on Alpha Zulu," Chunk reported, informing Dempsey that their primary, Arkady Zhukov, was not among the dead. "Setting charges now."

Dempsey flipped open the other bag, armed the second detonator, and slid it across the floor deep into the chow hall.

A soft whump echoed outside, followed by Munn whispering, "Tango neutralized."

"Three, get ready," Baldwin said, warning Chunk. "The north two sentries are converging on your position."

Unexpected gunfire erupted in the distance. Chunk and his boys taking on two of the remaining sentries.

"Five in position and ready to party," Saw said.

Dempsey exited the chow hall, turned right, and ran toward the northwest corner of the building. A Klaxon howled, shredding the silence, and the halogen floodlights kicked on, bathing the base in light. Dempsey flipped his NVGs up as he ran, rounding the corner to rejoin Munn and Trip. As he took a knee in the point position, he felt the familiar squeeze on his left shoulder telling him Munn had his six. Trip peeled off and sprinted north before disappearing into the trees, taking a hidden firing position from a different angle.

The dormitory door flew open and seven men and two women burst out, assault rifles slung over their sleepwear, legs pounding the ground in bare feet or untied boots.

Dempsey held his fire, deciding their biggest advantage was that, if Baldwin was right and this was primarily a training camp with a small operations center, then most of these shooters were students. He waited until he counted the ninth shooter to exit the dorm, then gave the order.

"Five, One—kick it off."

The dull whump of Saw's sniper rifle reverberated in the night, and the second man in the line of Zeta shooters pitched backward. As predicted, everyone froze, momentarily confused—apparently assuming that this was a late-night readiness exercise. It was not. The female behind the dead Russian looked down at her tank top in disbelief at the spatter of blood and brains. A split second later, the next sniper bullet took off the left side of her face and she collapsed.

Someone screamed something in Russian, and then the group spread out into a combat formation, moving left and right, searching for cover as they did. Dempsey noted how they moved like operators. Unfortunately for them, Ember had caught them with their pants down—literally. Without NVGs, body armor, and tactical support from their TOC, the Zeta recruits were hopelessly outmatched. Dempsey picked a target, placed the red dot of his holosight on the man's head, and squeezed. The Russian fell and the shooters around him wheeled left, taking aim at Dempsey's position just as shots rang out from Chunk and Riker from the north. Two more Zetas fell, and another sniper round from Saw dropped a sixth man. Dempsey tapped Munn twice on the leg, releasing Munn to loop around and set charges in the dormitory. Dempsey checked his internal clock: *four and half minutes left.*

"Three, did you get what we need?" Dempsey asked as he dropped number seven with a headshot.

"We got a pack full of good shit—laptops, hard drives, files and stuff—but y'all don't ever tell me what the hell we're looking for . . ." came Chunk's casual drawl, followed by more 5.56-sounding pops from the American assault rifles. The last two Zeta recruits fell—a second woman who was in a combat crouch, sighting over her AK-47 and a lanky, bare-chested brute who had turned to regroup but instead pitched forward like someone had hit him in the back with a sledgehammer.

"Spear, we have a problem," Baldwin said in his ear.

Of course we do . . .

Dempsey tensed, anticipating the bad news.

Smith's voice took over. "One, you have a QRF heading your way—two trucks with shooters, and they're way ahead of our schedule. You need to get to Redskins and get the hell out of there."

CHAPTER 31

I should be there.

I should be there

I should be there . . .

Those four words wouldn't stop echoing in Grimes's head as she watched her team on the streaming satellite feed on the big screen. Things had been going incredibly well, almost too well, which was why everything was about to turn to shit. The SEAL called Saw was clearly a helluva shooter, but if she'd been there, too, then clearing the incoming Russian QRF assaulters would have been that much easier. She understood the decision to keep her back was based not on her skills but rather her lack of training and expertise in maritime infil by SDV.

But damn it, I could have worked through it.

She could tell which figure was JD, even without knowing the order of battle, by his fluid, graceful movements. As two SEALs moved southwest along one building and a third slipped off the roof to join them, Dempsey surged forward, zigzagging impossibly fast like a character in a video game. They needed to blow the charges and get to water before the two QRF vehicles arrived.

"One, I'm afraid we have an even bigger problem now," came Baldwin's irritatingly passive voice.

"Bigger than the QRF?" Dempsey huffed.

"Yes . . ."

The monitor she was watching refreshed, and a split screen suddenly replaced the mono feed she'd been watching. The left half picked up the bird's-eye thermal imagery of the compound from before, and the right began streaming a crystal-clear satellite feed of a second, different site.

"We've got eyes on Pushkin military airbase outside Saint Petersburg—seventy-eight miles from Spear," Baldwin continued. "We're watching two Mi-28N Night Hunter attack helicopters spinning up. I'm rather certain they are about to head in your direction."

"Roger," Dempsey said. "How long do we have?"

"Thirty minutes tops, conceivably as short as twenty-five if they transit at top speed. These assets are every bit as capable as Apaches, and if you loiter much longer you are unlikely to survive their arrival."

"Check," Dempsey said as if he had just been given the results of a price check at the grocery store. "Three, time to wrap up. We gotta get wet."

"Check," Chunk said.

Grimes watched Dempsey take a knee as Munn's glowing thermal image dashed into the southeast building. She watched the heat signature move to the middle of the building and pause, then move back to the entrance. He was outside in under twenty seconds, his charges set.

Go, go, go . . .

"One, Two—charges set," Munn reported.

"Check," Dempsey said.

"One, Four—all charges are linked and will go on my command or timer."

Translation: *if I'm killed before I can push the button, they'll go off regardless,* said as calmly as if the SEAL were talking about a dinner reservation he'd made. This was the world her brother Jonathan had lived and died in—a world where the opportunity to make the ultimate sacrifice was always lurking just around the next corner.

And it was her world, too, now. As part of Ember SAD, she put her life on the line with every operation, just like her brother had once done. She'd faced down Death in Jerusalem and technically Death had won, but then Munn had somehow managed to snatch her soul from the Reaper's bony grasp and bring her back. Now, her team was in danger of falling, and she was stuck here, on a fucking garbage ship, where she couldn't do anything to help them.

I should be there.

I should be there . . .

Something on the left-hand side of the screen caught her eye. "Clubhouse, what's that moving down from the north? Oh shit . . . ," she murmured as a wave of nausea washed over her.

"Oh shit, what?" Dempsey said, not missing a beat.

"Ah, yes. Just getting to that, Mother. One—there appears to be a single Raptor fast-attack boat converging south on your position from Vyborg. Six heat signatures aboard. At its current velocity, it will block your exfil in . . . six minutes."

Six minutes! she thought in a panic. *That's not enough time.*

"Check," came Dempsey's cool reply. "Spear—rally at Redskins. Move now."

"Clubhouse, where the hell are these guys coming from? We had no indication of any facility capable of mounting a QRF north of Saint Petersburg."

"Well, Mother, it's the same question we're asking ourselves. The trucks and boat came out of Vyborg, so obviously there is either a military or police presence there that we missed," Baldwin replied.

She watched as an arc of thermal images—the six members of Spear team—unleashed lethal fire now at the remaining occupied building, which had four heat sigs. Grimes watched two thermal images at the corner return fire briefly, but then their red-yellow silhouettes fell to the ground. The six-man Spear team was moving backward toward the water, still firing inward from their arc, but they had a full kilometer to go.

They weren't going to make it.

They might beat the Night Hunters, but the fast-attack boat would be waiting for them at the water. The Russians would have night vision and thermal imaging to guide the QRF assaulters.

Spear was fucked.

Her mind raced furiously. There was something—something her brain was trying to remember—something she'd seen and her subconscious had registered but then neglected to inform her conscious mind of. She pulled her eyes from the horror show unfolding in slow motion on the monitor and shifted her attention to the hard-copy satellite images spread out on the table.

"Where is it?" she murmured as she sifted through the images. "Where the hell is it?"

On the fifth image, she noted the small corrugated building beside the oversize, mostly empty "parking lot." There . . .

"Clubhouse, this is Mother—zoom in on the parking lot area, the one with the wind sock we saw on imagery."

She watched the image shift and zoom in. On the west edge, facing into the lot she saw the thing her brain had been screaming for her to remember. As the satellite image zoomed in closer and closer, it became apparent that some of the trees in the northeast corner were not trees at all but what appeared to be a cammo tent.

"What is that, Clubhouse?" she said and used a computer mouse to put a red rectangle overlay over something sticking out of the cammo netting. "It's the nose of a helicopter, isn't it?"

"We see it . . . wait one . . . Mother, there's a ninety-two percent probability that we're looking at the nose of a Russian Kazan Ansat helicopter."

In Chunk's Tier One squad data files, she'd noted that one of the operators, Trip, had attended the flight training course in Florida—obtaining commercial, instrument, and multiengine ratings in both fixed wing and helicopters.

"Spear, Mother—there's a Kazan Ansat helo under a cammo tent on the northeast corner of the compound. Spear Four—can you fly that bird?"

Immediately she saw the thermal images of Spear Team pivot course a hundred and eighty degrees, now heading back toward the cluster of buildings they had just rigged for detonation.

"Depends," came Trip's tight voice, his breathing hard.

"On what?"

"On whether it's similar to a bird I know how to fly."

On that cue, Baldwin jumped in. "It should have flight characteristics analogous to the Bell 407—a high-performance version of the older Bell 206 Long Ranger."

"All right, I can probably fly it then," Trip said. "But it won't outrun their fucking Night Hunters. They probably got a thirty-five- or forty-knot speed advantage."

"Fifty to sixty," Baldwin corrected.

"It's your only option, Spear. Just get there," Grimes barked. "I have a plan. Clubhouse, what's the position of the trucks?"

"Three minutes out," Adamo said with pronounced tension in his voice. There was more on the line than just the mission, or even the lives of the operators. If Spear was killed or, worse, captured, then Vladimir Petrov would accuse the United States of an act of war, and he'd have the proof necessary to justify retaliation. It was no exaggeration to say that failure now could be the first domino to fall in a cascade of events that would lead to World War III.

"Where is Greyhound?" she asked, referring to the Proteus. The advanced minisub had returned to the *Zeus* during the day to swap crews but had since redeployed to loiter inside Vyborg Bay for a stealth pickup after things calmed down.

"I see where you're going with this, Mother," Adamo said, his voice betraying a modicum of hope. "It could work."

"I can calculate the rate of closure better once Spear is in the air. But it might work, indeed," Baldwin said.

"Mother, One—what are you thinking?" Dempsey asked.

A badass grin spread across her face as she laid out her plan for him. She might not be on her long gun, but she was still his overwatch, damn it, and it was her job to bail them out. No matter what . . .

CHAPTER 32

In war, the key to ultimate success was to find advantage in disadvantage—even in times of *great* disadvantage.

Most especially then . . .

It had been true in Leningrad in the Great Patriotic War. It had been true with the defeat of Hitler's army at Stalingrad. It had been true with the rebirth of Russia after the fall of the Soviet Union. And now, his task was to make the adage true tonight.

Arkady tapped a finger absently on the side of the aged coffee cup. *But how to do it?*

The phone rang.

He glanced at the number on the screen at the top of the phone and he sighed. The call was inevitable, but he had hoped to place it himself with a report of good news. He supposed that was wishful thinking. Petrov was not a patient man.

"The way of things," Arkady muttered and picked up the receiver. "Yes?"

"Really? That is how you greet me?" the Russian President said. "Bright Falcon is under attack!"

"I know."

"I shouldn't have to ask this question, Arkady. Is it the Americans?"

"I do not have confirmation, but who else could it be?" the old spymaster said.

"The audacity," Petrov shouted. "The unbridled audacity to attack us on Russian sovereign soil. This is an act of war, Arkady. An act of war I tell you!"

"It is aggressive and unprecedented, but we have been aggressive, too. We're *already* at war with the Americans; it's just neither side has the balls to admit it. Cyber offensives, false flags, propaganda, proxy operations—both sides have been doing it for a long time now. This is probably payback for Turkey. I think it's safe to assume Warner knows what you did."

"What *I* did? No, what *you* did. All that shit was your idea. Not mine. I went along with it because I trusted you, but now I'm starting to wonder if you're losing your edge. Maybe it's time for you to *actually* retire."

"You're upset, Mr. President. And you have every right to be, but now is not the time to make snap decisions you might later regret."

"Who are you to lecture me? I'm the President of Russia, not you, old man."

Arkady held his tongue until he'd quelled the urged to fire back.

You are a president of my creation, you ass. And you will remain so at my pleasure.

Instead he said, "You're right, you're absolutely right. I apologize. I overstepped my bounds."

Angry silence lingered on the line between them until Petrov finally said, "What are we doing about this, Arkady?"

Arkady took a sip of his coffee while he chose his words carefully. "I believe we can turn this event to our advantage. I think the Americans miscalculated the complexities of their operation. It is one thing to wander into the lion's den unscathed, but it is another matter altogether to get out. I'm surprised they discovered Bright Falcon. I'm even more surprised they hit it, but now I'll make them pay for their hubris. They're boxed in. There's nowhere to go. This is an opportunity to turn a small loss into a very big gain."

"What do you mean?"

"I mean that we've lost nothing of consequence in this assault on Bright Falcon. I have a dozen recruits there. So what? A radio station. Who cares? There's no intelligence of consequence to be had. All of my seasoned field agents and operators are deployed in their NOCs."

After Sylvie had been taken, Arkady had seen to it that all sensitive operational intelligence had been removed from the site at Vyborg. What the Americans harvested from her mind was another matter altogether, but not something he was keen on discussing with the volatile Russian President in the heat of the moment.

"What if they get the list of personnel? Huh, what then? It will be catastrophic."

Arkady laughed. "There is no list."

"What do you mean? You keep personnel files on everything, Arkady. I know you better than anyone, or have you forgotten?"

"Those files are locked in a drawer in my desk at Lubyanka," Arkady said. "They would have to invade Moscow and sack FSB headquarters to get those records, and everything else is in my head. No, Jarvis and Warner are the ones who have the problem, not us. Because we're either going to capture Ember's Special Activities Division and wring out decades' worth of valuable intelligence, or we kill them all. We may lose a rook and some pawns, but they lose their queen and a bunch of knights." When Petrov didn't say anything, Arkady added, "We just scrambled two Night Hunters to intercept. I have a maritime interceptor blocking egress to the sea and ground troops cutting off their escape by land. They're completely surrounded."

"Very well," Petrov said, collecting himself. "But we will hit them back. Warner can never believe he's gotten the upper hand. You will answer this outrageous provocation with an operation of our own, yes?"

"Of course, Mr. President. Arrangements are already being made."

"Make it hurt, Arkady. Make them bleed. I am losing patience for your covert, shadow puppet bullshit. I want you to execute an operation that makes Warner wake up in the middle of the night with colds sweats for the rest of his life. Do you understand, Arkady?"

More than you know, and sooner than you can imagine.

"Yes."

"Make him pay."

And the line went dead.

He heard the whine of the Mi-28N attack helicopters spinning up on the airfield outside. The Ember attack *had* caught him off guard. Jarvis had taken a bold and brazen stroke, but it was not enough. In sending his SAD team to Bright Falcon, he'd left his own castle unprotected.

Disadvantage turned to advantage . . .

Arkady pulled an encrypted satellite phone from his worn leather satchel and pressed "1."

"Prime," Valerian answered.

"We must accelerate the timeline."

"Why?"

Arkady clenched his jaw. Only a year ago his prodigy would have found the thought of such a question unimaginable, and yet now he could no longer even control his need to speak it. Arkady was right to begin the process of accession for the next Zeta Prime. Valerian was a remarkable asset, but he also had a deeply flawed psyche and was rapidly approaching his half-life.

"Because a new opportunity has unveiled itself," Arkady said. "The Ember assaulters are not in Virginia."

"And how do we know this?" There was confusion but also obvious disappointment in Valerian's voice. "And if the American ghost is not here, then what is the point of the attack?"

"The point of the attack is not your concern, Prime. You are a weapon. You are an instrument of policy, not its maker. That there is a point to my plan is all you need to know, and your mission is your mission. Is that no longer how you perceive your role?"

"Of course. My apologies. What is the timeline?"

"Soonest possible, and I trust you to use your own judgment. And because you are like a son to me, I will tell you . . . I know that the Ember operators are not in Virginia because they're here."

The silence this time was one of shock.

"In Saint Petersburg?"

"In Vyborg."

"What! How is this possible?"

"All you need to know is that the Americans are being dealt with. They are in the lion's den, my friend, and there is no way out. Escape is impossible. Now focus, Valerian. You have work to do."

He terminated the call, sighed, and sent a text message to Gavriil.

Are you with Prime?

The reply came almost immediately. No.

Arkady dialed the number "2" and Gavriil answered before the end of the first ring.

"Yes?"

"It's time. Are you ready to ascend?"

"Yes," the Zeta said, and Arkady could almost see the smile on Gavriil's face despite the thousands of miles that separated them.

"Good. Once this mission in Virginia is complete, execute the Mercury protocol and you will become the Prime."

"I understand," Gavriil said. No questions. No remorse. Blind faith and obedience, as was required of a Zeta Prime. "I will see it done."

"Very well. And Gavriil?"

"Yes."

"I want you to know, you're like a son to me. Be careful."

Arkady ended the call, stood, and arched his back to stretch out the kinks. His mind was a merry-go-round of thoughts, shifting from Valerian, to Petrov, to Gavriil, to Jarvis and back again. Allies and enemies. It seemed he had so few of the former and so many of the latter. *Maybe it is time to retire,* he thought as he walked over to the window.

No, not yet. I still have work to do . . . important work that only I'm capable of managing, he decided and then watched in silence as the Mi-28N Night Hunter helicopters disappeared into the dark.

CHAPTER 33

Dempsey stepped carefully over the bodies of the dead Zetas they'd bested just minutes earlier. To be cavalier now would be dangerous. It would take only one fighter assumed dead—who was in reality only wounded—to ruin your day. He'd seen it before. During a deployment in Africa, with SEAL Team Four—before the planes crashed into the Towers—he'd lost a teammate that way. Rich Rizzuto, a SEAL who hailed from Upstate New York, had taken a bullet from a "corpse" that ripped through his forehead—taking away his faculties and sentencing his body to a wheelchair for the rest of his life.

Dempsey scanned carefully over his rifle, sweeping the holographic red dot across the heads of the downed Russians as he advanced. To his right he heard a dull pop as Munn fired into one of the bodies that concerned him.

Munn had been in Africa, too.

"Pick it up, Spear," Smith said in his ear. The Ember Director's voice was as tense as Dempsey had ever heard it. But it still didn't have that subtle tone that signaled the battle was lost. "It's gonna be tight. Hopefully, it doesn't take Spear Four too long to figure things out."

"Yeah, well, Spear Four doesn't read fucking Russian," Trip said from the cockpit of the Ansat. "And all these controls are in Russian."

"Controls is controls, dude," Chunk said.

"You wanna come fly this bird, sir, be my guest," Trip fired back, but Dempsey knew that was just bravado talking, because he heard flipping switches in the background on the open mike.

"Two trucks are arriving at the south entrance in thirty seconds," Baldwin reported. "We hold two-dozen shooters on thermal in the convoy."

"Clubhouse, you got control of the detonation, right?" Chunk asked. Dempsey could see the SEAL officer now to his right, converging on his two teammates as they approached the small building beside the helicopter from the north.

"Yes, Spear Three," Smith said. "We got your six—focus on protecting your taxi ride out of there."

"Tell me when you're gonna light up the two buildings to the south," Dempsey whispered.

"About fifteen seconds," Smith answered. "Trucks are almost in the kill zone."

"Position of the Night Hunters?" he asked.

The Russian Mi-28s were his biggest worry. They would rip the Ansat helicopter to shreds. Even in the hands of a trained combat pilot, there was no outmaneuvering the twin threats coming for them. Separation and distance was their only hope.

"You'll make it if you hurry," Smith said.

Which was not an answer, Dempsey noted.

"Time on target, twelve minutes," Baldwin said.

Shit.

"Trucks are entering the blast zone. Blowing charges in three, two, one . . ."

Dempsey saw the flash and then felt the heat as a massive shock wave rolled through the camp. The explosion must have taken out the facility's power transformer, because the halogen spots all went dark and the camp plunged into darkness. Wasting no time, Dempsey was up and snapping his NVGs back into place. He moved fast in a low crouch toward the helo, with Munn paces behind him. He spied Chunk, Riker, and Saw converging from their position. Across the wide, square parking lot, Dempsey could now clearly see the shape of the helicopter beneath the cammo netting. Backlit in the cockpit, Trip was working feverishly on whatever abbreviated checklist he was improvising to start up the helicopter.

"I'm ready to spin up," Trip shouted. "Get that netting clear."

"Give me a hand," Dempsey said to Munn as he grabbed a corner of the cammo tent. The netting was draped over a box-shaped frame with wheels at the corners, constructed from aluminum poles connected like Tinkertoys. Together, he and Munn rolled the entire structure clear of the tail as the whine of the Ansat spooling up echoed in the night.

"Spear, you have at least six shooters headed toward you from the destroyed trucks. Everyone else appears to be down. Oops, it's five now—one of them has collapsed it seems."

"Check," Dempsey said, taking a tactical knee beside the helo and sighting south toward the dying flames of the burning buildings.

"Spear, the maritime patrol is on station, and they seem to be getting busy. You need to get the fuck out of there," Grimes said, her voice holding the bowstring tension that said she *needed* to be there instead of watching it all on TV.

The whine of the turbines rose in pitch, and the rotors above the helicopter began to turn in a slow circle overhead. Trip shot Dempsey a big grin and thumbs-up from the pilot's seat as Dempsey and Munn ran to the bird. They took a knee on either side of the open port-side door, scanning south and covering the approach as the three SEALs pulled themselves into the passenger compartment. Dempsey squeezed off two three-round bursts and jumped into the bird as Munn followed suit. Yellow-green flashes of rifle fire danced in his vision, and two rounds tore through the side of the helicopter beside his head.

"Go, Four, go!" he hollered and then leaned out the open door to return fire, hearing three-round bursts from Munn interspersed with his own.

The turbines screamed and the Ansat lifted off. Heart racing, Dempsey pulled a grenade from his kit and tossed it blindly in the general direction of the gunfire coming from the woods. The exploding grenade lit up white light in his NVGs, blinding him. Trip lowered the nose and banked hard to starboard. Saw grabbed Dempsey's kit and kept him from falling out as the little Russian helo began screaming west, just over the tops of the trees.

Dempsey nodded at Saw for saving his ass, then, turning to the group, said, "Nice work, guys."

"Yeah, well, the hard part's coming up," Riker grumbled beside him, the heavily tattooed SEAL voicing his first and only comment since the op began.

"How you doing, Four?" Chunk asked Trip, leaning forward into the cockpit.

"All the damn switches and instruments are labeled in Russian Cyrillic bullshit," Trip said. "Flying this thing's no picnic, but crashing it convincingly without dying in the process is gonna be a bitch."

Dempsey clenched his jaw. A year and a half ago, when he'd first met Chunk, they'd survived a crash in *another* Russian helicopter, an old military Mi-17, in the Iraqi desert. Now, it appeared they were going for double jeopardy.

"Just like old times, huh, One?" Chunk laughed in his earpiece.

"Yeah," he grumbled. "At least this time we're over water."

"Spear, turn to heading two-six-two degrees," Baldwin said. "I'm going to vector you right to Greyhound; after that, the rest is up to you. You have about eleven miles to go. The Mi-28s are vectoring to intercept. Hmmm . . ." There was an uncomfortable pause, and Dempsey looked at Munn, who shook his head, lips tight in a frown. "Is that your best speed, Spear?"

Dempsey felt the helicopter nose forward slightly, and the whine of the engine increased in pitch.

"That's all I got," Trip said.

"Oh . . . ," Baldwin murmured.

"Oh *what*, Clubhouse?" Dempsey said, his anxiety rising. "Give it to us straight."

"It's going to be close. Let's see here . . . Ah, yes. You will be over Greyhound with more than a minute to spare when the Mi-28s reach the edge of their firing range. They are making twelve knots slower than expected—head winds from the north, I'm assuming. Luckily that works out in your favor."

Yeah, lucky us . . . All we have to do now is survive the crash, swim down and find the Proteus on a single breath in the dark, and escape without the Russians dropping bombs and torpedoes on us during our six-hour transit back to the Zeus. Just another walk-in-the-park mission for Task Force Ember.

"It's gonna be all right," Munn said, his voice surprisingly calm, almost upbeat.

Dempsey eyed his friend warily. He'd already not liked their odds, but to hear the normally glass-is-half-empty Munn suddenly brimming with optimism was seriously making him nervous.

"You're the one always pointing out how dire and fucked up our situation is and how we're going to die, and you choose this, of all times, to become Mr. Happy?"

"Yeah," Munn said with a shrug. "My gut says Lizzie's plan is gonna work. If we make it to Proteus, we'll be the night. I'm telling you, that little mermaid is one stealthy bitch."

Dempsey couldn't find the words, so he just shook his head.

"Strip all your shit, guys," Chunk said, his voice all business. "Let's make sure we leave a debris field with lots to suggest a bad outcome. Kits and helmets. Shit from your pockets that will float."

Dempsey snapped his weapon off and dropped it onto the floor of the helicopter.

"Ease right, Spear," Baldwin said on the line. "To heading two-six-seven degrees."

He felt the bird bank slightly right for a second or so. Beside him Munn was bent over, untying his boots. The doc grinned up at him.

"Coupla boots floating in the flotsam's a nice touch, right?"

Dempsey nodded and began to tug off his own boots. It would make the long, deep swim easier as well. Next, he unfastened the wide Velcro cummerbund of his kit from around his waist and slipped the entire kit over his head and set it on the floor between his feet.

"You got a grenade, Four?" Dempsey asked, contemplating how this would best play out.

"Yeah, but it'll be easier if someone else does it. I'll hold a low hover while you guys jump, then last guy tosses a grenade into the cockpit. I'll pull the collective up and jump out after."

"Check," came back the group reply.

"Listen up, guys. Clubhouse is going to put us directly on top of Greyhound. Swim down fast. It's going to be dark as shit, and if you let the current set you, you might not find Greyhound before you run out of air," Chunk said.

Everyone nodded.

"We need this to look authentic. Like our bird took a hit in case they have eyes on from above. I'll toss a flash-bang in the back before we jump," Munn suggested.

"Good idea," Dempsey said, pulling a smoke grenade out of his kit. "I got the smoke if you do the flash-bang."

"And I'll drop a flare up front," Saw offered.

313

"It's a plan," Chunk said.

"Right on course. One minute," came Baldwin's voice. "Eight hundred yards."

Dempsey closed his eyes and began taking long, slow, deep breaths to blow off as much CO_2 as he could. It would be a long swim. The Proteus would come up to only forty feet.

"Five hundred yards."

Dempsey felt the helicopter slow, and Trip dipped so low Dempsey worried he would drag the skids in the surf and crash for real.

"Two hundred."

"The lead Mi-28 is coming into range, guys. Hurry it up," came Smith's tense voice. "They got laser-guided missiles on those things."

"Fifty . . . twenty . . . ten . . . hover."

Trip brought the Ansat to a hover, just a few feet off the water.

"Missile! Missile!" Smith hollered in Dempsey's ear.

"Forget the flare and grenades! Everyone out!" Dempsey commanded.

"Incoming in eight seconds," Baldwin said.

Dempsey watched the three SEALs in front of him leap out the open port door and then he jumped, taking a huge gulp of air just before hitting the frigid water. He heard Munn hit the water a fraction of a second later.

"Three seconds . . ." came a garbled voice in his earpiece, and he pulled and kicked with all his might, driving himself deeper and deeper into the black water. He pulled straight down, the salt water burning his eyes. He wouldn't have enough breath to make it back up if he didn't find the Proteus waiting.

His lungs were starting to burn, and the compulsion to exhale was overpowering. But he knew better than to give in. The breath in his lungs still contained precious oxygen, despite the rising concentration of CO_2 making him want to relieve the pressure. A wave of panic washed over him as he scanned the inky deep. He couldn't see the

Proteus anywhere. Chunk's words echoed in his head: *Swim down fast. It's going to be dark as shit, and if we let the current set us we'll never find it.*

Just when he was about to abort and pull for the surface, the missile above found its mark. A brilliant flash illuminated the ocean around him, and as the Ansat disintegrated into a fireball above, the Proteus materialized in his peripheral vision. A cigar-shaped shadow looming off to his right and on depth with him. Chunk was right; the current had set him on the descent. He turned and swam toward the Proteus, scissor kicking and pulling with everything he had. Suddenly, the light above went out and the Proteus once again disappeared into the inky black.

Noooooo!

He wanted to scream, but that was impossible of course. His chest was on fire now as he pulled with everything he had.

A red glow seemed to ooze from the darkness ahead, and it was getting brighter.

And more yellow . . .

The hatch of the Proteus opening?

He pulled toward the light, his lungs a toxic volcano ready to blow—demanding he exhale to release the pressure. He felt hands on his shoulder, pulling him into the hazy yellow rectangle—his vision blurry in the ocean water. Something was being shoved into his hand. He felt the familiar shape of the regulator and thrust it into his mouth, exhaling sharply and smashing two fingers on the purge valve. Compressed air blasted water from the mouthpiece, and he took the longest, most desperate breath of his life. The diaphragm of the regulator trembled as he sucked the air into his furious lungs. He exhaled quickly, exchanging air with deep, controlled breaths, flooding his bloodstream with fresh oxygen as he willed his heart rate down and held hyperventilation at bay. His wits returned a moment later, and his thoughts went to his teammates.

Am I the first one? The only one? No, there had to be multiple rescue divers helping.

The diver who had handed him the regulator dragged him inside the SDV, and Dempsey pulled himself to the bench seat across the long hatch and felt something else shoved into his hand. He pulled the mask over his head and into place on his face, then pressed the heel of his left hand against the top, sealing it against his forehead and exhaling sharply through his nose. As he cleared his mask, the world came into view. Inside the yellow glow of the interior of the Proteus, he watched two other divers assisting his teammates. He counted them off by call sign: Two, Three, Five. His heart rate spiked as he identified each of the men.

Trip was still missing . . .

Dempsey grabbed the diver closest to the hatch and squeezed his shoulder. The diver met his gaze, and Dempsey held up one finger and pointed out the hatch. The Brit, who had a dive helmet on, nodded and said, "I know, mate. I'm going to go look for him." He launched himself out the open hatch and disappeared into the black.

Who knew where Trip's drop had been relative to theirs? If the helo had drifted or he'd made a last-second maneuver, he could have splashed down ten or fifteen yards farther away. And the longer he was out there, the more the current was separating him from the Proteus, which was station-keeping with its thrusters. Jaw clenched on his regulator, Dempsey scanned the inside of the Proteus for a weight belt and fins. A firm hand gripped his shoulder; he whirled and saw Munn, who'd already changed over to a full-face mask.

"They got him, JD. He's okay," Munn said and pointed to the open hatch where the SBS diver was shuttling Trip inside, the SEAL breathing from an octopus on the Brit's rig.

Dempsey closed his eyes in relief as the hatch swung down into place behind them.

Thank God in heaven—everyone had made it.

Dempsey followed Munn's lead and swapped into a dive helmet and purged the water out with a dull, echoing hiss.

"Looks like we're two for two in helo crashes," Chunk said from where he sat on Dempsey's left, the SEAL officer's voice tinny in the helmet's headset. "Wanna go for a hat trick?"

"Total silence, please," came a whisper on the open channel in Dempsey's helmet—from the diver in the cockpit. "We have lots of tech to make us invisible from the surface, so let's not get found cuz they hear us bullshitting."

Dempsey winked at Chunk, then wrapped his arms around himself and shivered as his body ceded all its heat to the frigid water. Yes, they had once again pulled off an impossible mission with a miracle escape, but what was the point if he died from hypothermia over the next six hours? He closed his eyes and visualized maintaining his core body temperature when he suddenly felt a current of warm water begin to circulate inside the cabin. A lazy, relieved smile spread across his face.

God bless the nerds who had designed this thing.

They really had thought of everything.

PART III

The modern American wartime strategy is governed by a zero-friendly-casualty premise. I can assure you, your Russian counterpart has no such illusions or constraints.

—Levi Harel

CHAPTER 34

Ember Boeing 737
42,000 Feet Over the Atlantic, 120 Miles West of Spain
June 25
1530 Local Time

He wasn't ready to be in his rack, despite the aching, bone-weary fatigue, so instead Dempsey stretched out in an oversize leather recliner in the jet's lounge. Remote in hand, he was staring at the black screen of the TV he'd yet to turn on. He wanted his mind to drift to nowhere, but it refused. For some reason he couldn't articulate, instead of feeling like they'd just gained the upper hand on Zeta by disrupting their command and control, he felt like they'd fallen another step behind. Neither Arkady Zhukov nor Malik had been among the dead, which meant the mastermind and his agent were both still out there.

"John Dempsey retired to his easy chair," said a female voice. "Now there's something I wouldn't have believed."

Dempsey startled and looked over at Grimes, smiling at him from the door to the bunkroom.

"Ha," he laughed. "Believe it, sister. One day, when all the work is done . . ."

"So never."

He smiled. "Right—never. But a guy can dream."

Grimes slid into the chair next to him, smoothed a runaway hair from her cheek, and tucked it behind her left ear. "You good, JD?"

"All good," he said. "Five by five."

"So what do you think his next move is?"

She didn't need to specify. They both knew who she meant.

"I don't know, Lizzie," he said honestly. "Chunk grabbed a bagful of drives and laptops from their ops center, but who knows if there's anything useful, much less something that can tell us their next move." He sighed and rubbed his eyes, then looked back up at her and tried to smile but failed. "But if anyone can figure it out, it's Baldwin and his boys. Once they get started on the shit we bring them from the X, miracles tend to occur. Taking out Vyborg might slow Zeta down enough for us to figure out their next move before they hit us back."

She nodded, but her lips were pursed. "You think that's true?"

"I don't know. From what I saw, Vyborg looked more like a training facility than a command and control center—at least the way we're used to it. I can't put my finger on it. I know that we do things differently than the Russians, but this just didn't feel like we took out anything important or killed anyone that mattered."

Grimes nodded, staring at a point off in space. "My gut's screaming the same thing. If taking out the site in Vyborg would cripple Zeta, then why was it so easy to do?"

Dempsey leaned in and stared at her, a smug smile and raised eyebrows.

She rolled her eyes.

"You know what I mean. I know you guys are the wonder shit and no one else on earth could have pulled it off, but where was the security?

Why were the buildings so easy to breach? Where was a two-minute QRF instead of fifteen? Don't you feel that way, JD?"

"Hide in plain sight, right?" he said, but he wasn't convinced, either.

"I get that. That's what we do—hide in plain sight as a security consulting firm's corporate flight department at a medium-size commercial airport. But if someone tried to hit Ember, they'd get nowhere. The TOC is in a secure bunker with no access and no way to guess what's going on underground. Even satellites see nothing but a boring flight hangar. And if you did get in, you'd be in for a helluva firefight. But Vyborg was just a bunch of shacks in the woods. Chunk said their 'operations center' wasn't a real TOC, more like a couple of computer workstations you might find in a small business."

"So what are you saying?" Dempsey asked. "That we got tricked? That Vyborg was a decoy facility?"

"I don't know," she said, but her eyes said the gears in her mind were turning. She shifted in her chair. "What if this Zeta unit is a collection of fully autonomous operators, centralized under the control of just one individual? What if Buz is right, and Arkady Zhukov—not Petrov—is the mastermind behind everything? All along we've been hunting Malik, referring to him as the Russian ghost, but he's like us. He's a weapon, not command and control. Arkady is the *real* Russian ghost. The man hasn't been photographed in more than fifteen years."

"Yeah, but how is that any different from Ember? Jarvis created us and runs the show, and we operate in the shadows."

"It's not the same. Jarvis is the DNI. He's highly visible and fully vested into the IC hierarchy and chain of command. Yes, we operate in the black, but there's lots of communication up and down the chain; Smith, Jarvis, and Warner all provide input, and we operate as a collective unit. Don't get me wrong, I'm not saying Ember's a democracy, but we are highly integrated and use a team model. What if Zeta doesn't work like that? What if Zeta trains up their operators, puts them out there in their NOCs, and then activates them with a text message or single code word phone call? Maybe Zeta is the evolution of the Soviet Union's Cold War illegals program in the 1980s. It appears to have some of the same hallmarks."

"Maybe, but Malik is more operator than spy. And we know he coordinates with other assets. We saw that in Turkey and the Baltics."

"Yeah, but I don't think those assets were Zetas—I think they were *his* assets. In Turkey, he was using a PKK splinter faction. In Narva and Klaipėda it was Amarov's Vory hit men. What if Arkady's modus operandi is to have every Zeta operative stand up his or her own autonomous networks and use those networks to execute missions locally?"

"It doesn't seem very efficient," Dempsey said, screwing up his face. "The proficiency and talent of the team would be far below our level. We'd kick their ass in every engagement."

"Yes, but in ninety-nine percent of the missions, they're not up against Ember. Hell, most of the time they're up against local law enforcement or civilians. We've all heard the old expression—perfect is the enemy of good. Well, that's Zeta. I think Arkady is using a different paradigm than Jarvis, and as much as I hate to say it, Arkady's approach—for the type of operations he's focused on conducting— might be more effective. We're trying to stop anarchy, mayhem, and terrorism, whereas he's trying to cause those very things. Imagine having a hundred Zetas, all over the globe, hiding in their NOCs ready to go. If one dude gets taken out, no big deal because the organization does not rely on him for any other mission than the ones his network can handle. Moreover, there's nothing tying that agent's network back to Russia. It provides Arkady arm's-length separation and plausible deniability for every operation that goes bad. It worked on us in Turkey. We were hunting the PKK command and control for the ringleader. It wasn't until that Screen unit showed up to grab Allen that we confirmed Russian involvement. And I bet that wasn't Malik's call. He'd exfiltrated already. My point is, a dozen Zetas working autonomously and independently with their own network of paid assets would be far cheaper and more stealthy than standing up a dozen Task Force Embers to try to do the same work."

Dempsey contemplated that a moment. "Jesus, Lizzie, do you think that's what's really going on here?"

"It's the theory Buz and I have been teasing out over the last hour."

"Well, that's scary as shit."

"Yeah," she said with a solemn nod. "Because no matter how hard we try, even if we devote all our time and resources to the problem, we'd never get them all."

"Then we shouldn't bother trying," Dempsey said, rubbing his stubbled chin.

"What do you mean?" she said, taken aback.

"I mean you're right, it would be a waste of time because we'd fail. It's an endless and frustrating game of whack-a-mole. We'd be better off taking out the man in charge of the tasking. We'd be better off focusing all our efforts on finding and killing Arkady."

"And pray there isn't just someone else who inherits the code words from him when he's gone."

He nodded and rose from his chair. "I'm gonna get some sleep," he lied.

"John?" she said, stopping him at the door.

"Yeah?"

"Nice work tonight. I wish I could have been there with you guys."

"Thanks," he said, turning to look at her. "I'm kinda glad you weren't this time."

"Why's that?" she asked, her voice a little hollow.

He smiled warmly at her. "Because if you had been on the X, we'd all be dead. Your quick thinking and attention to detail is the only reason we made it out. Thanks for, well, being you."

Her cheeks went rosy at this, and nothing else needed to be said.

He turned and headed for the bunkroom. Three minutes later, he was lying on his back staring up, eyes open but out of focus. Instead of obsessing about Elinor, his mind was fretting about a new worry—Grimes and Buz's terrifying Zeta network theory. Because if they were right, the Russian ghost was not their only problem. Malik wasn't alone out there, and God only knew how many others just like him had been tasked to unleash payback for what Ember had just done in Vyborg.

CHAPTER 35

Valerian stared out the window of the bizjet thinking about war.

Russia and America were both very, very good at it, but they approached warfare from completely different perspectives. In a strange way, their national symbols embodied these fundamental differences. The bald eagle, the majestic symbol of the USA, was the ultimate embodiment of finesse in nature—soaring above, navigating complicated thermals and winds, observing its prey from on high waiting until the perfect moment of weakness or inattention to strike. And when the eagle finally decided to make its move, it did so with perfect timing, trajectory, and speed, striking its prey with superior precision, delivering a razor-honed talon to the jugular.

Russians were not eagles and held no such illusions.

The Russians had correctly chosen the grizzly bear to symbolize their national identity. Unlike the eagle, which prefers to soar above nature's war zone, only participating on its own terms, the bear lumbers his entire life in the trenches. The bear doesn't migrate to flee the hardship of winter, nor does the bear fly away from a challenge. The bear endures, the bear suffers, and the bear must establish his dominance over every challenger in his dominion over and over and over again. In a fight, the bear mauls—calling upon his mass, his strength, and his tenacity to crush, dismember, and outlast his adversary.

The problem with how Valerian had been engaging the Americans was that he had forgotten his identity. As a Zeta, he had spent so long acting like an American operator, he'd forgotten how to be a bear. Valerian blamed Arkady for this. The old man had eschewed the traditional Russian paradigms and trained each Zeta to be a bird of prey. He'd even christened the Vyborg training facility Bright Falcon. But in aerial combat, a falcon will lose to an eagle nine times out of ten. Valerian was tired of fighting the Americans on their own terms. And so, when planning how to attack the Ember facility, he had decided it was time to return to his Russian roots. In this engagement, he would be a bear, not a falcon. This mission was not about finesse and precision. Tonight, he was going to maul his adversary to death, and when he was done the carcass that remained would be ripped to pieces and unrecognizable.

The private jet he'd chartered to fly him and his Zeta colleagues to Newport News had just finished taxiing. The commercial hangar was located across the tarmac from the main terminal and therefore across from the Ember hangar just north of the main terminal, near the end of the row of hangars containing various commercial operations. Valerian glanced out a port window at the target. Arkady's high-placed spy, Catherine Morgan, had provided Gavriil with sufficient information to plan the operation. Initially, the other three Zetas had balked at Valerian's tactical pivot, but he was very persuasive—and as Prime he had the privilege of pulling rank. Tonight, they were going to hit

Ember with a sledgehammer so hard that all the Americans' high-tech surveillance and security countermeasures would be useless.

The cockpit door opened, and the copilot stepped out to greet them.

"Hey, fellas, looks like we got you here a few minutes early. You're going to disembark on the tarmac and head into the terminal, where we'll get your luggage delivered. Let me just get the door open and you can be on your way," the pilot said, his gaze ending on Valerian.

"Thank you, but if you could just tell the baggage handlers to set our luggage on the tarmac, we'd prefer to carry it ourselves," Valerian said, adopting a generic American accent. "Some of the contents are quite delicate and expensive. We'll just wait on board until its ready."

The pilot shrugged and unlocked and lowered the air-stair. "Suit yourself," he said. "This was our last flight for the evening, so that's fine."

Five minutes later, the copilot notified him that the baggage had been unloaded and was waiting for them on the tarmac. Valerian and his four Zeta comrades exited the jet and found their bags and hard crates stacked in a pile. A luggage handler was standing next to a Mule ATV hitched up to a small flatbed trailer.

"You sure you guys don't want me to drive this stuff over to the terminal for you?" the man said. "It's quite a bit of stuff."

"No, thank you," Valerian said, going straight to his bag. He unzipped the lower compartment, reached his hand inside, and his fingers found the HK VP9 pistol with suppressor installed. In a swift, fluid movement he pulled the weapon out and shot the luggage handler in the forehead before the man even knew what was happening. He then calmly walked back up the air-stair and into the jet, where he killed the pilot and copilot with a single round to the head each.

By the time he returned to the tarmac, two of his teammates had tossed the body of the luggage handler into the luggage compartment in the belly of the plane and were shutting the hatch. Meanwhile, Gavriil had opened the largest of the plastic hard cases and was quickly and expertly priming the EPFCG—explosively pumped flux compression generator—one of dozens of such units that Russian Zetas had smuggled into the United States and had hidden in major US cities to take down critical telecommunications and power grid infrastructure in the event of a nonnuclear conflict with America. These units were the result of fifty years of refinement of the original electromagnetic pulse generators first developed in the Soviet Union in 1951. Their device used explosive charges to rapidly compress a magnetic field, thereby releasing a single concentrated, and immensely powerful, burst of electromagnetic energy. The resulting EM wave would fry electrical components and render them dysfunctional unless protected with EM shielding or a Faraday cage.

"Ready," Gavriil said, stepping away from the open crate and moving toward the Mule 4x4, where Valerian and the two other Zetas were loading the last of their bags in a trailer.

A moment later, all five men were sitting in the ATV, speeding across the tarmac toward the Ember hangar. As they crossed the runway, Valerian glanced left and saw the descending aviation lights of an aircraft on approach. A malevolent grin crept across his face. *This ought to be interesting,* he thought. Twenty seconds later, he braked to a stop outside the Ember hangar and turned to Gavriil.

"Now," Valerian said, and Gavriil pressed a button on the remote control.

At first, nothing happened and he was about to tell Gavriil to press the button again, but then he heard a muted pop and the entire airport went dark. A nonnuclear EMP wasn't like a bomb—no brilliant fireball, flying shrapnel, or concussive shock wave. In fact, Valerian couldn't even tell a tsunami of electromagnetic energy had just rolled through every cell in his body; it was as if nothing had happened.

The incoming plane, a modern fly-by-wire passenger jet, told a different a story, however. He watched the jet, which was mid-flair, immediately yaw and then hit the ground so hard its starboard landing gear collapsed. The plane tilted, spun, and skidded off the runway with a horrendous crash.

A nice distraction for emergency services to focus on, he thought. *Rescue the civilians over there while we slaughter your shadow warriors over here.*

He turned his attention back to the Ember hangar, which was now completely dark, and got to work. Despite having never operated together before, his four-man team moved quickly, silently, and with hive-like purpose. While Gavriil opened the second hard case, an electromagnetically shielded box that had kept their electronic gear protected during the EMP blast, Valerian passed out body armor and weapons. Yukov unpacked the explosives while Franco prepped their gas masks and Kostya handed out CS/OC gas grenades. Thirty seconds later, they were fully kitted-up with respirators on, comms up, and eyes on the target.

Valerian and Gavriil split left while the others went right. In addition to the massive hangar bay doors, the building had traditional swing doors on the north and south sides of the building. The original plan was to breach simultaneously and enter from both sides to clear the hangar bay with converging two-man teams, but one look at the setup and Valerian changed the plan. The main doors were stout—engineered ballistic slabs with hardened steel frames that probably used multipoint locking bolts.

"Fuck these doors," Valerian said over the comms channel. "It will be easier to blow a hole in the hangar bay door."

"Check," Yukov said on the radio.

Gavriil nodded his agreement and sprinted around the corner back to the hangar bay door and set a massive breacher charge. Five seconds later, he was back around the corner, huddled shoulder to shoulder with Valerian.

"Clear," Gavriil said.

"Blow it," Valerian said, covering his ears.

The explosion that followed shook the wall they had their backs pressed against and was the loudest breacher detonation Valerian had ever heard. But it didn't matter. Time was their enemy, and Gavriil knew this. He had to err on the side of overkill because they didn't have time to try again until they got the yield just right. Valerian and Gavriil were on their feet a heartbeat later and sprinting around the corner. Through a jagged, gaping four-foot hole in the hangar door, the inside of the hangar glowed a dim, eerie amber.

"They have chemical emergency lights," Gavriil said, annoyed.

Even through the face mask, the expression on Gavriil's face told him the other man was running the same risk-reward calculation he was. Odds were good they would take fire on entry.

"Three, gas," Valerian said.

Franco stepped up next to the hole and pointed the wide-mouth barrel of his Russian 6G30—a revolver-style grenade launcher—into the void. He squeezed off three rounds, each making a hollow *thrump* sound as he covered the left, middle, and right sides of the hangar.

"Thermals?" Valerian said to Gavriil.

The operator pulled up a handheld thermal imager and scanned the inside of the hangar. "Two bodies, both armed, but they're running toward a plane."

"Go, before they get inside the plane," Valerian said to Yukov, who was standing by with his assault rifle at the ready, his laser target designator switched on.

The Zeta slipped into the hangar, and Valerian heard three shots followed a second later by "Clear" over the radio. "Two KIA."

Valerian and his three teammates ducked through the hole and into the hangar, which was rapidly filling with billowing clouds of tear gas. Valerian scanned the completely ordinary-looking building for the hidden entrance that Catherine Morgan had described.

"There," Gavriil said and pointed to a metal cabinet-style locker with double doors positioned against the wall on the south side of the building. "It is the hidden access to the elevator. You need a code to open the doors and to call the elevator car."

"Blow it," Valerian said.

Gavriil sprinted to the locker and set another large breacher at the base of the cabinet in the middle of the doors. He stepped back, quickly assessed the placement, then took cover and blew the charge. The metal cabinet exploded, sending hunks of twisted sheet metal in every direction, with the bulk of the cabinet landing intact with a resounding thud twenty feet away.

Valerian moved toward the hidden access, Franco, Yukov, and Kostya running stride for stride at his side. Where there had once been a cabinet, there was now just a gaping hole rimmed by twisted rebar protruding from the concrete floor. He looked down the shaft and saw the top of an elevator, which, thanks to the EMP, was stuck inoperable at the bottom. Valerian looked at Yukov and gave the order with his eyes. The stout Zeta nodded and tossed an entire brick of C-4 wired with a remote detonator down into the shaft. They moved back as a unit, covering their ears.

Yukov pressed the wireless detonator button, and the C-4 turned the elevator shaft into a giant vertical cannon—shooting a column of flame to the ceiling of the hangar, along with massive hunks of shrapnel that punched holes in the roof. Once the flames collapsed, the Zetas moved back to the smoldering hole and in unison each man pulled a black nylon climbing rope from a pouch, tied one end off, and threaded the other end through a pulley rig clipped to the front of their respective kits. Before descending, Franco fired a single tear gas grenade down into the hole. Valerian held them for a five count, giving the gas time to fill the shaft and obscure their descent from anyone who might try to sight up from below. On his hand signal, they silently rappelled down the charred elevator shaft. Tiny flames flickered here and there as pieces of exposed insulation burned, sending tendrils of darker gray smoke spiraling upward within the rising cloud of gas.

When he reached what was left of the elevator car, he halted the team in midair to survey the access point. The top of the car was completely obliterated, and the double doors leading from the shaft into the Ember compound were bowed out, creating a narrow gap. Valerian eyed the gap and prayed they could squeeze through it, because prying the misshapen doors open on their tracks would be impossible. And if they had to ascend to set off another charge, then the mission would be so far off the timeline they would probably fail.

"More gas," he said, turning to Franco. "Two through the gap, then toss a flash-bang."

Franco nodded and slid down to the bottom of the shaft, landing softly. He fired his last two gas grenades through the gap between the elevator doors, dropped the launcher, yanked a flash-bang from his vest, and tossed it through the gap as well. The flash-bang detonated while Valerian and the other three Zetas landed beside Franco, who had taken a knee and was now unloading a prolonged volley through the gap. The Zeta emptied his entire magazine, blindly but systematically hosing down whatever and whoever was on the other side.

Franco scooted aside to change magazines while Yukov took the initiative to squeeze through the gap between the elevator doors. Gavriil went next, followed by Franco and Kostya, with Valerian going last into the smoky, gas-filled Ember compound. His respirator hissed in cadence with each breath as he advanced into the enemy's den. His crimson laser sight carved a menacing line through the swirling noxious fog as he searched for his first target.

Without warning, a three-round burst of gunfire shattered the silence—the rounds zipping past inches from his left ear.

And so it begins, he thought. At long last he was able to turn the killer inside loose with no restraints, no restrictions, no limits.

Tonight, the winner of the battle between Zeta and Ember would be decided.

And the war between Russia and America would begin.

CHAPTER 36

Ember Director's Office
Ember Complex
Newport News/Williamsburg International Airport
June 26
0110 Local Time

After thirteen years in Army Special Forces, much of it with the elite Tier One Delta Force combating terrorism, Shane Smith had allowed himself the luxury of believing he'd lived a charmed life. As an operator, he'd led teams into the world's darkest places, faced the most violent adversaries, and yet emerged on the other side with few scars to show for it. The last-minute plan always worked out, the enemy's bullet always narrowly missed, and when the shit hit the fan, the cavalry always arrived just in the nick of time. And through it all, he'd smiled and found himself thinking—*if I was supposed to die, I'd be dead already.*

But when mainline power went out and an explosion shook the complex so violently the glass wall of the conference room shattered, he wondered if Newport News had been hit with a tactical nuke. Now, as noxious smoke filled Ember's "unbreachable" underground fortress, all his delusions of invulnerability disintegrated.

In the event of a normal power outage, Ember's robust battery backup system would instantly restore power and bring all the systems back online. But for some reason, that hadn't happened. Only their critical systems, those that were electronically shielded, were operational. All topside security cameras and hangar systems had been bricked, which lent credence to his tactical nuke theory. Thankfully, the engineers who had built this facility had designed it to withstand an electromagnetic pulse that would normally wipe out all their systems. EM shielding and buried cable that ran up to a secondary antennae tower two miles away ensured that his distress signal to Jarvis was transmitted. He didn't know how long it would take the DNI to mobilize a QRF from Camp Peary to the north or the SEAL Teams in Virginia Beach to the south, but what he did know was that it would be too long. The inbound Ember Boeing with Dempsey and the gang was their best hope, and they were ten minutes out. By the time the cavalry arrived, whatever was about to happen here would be over.

Ten minutes—that's all. That's the difference between life and death. If the Boeing had left just ten minutes sooner, if the winds had been only slightly less on their nose, if they had carried just a couple of knots more airspeed—if any of these things had happened, then Ember's Special Activities Division would be engaged with the attackers already. And we would have a chance.

But they didn't have those minutes, did they? So it fell to him, Martin, and Latif to hold the line. Adamo and Buz Wilson were capable with firearms, but they weren't seasoned operators. The rest of the staff here tonight, including Chip and Dale and Amanda Allen, needed to be protected. And then there was the business of destroying everything that could be taken and harvested by the enemy . . .

Smith opened the application and typed in his user ID and password.

Emergency Protocol Omega. Activate?

He double-clicked on the **YES** icon beneath the prompt.

Authenticate?

A grenade exploded and automatic rifle fire echoed outside his office as he typed in his seventeen-digit command code—a code he never in a million years envisioned using. Ember was darker than black. Only a few people on earth even knew they existed, and fewer still knew about this facility, let alone its exact location.

How the fuck is this possible?

After the last keystroke, he hit "Enter."

Executed . . .

Smith slipped his body armor kit over his head and grabbed a SOPMOD M4 assault rifle as the scorched-earth program began to run. It would spread rapidly through the entire Ember network, destroying every file on every server, hard drive, and even laptop connected to the system.

SOPMOD M4 fire joined the mix, and he knew Martin and Latif were in the fight.

He tapped the earpiece to activate his comms and moved to the office door.

"Ember is One. One, Two, and Three will hold the TOC while Four and Five egress the rest of the team to Omega," he said, referring to the virtually impenetrable safe room at the very back of the complex. The Omega room had a twelve-inch-thick concrete floor, walls, and ceiling with a titanium liner. The O2 tanks and CO2 scrubbers were internal, and the room had its own emergency comms gear with a dedicated buried hardline and ample food and water stores. The entire

Ember staff could survive inside for up to five days—if they could get there in time to seal the door.

Smith scanned over his rifle, turning left and right, as he exited his office and moved down the short hall behind the TOC. He found Adamo crouched on one knee, firing a rifle into the TOC, the thick glass door propped open against his thigh. Wilson was beside him, firing his own rifle into the fray. Smith noted that neither of them had headsets or radios, so his last command had fallen on deaf ears. Allen stood behind Adamo, firing a pistol over the Operations Officer's shoulder. She turned and looked at him, her eyes wide.

"What's happening?" she asked, her voice cracking.

"I don't know, but I need everyone to pull back to Omega," Smith commanded.

Allen remained frozen, her eyes on him.

"Who are they? What do they want? We already moved Sylvie Bessonov and Amarov to a CIA black site."

He put a hand on her shoulder, and her eyes flickered back to the present.

"If this is the Russians, then they don't know that. Now move," he commanded.

"You need me here," Adamo said in between controlled bursts from his rifle. "Martin is down."

"Fine. Allen, get the hell outta here. If the breachers make it to the safe room before we do, secure the door."

"Without you?" she asked, her mouth hanging open.

He nodded. "But don't worry, we'll be there."

Smith turned his attention back to the TOC, where he saw Luca Martin sprawled facedown on the floor, lying in a pool of blood beside his rifle. The glass doors across from theirs were completely gone. "Go," he barked, and Allen sprinted down the hall, toward the wooden door leading to the common room.

To his left, Latif was firing regular three-round bursts from behind a toppled desk. Through the smoke that now filled the TOC, Smith saw motion and crossing beams of laser designators in the small antechamber lobby.

"Reload," Latif hollered from where he was crouching.

Smith leaned in over Adamo, firing two three-round bursts into the smoke while Latif changed his magazine. In his peripheral vision, Smith saw a red targeting laser find its way to the side of Latif's head, but before Smith could yell a warning, the ex–Green Beret pitched backward, blood spitting out of the other side of his head.

Martin and Latif . . . both gone.

The unmistakable odor of riot gas hit Smith's nostrils.

Oh fuck . . .

"Pull back to Omega," he shouted, squeezing Adamo's shoulder and nodding to Wilson beside him. Wilson fired a burst into the converging cloud of noxious gas while pedaling backward. Holding his breath, his eyes beginning to tear, Smith fired a final volley at an advancing shadow.

"Grenade!" Adamo hollered, and Smith felt sharp pain as Adamo barreled into him, hitting the left side of his rib cage hard enough that Smith felt a crack. The tackle propelled him down the hall. He stumbled to his right knee and caught himself with his outstretched left arm, both of which stung with pain on impact. The blast concussion hit him next, enveloping him in heat, and the world disappeared in a white flash that left him light blind. He spun left and pulled his rifle up, squeezing his eyes tight. When his vision returned a half second later, a man in black Nomex wearing a gas mask was rounding the corner through the door. The assaulter held a subcompact machine pistol and was spraying bullets in an arc. Reflex took over, and Smith placed his red dot on the man's head and squeezed. Three rounds, milliseconds apart, tore through the man's head.

"Pull back, Buz," he coughed, yelling at the man behind him. Tendrils of tear gas pursued them with serpentine malevolence. "We're overrun."

He flicked his rifle to single-round mode with his right thumb, more on instinct than a conscious decision, as he retreated down the hall. A second assaulter came through the door of the common room and Smith fired, but the asshole pulled back just in time.

"Where's Adamo?" Buz yelled, shooting while backpedaling.

Smith glanced long enough to see what was left of Adamo on the floor where he'd saved Smith's life.

"He didn't make it."

A wave of angst and fury swept over Smith and he turned back to unleash hell on the encroaching assaulters, but instead of seeing enemy shooters a second grenade came bouncing down the hallway. Smith turned and tackled Wilson, driving them both through the partially opened door to the common room. The blast propelled him the rest of the way into the room, and he felt searing pain in his trailing left leg—like someone had burned him with a blowtorch. He landed on top of Wilson, who quickly scrambled out from under him.

"We gotta move, Smith," Buz said, grabbing him under the left armpit.

Smith flicked his M4 back to three-round burst and fired several times as Wilson towed him by his kit. Smith kicked his legs, heels slick with blood, slipping as he tried to get traction. He fired again and again at the doorway behind them as Wilson dragged him across the room with incredible speed. The next thing he knew, they were through the common room and into the bunkroom. Wilson hoisted Smith to his feet and met his eyes.

"You good, man?" the CIA man asked, his face tight and bathed in sweat.

Smith shifted his weight to his injured left leg, felt a stab of pain and warm blood flowing freely into his boot, but the leg held his weight.

"Good," he coughed and sucked in several lungfuls of clean, uncontaminated air. He wiped away the river of snot running from his nose and blinked the tears clear as Buz came into steely-eyed focus. "Jeez, you're badass for like a . . . what? A seventy-year-old?"

"Fuck you, kid," the CIA man said through a combat smile and then tugged at his kit. "Let's go."

A burst of small-arms fire peppered the closed door behind them as they sprinted across the bunkroom and exited into the cage lockers where they kept their weapons and gear. He was limping now, his left leg screaming in protest despite the adrenaline fueling his retreat. They ran the gap between the parallel rows of cages—six large ones holding the SAD team members' gear and then smaller cages for the analysts and administrators, the latter of which he suddenly realized included him, despite one large SAD cage still having the name "SMITH" beside the unlocked gate.

The compulsion to grab a fresh magazine was overpowering, but there was no time for that. A massive explosion shook the bunkroom behind them, followed immediately by machine gun fire as the assaulters methodically worked their way toward them—tossing grenades before each doorway breach. Smith felt a wave of dizziness and then nausea sweep over him as they exited the equipment room, and he stumbled against the doorjamb before weaving into the corridor behind Wilson. Numbness now replaced the pain in his leg, though somehow the limb was still heeding his commands. He looked down and saw his left pant leg soaked bright red.

Clipped a fucking artery. I'm bleeding out . . .

A door on the right side of the corridor cracked open and light flooded in. He raised his rifle, noticing that it felt impossibly heavy and he had a hard time keeping it steady. But instead of masked assaulters, Amanda Allen's face appeared in the gap with Baldwin's young protégés, Chip and Dale, behind her. He lowered his weapon, and the trio emerged from the conference room and stepped into the corridor.

"The Omega room is two doors down," someone said.

"Hurry," someone else said.

"Where's Baldwin?" Smith asked as a wave of light-headedness washed over him.

"He's not here tonight," Chip said—or was it Dale? He heard a chuckle and realized it was him, laughing for some reason.

"I didn't know the access code," Allen said as they shuffled down the corridor. "He doesn't look so good," she added, but now he thought she was talking to Buz.

He nodded, his head light again.

I'm still seeing in color. I got some time left to get a tourniquet on.

"Shane, none of us knows the code," Buz said, propping him up against the wall beside the titanium door. "You're going to have to do it. Hurry."

He swallowed and looked at the biometric scanner and keypad on the wall beside the door. He pressed a button and the panel flipped out ninety degrees, revealing a flat piece of black glass behind it. Smith wiped his bloody palm on his shirt, then pressed his right hand onto the plate. The reader flashed green and he tried to enter the six-digit code, but his index finger couldn't find the right buttons.

"I'll do it for you," Allen said. "What's the code?"

He looked at her and she looked so pretty . . . glowing . . .

"Shane, what's the code?" she said with urgency.

"It's four, nine, nine, seven, two, four," he said and was surprised how quiet his voice sounded.

He felt a tap on his arm and looked up at Wilson, confused for a moment, but Wilson pointed back down the hall and he understood. They were coming. He raised his rifle, barely able to lift it now, and watched the targeting dot dance unsteadily on the door to the equipment room. Beside him, he heard a beep and a hiss as the door to the safe room opened outward into the hallway.

"Everyone in," he hollered. His voice sounded tinny in his cotton-filled ears. "Hurry." Even to him, the command sounded slurred.

Shadows moved in front of him and he fired, aware that Wilson, beside him, had already been shooting. Muzzle flashes danced in front of him as enemy bullets whistled down the corridor at them. In his peripheral vision, he saw his people ducking and scrambling through the gap to safety.

"Let's go," Buz hollered as enemy fire pounded the floor and walls around them.

A rifle shot rang out and the slender young man they called Dale, who always wore a classic rock T-shirt and cradled a foamy latte in his hand, pitched forward as if someone had smacked him in the back of the head with a two-by-four, and his body collapsed across the threshold, half in, half out of the safe room. Allen screamed something as she grabbed Dale by the wrists and pulled him inside. Smith saw the black shadows advancing rapidly, almost upon them. With a surge of adrenaline from somewhere deep inside, he grabbed Wilson and shoved him through the door just as a bullet tore through the side of his left shoulder. His chest immediately felt tight and heavy and he wobbled on his feet. To his dismay, Allen stepped into the gap and reached to pull him into the room, but then she froze, looking past him, her eyes wide.

"You . . . ," she said, her voice a long, hot breath.

Smith turned, in what felt like slow motion, to face the enemy—an operator holding a compact machine gun in one hand and a gas mask with the other.

For a moment he thought it was Dempsey, there to rescue them, but then the dark-haired Dempsey clone said, "What an unexpected surprise. How lovely to see you again, Amanda." His teeth gleamed behind a vulpine grin.

It was him—Malik. The Russian ghost. Dempsey's nemesis.

With all the strength left in his body, Smith shoved Allen backward into the safe room.

"No!" Malik screamed.

Flashes of white light popped in his visual field as what felt like four consecutive hardball pitches hit his chest. Desperate hands clawed at his kit through the closing gap, but Smith batted them away as he used his body weight to slam the door shut. As he slid down the slab, his legs going to jelly, he heard the magnetic lock click, securing the room behind him.

"No, no, no . . ."

He couldn't remember who was yelling at him or why.

Reality morphed, like an iridescent bubble expanding around him, and he was lying on the pitcher's mound after the line drive had hit him in the right side of the chest. It burned like fire as he tried to pull in a breath . . . and then his dad was standing over him, staring down with love and concern, his woodland cammo hunting jacket dark against a summer blue sky.

You okay, son?

He wanted to be a man. He wanted to be like his dad, but it hurt so bad.

"I'm okay," he gasped, and his dad smiled.

But that wasn't right. His dad was dead. Dead and buried.

His dad spoke softly, haloed by the sunlight behind him.

That's my little man.

"Where is the American operator? Where is the man you thought could kill me?"

Smith looked up, his dad's face winking in and out of existence. He reached back with his left hand, felt the nearly imperceptible seam of the sealed door, and smiled a sticky smile, his lips pulling apart in the blood.

"Coming for you," he said to the Russian ghost and tried to laugh, but all that came out was a gurgle as a bloody bubble grew from his lips and popped.

"Good," the Russian said. "Then he can join you in hell."

Smith tried to choke out a "fuck you" but couldn't, so instead he slowly raised the middle finger of his left hand as the Russian ghost faded and his dad rematerialized.

I love you, Dad. I hope I made you proud.

"You did, son. You always did."

He didn't see the muzzle trained on his forehead.

He didn't hear the crack of gunpowder as the rifle discharged or feel any pain as the slug entered his skull . . .

Just a brilliant white light, and peace, and the dying certainty that Ember was still standing and this was not the end of all he had built.

CHAPTER 37

Valerian looked away from the American he'd just executed and checked his watch. *One minute behind the timeline.* All gunfire had ceased, and he presumed his men had taken the facility, but there were still rooms to clear.

"SITREP," he said into his mike.

"Three is KIA," Gavriil said, referring to the Zeta called Franco. Gavriil was standing a meter away, still scanning over his rifle, and he could hear the man's voice both over the open mike and aloud in the room beside him a microsecond later.

"Four and Five are fully operational," Kostya reported, answering for him and Yukov. "We're clearing any spaces we missed back to the entry, and then we'll harvest intel from their operations center."

The riot gas had reached the back corridor now, and while the concentration was low, the potency was high, and Valerian had to put his mask back on. Because they'd used gas on the entry, it was highly unlikely that American threats were lurking behind them. It was simply impossible to hide when you couldn't take a single breath without coughing.

"We're one minute behind the timeline," he said into his mike. "Four and Five clear back to the entry, but I want you topside to secure the hangar in preparation for egress. Two, go to the ops center to harvest data, and I'll search the remaining rooms for our captured comrades."

"Check," came the reply from Kostya.

Valerian turned to find Gavriil standing behind him, rifle at the ready. "Do you want me to help you clear?"

"No," Valerian said. "There's no time. Our chances of escape are already dwindling. And an American QRF is undoubtedly en route."

"And if you find Amarov and Sylvie here, what then?"

Valerian dragged his index finger across his neck.

Gavriil nodded, but Valerian saw a momentary flicker in the other man's eyes. *Anger, regret, frustration . . .* he couldn't be sure. What he was certain of, however, was that Gavriil had his own set of orders from the old man, orders that Valerian was certain involved putting a bullet in his brain. Were their situations reversed, Valerian would do the deed while they were still underground. He would use Gavriil to assist him up until the very last moment—helping to harvest intel and clearing rooms—because the timeline was already too short to do it alone. He would insist on being last man and let Gavriil begin the climb up the elevator shaft so that his hands were occupied, his weapon stowed, and his attention focused on egress. That's when Valerian would pull the trigger.

Or, he could do it right now . . .

"Is there something else?" Valerian asked, willing his finger to stay on the trigger guard.

"No," the other man said, turning and jogging away. "It's just a shame; I liked Sylvie."

Valerian watched him disappear through the door at the other end of the corridor. When he was satisfied it wasn't a feint and Gavriil wasn't coming back, he brought his rifle up and scanned the corridor for other rooms and exits. The elevator could not be the only method to access the Ember facility. In a fire, the Americans would not expect their premier clandestine service to climb out of an elevator shaft. No, there had to be an emergency egress hidden somewhere.

He quickly cleared the only other rooms in this back corridor, an empty SCIF and a mechanical room. The mechanical room was equipped with pumps, valves, air handlers, and a row of cabinet-size battery packs. At the far end of the room, damage-control gear—EABs, heavy fire-retardant jackets, boots, and helmets—hung on a large roller trolley. If he hadn't been hunting for a hidden exit, he would have completely overlooked the door behind it. He trotted over to the rack and shoved it out of the way, revealing a metal slab door with a simple placard that read EXIT. It had no handle or rocker bar, but it did have a three-point magnetic locking system and a small video screen embedded in the center of the slab. When he got within two feet of the door, the screen woke up and displayed a live camera view of what was on the other side—the twenty-first century equivalent of a "peephole."

"Clever," he murmured and pushed on the door, but it did not budge. He scanned the doorframe, saw a red plunger-style button, and pushed it. The locking bolts shifted with a triple click, and on his second push the door opened into a concrete tunnel lit by dimly glowing yellow lights in the ceiling.

"One, Two," Gavriil's voice said in his ear. "Looks like they ran a scorched-earth program on their servers. I've extracted four SSDs and some files from the Director's office that weren't in a safe, but that's all we have time for."

"Check. I finished my sweep; our people are not here. They must have moved them to another site," Valerian said. "Start your egress and move to the rally point. I'll be right behind you."

"I'll wait for you," Gavriil said. "Hurry."

Valerian smiled and pulled the rolling equipment rack back in front of the door. "*Da,* I'll be right there."

He eased the emergency door gently back against the frame so as not to make a sound and then took off at a full sprint down the tunnel. Neither the exit nor the tunnel had been reported by Catherine Morgan, and he'd not seen anything on satellite imagery indicative of where this tunnel ended. He might pop his head up into the middle of a deserted field or, just as likely, he might step out into a secure building where he would be greeted at gunpoint.

A fatalistic grin spread across his face at this cosmic roll of the dice that was about to decide his fate. Whatever happened next, at least he had the satisfaction of knowing that if it was his time to go, he would leave the world on his own terms and not those prescribed by the man he'd once embraced as father.

CHAPTER 38

Taxiway to the Corporate Hangars on the General Aviation Ramp
Newport News/Williamsburg International Airport
June 26
0125 Local Time

Dempsey shifted his weight back and forth on booted feet trying with futility to dissipate the anxious energy building inside him. His left hand flew across his kit, checking his loadout. It had been ten minutes since they'd lost comms with Ember. The last message had been an encrypted report from Smith that the Ember compound was under attack and that he was moving everyone to the Omega bunker. Since that transmission, the silence had been deafening. They had attempted to reach the DNI, but to no avail, relaying information through the watch commander at NCTC, who reported that the Newport News airport had been hit by an EMP, knocking out all power and communications. The air traffic control tower was dark, and all inbound traffic was being diverted to Dulles, Norfolk, and BWI—all traffic except for the Ember Boeing, which had touched down safely just seconds ago on a runway lit by emergency flares and flashers.

"I'll have you there in thirty seconds, JD," came the pilot's tense voice in Dempsey's ear. "Where do you want me to park this whale?"

"West corner of the hangar, nose in for cover as we egress," Dempsey said, checking that the safety was off on his assault rifle for the third time. "And watch for fire—I don't need you guys taking a hit."

"Check," the pilot said as the aircraft lurched through the turn off the taxiway and onto the ramp at dangerously high speed.

Dempsey reached up to steady himself using the overhead and felt Grimes's hand on his arm as she caught her own balance, the foot difference in their heights making it impossible for her to steady herself using the ceiling as he did. Munn and Chunk were pressed in close behind her, all of them primed and ready beside the hatch. Dempsey struggled to chase away the worry he felt for his Ember team family. Flashbulb memories from the surprise ambush two years ago in Yemen that had wiped out his entire Tier One SEAL Team played unbidden in his mind, distracting him at the worst possible time.

It's happening again, he thought. *Only this time on American soil.*

"How's this gonna work?" Chunk said, the normally easygoing southerner's face a mask of tension.

The question snapped Dempsey back to the present. He needed to focus on taking control of the crisis at hand instead of fretting over which of his Ember brothers and sisters he might be losing.

"We start by clearing the hangar," he said, leaning into another hard turn as the Boeing's tires squealed loudly. "Once we've secured topside, we split and retake the underground. You, Munn, and your guys will breach via the main entrance, and me and Grimes will make a stealth entry via the emergency exit tunnel. It's concealed in the woods outside the airport perimeter."

Chunk nodded. "But when you say the main entrance, you mean that hidden elevator thing Munn was telling me about?"

"Yeah, except it's coin-flip odds whether the elevator is serviceable. We need to be fluid. I might divert some of your guys to come with me if you're access limited in the hangar. Otherwise, the plan is to meet in the middle, two converging squads. Kill everyone who's a shithead. We leave Ember non-shooters in the Omega bunker until we've got everything else locked down. I'm not taking any chances."

Chunk nodded, and Dempsey watched the SEAL checking his own weapons and gear. He knew the man wanted to ask so many questions—like how long had Ember operated in plain sight out of a civilian airport a stone's throw from the East Coast SEAL community—but Chunk was a pro and he didn't go there.

"Who am I with?" Wang said, stepping up and holding an HK.

"You're staying here," Dempsey said, noting he'd never seen the young man so serious.

"But, John . . ."

Dempsey raised a hand, cutting the kid off. "I'm not keeping you out of the fight because I don't want your help. I'm holding you back because I need you here. Get on your computer and do that voodoo shit you do. Hack into the Zeta comms. Link with NSA and be my eyes and ears. Get me satellite coverage. There is no Ember anymore, Richard. You're my TOC, and we're going to need you."

Wang gave him a grim nod and said, "You can count on me."

"I know," he said and gave the boy genius a parting squeeze on the shoulder.

"Five seconds and the air-stair comes down, JD," the pilot announced.

"Check."

He rolled his head and twisted his shoulders right and then left, getting a half-dozen audible and satisfying cracks.

"Spear One, this is Liberty Crossing. SITREP?" said a new and familiar voice in Dempsey's ear—a voice that immediately knocked the edge off his nerves. From the day he'd joined the Tier One, and through all his time at Ember, no matter how terrible things got, Jarvis had been the one unwavering constant in his life. With Jarvis finally on the line, Dempsey felt his confidence surge and the fatalism he'd been battling melt away.

"We're at the hangar. Breaching in ninety seconds," Dempsey answered as the plane rocked to a stop and the grind of the pneumatic system signaled the air-stair coming down.

"Check," Jarvis said with total calm. "We have comms with Wilson. Omega is secure, with four souls, one urgent surgical among them. Four members outside of Omega, condition unknown, presumed urgent surgical or worse. These include One and Two as well as your two operators."

One and Two—meaning Smith and Adamo. Your two operators—that was Latif and Martin. Presumed urgent surgical or worse—translation: they were all casualties.

He heard Grimes suck in a breath and Munn mumble a tense "shit" behind him as they heard the news.

Fuck . . . I can't lose them; I won't do this again.

He fought the emotional upwelling, swallowing it down to a dark place to be dealt with later. As the air-stair reached the halfway point in its descent, he moved onto the platform, eager to go.

"We have satellite coverage in place," Jarvis continued. "No ability to penetrate the compound but suspect five assaulters in the initial breach. We hold two thermal signatures inside the hangar and one possible squirter who exited the hangar and is running toward the plane crash. He might be going for a vehicle or trying to get lost in the commotion. Shooter one in the hangar is in the north corner covering your approach through the hangar doors. Shooter two is in the west corner covering the main entrance access from the parking lot."

Dempsey was down the stairs moving to Munn's right as they quickstepped along the starboard side of the aircraft, the rest of his assault team two by two in trail. They were using the same call signs from the Vyborg mission, which felt like another lifetime ago even though it had been less than twenty-four hours since they'd executed a mirror image operation on Russian soil.

"Four and Six, you guys go after the squirter. We don't need him setting up on our six and we sure as hell don't want him getting away. Liberty, we need eyes for Mother—now aboard the Boeing," Dempsey said, referring to Wang in the mobile TOC on the jet. After the Vyborg op, Baldwin had taken a rare night off to celebrate his wedding anniversary. With Baldwin out of pocket and the rest of the Ember ops personnel either dead or incapacitated, that left only Wang to assume all signals and cyber duties for the team. "Mother, I'll need you to guide them to that squirter." Dempsey glanced over his shoulder at Trip and Riker.

The SEALs nodded at him.

"The rest of you are with me."

"Roger, Spear. Be advised, we have a QRF less than ten minutes out—a platoon from SEAL Team Four arriving by helo will be up in a few on this common frequency. Airport is under lockdown and all flights on hold," Jarvis said.

"Check," Dempsey said, moving to the corner of the hangar. He took a tactical knee as he surveyed the scene and saw the gaping hole the enemy assaulters had blasted in the hangar doors. The team fell in around him, with Chunk on his immediate right.

"Why'd they breach the hangar door like that?" Chunk said.

"Because the regular doors are hardened. We'll have trouble breaching them ourselves."

"It's suicide to go through that hole. We'd be fish in a barrel to those two shitheads in the hangar."

"Agreed," Dempsey said as an idea came to him and he turned to the SEAL sniper. "Saw, is that a telescoping ladder pole on your back?"

"Check," Saw said. "I always carry it so I can get up to balconies, rooftops, and shit."

The corner of Dempsey's mouth curled up. "Perfect, because there's a maintenance hatch on the roof of this hangar. I want you to climb up, open that bitch, and unload on these assholes. It will take them by surprise and—"

"The covering fire will give us a chance to duck in through that hole," Chunk said, finishing Dempsey's sentence.

"Exactly."

"I'm on it," Saw said and pulled the slick tactical accessory from his pack. The three-foot-long carbon-fiber telescoping pole had a hook on the end and extended to sixteen feet in length. Saw hooked the claw over a gutter strut and used the tiny interspersed foot cleats that popped out when the pole was fully extended to climb up to the roof. With apparent ease, he hauled himself up on to the gently domed metal roof and disappeared. Ten seconds later, he reported in: "Five at the hatch, opening now . . ."

"Spear, this is Mother," said Wang's voice in his ear, his timing impeccable. "I have good eyes. Tango One is positioned high on the north wall scaffold. Tango Two is behind the Citation jet beside the Ember elevator on the west side. I can't decrypt their comms, but say the word and I'll commence jamming."

"Do it now," he said, loving the fact that Wang was in the zone—giving them the exact information they needed when they needed it and hamstringing the Russian bastards so they couldn't communicate.

"Roger . . . jamming."

Dempsey chopped a hand, signaling for Chunk, Grimes, and Munn to follow him to the breach in the hangar door. They moved in unison, quickstepping in tactical crouches, and took bookend paired positions on either side of the gaping hole.

"God's up, copy all, Mother," Saw whispered. "On your mark, One."

Chunk touched his chest, then gestured to the hole, signaling that he wanted to go first. Dempsey was about to shake his head but saw a fire in the SEAL officer's eyes that said, *Let me do this.* He nodded and Chunk shifted into position. Munn scooted up behind him, making clear his own intention to be number two in the stack.

"Go," Dempsey said, and a heartbeat later Saw opened fire.

A second and a half later, after three bursts of fire from Saw, Chunk shot the gap with lightning speed and Munn followed. They went to work immediately, with their SOPMOD M4s echoing loudly as they engaged the enemy shooters.

"North tango, KIA," Saw reported.

"West tango, down," Chunk said as Dempsey stepped through the hole with Grimes right behind him.

"One, Mother," said Wang's voice in his ear. "Both shooters down. No other thermal signatures except your four friendlies."

"Check, Mother," Dempsey said but continued to scan the hangar, never relying fully on ISR, even from Wang. He spied a tennis shoe–clad foot and shifted left and saw the dead pilot beside the King Air 350, a short MP-7 machine pistol beside the body. Chunk was moving across the front of the hangar, and then he heard the crash of the pilot's lounge door being kicked.

"Lounge clear," Chunk said. "Two angels—a pilot and it looks like a mechanic."

With everyone's eyes on him, Dempsey chopped a hand and moved toward the metal shards ringing a hole in the floor that used to be the concealed elevator access to Ember. Five black nylon ropes were tied off to pieces of rebar, and the warped remains of metal elevator supports dangled down into the smoke-filled pit below.

"Smells like they went in with riot gas," Chunk said, crinkling his nose.

"Explains why my eyes teared up when I opened the hatch," Saw said. "That shit vented right into my face."

"I saw gas masks on those dudes' kits we shot," Munn said.

"All right, Two and Three, you guys take their masks and descend the shaft," Dempsey said. "Five and Seven are with me. We're heading to the emergency exit and we'll meet you in the middle."

"Copy, One," Saw said. "Five coming down from the roof."

"What are you guys going to do for masks?" Chunk said to Dempsey.

"The emergency egress tunnel connects to the Ember mechanical room, which is where we keep our DC gear," Dempsey said. "There are EABs in there we can put on when we breach."

Chunk nodded.

"Let's go," Dempsey said to Grimes. Once outside, he turned left and felt Saw pull in beside him. In combat crouches, they ran across the tarmac toward the narrow service road that paralleled the runway. At the end of the drive, Dempsey led them off the paved surface and into the grass. He pulled his NVGs down and powered them on as he ran, staying low until he was at the edge of the tree line.

"Four. SITREP?" he asked, checking in with Trip on their pursuit of the dude who'd squirted from the hangar.

"It's a shit show over here," Trip came back. "A plane ran off the runway and crashed, and we've got what looks like two hundred people milling about down here. We think he's in the crowd because we found a kit and rifle in the grass behind the hangar."

"Check, keep working it," Dempsey said.

"One, I have a second squirter—a lone figure coming out of the Ember emergency exit now! He's moving north toward the perimeter fence," Wang said, his voice tense but controlled.

"Shit," Dempsey barked and took off at a full sprint. On his second day at Ember, Smith had shown him the "storm drain in the woods," but that was two years ago, and he'd never actually used the emergency egress. He ran in the general direction he remembered, inside where the service road intersected a perimeter road that curved ahead of him.

"Mother, am I going the right way?" Dempsey huffed.

"Vector left fifteen degrees," Wang said.

Dempsey veered slight left with Grimes and Saw in tow.

"Fifty yards, you're on track now . . ."

Moments later they came upon a cement collar—like a toy submarine conning tower—coming two feet up from the floor of the woods. The heavy steel manhole cover lay tipped on its side, leaning against the cement cylinder.

He turned to Grimes. "Breach with Saw as planned. Kill anyone who's not us."

"Where are you going?" Grimes asked, her voice sounding almost more jealous than concerned.

He held up a hand and said, "Mother—do you and Liberty Crossing still have comms with Omega?"

"Affirmative."

"Let them know we have friendly shooters breaching the compound. Tell them to shelter in place until Clubhouse is secure. Code word access to Omega only."

"Check, Spear One."

His eyes met Grimes's gaze. "The fucker who just squirted from here is Malik, I'm sure of it, and I'm going to get him."

"We don't know that, JD. We don't even know if he's here."

He held her eyes. "It's him," he said. "I know it."

He realized he almost desperately needed her to believe him—if only so he could believe it himself.

She nodded, not arguing. "Then be careful, John. Because if it is him, this guy is a dangerous, tricky bastard."

"I know, but so am I," he said. Then he turned and took off north through the woods in pursuit with Wang playing wingman in his ear.

CHAPTER 39

One of the first lessons a climber learns is to inspect his ropes before each use. A woven line is comprised of dozens of strands—each insufficient to bear any weight alone, but capable of bearing tremendous strain when braided together and working in concert. Nick the rope, however, and the intact strands become overstressed and begin to fail. The rope frays, rapidly deteriorating under the tension until finally the load is too great to bear and *snap*—

A fraying rope—that was what Valerian felt like.

The nick had happened only one month ago, when the American operator had bested him in Istanbul. *How quickly I've come apart since then.* The worst part, however, was that he could feel it happening. He could feel himself fraying, psychologically and emotionally, strand by strand by strand. The tension now was so great . . . it wasn't a question of whether he would snap, but when.

Seeing and losing Amanda Allen again had done a number on his head. The look on her face, staring at him through the gap in the safe room door, was seared in his memory. Like a photo negative, the ghost image tortured his mind's eye. *Fear and longing*—he had seen both in her eyes. He'd gotten to her, just like she'd gotten to him.

A strange schizophrenic war between two parts of his ego raged as he ran. The practical side, the Zeta within, recognized that this mission was over. There was no combination of possible circumstances that would lead to the outcome he desired: the American operator dead and Amanda Allen in his possession. Best-case scenario, he avoided capture and escaped with his life, but to do so would require abandoning both of his objectives.

The other part of him, the conflicted soul that Arkady had worked so desperately to purge, didn't care about self-preservation. To leave the world without besting his adversary—to leave in defeat—was more than he could bear. He could end things here, in the woods, setting a trap for the American ghost who was almost certainly on his trail. He could take one final scalp, achieve one final and glorious act of defiant victory, before the American forces surrounded him and cut him to shreds.

I didn't train you to be stupid, Arkady lectured in his head. *You need to think two moves ahead.*

Valerian didn't slow as he approached the seven-foot perimeter fence, topped with razor wire, that surrounded the airport complex. He'd been practicing parkour since he was a teenager, and barely breaking stride, he planted a foot mid-wall, bounded upward, and then rolled over the top, the razor wire cutting harmlessly into his black vest as he dropped to the other side. He pulled the micro-earpiece from his left ear, dropped it to the ground, and crushed it beneath his right heel. Completely cut off and alone now, he took off in a sprint, ditching his assault rifle in a retention pond behind a row of townhouses along Old Denbigh Boulevard. Lastly, he yanked apart the Velcro straps of the vest and tossed his kit.

The 9 mm pistol he would keep for now. That would be the last to go.

The Americans were undoubtedly watching him on thermal imagery right now, so hiding was out of the question. To disappear, he needed his thermal signature to become lost in a sea of others. After that, he would alter his physical appearance enough to defeat probing eyes and facial-recognition software. Fortunately, there was a place nearby where he could achieve these objectives and disappear—Mary Immaculate Hospital. This morning he'd parked a car in the hospital's basement parking structure. From there, he would drive south to Virginia Beach and then across the Chesapeake Bay Bridge-Tunnel to the Delmarva Peninsula, where an ally waited for him with a small plane. The hospital emergency room would soon be packed with trauma victims from the plane crash, allowing him to blend in, lose himself, and disappear. But the emergency response at the airport was hampered by the EMP and slower than he needed. Gritting his teeth, he realized he would need to inflict more trauma to generate additional confusion and casualties for law enforcement to manage. An active shooter scenario in the retirement home would add to the chaos and further overwhelm the system.

He crossed the rear of the row of townhouses and moved east, then crossed back across Old Denbigh Boulevard to the south, weaving around the gated guard shack and then crossing the parking lot. He stayed to the shadows until he reached his intermediate objective—Warwick Forest Retirement Community. He slowed to a jog as he crossed the facility's manicured grounds and pulled his 9 mm pistol from his waistband. Leveling it at the parking lot in front of the drop-off circle, he unloaded three rounds into three different parked cars. Horns blared and lights flashed as two of the three car alarms went off.

Valerian turned toward the front of the building and fired two more rounds through the glass doors of the entrance. He untucked his shirt, stuffed the pistol underneath in his waistband, and ran through the double doors into the lobby. As he crossed the threshold, he transformed from stone-cold killer to panicked victim—frantically scanning this way and that. A placard with a large yellow arrow read "Health Station" and pointed down the hall to his left. He took off toward the circular desk, where he could see the tops of the heads of at least three people ducking behind the workstation.

"Help me, please! They're shooting us. Someone help!" he called, his footsteps echoing off the tile floor.

He watched as the head in the middle rose just enough for brown eyes to peer above the Formica countertop. The woman's hair was peppered with gray, and her eyes, framed with deep crow's-feet, were wide with fear.

"Around this side," she breathed, her voice shaky.

He followed her instructions and dropped to his knees behind the counter. "There's at least three of them," he choked out. "They killed the security guard right in front of me. What do they want?" His voice cracked, and a tear spilled onto his stricken face while at the same time he reached behind him and grabbed the pistol from the waistband of his trousers.

"It's okay. We're going to be okay." The woman managed a smile and put her hand on his arm. "We're going to make it out."

He smiled back at her.

"I'm not so sure," he said as he whipped the pistol around in a tight arc and fired twice into the center of her face. She pitched backward as Valerian turned a few degrees and fired into the temple of the heavyset black man beside her. The last man of the trio raised his hands over his head. His hair was a shaggy mess of dirty blond, and he wore the same dark-blue scrubs as the dead man beside him.

"Please! Please don't. I can help you," the man begged.

Valerian lowered the pistol, pointing it at the floor between them, and smiled.

"Okay, I'll let you help me, but you must be quiet. Do you understand?"

The man nodded.

Valerian looked him up and down. He was a bit thin, but he was at least six foot three. And hospital scrubs were cut wide, with a drawstring, in any case.

"Take off your pants," he said.

"Wha . . . ?"

Valerian raised the pistol but kept his voice and expression calm. The last thing he needed was the man to piss in the scrub pants he would be wearing momentarily.

"Okay, okay . . ."

The man kicked off his sneakers and scrambled to pull the scrub pants off. Then he raised his hands over his head again.

"And the shirt," Valerian commanded, pulling the pants out of the way so they wouldn't get blood on them. The man pulled the shirt over his head and handed it to him, his hands rising again.

The 9 mm bullet made a hole directly over the bridge of the man's nose.

Valerian donned the scrubs, shoving his shirt and tactical pants into a file drawer, and swapped his boots for the man's sneakers as he picked up the desk phone and dialed 9-1-1.

"9-1-1—what's your emergency?"

"They're shooting at us! Someone is killing people at the Warwick Forest retirement home. I saw three of them and they're killing everyone." He sobbed uncontrollably.

"We received other calls already, sir. Help is coming. You need to shelter in place. Can you stay with me on this line?"

Valerian smiled and then screamed "Nooooo!" and then fired the pistol twice beside the phone and hung up. Then he was up, moving around the desk. It would help to have someone in his ear right about now. Timing his egress with the arrival of the police response, but before the EMS and fire trucks, would be ideal. He missed Sylvie, as irritating as she could sometimes be.

He'd just have to wing it.

He kicked in the first door on the left as he went down the hall, the brown wooden plaque on the wall beside the door announcing that

THE PATTERSONS lived in the small apartment. He followed his pistol through the door and stepped inside.

"Hey, what the hell?" shouted a man watching late-night TV in an easy chair. He was snacking on peanuts and wearing a dark-blue ball cap with "USS *Oriskany*" stitched in yellow across the crown.

"I need your help," Valerian announced.

The man looked at him, confused. Then Valerian smashed the butt of the gun into the man's temple, knocking him unconscious. He fired a single round through the man's chest. The bullet would tear through lung and blood vessels, but nothing that would kill him quickly. He would develop a pneumothorax, perhaps a hemothorax as well, but he would be alive long enough to serve his purpose.

"No . . . ," a trembling voice cried from behind him.

He turned to face the wife, awake now and sitting up in bed.

"Sorry," he said with a measure of sincerity. Then he shot her in the abdomen.

She wailed in pain and began to sob. Valerian walked over and punched her once, hard, in the left side of the head, knocking her unconscious. He darted to the door, ducked his head into the hall, and spied what he needed near the nurses' station—a rolling hospital bed. He retrieved it and wheeled it to the door of the Pattersons' suite. Then he scooped the old man out of his chair and onto the bed. He took the wide, heavy-framed eyeglasses from the man's face and slipped them on. The world was a little hazy, but the distortion of his face would slow down most facial-recognition programs, especially if he could add some shadows. He grabbed a ball cap from a coatrack beside the door—this one gray with a subdued American flag—and pulled it down onto his head. A moment later he tucked the man's dying wife in beside him and then pushed the bed quickly down the hall toward the exit.

"What's happening?" a nurse asked, running up to him. She was short—no more than five feet tall—and her thick arms were covered in sleeves of tattoos.

"Thank God," Valerian said, digging deep in his repertoire of American accents and adopting a heavy southern drawl. He pushed the thick glasses up on his nose with a middle finger. "Y'all gotta help me. There's terrorists in the building. They killed the nurse and the aides and shot some residents, but these two are still alive. I'm trying to get them out of here. If I can get 'em over to the trauma center, I think the docs could save 'em. Are you a nurse?"

The woman nodded but advanced slowly. "Yeah," she said. "Who are you? I've never seen you here before."

"Name's John, but everybody calls me Buddy Ray. I'm an LPN in the urgent care. I've only been working here since Tuesday. Please, you gotta help me. They ain't gonna let EMS in here while there's a shooter in the building."

The nurse nodded and grabbed the corner of the stretcher and helped wheel it toward the exit. "I'm Miriam. How bad are they?" she asked, taking charge.

"Hurt real bad," he said, forcing his voice to crack. "It's my fault. Them two guys was shooting everyone down in urgent care, and I hid in the room with Mr. and Mrs. Patterson. I just hid in the closet like a coward."

"It's not your fault, Buddy Ray," the nurse said.

Valerian knew he was giving her just what she needed, to be focused on helping someone else. He began to sob, and she squeezed his arm firmly.

"They would've killed you, too," she continued. "There's nothing you could have done. But we're gonna save the Pattersons, okay? We're gonna get 'em to Mary Immaculate and they're gonna be okay."

"Okay."

"Come on, hurry," she hollered at him, practically running toward the double glass entry doors.

He could see the sea of flashing blue lights beyond the guard shack at the gated entrance. To his left he saw two high-top white vans, both with blue handicapped symbols on the sides, used no doubt to take residents to various medical appointments. He maneuvered the stretcher toward the rear of the nearest van, opened the back door, and pulled the heavy stretcher inside, pulling hard as Nurse Miriam pushed from below.

"Do you know how to drive this thing?" he asked, his eyes still wide with fright. "I'm sorry, but I'm shaking so bad, I know I can't do it, Miss Miriam. If you drive, I can stay with the Pattersons in back."

The nurse squeezed his shoulder and headed for the driver's seat. "It's okay, Buddy Ray. You did good. I got this." He heard her rummaging around and then she called back, "I got the keys. Here we go."

The engine roared to life, and the van tore out of the parking lot and onto Denbigh Boulevard toward the hospital.

He leaned over the body of Mrs. Patterson. From her gray pallor, he realized she was already dead. "Hurry, Miss Miriam! Mrs. Patterson's got a pulse, but she ain't breathing. I'm gonna give her mouth-to-mouth!"

"Hang in there, Buddy Ray. You're doing great."

He felt the van slow and stop at a police roadblock—a newly materialized checkpoint to control traffic in and out of the airport. He'd need to put on a helluva performance, not to mention a little help from his unwitting accomplice, to get through this mess without killing cops. He leaned over the dead woman and pinched her nose, then opened his mouth and blew.

"Ma'am, we need you to exit the van, please," Valerian heard the officer at the window say. "Who's in here with you?"

"Listen to me, young man. There are terrorists shooting up the retirement center. I'm a nurse there, and they killed at least three people. We got two critically injured residents in the back who are gonna die if we don't get them to the trauma center right now."

"You have ID?" the officer said.

Valerian blew again, his own breath now blowing back at him, mixed with a nauseating stale, acidic stench from the old woman's corpse.

"Yes, sir," she said, handing him her Warwick Forest ID, he assumed.

"Who's in the back?"

"John—we call him Buddy Ray—he's an LPN from the urgent care. Please, Officer, we're losing one of them already."

"Okay, ma'am. We're gonna send an escort with you."

The rear cargo door swung open, and a young officer, his hand clutching the rifle in a combat sling on his chest, climbed in.

Valerian looked up, meeting the policeman's wide-eyed gaze. "Do you know CPR?" he asked. "I need you to do compressions."

The officer came in beside him, shifting his rifle under his left armpit, and began to do compressions on the dead woman. Valerian felt the van lurch forward and resisted the urge to smile. Manipulating people was just too damn easy. But as he leaned in to give the dead woman a puff of air, something strange happened—a ghost from another corpse, dead now almost six weeks, invaded his thoughts.

He'd killed Melania Kartevelian, wife of a Georgian media magnate, in her home while her husband watched. Unlike most of his victims, her courage in the face of death had left an impression on him. And as his lips pressed to dead flesh, her final words echoed in his mind: *I know you, son of Georgia. Proud chin, strong jaw, slate-blue eyes—you are one of us, except you . . . you are a* moghalate. *You think they will accept you? You think they will let you rise? You will never be Russian. You are their dog. A pet. Nothing more.*

A chill raced down his spine as he contemplated his tenuous future. After tonight, he would be disavowed—no longer a Zeta, no longer a Russian. Melania Kartevelian's dying insult had proved prescient. He was a dog, abandoned and kicked to the side of the road.

And worse, he would be hunted . . . hunted by the Americans and hunted by his own people for the rest of his days.

CHAPTER 40

"Spear One, I have your tango crossing south toward a large commercial building two hundred and fifty yards to your east."

Dempsey veered left, hugging the tree line, as Jarvis's last report echoed in his mind.

Presumed urgent surgical or worse.

Or worse . . .

No new info had crossed the wire since Munn and Chunk had led the assault into the Ember compound. How many of his Ember teammates had fallen? How many more brothers could he add to the list of the dead?

"Spear One—did you copy my last? Your tango has just entered the building—it's an old folks' home."

Dempsey shook his head clear. "Copy. It's gonna be hard to track him if he leaves in a crowd."

Dempsey picked up the pace. He knew exactly what Malik was planning to do—create mass havoc and then try to slip away in the crowd of other signatures. And he had to assume that the Russian operator knew he was coming—that someone was in Malik's ear reporting Dempsey's movements.

Well, get ready, motherfucker. Cuz I am coming for you, and this time's not gonna be like Istanbul.

He emerged from the woods and crossed a street, finding himself in a well-lit parking lot between single-story office complexes. He heard the gunfire before he heard Wang in his ear.

"An alarm was sent out from the Warwick Forest Retirement Community—an intruder alarm, with shots fired. They're calling it an active shooter situation. What the hell is this guy doing? Going out in a blaze of glory?"

Dempsey ran between the office buildings and vaulted over the four-foot wrought-iron fence onto the sprawling property of the retirement community.

"I gained access to their security system," Wang said, fingers typing furiously in the background. "Running a real-time facial-rec program on their camera feeds for Malik, but we don't even know if this is him . . ."

"It's him," Dempsey growled and took a knee at the rear corner of the wide-open grassy park behind the main building of the retirement home.

If I were Malik, what would I do?

He pulled his tablet from his left cargo pocket.

"Stream me the imagery you're using," he said to Wang.

The screen flickered and he was looking down at himself—literally watching the thermal image of himself crouching over his tablet in the dark corner of the park. He could also now see the thermal of a mob of panic-stricken people pouring out of the rear and sides of the building. He quelled the impulse to sprint to the rear door, breach, and hunt down the shooter. The Russian was strategic, even when being chased. Dempsey had learned how quickly Malik could turn the tables in Istanbul.

This asshole has a plan. What is it?

"What's this big building to the south? Is that the hospital?" Dempsey asked, looking at the tablet and then a structure six hundred yards south of his position.

"Yes—that's Mary Immaculate Hospital on Denbigh Boulevard."

Dempsey knew the hospital was there but had never appreciated how close it was to the Ember compound as the crow flies.

"There's an emergency services response now from Newport News Police," Wang said. "They're setting up a perimeter, and the SWAT operators will be on scene in eight minutes. It looks like FBI has been notified."

"I know where Malik's going," Dempsey said and slipped the tablet back into his cargo pocket. Maybe he could stop him here, at the retirement home, now that he knew what the Zeta had planned. "Status at Ember?"

A painful pause hung in the air before Wang answered. "No news, but we have a helo arriving in less than two minutes with operators from SEAL Team Four and another QRF from the north in ten."

"Copy," Dempsey said, checking his emotions and forcing himself to focus. "You need to let Newport News PD know I'm here," he said, moving in a combat crouch across the grassy park toward the rear entrance of the facility. "Don't wanna get shot by law enforcement."

"On it," Wang said.

"There's people getting into that van," Dempsey said as he closed on the building. "They loaded a stretcher. Send me any images you have from the cameras when they wheeled it out, including the patients on the stretchers."

He picked up his pace, heart pounding as the van sped away.

"Working on it . . . stand by."

It's him, I know it's him, Dempsey thought as he watched the van get stopped at a police blockade. He paused, debating whether to head into the retirement home or make a beeline to the hospital.

"Nothing popped on facial recognition." He'd never heard Wang sound more stressed out—no joking, no arrogant banter. "But I got a decent screen-capture image of them leaving the lobby."

"Send it," Dempsey demanded. He pulled the tablet from his pocket as the picture arrived. The people on the stretcher were an old couple. The one scrub-attired worker at the end of the stretcher was a short, heavyset nurse. The other . . . He zoomed in.

"It's him," he said and took off at a full sprint toward the hospital.

"The van got through the police blockade . . . shit, they have a police escort. What do you want me to do?"

"Track him. Zoom in and tell me exactly where he goes. Don't you lose him, Mother."

"I won't. They're on Denbigh Boulevard, just about to pull onto the hospital road."

Dempsey cleared a five-foot chain-link fence at the back of a townhome complex without slowing down, then crossed a park. Seconds later, he emerged from a grove of trees into an empty parking lot at the north end of the enormous medical complex.

"They're entering the hospital complex from the south. The ER and trauma center entrance is on the southeast corner; that's where they're going. Forty-five seconds . . . okay, they're pulling up now."

Dempsey slowed at the corner of a building, then stopped. The ER would be on full alert and he was coming alone, fully kitted up, and looking pretty fucking dangerous. He needed to switch from SEAL to spook. He untucked his shirt, pulled off his kit, and stashed his weapons in the bushes beside the building. Next, he unbuttoned his shirt several buttons. He paused to catch his breath and think . . .

There's going to be an enormous police presence in the ER. I could get Wang and Jarvis to clear me in hot, but that would tip off the Russian and he'll squirt. Damn it . . . I'm going to have to go in vulnerable.

"What's your plan?" Wang asked.

"My plan is to hunt this sonuvabitch down and kill him, that's my plan," Dempsey growled. He pulled a folding knife from his pocket and cut a small gash inside the hairline at the top of his scalp above his right ear. Scalps were vascular, and even this small laceration would bleed like hell, without impacting him physically. Dempsey felt the blood instantly running warm down the side of his head, and he wiped it all over his ear and the side of his face. Making no attempt to staunch the wound, he let blood run down his neck and stain his white T-shirt red at the collar. Hoping he looked battered enough to fool the first responders, he ran toward the ER entrance, stumbling and weaving as he did.

The Warwick Forest van was parked in front of the ER entrance—back doors open and the rear compartment empty. Two cops stood beside the van. Both looked up as soon as they noticed him, hands going immediately to their weapons as he approached.

"Help," he hollered, forcing a sob into his voice. "They're killing people at Warwick Forest retirement home. Please help me—I've been shot!"

He stumbled to his knees, and the cops raced toward him, hands still on their weapons. Dempsey drooped, cradling his head in his hands.

The cops were beside him, one kneeling to his left and the other a few feet away, hand at the ready on his weapon. "What happened? Where are you hurt, buddy?"

"Terrorists, shooting everyone . . . Something's wrong with my head," he said, slurring his words and holding out his bloody palm.

The cop frisked him quickly, and Dempsey was glad he'd left his weapons behind. Then they pulled him up, hands under his armpits. He let his legs go to jelly as the two cops dragged him toward the ER entrance.

"We have a gunshot wound here," one of the cops hollered.

And then he was surrounded by people, lifting him, putting him on a stretcher.

"Trauma three."

"Get me someone from the surgery team and a trauma nurse."

"Send the alert."

Dempsey moaned as a nurse pushed the stretcher across the hall. He let his head loll back and forth, using the opportunity to scan the

ER, which was divided into what looked like six open bays separated by curtains, all of which were pulled back against the walls.

"Let's get anesthesia over here. This guy is a GCS less than eight. We need to intubate."

Across from him, a group of green scrub–clad workers were packed in around two different patients. They were doing CPR on one of the figures on the stretchers, but he didn't see Malik in the crowd. Then he spotted a nurse from the retirement community standing alone next to the van.

He sat bolt upright.

"Easy there, man," said a young doctor. "We need to lay you back down."

He turned to the doctor, his eyes now open and clear, certain his voice would do the rest. He leaned in close. "Listen to me. I'm fine. I'm an American Navy SEAL hunting the active shooter from the retirement center. There was a guy in eyeglasses and blue scrubs who just brought in two wounded from Warrick. Did you see where he went? Did anybody see where he went?"

"Navy SEAL, huh?" the doc said while attempting to press Dempsey's chest back down onto the stretcher. "And I'm with the CIA. Can I get some succinylcholine here? I got a confused patient with a GSW—"

Dempsey didn't have time to negotiate. An adrenaline dump sent liquid lightning into his veins and he spun hard left, rolling off the stretcher. He landed in a combat crouch, squaring off against four wide-eyed faces staring at him over surgical masks.

"Hey, you can't just—"

To his left Dempsey saw Malik trying to slip away unnoticed along the opposite wall.

Time slowed, and the Russian Zeta turned to look at him. He pulled the heavy eyeglasses from his face and peered at Dempsey with slate-blue eyes full of malice. At the same time, a security guard came charging by, running to help subdue Dempsey, oblivious of the killer just ten feet away.

Dempsey predicted what would happen next but could do nothing to stop it. As the security guard ran past, the Russian backhanded his left forearm into the side of the guard's head, then twisted, spinning the man's head under his armpit as he drove the palm of his right hand hard into the man's shoulder. Dempsey heard the crunch of the guard's neck bones snapping, and then the guard slid to the floor. His Glock service pistol was in the Russian's right hand.

"Everyone down!" Dempsey shouted, grabbing the two closest members of the trauma team and pulling them to the ground. Three cracks from the Glock echoed. The anesthesiologist spun on his heels as the first bullet impacted his jaw, spraying blood across the monitors beside the bed as the doc collapsed on top of Dempsey. He rolled the body off his back and glanced up in time to see Malik streaking away to his left.

"Help me," a tiny voice said.

Dempsey looked up to see a young nurse, her eyes wide as she looked down at her abdomen where a bloodred flower bloomed on her scrubs. He eased her onto her back and placed her hands on top of the wound and said, "Put pressure here."

"Don't leave me," she said.

"I've gotta stop this guy. Hang in there. Help is coming."

Jaw clenched with rage, Dempsey sprinted across the bay to the security guard Malik had just killed. "C'mon, please be there," he murmured as he hiked up the guard's pant legs one at a time looking for an ankle holster. "Thank you, God," he said as he pulled a palm-size Smith & Wesson M&P Shield concealed-carry pistol from the holster. He quickly checked his six to make sure he wasn't about to get shot in the back by an anxious cop, and his heart sank as the two officers he'd duped at the ER entrance came charging straight at him with weapons drawn.

"Drop your weapon and get on your knees," the younger of the two officers yelled, taking aim at Dempsey's chest.

"Listen, fellas, I'm not the shooter," Dempsey said, slowly setting the pistol on the linoleum floor. "My name is John Dempsey. I'm a member of a government counterterrorism task force, working in plain clothes, pursuing an international terrorist who has infiltrated this building."

"That shit ain't going to work again," the other officer said. "You might have fooled us on the way in, but looking at you now, I see a man who matches the description of the shooter to the letter. Six foot two, dark hair, muscular build, scar on the left cheek."

Fuck you, Malik, for looking like me, he thought.

"A little help, Mother," Dempsey murmured. "Can you get the DNI on the horn to talk to these guys?"

"Working on it," Wang came back. "Looks like I'm going to have to get creative here . . ."

"Put your hands behind your head or I shoot you," the young officer said.

Dempsey complied, knitting his fingers behind his head and easing back onto his haunches.

"Mother, do something now," he said through gritted teeth.

The senior officer, gun trained on Dempsey's head, began a slow, arcing sidestep to get behind Dempsey. Unfortunately for everyone involved, there was no way in hell Dempsey was going to let himself get cuffed. He tensed his muscles, ready to—

"Wait," an anemic female voice called from across the bay. "He's telling the truth."

The officer facing Dempsey glanced at the nurse who'd been shot in the stomach. "Ma'am, did this man shoot you?"

"No, it was the other one," she said.

"What other one?" the officer asked, but they were all cut off by the hospital loudspeaker.

"Attention, law enforcement officers at Mary Immaculate Hospital," a commanding male voice said over the PA system. "This is the Director of National Intelligence, Kelso Jarvis, talking to you from the National Counterterrorism Center. I have a plainclothes agent working undercover and pursuing an international terrorist. Do not attempt to impede, detain, or arrest my agent. All hospital personnel and patients are directed to shelter in place. Law enforcement officers are ordered to set up a perimeter around the hospital and detain any and all vehicle and foot traffic from exiting hospital grounds."

"I'm going to need name confirmation," the senior officer shouted, his gaze locked on Dempsey.

"They need my name, boss," Dempsey said, unsure if Jarvis would have heard the cop through his transceiver.

"Very well," the DNI said. "My operator's name is John Dempsey."

The senior officer nodded at Dempsey and lowered his weapon.

"Thanks, boss," Dempsey said aloud, reaching for his pistol as the two police officers stood down.

"Help is on the way," the DNI said on the loudspeaker, and then in his earbud Jarvis added, "And John?"

"Sir?" Dempsey said, pressing to his feet and turning to finish the hunt.

"Shoot to kill."

CHAPTER 41

Valerian moved swiftly up the stairs, taking them two at a time to the third floor. He barely stopped to register surprise when the American DNI made an announcement on the hospital PA. From the sound of it, the police had just tried to arrest his American doppelgänger, and it had taken intervention from a higher authority to shut that down. Good. It had bought him the precious time he needed.

He stepped out of the stairwell into a well-lit hallway just as a Klaxon began to blare and white lights flashed at both ends of the hall.

"Code White. Shelter in place. Code White. Shelter in place," a prerecorded voice said robotically over the hospital intercom speakers.

His mind was racing as he considered his dwindling options. Escaping by car would be difficult, if not impossible, in the midst of the lockdown. The DNI knew he was here, and soon the hospital would be swarming with operators. The rational part of him conceded that the time for running was past. The other part would never surrender.

He looked right, past the elevator bank, and saw double doors with a security punch pad and the words CARDIAC ICU above them in block letters. He turned the other way, jogged a few yards, and stopped at a door marked PHYSICIAN LOCKER ROOM. He kicked the door open, knocking it nearly off its hinges, and stepped inside. A doctor in a white coat, gray slacks, and a green scrub shirt cowered beside a leather couch, arms over his head, hands shaking.

Valerian shot him in the temple.

He leaned over the doctor, snatched the ID badge from the man's lapel, and then grabbed one of three clean white lab coats hanging on a rack and shrugged it on. He trotted across the locker room to another door, where he swiped the badge across a card reader until it beeped and pushed through into the Heart and Vascular ICU. He entered the ward behind a long, rectangular nurses' station that took up most of the space. Beyond, eight patient rooms lined the opposite wall in a row. Each bay was separated from its neighbor by a floor-to-ceiling divider wall for privacy. But the front of each bay was equipped with a floor-to-ceiling glass wall and sliding glass door, allowing the nurses to peer in at any time to check monitors and observe a patient's condition. The nurses' station was vacant, and he assumed the staff had hidden in a lounge or in the patient rooms, most of which he could see had patients inside.

He leaped over the nurses' station desk, quickly assessed sight lines in the ward, and judged bay three to be tactically superior to the others. Through the glass, he saw an unconscious man lying flat on his back in the bed. The man's belly ballooned in and out as a ventilator hissed air into his lungs via a clear plastic tube in his throat. He pressed a button to open the sliding glass door and stepped inside.

"Quick, Doctor—hide with me back here," a female voice said in hushed tones.

He looked over the obese man and saw a young woman—pretty, midtwenties—crouched in the corner. She wore light-blue scrubs, and her eyes were wide with worry. He smiled. With no bullets to waste, he crossed the foot of the bed and then knelt beside her.

"What's going on?" he asked, dropping his American accent. God, it felt good to become himself again, but it didn't have the desired effect on the nurse. Awash with fresh fear, her eyes darted from him to the door and back again.

"I don't know," she said after a moment of hesitation. "The alarm went off for an active shooter. We thought we heard gunshots somewhere and . . ." She looked down at the name on his white coat. "Wait— you're not Dr. Beck," she said and tried to scurry away from him.

He spun her pretty head nearly all the way around until her neck made a horrible crunch, followed by a gurgle. Her face turned purple and immediately swelled to twice its normal size. He laid her gently on the floor, her terrified face looking impossibly backward behind her and up at the ceiling.

He covered her face with a towel, then pulled the pistol from his waistband.

Bloodlust had all but consumed him, that rabid yearning to kill without restriction.

The rope was fraying quickly now, and he felt himself coming apart at the core.

I just need to keep it together long enough for one more murder, he told himself.

He exhaled, silently mouthed his Zeta mantra, and found his center. His American rival would come bursting through the door any second, and when he did, Valerian would be ready.

CHAPTER 42

Dempsey exited the stairwell in a tactical crouch, knees flexed, weapon at the ready. He cleared left, then right in rapid succession, fully expecting to hear the crack from the Russian's Glock and the burn of a bullet entering his flank, but the pain never came.

The hallway was deserted.

After Jarvis's announcement, the hospital had initiated its active shooter protocols. A white light flashed, an alarm blared, and every ninety seconds a computer voice instructed people to shelter in place. Dempsey moved left, scanning over his acquired Smith & Wesson. He was happy to have a .40 caliber but wished he had more than the seven-round magazine. The Russian's Glock carried twice that many bullets, though Malik was down at least three.

Halfway down the corridor, something in his peripheral vision caught his attention—a door partly off its hinges, the bottom corner sticking out in the hall.

"Mother, One. You got thermals?"

"Yeah," Wang said. "But this is a three-story building. It's hard to sort out elevation from a single bird's-eye view. I have thermals all around you, but they could be above you or below you."

"They are," Dempsey said. "I'm alone. Do you see me sweeping?" He swiveled left, then right as he advanced on the door.

"Yes. I hold you moving north. If you're alone, then I have seven images in a line on the other side of the wall from you—patients I assume? First one like fifty or sixty feet north of you. Some rooms have tightly grouped pairs. Staff sheltering in patient rooms perhaps? Then near the far north outside wall I have a group of about nine people all clustered together in a single space. Does that help?"

He didn't answer as he stepped through the doorway and cleared the open room. A single man, dead, lay slumped beside the couch.

"Body, like, four feet from you," Wang reported.

"Yeah. A dead body. Very helpful, Mother. Stand by." He eyed a vacant bathroom with a single toilet behind the dead body. "Anybody behind the door in that bathroom?" he whispered.

"Negative."

He swiveled right toward a closed door with an electronic key card access pad beside it.

Malik came through here, killed the doc, stole his badge, and went into the secured ward beyond. He knows I'm coming, and he's waiting in ambush. He'll be in cover, but he'll have a line on this door for sure.

The SEAL inside decided it was tactically preferable to come from the opposite direction, so Dempsey backed out of the lounge, turning and clearing the hallway again as he did. Sighting over his pistol, he approached the main access to the ICU, a pair of magnetically locked double doors.

"How long to hack into the hospital's security system?"

"Already in. I didn't have anything to do, and I was, like, he might need me to . . ."

"Can you release the magnetic locks of the doors in the secured areas?"

"Of course. Which ones?"

"All of them."

"Now?"

"Now."

A soft metallic click followed a heartbeat later. Dempsey positioned himself to the left of the double door and then pressed the metal plate on the wall that said PRESS TO OPEN. The door hissed open, the left swinging in and the right outward. Before advancing, he scanned the ward. Eight patient rooms were situated in a row along the left wall. The front of each had a glass slider door, allowing ease of monitoring from the nurses' station on the right side of the ward. From Dempsey's perspective, only the third patient room would have a firing line on his position. He glanced up and saw a globe mirror above the door to help the nurses at the desk see who was coming and going. From where he stood, he was still hidden, but a few paces into the ward and the Russian could see him from almost anywhere in the ICU.

Bay three—that's where I'd take position . . .

Dempsey exhaled and let himself drift into the slipstream—becoming one with his weapon, his body, and his surroundings. He crept forward, his shoulder pressed against the glass door of bay one. The room was empty but staged to receive a patient with a bed, monitoring equipment, and a tray of instruments on a roller stand at the head of the bed. He glanced up and saw his distorted reflection in the globe mirror and stopped; a tactical paradigm shift came to him. Instead of advancing farther, he slipped into the room. He wasn't behind enemy lines, with an enemy QRF bearing down on his position. This time, he was on American soil. He had all the time in the world.

Malik didn't.

In short order, Jarvis would send backup to the hospital, if it wasn't en route already. Malik's internal timer was counting down—a situation Dempsey had been in too many times to count. To avoid capture and survive, Malik would have to act and act quickly.

Yeah, that's right, come and get some, asshole, he thought with a grin as he took cover behind the rolling hospital bed. After what felt like an eternity crouching, he whispered, "Mother, report movement."

"Lots of milling around at the end of the unit. I think I have the overlapping thermals figured out. Baldwin wrote a program once that uses head circumference to mathematically predict whether an image is above or below a target image. I'm using you as the target image right now to monitor the other thermals and figure out who is on what floor."

"Check."

Dempsey hunkered down and waited.

The ward was still and quiet, except for the *hiss—click—hiss* of ventilators running in multiple rooms. Then suddenly, his ear pricked to a new noise . . . a faint squeak. A rubber sole on a polished floor? From his squat behind the empty bed, he shifted his gaze to the globe mirror above the door.

"One of the thermals is up," Wang said. "The program indicates he's on your floor. Moving slowly toward you. Shit, this could be your guy. His body position suggests he has a pistol."

Dempsey tightened his grip on his weapon. Eyes on the mirror, he watched a distorted figure step into view. Reflexively, he pressed himself deep into the corner. If he could see the Russian in the mirror, then logic held the Russian could see him, too.

"Figure coming down the hall toward you. Can you see him? The head size algorithm says you're on the same horizontal plane . . . One, do you copy?"

Dempsey didn't answer.

Despite the distorted reflection, he knew the man in the mirror was his Russian counterpart. He could tell by the fluid movements, by the way he pivoted—silently clearing his corners. The Russian advanced, body in a low crouch, shoulder forward, pistol steady with elbows slightly bent. Dempsey let out a long, slow breath and moved his finger onto the trigger. In seconds, Malik would step into view and he'd have him, except there was one complication.

The glass slider door was going to be a problem. When the slider was open, as it was for his room, the two glass panes overlapped. A single pane would change his bullet's trajectory, but two would guarantee a miss. He had no idea what kind of rounds were in his weapon, but a hollow point would tumble after impact, maybe not even be lethal after punching through two heavy panes. He only had seven rounds in the little subcompact 9 mm, which meant he couldn't pull the trigger until Malik stepped past the edge of the panes. He'd have to hope the Russian didn't notice him crouched behind the hospital bed until it was too late.

A swell of uncharacteristic nervous energy hit him. He felt heat rise in his face but forced it down with a long, steady breath.

"He's right on top of you," Wang said in his ear as the Russian assassin stepped into view. Dempsey stared at the man in profile. The chiseled face could almost be his own. The body could as well, and the way he moved could be any of the Tier One SEALs he'd spent his life with. The Russian stopped, staring straight ahead, his pistol pointed at the double doors as if he expected them to burst open. Dempsey just needed him to take four more paces toward the exit and he would have a clean line on the back of the bastard's head . . .

The Russian took a single step forward and then hesitated.

Three more feet . . .

Come on, damn it, what are you waiting for?

Dempsey resisted the overwhelming compulsion to fire through the glass panes. Unexpectedly, his Zeta doppelgänger relaxed and stood up out of his tactical crouch. The Russian lowered his weapon and took an easy step forward. But it was all subterfuge, because on the next step he spun on a heel to face Dempsey, brought his muzzle up, and fired multiple rounds into the glass. The two panes exploded in rapid succession, sending a million gleaming shards in all directions. Like a special effect from a movie, the Russian stepped through the vortex of flying glass, tongues of fire leaping from the barrel of his outstretched gun.

A slug slammed into the metal side rail just above Dempsey's head, ricocheting with a metallic ping. Dempsey shifted right, out of his corner, and sighted in to return fire. Impossibly, the Russian was not there—or anywhere. A warm trickle of blood ran down his left cheek as he glanced up at the globe mirror to check which side of the bay Malik had dodged to. A blur to his left answered the question, and a muzzle flash exploded from the corner just as he ducked. Dempsey grabbed the end of the hospital bed and like a fullback pushing a blocking dummy, he drove the bed into Malik, doubling the Russian over at the waist and sending the Glock flying out of his hand. He plowed his doppelgänger all the way across the ward and slammed him into the nurses' station desk with a resounding thud.

Malik grunted, and Dempsey felt a smile cross his face as he brought his gun up to end the bastard. But the bed reversed course before he could squeeze the trigger, propelling him backward as the Russian somehow shoved off the desk with both feet. Dempsey's heel caught and he tumbled backward, landing flat on his back, his head smacking the tile floor. Stars filled his vision. He blinked hard and looked up as the Russian seemed to fall from the heavens, straight down onto him from an impossible height.

Dempsey got his pistol up and squeezed off a round a split second before the Russian landed on his chest. But the bullet missed and Malik's left hand shot out at lightning speed, impacting Dempsey's right arm just above the wrist with enough force that Dempsey thought he felt a bone break. His fingers went numb and his pistol went skipping across the tile floor. At the same time, the Zeta's full weight on his chest punched all the air out of his lungs, and Dempsey felt a crack accompanied by a tearing pain on the left side of his rib cage. He threw a weak punch with his left arm, but too late. Powerful hands wrapped around his throat, the thumbs pressing so hard he thought his Adam's apple was going to implode. The Russian's grip tightened, and Dempsey felt his vision go gray as the blood flow to his brain was suddenly cut off.

"This is how it should be, my friend. Me watching the life drain out of you as I crush your throat. You tried to take everything from me, but in the end, I will take that which is most precious from you," Malik said in Russian-accented English.

As a black cloud descended on Dempsey, muscle memory took over. He kicked his left leg up beside the killer, bending at the knee, and then shot the leg between them, spinning right as his heavily muscled leg smashed into the Russian's forearms. Malik's grip on his throat loosened for a split second, and Dempsey slurped in a lungful of air. His wits momentarily refreshed, he scissored his left leg backward, knocking the killer off him. He rolled hard to hands and knees and tried to crawl away, but the Russian leaped onto his back. With an animalistic bellow, Malik wrapped a thick forearm around his neck and locked it in place with his other arm into a wicked choke hold. At the same time, Dempsey felt his adversary's strong legs wrap around his waist. He tried to shove his left hand and forearm between Malik's arm and his throat, but to no avail.

Not like this, he thought as his vision began to gray. *After everyone I've lost, everything I've sacrificed, I'm not going out like this . . .*

A glimmer on the floor caught his attention. When he pushed the bed out of the room, he'd knocked the instrument tray over, scattering all the surgical implements. Straining, he reached for the flash of silver. Dark clouds began to close in from the sides, and he felt the muscles in his arms and legs going sluggish.

Focus, the SEAL inside him commanded, and then the voice began reciting the SEAL ethos:

I will never quit.

His fingertips found the handle of a cold steel implement.

I will persevere and thrive on adversity.

He closed his hand around it and saw he was clutching a scalpel, blade tip down.

My nation expects me to be physically harder and mentally stronger than my enemies.

The Russian, who was riding his back like a bull rider, tightened his stranglehold and in that instant Dempsey felt like his head might pop off his shoulders.

If knocked down, I will get back up every time.

The world was a gray black now, and his oxygen-starved brain was about to lose consciousness.

I will draw on every remaining ounce of strength to protect my teammates and complete the mission.

With all the strength left in his body, he rolled right, flipping the Russian onto his back. Then, he reached back and dragged the blade across the face pressed hard against the back of his head. He felt the scalpel tear through flesh and felt warm blood spray the back of his hand, but Malik's grip on his neck did not wane. The Russian operator didn't so much as grunt from the deep slash to his face.

I am never out of the fight.

Gritting his teeth, Dempsey plunged the surgical blade into the Russian's left wrist. He drove the scalpel deep, then sawed away, cutting and slicing through blood vessels, tendons, and ligaments. This time Malik grunted in pain, and the grip on his throat weakened.

His brain now screamed a more personal plea:

I will see Jake graduate from BUD/S.

I will mourn my dead Ember brothers.

And I will avenge what's happened today . . .

He wrenched the blade free and struck again, this time hitting Malik's muscular forearm. Unfortunately, the scalpel handle was now so slick with blood that when he tried to inflict more damage the handle slipped from his grip. Desperate for air, Dempsey rolled hard to his left, twisted violently, finally breaking the Russian's leg hold around his waist. He reached back and clawed at the gash in the Zeta's face, ripping flesh. Malik recoiled, releasing him, and the next thing Dempsey knew he was free.

With a gasp, he popped to his feet and whirled to face his doppelgänger.

The man's cheek was flopped over on itself, his left wrist was pumping spurts of blood across the room, and the scalpel was sticking out of his right forearm. Despite the damage, the Russian was smiling, his piercing blue eyes bright and possessed with malice the likes of which Dempsey had never encountered.

Is he my reflection? Is that my face when I'm working?

The Russian looked down, grabbed the handle of the blade, and pulled it out. He tossed it aside and it clinked on the tile seven feet away. Then, with superhuman speed, the Zeta turned and fled. The retreat caught Dempsey off guard, and for a split second he didn't react. Reflexively, he scanned the floor for his weapon. He spied the little pistol up against the wall beside the first bay and picked it up on the run as he chased after Malik.

"Wang, you got eyes on him?" he called, not sure if his earbud was still in his ear.

"Holy fucking shit, dude, are you okay?" the cyber boy wonder asked.

"No, I'm not," Dempsey coughed as he charged out of the ICU. "Report!"

"He's in the stairwell, the first door after the elevator on the right. Same one you took up."

"Check," he said, legs churning.

"My God, he's fast," Wang said. "I think he's leaping down the half flights."

Dempsey hit the stairwell door at a sprint and sent the slab careening into the doorstop with a resounding shuddering crash. He hit the stairs in stride and looked down over the railing to see—just as Wang described—the Russian descending the stairwell in leaps and bounds like a comic book character.

"I think he's going down to the parking garage," Wang said. "I'm going to lose him down there with all the structural interference."

"Check," Dempsey huffed, taking the stairs as fast as humanly possible without flying.

"Lost him," Wang said two flights later. "Sorry, Spear."

"Tell Munn where to find me," Dempsey said as he descended the final half flight. "In case things go bad."

"Dude, what are you doing?" Wang came back.

He didn't answer.

"Dempsey, what's going on?" Wang said, breaking call sign protocol, his voice tight.

Dempsey didn't answer and instead fished the earbud from his left ear canal and stuffed it in his pocket. He'd never intentionally severed comms in two decades as an operator. But this was one battle he had to finish on his own—no commentary in his ear, no distractions.

He dropped into a crouch and approached the heavy metal fire door leading to the underground parking garage. His bruised throat burned, and his left wrist and rib cage were screaming in pain. He ejected the magazine from the little M&P9 and counted two rounds—plus one in the chamber made three.

Three rounds, this battered body, and my wits . . . it'll have to be enough.

He exhaled once, found his center, and turned off the pain.

Then, with nerves on fire, he pushed open the parking garage door.

CHAPTER 43

Dempsey entered the parking garage.

He cleared right, then left and eased the heavy metal door silently closed against the frame. The Russian had undoubtedly prestaged a car here for his escape. To both his surprise and relief, the parking garage was a ghost town. The last thing he needed was more civilian lives to worry about and deaths on his conscience. This is the way it was supposed to be—operator versus operator, two gladiators in the arena facing off.

He scanned the garage for movement.

Listened for sound.

So many places to hide—among the rows and rows of parked cars, behind any of the dozens of concrete pillars.

Despite being the one holding a weapon, he felt like the combatant at a disadvantage.

He crept toward the first quadrant of parked vehicles, which unfortunately were mostly SUVs, with tall sides and tinted rear windows. He angled wide, moving into the middle of the driveway between two rows. He advanced in a low tactical crouch, keeping his weapon trained straight ahead while he swiveled his head right and left as he moved from bumper corner to bumper corner. His instincts told him to drop low and scan the ground under the vehicle undercarriages, but before he did, he checked his six to make sure Malik wasn't stalking him. Clear behind, he took a tactical knee and dropped his head low enough to look beneath the vehicles. He scanned the row to his right first, then his left—

A car alarm wailed, piercing the silence and making him flinch.

He whirled in the direction of the sound.

A second alarm went off, then a third, and a fourth. Horns blared, lights flashed, and the once silent garage was transformed into a cacophony of chaos. Dempsey moved in the direction of the ruckus, sighting over his S&W, legs gliding beneath a static torso. When he reached the quadrant where the alarms were going off, he scanned for the Russian, making a broad 180-degree sweep. Seeing nothing, he dropped to a knee for a second undercarriage survey.

And that's when it happened.

Impossibly, Malik fell on top of him, attacking from the one place Dempsey had failed to consider . . . *up*. Dropping from where he'd been hanging from an overhead plumbing run, the Zeta knocked the gun out of Dempsey's hand and slammed an elbow in between his shoulder blades. An electric stinger shot down Dempsey's left leg and blew up his big toe as the old vertebrae injury bore some of the brunt from the blow. Dempsey twisted, swinging his left arm around, and caught the Russian with a backhand hammer fist across the jaw. The strike bought him time to find his footing and square off against his adversary.

Malik shook his head, as if trying to clear his vision, and then brought his fists up.

Dempsey shifted into a close-quarters combat stance and it began.

Kick, punch, elbow, knee . . .

The fight happened at reflex speed—driven not by conscious thought but rather by decades of training, combat experience, and muscle memory. Dempsey would sense movement, duck, and weave.

391

He'd counter with an elbow or a punch, but instead of connecting with soft tissue he'd feel a stab of pain as his blows were blocked. With each deflection, he'd transmit the kinetic energy into his next movement, be it strike, feint, or block.

Ridge hand, swivel, palm strike, block, knee, hammer fist, punch . . .

As he tired, more of the blows from Malik began to find their marks. He felt warm blood spilling down his face, and his left eye was a pinkish blur. His breath rattled in his chest, and staying upright was an agony as the Russian hammered his torso—more than one rib almost certainly broken. An elbow struck him in the left temple, spinning him in a full circle, and he felt himself falling.

It was over . . .

Dempsey was on his knees, bruised and breathless, with Malik standing over him.

Despite the ruined left wrist, the Russian had bested him.

Fireworks of exploding light filled Dempsey's vision. His mind screamed at him to get up, but every fiber in his spent, battered body resisted the call. He knew the Russian was looming over him, about to deliver the killing blow that would end it all, but his mind decided to show him something else. For a fleeting moment, he was transported in time—back two years to the basement of his nearby Virginia home. The memory flashed through his brain in a microsecond that felt much longer. He was working a heavy bag, punching, kicking, and striking with all his fury and hate and angst. He was lost and ruined, dead and alone. And in his darkest moment, Shane Smith had walked down the stairs.

I remember that day . . .

It was the day of his christening—the day John Dempsey had been born.

"Good Lord," Smith said, clinking two beer bottles together in applause. "You hit like Jack Dempsey reborn . . . You do know who Jack Dempsey was, right?"

"I've heard the name."

"Heard the name?" Smith said, shaking his head. "Shit, Kemper, the man is a legend. They called him the Manassa Mauler. He won more than fifty of his fights by knockout. Seven years as a world heavyweight champion. Dempsey was one of the greatest boxers of all time . . . They don't make fighters like Jack Dempsey anymore."

"Sure they do," he'd said. "They're called Navy SEALs."

Dempsey looked up.

Shane Smith—his friend, his baptizer, his brother—was standing beside the sneering, blood-drenched Russian. Smith grinned at him with that easygoing *it'll all work out* smile he always wore. In that moment, Dempsey knew he was looking at a ghost. His first Ember brother was gone, murdered by Malik, and was here with him now.

"Get up, Dempsey," Smith said. "Get up and do what you were trained to do, what you were made to do, what you always do. Get up and do it for Ember—for Latif, for Adamo, and for me."

"The thing is," Malik interrupted Smith's ghost, breathing hard and heavy, "without a gun, you're nothing—just a tired, burned-out American fool. I'm younger than you, faster than you, and stronger than you."

"Yeah, that's true," Dempsey said, gathering his fury. "But I'm tougher than you."

Like a sprinter from the blocks, he exploded upward, slamming his right shoulder into the Russian's solar plexus. He found his footing, balled his fists, and then channeling his namesake, Jack Dempsey, went to work.

Hell yeah, Dempsey, the ghost of Smith screamed in his head. *Get some, brother.*

Like an avalanche, his punches came so fast and furious there was nothing the Russian could do. His mind filled with images of Smith: kitted up in the field when he was Ops O, in the Ember TOC as Director, deep-sea fishing with a beer in hand, and a half-dozen other times where Smith had always had his back. Every blow against the Russian ghost was cheered on by his dead brother, and impossibly each blow carried more fury and power than the last. The Zeta's nose broke first, followed by his jaw, his right eye socket, and then his left. Then the Russian was on his back and Dempsey was on his chest, a supernatural strength driving each frenzied fist and elbow. He felt warm tears mixing with the blood on his own face. And with the parade of memories and cheers from his dead teammate, Dempsey pounded his reflection into a bloody, unrecognizable, gurgling pulp.

When it was over, he was left kneeling on the Russian operator's lifeless chest, sobbing. He wasn't sure how long he lingered like that before he slowly and painfully got to his feet. As he headed toward the ramp that led out of the underground garage, he found the earbud in his pants pocket and put it back into his left ear.

"Mother, this is Spear One," he said, his throat slick with his own blood, his voice a hoarse, grating rasp. "The target is down."

"Oh, thank God," Wang said. "You're back. I thought we'd lost you."

The next voice on the line belonged to Jarvis. "Copy all. Good work, Spear One."

"I'm heading back to Ember," Dempsey said, his voice barely his own as he felt his throat and neck continue to swell.

"No need, One," Jarvis said. "Clubhouse is secure. I have Spear Two and Three headed to you. Stay in place."

Dempsey heard the order, but he just kept going, walking toward the only home he'd known for the past two years . . . with Shane Smith walking at his side.

CHAPTER 44

Sentara Norfolk General Hospital
Trauma Surgery ICU Waiting Room
Norfolk, Virginia
June 26
0630 Local Time

Dempsey cleared his throat—not to get attention but because the coppery-tasting phlegm kept piling up back there, making it hard to breathe. He swallowed it down. If he coughed up blood again, Grimes—maybe even Munn—would force him to go back to the ER. The X-rays showed no fracture of his windpipe, but he did have a broken rib, a hairline ulnar fracture in his right wrist, and several cracked bones in his shredded hands from the final fight with Malik. The hospital doc had recommended a CT angiogram of his neck to look for blood vessel injuries to explain the massive swelling, but he'd declined, of course. Munn had been watching him like a hawk ever since.

"Be right back," Munn said, getting up. "I'm going to go check on things."

Dempsey nodded but didn't move.

Grimes was waiting for news on the fate of Luca Martin, who despite taking multiple rounds to the chest had survived, and of Chris Noble—the young genius everyone called "Dale," the injured half of Baldwin's protégés.

Strange that after two years, I never once asked what the kid's real name was.

Grimes made a noise, and he looked over at her. She was sitting across from him, staring at her feet, hands limp in her lap. He wanted to say something to her, but he just didn't have the emotional energy.

A hand squeezed his shoulder, and he looked up to find Buz Wilson staring down at him, his dark eyes brimming with empathy. Buz had changed his ruined shirt into a borrowed scrub top Munn had brought, but the T-shirt underneath was still badly stained in soot and blood.

"Didn't mean to sneak up on you," Buz said and took a break from his pacing to drop heavily into the seat beside him.

"No problem," Dempsey said, studying the man next to him, brilliant young eyes set in a weathered visage carved with wrinkles of a life hard fought and well lived. He had proven himself a teammate in every sense of the word since coming aboard. Even now, when he could be home with his wife, Buz was here, with his adopted Ember brothers and sisters waiting for word on men he barely knew. More than thirty years in the CIA—Dempsey wondered how many times the man had sat in waiting rooms like this. Too many, probably.

"How long did you know Shane?" Buz asked softly.

"A lifetime," Dempsey said, not explaining the metaphor. Smith was the first person John Dempsey had met in *this* life. Since that day in the basement, the day of his christening, they'd been friends, teammates, and brothers. He looked over at Buz and gave a sad smile.

"He was a good man," the old-timer said simply, sensing that anything more would be too much.

The door opened and Munn came back, saving Dempsey the pain of talking about Simon Adamo and June Latif—the other two Ember teammates confirmed dead. Munn looked tired and much older than he had this morning. Grimes shot to her feet, hands on her hips. Dempsey found he couldn't stay in his seat either and rose, hands clasped in front of him.

"Luca is in the Trauma ICU now," Munn said. "The surgery went very well. He lost a lot of blood, but he's young and basically a professional athlete in our business. The civilian docs are being guarded, but I say he's going to make it."

"Full recovery?" Grimes asked, her voice cracking.

Munn nodded. "I think so. They had to staple off a piece of his right lung to stop the bleeding in his chest, but he'll tolerate that fine. The bullet went through his diaphragm and liver, which is where all the blood went. They stopped the bleeding without removing any liver and fixed the hole in his diaphragm. He's stable."

Dempsey watched Grimes shift her gaze to the middle distance, her right hand going to the side of her chest, fingers light on the fabric of her shirt over her own scar. Was she thinking about the pain of her own recovery? Was she thinking about what Luca had ahead of him? About Smith, Adamo, and Latif?

All of that and more.

"And Chris?" Buz asked.

Dempsey smiled. Only the fucking new guy would call Dale by his real name.

Munn's face clouded. "Dale is stable," he said, "but the bullet tore through his spine at C6—that's the sixth neck vertebrae. He's paralyzed."

"For life?" Grimes asked, but her voice said she knew the answer.

Munn gave a solemn nod. "His level will be either C6 or C7—hard to tell just yet. He'll be in a wheelchair, but with some arm muscles still working. He'll have his diaphragm and all his respiratory muscles, so he can breathe. They had to do a tracheotomy because the bullet injured his trachea, but that will be temporary."

Munn crossed his arms and gave them time to absorb all he'd told them.

"How long in the hospital?" Buz asked.

"A long time for both of them. Weeks here, and for Dale it'll be months of PT and rehab after. As for the immediate future, I think it's probably a good time for everyone to take this opportunity to get some sleep. There's not much we can do here at this point."

"We'll stay," Grime said and took her seat.

Munn nodded. He got it.

Dempsey spoke up. "We'll take shifts in the hospital so someone is always here with them. I'll take the first shift; you guys can go get some rest."

"And where am I supposed to go to do that, John?" Grimes said, a flash of anger in her voice. "I can't go home because we don't know if the Zeta threat was completely neutralized, and I can't go to Ember because Ember is ashes."

"Jarvis has quarters set up for now at Naval Station Norfolk," Munn said. "They have officer housing we'll share together, except for Buz who will be in married quarters on station with his wife. Little Creek is too far from the hospital."

"And after that?" she asked. "What's happening to Ember?"

"We'll set up shop wherever the DNI finds a place for us," Dempsey said. "The Newport News facility is toast. Even if we rebuilt it, the cat is out of the bag. Ember is going to have to find a new home."

She nodded, and he could see her contemplating the implications of a move. "Probably for the best," she said through a sigh. "Even if we could go back to the hangar, I don't know if I'd want to."

Buz squeezed Dempsey's shoulder. "Wherever home is, I want you to know I'm with you, brother."

It was the perfect thing to say.

Dempsey suddenly realized he needed to get out of the waiting room. It was like the end of a long, cold dive at night when you'd give almost anything to get out of the dark and the cold and breathe normal air.

"I'll be back," he mumbled and left through the large double doors of the waiting room.

The hall outside was glass from waist high to ceiling on the right side, looking out over the Elizabeth River. He could see the city of Portsmouth across the river and the sprawling naval hospital that took up the entire east corner of town. He stopped and craned his neck, trying to see farther north, where the Atlantic fleet sprawled along the shoreline at the confluence of the York and James Rivers. He loved this town. He'd served here with SEAL Team Four. He'd had quarters at the Ocean Front in Virginia Beach and later, after marrying Kate, moved into a small house in Chesapeake. There was history here—for him and his beloved Navy.

Dempsey collapsed onto one of the padded benches along the curved glass wall and leaned forward, elbows on knees. Head hanging, he stifled a sob as fresh tears blurred his vision.

"Thought if I waited long enough you'd find your way here," a familiar voice said.

Dempsey looked up at Jarvis, who was standing and staring out the wall of glass, hands clasped in front of him. The DNI was alone— almost unheard of these days. Seeing Jarvis sent a wave of emotion crashing over Dempsey, and he didn't even try to wipe the tears from his face. Jarvis was the closest thing to family he had left in the world, and ignominy didn't have a place in their bond.

"I can't believe Shane's gone, sir. I just . . ." Dempsey's throat closed up, and he looked at his lap. He squeezed his eyes shut.

Jarvis placed a hand on Dempsey's shoulder. Dempsey felt the man's strength, interrupted by a momentary tremor of emotion before going rock steady again.

"I know how Dale and Luca are doing, so save yourself the pain of telling me, son."

Dempsey couldn't help but smile.

Son. Nobody's called me that in a very, very long time.

But here, now, and especially from this man, it fit.

Jarvis let the silence linger a moment longer before taking a seat beside Dempsey.

"I won't insult you with a pep talk," he said through a sigh. "I won't eulogize our dead with details you already know or tell you how they gave their lives willingly for a cause that was deeply important to them."

Dempsey raised his head. "Then what will you tell me, sir?" he asked, looking at Jarvis in profile as he stared out the window.

"That this isn't over, John. Not by a long shot." The DNI turned to him, his eyes at once cold as steel and hot with passion. "We lost a battle today, but the war has just begun. We're going to finish the mission we started in Vyborg. We're going to hunt down and kill every last Zeta, including Arkady Zhukov."

"Is that an order, sir?" Dempsey asked, feeling a fire ignite in his gut.

Jarvis nodded. "And there's something else."

Dempsey felt energy, the directed energy of galvanized purpose, flowing through him now.

"Sir?"

"Before coming here, I was at the White House debriefing the President, and at the end he posed an interesting question to me," Jarvis said, getting to his feet, his voice a low growl. "He asked me if I thought, *hypothetically*, whether Ember could eliminate the Russian President."

The words were too much, inflating and lifting him to his feet beside his boss.

"And what did you tell him?"

"Hypothetically?" Jarvis asked, his right eyebrow raised and eyes glowing.

"Of course."

Jarvis grabbed him by both shoulders and squeezed tightly. "I told him I had the perfect man for the job."

Dempsey nodded as Jarvis released him and turned to look again out the window.

"Mourn your dead, John. Care for your wounded. But keep the rest of the team sharp and focused. When the dust settles, we're going back to work."

"Yes, sir," Dempsey said.

Without a backward glance, Jarvis turned and left, his broad shoulders disappearing around the slowly curving hallway.

Dempsey placed his hands on the windowsill and fixed his gaze across the river, where a tug pushed a *San Antonio*–class vessel toward the shipyard dry dock. On board, dozens and dozens of Navy men and women were preparing for the long and arduous task of tearing their ship apart, a necessary first step so that they could make a laundry list of repairs and improvements. That was the thing about overhauls—as exhausting and terrible as they were, they were the only way to make a ship more capable and battle ready for the ever-changing threat landscape.

A wan smile spread across Dempsey's face as he recognized the irony . . . the overhaul process for Ember was starting today as well.

CHAPTER 45

6602 Eames Way
Bethesda, Maryland
June 29
1930 Local Time

For the second time in a fortnight, Catherine Morgan stepped into her home to find an uninvited guest waiting for her. This time, however, going for her Glock in the drawer beside the refrigerator was not possible, because the DNI's Chief of Staff was pointing it at her chest.

"Hello, Petra," Catherine said as she set her purse down on the counter. Her heart rate spiked from the adrenaline dump and her senses sharpened. Her gaze ticked from Petra's eyes to the weapon, where she noted that Petra's gloved left index finger was on the trigger, not the guard. Irritation bloomed in her chest. After her last visit from Gavriil, Catherine had added multiple cameras and sensors tied to an app on her phone—a home security upgrade that had proved useless tonight. "I see you figured out how to defeat my security system."

"Baldwin volunteered to help me," Petra said, coolly. "He's not in a good place right now . . . and neither am I."

Catherine studied her adversary's face for signs of weakness or doubt. She needed a crack she could exploit—empathy, logic, naivety, patriotism—anything she could focus on to edit the narrative Petra had written in her head. This skill was why Arkady had chosen her for the assignment in the first place. She was very good at persuasion; manipulation came naturally to her. "I can see you're upset," she said. "We're *all* very upset about what happened. Why don't you put the gun down, Petra, and we can talk about it."

"I'm not here to talk, Catherine," Petra said, unflinching, "or whatever your real name is."

"Whatever you think I've done, however you think I'm connected to the attack, I can assure you I had no part in it."

"I don't believe you."

"Petra, put down the gun. You're scaring me," Catherine said, adjusting her posture and the tenor of her voice to ooze vulnerability. But her plea fell on deaf ears, and Petra kept the muzzle of the pistol trained dead center of mass, the Glock unwavering in her grip.

"The problem with catching a mole," Petra began, "is that everybody always gets hung up on looking for evidence. It makes sense. That's how criminal investigations are conducted, and it's how I started my search. But in no time at all, I became frustrated. You covered your tracks so effectively, I couldn't find any hard evidence." She watched the former intelligence operative circle her slowly and felt a chill as a smile spread across Petra's face and she let out a soft chuckle. Fear clutched her—more than she had felt when the Zeta operator had been in her house. That had left her with resignation, but this . . . she was a traitor to this woman, not a burned asset.

"I'm sorry," Petra was saying, the Glock never wavering in her hand, "I don't mean to laugh, but I can't help but find humor in the terrible irony of your fate. You see, Catherine, for all these years you did your job *too* well. Your competence forced me to abandon a traditional investigative approach and reframe the problem. That's when epiphany struck. Catching a mole doesn't have to be complicated; it's just a process of elimination. In fact, the way I caught you was surprisingly simple—I used a Venn diagram. The key to my approach was to choose highly compartmentalized and targeted pieces of information, and by targeted, I mean information that was strategically exploited by your boss in Russia. In the first circle, I listed all the personnel who knew that the Ember compound was located below the hangar at Newport News. In the next circle, I listed all the personnel that knew about the President's decision last month to make an emergency and unannounced trip to Istanbul . . ."

As Petra talked, a fresh upwelling of panic roiled Catherine's insides. She wasn't going to be able to talk her way out of this one. She glanced at the cutlery block three feet away on the counter, which held a full complement of kitchen knives, plus one throwing knife with a matching hilt she was proficient at using. She looked back at Petra, noted the other woman's firing stance and the way she held the Glock—two reliable indicators of firearm handling competency—and decided that going for the knife would be suicide.

" . . . And in the third circle, I listed all the personnel who knew that Anne Parsons was murdered in a park in Simferopol, Crimea, after secretly meeting with a Belarusian informant with ties to the FSB." At that, Catherine felt the blood drain from her face and was unable to stop her mouth from falling open. "Oh, I see I have your attention now. That's good. I was hoping it would click for you like it did for me," Petra said, a hint of smug satisfaction creeping into her voice. "Fortunately for you and your boss, Anne Parsons's murder was completely overshadowed by the terrorist attack on DNI Philips's estate last year. In the aftermath, everybody forgot about Anne, everybody except for one person . . . a person who every day, on his way into work, walked past a marble wall with one hundred and thirty-two black stars inscribed beneath the words 'In honor of those members of the Central Intelligence Agency who gave their lives in the service of their country.' This person knew that Anne was working to turn a Belarusian FSB asset. This person understood the significance of a missing thumb when her body was discovered. And this person recognized that the nature of Anne's murder had all the hallmarks of an Arkady Zhukov assassination operation."

"You're talking about the new Ember guy, Buz Wilson?" Catherine said, meeting the other woman's eyes.

Petra smiled. "It takes a village."

Catherine found her center, steeled herself, and said, "I think, Petra, that you're tired. You've been under a lot of stress. You've just been through a traumatic loss, and you're looking for someone to blame. Also, you're sleeping with your boss, and you're worried about his health. Now, I know that you think what you're doing here tonight is an act of patriotism, but accusing me of treason and hauling me in is not the solution. You said it yourself: you don't have any evidence. Courts don't pass judgments based on Venn diagrams. Convictions require evidence, and you don't have anything here but tenuous and circumstantial dotted line connections between me and the incidents you've described."

"You're right—no jury would convict you based on my method-ology. No judge would pass sentence based on my logic proof. But tonight, I don't have to convince a jury." Petra's words turned her blood to ice. "I know you're guilty. I know you're a Russian mole, and your handler is Arkady Zhukov."

Fear gripped her now, more than she'd felt when she thought Arkady planned to retire her. No post-mission obligations—wasn't that what Gavriil had said? She'd known there was a good chance that giving up the location of Ember would blow her cover, but it was all happening too fast. She thought she'd have more time to get out.

"It's time to head down into the basement," Petra said, glancing at the doorway to the stairs.

"No," Catherine said, setting her jaw. "You'll have to shoot me where I stand."

"I'm prepared to do that," Petra said, her mouth a hard line. "Just because you didn't participate in the assault on Ember doesn't mean you don't have blood on your hands. Your treason killed my countrymen, Catherine, as surely as if you'd pulled the trigger. Two decades I've worked in the special warfare and intelligence communities. I might not wear a trident on my chest, but that doesn't mean I'm not a warrior. And just because you and I don't kit up for work every day doesn't mean we're not soldiers in this war. Your country attacked mine, and that cannot go unanswered."

In that moment, Catherine understood. Her suspicions that Petra was a Zeta had been the product of her own paranoia. This woman was not her replacement, nor was she Arkady's acolyte. Petra Felsk was exactly who she claimed to be—an American avenger, forged of the same metal as Kelso Jarvis.

Petra gestured toward the door to the basement. "There's someone who would like to talk to you downstairs."

"Who?"

"Why don't you lead the way and find out."

Catherine scratched the side of her neck, contemplating her pitiful options. If Jarvis was in the basement, maybe she could manipulate him into pursuing the path of prosecution instead of revenge. "Okay," she said and slowly walked from the kitchen to the basement steps, looking for a mistake to exploit in the process. The movement to the door and down the stairs would be her last chance to disarm Petra and kill her. But there was no such opportunity. Petra was too good and maintained a proper standoff the entire time.

The wooden stairs creaked with each step as she descended into the unfinished basement. A flickering light bulb overhead provided barely enough illumination to navigate down into the musty space she used for storage. As she stepped off the last stair tread and onto the concrete floor, a noose dangling from the ceiling off to her right caught her eye. The thin noose was tied from black nylon paracord and strung through an eyelet screwed into the bottom of a floor joist. A step stool had been positioned directly beneath, with a length of paracord tied to one of the four legs and stretched out ten feet snaking along the floor. Catherine's stomach went to knots and her mouth turned to cotton at the sight of the executioner's suite.

"Keep moving," Petra said behind her. "Toward the stool."

"There's no one else here, is there?" Catherine asked as she slowly turned to face Petra.

"No, I just said that so I wouldn't have to shoot you in the kitchen. It's better this way."

"For you," Catherine said.

"For everyone."

As she walked to the stool, she was surprised at her resignation to her fate. She'd always wondered why prisoners marched so compliantly to their demise instead of fighting tooth and nail. Now, she understood the repressive power of inevitability. She stepped up onto the stool, wobbling a bit at first until she regained her balance. She exhaled and, without being told, slipped the thin nylon noose around her neck, which Petra had hung with perfect measurements. Petra, for her part, kept her distance, covering Catherine with the pistol the entire time. Eight feet away, she knelt and picked up the loose end of rope on the floor that was tied to the leg of the stool.

"I took this paracord from Shane Smith's smoldering cage at Ember," Petra said as she took a step back to take the slack out of the nylon rope tied to the stool. "I thought it was poetic."

"Did you write a note for me?" Catherine asked, surprised to hear the question spill from her lips.

"No," Petra said with sobering exactitude. "I decided you didn't deserve one."

Petra's words hit Catherine like a slap across the face. It made the leaving feel hollow and her life pointless. But then, as if in response, Arkady's tranquil baritone voice spoke in her head, giving her comfort: *Do not be afraid, Maschenka. Face your death like you did your life—fearless and unapologetic. What you did, you did for love and country. So take solace, proud daughter of Russia, and know that we'll be together soon . . .*

With this, her fear melted away, replaced with resignation and regret at things left unsaid. It was this regret that spilled tears onto her cheeks. Time slowed. Arkady's shared verse began to echo in her head:

> ". . . My only regret is bittersweet
> That Death must take two 'fore again we meet."

She whispered goodbye to the man she'd always loved but had never had the courage to confess her truth to. With a long, resigned sigh, she closed her eyes.

She heard the scrape of the stool yanked from beneath her feet . . .

Sensed the unforgiving pull of gravity as her body fell . . .

And felt Death's kiss on her cheek as the paracord noose went impossibly tight around her neck . . .

CHAPTER 46

1650 Tysons Boulevard
McLean, Virginia
June 29
2115 Local Time

Jarvis tapped the icon on his work phone to disconnect the late-hour call with NCTC Director Reggie Buckingham. As he set his phone down on the dark marble countertop, he studied the slight tremor in his hand with clinical detachment and contemplated how strong he felt today. In the three days since the Ember attack, he'd felt more energized and powerful than he had in months. Was he operating on adrenaline, or was something else fueling him?

Rage?

Renewed purpose?

Maybe both?

He snapped his fingers shut into a hard, steady fist. He owned the tremor, it was his, and he wouldn't let it control or define him. He was, above all else, a United States Navy SEAL, something no disease or misfortune could ever take away from him. The doctor's prognosis was not a death sentence; it was an opportunity. Knowledge begat action. It afforded control. Overcoming this new adversity was his mission now, and he was never out of the fight. The same was true with Ember. The healing would take time, but the rebuilding process was already underway. In the coming months, the Ember team would need him, and he intended to be their rock.

There was a rap on the door. Tap, tap . . . tap.

Petra.

He walked to the door and let her in. "Where's your key?" he asked.

She greeted him with a smile, but there was a heaviness in her shoulders—as if she was suddenly carrying the weight of the world on her back.

"I thought we decided against me having a key for the time being," she said, holding his gaze but her eyes giving away nothing—no judgment, no complaint, no animosity.

"Something happened," he said with a sudden pang of worry. "Are you okay?"

"We need to talk," she said and took a seat on one of the barstools.

"You found the mole?" he said, a surge of anticipation whisking away the anxiety from a moment earlier. It was all the two of them had talked about since the attack. From the heavy dark circles under her eyes, he knew she'd barely slept since that night. Looking at her now, he wondered how he'd ever suspected her in the first place.

"I did," she said, slowly nodding.

Staring into her eyes, logic trees suddenly populated the whiteboard in his mind. He'd been so distracted with his own personal demons and national security crises that his mind hadn't been operating at normal capacity. But in this moment, the old Jarvis was back, and the calculus proof that had eluded him for weeks was suddenly axiomatic.

Catherine Morgan.

There had been plenty of hints along the way, self-evident now, that he'd ignored at the time. Her dismay at being dismissed from the Oval Office meeting when the subject turned to Petrov. The way she'd frowned when she'd found out he'd recruited Langley's Arkady expert for Ember. The way she'd befriended Secretary Baker and pushed policies in Turkey that risked turning President Erodan away from Warner and into Petrov's open arms. Dozens of little snippets—each innocuous in its own right—played like a movie reel at high speed in his mind. He remembered each incident with perfect clarity, just like he remembered rejecting his suspicion as preposterous.

Morgan's three-decade career had been exemplary. She'd fooled everyone and done it for a lifetime. So trusted and respected was she that President Warner had made her acting DNI for a time. And when Jarvis had succeeded her, he'd kept Catherine on and created a position for her at the nexus of the American intelligence apparatus. How could he have been so blind? So foolish? A clean ledger appeared in his mind, and the pages began to fill with data. How much damage had she done over the years? How many secrets had she siphoned, how many NOCs had she pierced, how many networks breached, how many plans foiled, how many technologies stolen? A tidal wave of emotion washed over him. Fury, shame, ire, disgust. He shut it all down, before it drowned him.

"It's Morgan, isn't it?" he said.

Petra nodded.

"How did you figure it out?" he asked, taking the stool next to her.

She blew air through her teeth and looked at the ceiling. "I'm not ready to go into the details right now. Is that okay?"

"Yes and no," he said, his thoughts already racing ahead to next steps. "We need to get all your findings and documentation over to NCTC so I can have Reggie—who I was just talking to, ironically— put a team together to take Catherine into custody before she destroys evidence or tries to run."

Petra met his gaze and said, "We don't have to worry about that."

"And why is that?"

"Because it's my understanding that Catherine took her own life. Hung herself in her Bethesda townhome a couple of hours ago."

As she spoke, his synesthesia went into hyperdrive, and her words reverberated with both musicality and color. A lone oboe began to play in his mind—*Tchaikovsky's "Arabian Dance"*—and he remembered his fever dream in the MRI machine. He gazed at her and realized that although their bodies were at rest, they were dancing.

An intricate duet . . .

Male and female . . .

Strength and grace . . .

Power and seduction . . .

A golden aura materialized around her, and he understood what she had done.

"Are you angry with me?" she asked, breaking the silence.

"No," he said. "Quite the contrary."

For an instant, he was transported back in time two years ago to a luxury DC home. Back then, he was the Director of Ember pursuing the man responsible for the massacre of Dempsey's Tier One unit in Yemen. On that fateful night, Robert Kittinger had been the traitor to their country, and Jarvis had been the angel of death, exacting—not vengeance, so much as a reckoning. Tonight, history had repeated itself, with Petra meting justice. She had done it for her country. She had done it for him. They were kindred spirits, avenging angels, tethered in fate and purpose.

Tethered forever.

She slipped off the stool and tugged gently on his hand for him to do the same. He obliged, and when he was standing in front of her, she collapsed against his chest.

"I know it's a breach of our agreement, but I don't want to be alone," she said through an unsteady breath. "Can we make an exception tonight?"

"Yes," he said, wrapping her in his arms. "From now on, everything we do, we do together."

"Tethered," she whispered, reading his mind.

"Forever."

EPILOGUE

Arlington National Cemetery
Section 60
July 4
1430 Local Time

They had never talked about it—coming here and visiting her brother together—although Dempsey was certain it had crossed both their minds a hundred times. Today it just happened—with Grimes climbing into the passenger seat of his black Tahoe without a word and him driving without discussing where he was going.

They'd spoken very little on the three-hour drive up from Norfolk and then mostly about Luca Martin and Dale. Martin was out of the ICU, all but one of the tubes snaking out of his chest already removed, which Munn said was remarkable. When Dempsey had informed Martin about the deaths of Smith, Adamo, and his close friend Latif, the former Marine had said nothing. He'd just sat up straighter in his chair and started asking questions about his rehab regimen and timetable. Dempsey understood. There were multiple fights in need of fighting.

The Ember relocation and "reconstitution" was already underway at MacDill Air Force Base in Tampa, where Dempsey and the SAD team would be heading very soon. Once they were fully operational, the hunt for Arkady Zhukov and the rest of the surviving Zetas would begin in earnest. They would hunt them down and do what they always did—mete out Ember's own divine form of justice. Martin, it appeared, had every intention of being part of that operation when the time came.

Baldwin's protégé, Dale, was in a very different place, however. The kid spoke little and ate even less. The medical team was now threatening him with a feeding tube if he didn't knock it off. Baldwin had flown up from Tampa and spent a full day and a night with the kid, and that seemed to have helped. It would take time, but Dempsey believed the boy would be okay eventually.

A bright yellow sun hung high in a cloudless blue sky. Birds chirped, and the grass looked especially green and vibrant today. They'd walked in silence, side by side, since their arrival. At some point, Elizabeth had taken his hand—her touch warm, but limp. From time to time, he would feel her tremble and when he did, he squeezed her hand gently. He led her through the grounds, as he knew the way intimately. Hell, he'd walked the green grass paths between white stones in his dreams. They had many stones to visit today. But they would start at the place of their mutual and most hollowing sadness.

Eventually, they reached the south end of the graveyard known as Section 60—a plot that was filling all too rapidly it seemed. He stepped off the paved path and guided her to the spot, where he stopped, released her hand, and dropped to his knees. His breath caught in his throat, and he sat back on his heels, not quite ready to look at the carved words on the white stone. She knelt beside him, wrapped an arm through his, and leaned her head on his shoulder.

"I miss him so much," she said, sobbing for her brother, Special Operator First Class Jonathan Clarke—known as "Spaz" to Dempsey and the other Tier One SEALs.

"I know," he whispered, his voice cracking. "I miss them all."

So many gone. And in a few weeks, they would be back here in Arlington again, to watch Barry Pozniak, US Army Special Forces, known to them as Shane Smith, get laid to rest. June Latif would be buried in the VA cemetery near his parents' home. And Simon Adamo had been interred already in Ohio.

Dempsey looked up and, wiping tears from his cheeks, read the stone aloud:

HERE LIES

THE

UNIDENTIFIED

REMAINS

OF

OPERATION CRUSADER

YEMEN

2016

When he was finished reading, he held Elizabeth's hand and they mourned together.

It should have felt like an ending, but it didn't.

This was just the beginning.

A long, unfamiliar road lay ahead of them, one they had silently, wordlessly, committed to walk together as teammates, as operators, and most important, as Americans.

GLOSSARY

- AIP—Air-independent propulsion
- AQ—Al-Qaeda
- BDU—Battle Dress Uniform
- Bright Falcon—Code name identifier for the Russian Zeta Operation and Training Center in Vyborg, Russia
- BUD/S—Basic Underwater Demolition /SEAL training
- CIA—Central Intelligence Agency
- CO—Commanding Officer
- COMSUBLANT—Commander, Submarine Force Atlantic
- CSO—Chief Staff Officer
- DC—Damage Control
- DCS—Distributed Command System
- DNI—Director of National Intelligence
- DoD—Department of Defense
- DPU—Dive Propulsion Unit
- DS&T—Directorate of Science and Technology
- EAB—Emergency Air Breather
- EBE—Emergency Breathing Equipment
- Eighteen Delta—Special Forces medical technician and first responder
- Ember—America's premiere black-ops counterterrorism task force

- EMP—Electromagnetic pulse
- EXFIL—Exfiltrate
- FOB—Forward Operating Base
- FSRU—Floating Storage and Regasification Unit
- GSW—Gunshot wound
- HALO—high-altitude, low opening
- HUMINT—Human Intelligence
- HVT—High-Value Target
- IC—Intelligence Community
- INFIL—Infiltrate
- ISR—Intelligence, surveillance, and reconnaissance
- JO—Junior Officer
- JSOC—Joint Special Operations Command
- JSOTF—Joint Special Operations Task Force
- KIA—Killed in Action
- LAN—Local Area Network
- LNG—Liquefied Natural Gas
- MARSOC—Marine Corps Special Operations Command
- MEDEVAC—Medical Evacuation
- NCTC—National Counterterrorism Center
- NOC—Nonofficial Cover
- NSA—National Security Agency
- NVGs—Night Vision Goggles
- ODNI—Office of the Director of National Intelligence
- OGA—Other Government Agency
- ONI—Office of Naval Intelligence
- OPSEC—Operational Security
- OTC—Officer in Tactical Command
- PJ—Parajumper/Air Force Rescue
- QRF—Quick Reaction Force
- RPG—Rocket-Propelled Grenade
- SAD—Special Activities Division

- SAPI—Small Arms Protective Insert
- SBS—Special Boat Service
- SCIF—Sensitive Compartmented Information Facility
- SDV—SEAL Delivery Vehicle
- SEAL—Sea, Air, and Land Teams, Naval Special Warfare
- SecDef—Secretary of Defense
- SIGINT—Signals Intelligence
- SITREP—Situation Report
- SOAR—Special Operations Aviation Regiment
- SOCOM—Special Operations Command
- SOG—Special Operations Group
- SOPMOD—Special Operations Modification
- SQT—SEAL Qualification Training
- TAD—Temporary Additional Duty
- TOC—Tactical Operations Center
- TMT—Tactical Mobility Team
- UAV—Unmanned Aerial Vehicle
- USN—United States Navy
- VEVAK—Iranian Ministry of Intelligence, analogue of the CIA
- Zeta—Clandestine Russian covert action and espionage activity

ACKNOWLEDGMENTS

We would like to thank and acknowledge our spectacular developmental editor, Caitlin Alexander, for being an astute and percipient contributor during our Tier One journey. We've learned so much from working with you and we are better storytellers because of your guidance. Also, we want to give special thanks to our amazing copyeditor, Jon, and proofreader, Liz, whose attention to detail and subject matter knowledge is second to none. The stories would not be the same without your commitment, talent, and insights.

ABOUT THE AUTHORS

Photo © 2012 Jennifer Hensley

Photo © 2015 Wendy Wilson

Wall Street Journal bestselling author Brian Andrews is a US Navy veteran, Park Leadership Fellow, and former submarine officer with degrees from Vanderbilt and Cornell Universities. He is the author of three critically acclaimed high-tech thrillers: *Reset*, *The Infiltration Game*, and *The Calypso Directive*.

Wall Street Journal bestselling author Jeffrey Wilson has worked as an actor, firefighter, paramedic, jet pilot, and diving instructor, as well as a vascular and trauma surgeon. He served in the US Navy for fourteen years and made multiple deployments as a combat surgeon with an East Coast–based SEAL team. The author of three award-winning supernatural thrillers—*The Traiteur's Ring*, *The Donors*, and *Fade to Black*—and the faith-based thriller *War Torn*, he lives with his wife, Wendy, and their four children in southwest Florida.

Red Specter is the fifth novel in the Tier One Thrillers series. Andrews & Wilson also coauthor the Nick Foley Thriller series (*Beijing Red* and *Hong Kong Black*) under the pen name Alex Ryan.

To stay up to date on their latest releases, follow Brian and Jeff on their Amazon author pages or visit www.andrews-wilson.com to subscribe to their mailing list.